UNDER ATTACK!

"They're still coming up our wake and we have them under fire," Smith shouted above the continuous thundering crack of the gun and the equally thunderous hammering of the rain.

Madeira, looking aft, could see nothing at all. Not even the helipad and the gun crew. "What's their range now?"

"Twenty-five yards, maybe."

"I don't think they're trying to board us, Bud."

"Well then what the hell *do* you think they're trying to do?"

"Shoot us up! Sink us! In these seas they've got to get close just to hit us."

Still looking aft, Madeira spotted a bright flash astern of the gun and off to one side. It started small and seemed to grow.

"Congratulations!" he shouted into the phone, the awful pounding in his head momentarily forgotten. "Wasn't that a hit you just got?"

"Say again?"

"I just observed a big flash aft."

"Yes, I saw it too but I'm not sure. . . . Oh Shit! No!"

"What?"

"That wasn't a hit. They just fired a goddamn missile at us!"

Other *Leisure* books by William S. Schaill:
SEAGLOW

THE WRECK OF MISERICORDIA

WILLIAM S. SCHAILL

LEISURE BOOKS NEW YORK CITY

A LEISURE BOOK®

June 1999

Published by

Dorchester Publishing Co., Inc.
276 Fifth Avenue
New York, NY 10001

ISBN 0-8439-4544-3

The name "Leisure Books" and the stylized "L" with design are trademarks of Dorchester Publishing Co., Inc.

Printed in the United States of America.

Part One

July 1959

One

"Pick it up!" shouted one of the guards, waving his club-like truncheon. It was Uribe, the short, skinny guard everybody had warned him against antagonizing.

Antonio Perez, his head pounding, looked down at the rocky ground and the sack of cement he'd just dropped. He shuddered as his already liquified bowels convulsed yet again. There was little left within him to be expelled; only the merest trickle of vileness, which worked its way down his filthy cotton trousers to the even more filthy sandals on his feet.

Antonio was certainly not the only prisoner who was sick and overworked. There were countless others just like him at *Angel del Llano*. For that matter, there were an even greater number outside the prison—law-abiding honest citizens—who suffered as much as he.

But none of that mattered in the slightest to the tall, very boyish-looking prisoner. Antonio was what mattered to Antonio, and at the moment, Antonio was understandably overwhelmed by his own misery.

His guts were on fire, his muscles screaming in agony from the hard labor. His feet were badly bruised and slashed from the sharp rocks and knife-like palmetto leaves that grew in the dry soil. His mouth and throat were parched by the dust and heat.

Worst of all, he was now a nobody, a filthy, shit-covered nobody, and he would die a nobody.

And once, he reminded himself, he had been a somebody. A *joven formidable*. A young man very much to be reckoned with.

He turned to face Uribe. "Fuck yourself!" he screamed at the guard, neither imagining nor caring that the misery he was currently experiencing might possibly be improved upon a thousand-fold. "Fuck your mother and fuck your grandmother too!"

He was stunned when the club first slammed into his head. Then, a second or so later, the pain erupted, a pain so intense and overpowering it dominated the universe and temporarily destroyed his sense of self. So absorbing was this pain that he was almost unaware of the destruction when the second guard's rifle butt slammed into his nose, then his jaw, and finally, his groin.

Bent over, whimpering and sweating under the hot summer sun, Antonio was forced to double-time three long, dusty miles back to *Angel del Llano*. Unable to get so much as one whole breath, he was driven every terrible step of the way by the laughing guards' kicks and blows.

Two weeks later, with nothing in any way healed, he was released from the prison hospital.

Waiting for him at the clinic door was Fuentes, a very big, and very mean prisoner who, in return for maintaining a certain amount of order, was granted certain privileges.

"My child," said Fuentes in a soft voice, his huge, melancholy eyes studying Antonio's, "you picked the wrong guard to fuck with. You shouldn't be such a smart-ass. But don't worry, I'll take care of you from now on."

One evening, not long after Antonio was able to eat with only limited pain, Fuentes—who was drunk, as he often was, on rum the guards provided him—put his arm around Antonio's waist.

"My child," he whispered, "haven't I taken good care of you? Now, you will take care of me. Make me feel good, my love."

Before Antonio grasped what was happening, the larger, older prisoner had forced him to his knees, laughing in rich anticipation as he did.

Nothing, not even Uribe's beating, had prepared Antonio for the servitude imposed by Fuentes. Now, in his own eyes as well as those of the other prisoners, he was even lower than a shit-covered nobody. He was the shit itself.

Antonio came to long for death, yet could not find the will to bring it upon himself.

Several weeks later, just when he'd about given up hope of ever regaining his manhood, and had become reconciled to spending the rest of his life in Hell, salvation presented itself.

Late one night Antonio and Fuentes were returning to their cell from a party. Fuentes, roaring drunk, had one arm wrapped around Antonio's neck while an almost empty rum bottle waved at the end of the other. They had the corridor to themselves.

On either side of the couple were dark concrete-block walls, walls discolored by mold and misery and stinking of sweat, pain, and fear.

Ahead lay the dimly lit steel staircase.

Antonio had gone up and down those stairs countless times without ever noticing them. They were just stairs.

But that night, out of the blue, his perception of them had changed forever. Once he'd recognized them for what they really were, they radiated a hope even greater than the hope his mother had derived from the paschal alter at the great cathedral in Havana.

The two started down the fate-filled stairs slowly, Fuentes singing, Antonio gagging at the pig's stench.

He had to move swiftly, he reminded himself, and with force. If he failed, Fuentes would kill him. Or worse, force him to continue living as he was.

When Antonio's right foot descended toward the top step, Fuentes reflexively tightened his hold around the boy's neck as their body weights shifted forward. Antonio was holding on to the railing and Fuentes was holding on to Antonio. Then, when one of Fuentes' feet reached the step, his hold on Antonio relaxed slightly.

Antonio was ready. He ducked down and twisted out of Fuentes' grasp. Pushing fast and hard against the railing, he snapped up behind the beast and shoved hard against his shoulders, desperately kicking the man's feet out from under him at the same time.

Antonio's former master, already off balance,

tumbled head over heels down the stairs, making a dull thunking sound as he went.

When Antonio reached him, Fuentes was lying at the bottom of the stairs. Blood was oozing from his mouth, nose, and eye sockets and he did not seem to be breathing.

Not wanting to take any chances, Antonio grabbed the neck of the shattered rum bottle and hacked his tormentor's throat to bloody ribbons.

Within moments Antonio was seized and isolated from the other prisoners while the authorities considered what, if anything, to do about him.

It was during the second week of his isolation that Ramirez first came to visit.

"So," said the trim, young intelligence officer as he stood in the door of Antonio's cell, his khaki uniform showing no sign of sweat despite the heat and humidity, "you have now killed two men."

Antonio, who was crouched in the corner, just looked up at the him, and realized that he was only a few years older than himself.

"Yes," he finally replied.

"Everybody seems to think you should die for your crimes," continued Ramirez as he stepped into the cell. "The prisoners, the warden, even Fidel himself. And several of Fuentes' friends have asked that you be given to them."

Antonio could only shudder, as if he had suddenly been thrown into icy water.

"But I think you have great value," Ramirez said. "You have learned about pain and you have learned humility and you have absolutely nothing to lose. Now it is time for you to learn purpose, commitment, and loyalty. Eventually you may even learn something about rewards."

13

Utterly confused, Antonio remained crouched in the corner of his cell, staring at Agustin Ramirez. Only much later did he realize he the figure at which he had been staring was, in fact, The Creator.

Part Two

May 1990

Part Two

May 1990

Two

The night was cool—deathly cold, in fact—as even a warm night at sea often seems shortly before first light.

Al Madeira stepped out onto the boat deck, the weather deck behind and one level below *Irving Johnson*'s bridge, with a cup of hot coffee in his right hand. He turned and used his free hand to close and dog the watertight door through which he had just stepped, and congratulated himself for not spilling even one drop of coffee in the process. He then paused and looked around, allowing his eyes to adjust to the motion-filled darkness that surrounded him.

Off to port—faintly visible through the thick, damp Gulf air—he could see the distant lights, white and red, of several northbound ships. Well beyond them, so far to the east as to be invisible, loomed the lights of Tampa/St. Petersburg.

To starboard, he could see nothing but night.

He could feel the ship roll slightly, feel the vibration of her two big diesels. He could sense her surging forward, through the water and the night, without even looking over the side at her white bow wave as it rolled past.

There was something, he thought, that wasn't quite right, but damn if he could put his finger on it!

It would come to him, he concluded. In a minute. As soon as he woke up a little more.

He smiled slightly to himself he walked aft a few paces to the steel rail that ran across the back of the boat deck. He leaned on the rail and looked down into the great, dimly lit, drydock-like well that constituted the aft two thirds of the ship. Nested in the well he could see the pale white outline of MOHAB.

MOHAB was the first mobile underwater habitat ever put into service and the reason for *Johnson*'s existance. MOHAB was essentially a small submarine with a very small motor, a set of sled-like runners on which to settle, and very large banks of oxygen tanks, fuel cells, and storage-battery-like capacitors called Pfeifer Units. She was designed to transport scientific researchers and other underwater workers down to four thousand feet. Once there, she would serve as their base and workshop for up to ten days—and one or two more in a pinch—without returning to the surface.

The habitat hadn't made the cover of *Time* Magazine, at least not yet, but in certain circles she was already hot stuff. Not only had *Maritime Engineering News* run a feature on her, but *Popular Science* had devoted four full pages to explaining her to its millions of fascinated readers.

MOHAB was now headed out on her first paying mission, and Madeira was starting his first civilian job—as MOHAB's Operational Director—after twenty three years in the Navy as a salvage and deep-diving officer. The job, as boss of the entire system, was a plum, and he still wasn't totally sure how he'd managed to get it.

But, he thought with a good deal of satisfaction, he had.

He felt the ship turn to starboard, and wondered why. Then a dilute slug of stack gas, hot and acrid, swirled down on him from the top of the funnel. He coughed as the foul gas forced its way into his mouth, nose, and eyes.

"BARUUP!"

Even before he'd had a chance to catch his breath, the shock wave generated by *Irving Johnson*'s air whistle slammed like a giant's opened palm into his chest and face.

One short blast, he thought. My rudder is right.

The stocky, dark-haired retired Naval officer looked around to each side and astern, but could see nothing in the damp pre-dawn darkness, nothing close enough to be exchanging steering signals with. The problem, he decided, must be ahead; something he couldn't see from where he was standing.

"BARUUP! . . . BARUUP! . . . BARUUP! . . . BARUUP . . . BARUUP!"

The danger signal! Every one of the five body blows struck him hard. The impacts—fast, desperate, almost continuous—generated the intended sense of near-hysterical urgency.

His breath catching, Madeira slammed his coffee cup down and wedged it into the housing of a small winch, spilling most of it. He then launched himself forward and up the ladder to the bridge, taking two steps at a time, the ladder clanging with each footfall.

He was in the darkened pilothouse before the reverberations of the last blast had stopped ringing in his ears and pummeling his racing heart.

"What's happening, Paul?" he asked Paul Hawkins, the mate of the watch.

"Come right another forty degrees," Hawkins said to Bobby Bell, the seaman who was standing behind the large, curved control console with one hand on the helm. "Steer two-eight-five."

Then, turning to Madeira, he replied, pointing over the port bow, "That son of a bitch's hogging the whole damn Gulf."

Now fully alert, Madeira couldn't help but note the strong mix of emotions present in the younger officer's voice—indignation, anger, and a very real fear—and the size of his eyes, whose whites reflected the faint, colored lights flickering on the console.

"I spotted him on radar about an hour ago. He was on our reciprocal. I came right thirty degrees and figured he'd do the same and that'd be the end of it. I mean it *was* a simple meeting situation."

As Hawkins spoke, Madeira's eyes followed the mate's pointing arm out ahead of the ship and up. He first spotted two running lights, one red and one green. Then, looking up even more, he saw the two white range lights.

The lights were all standing far too high above the horizon for comfort. They had to belong to what was either a very large ship, or a very close one. Or both.

And her bow was pointed directly at them.

"What's his range now?" Madeira asked.

"About two miles. Maybe less."

Christ! Madeira thought. Assuming the other

ship was making the same speed as *Johnson,* a collision was less than two minutes away.

"Your last course change should get us by him."

"That's what I thought the last three times, but every time I come right he comes left. Should I stop? Back down? The bastard's in one hell of a hurry to get to Galveston and refuses to go one inch out of his way. He doesn't seem to give a damn about traffic lanes either."

"Have you called him on the radio?"

"I've tried a hundred times," Hawkins said as he passed his hand through his curly blond hair. "He refuses to answer or his radio's fucked up or turned off."

Cold sweat began to form under Madeira's arms and dribble down his spine. Two ships, totaling possibly hundreds of thousands of tons of steel, blundering toward each other, seemingly hellbent on occupying the same tiny spot of water.

"It's too late to stop or back down. We've got to continue as we are and hope he's turning astern of us right now. Have you called Captain Reilly?"

"Yes. Twice. He knows what I've been doing. He didn't seem all that interested."

The whole process is so damn routine, Madeira reassured himself. It's just a matter of waiting until the results of Hawkin's actions, along with those the other ship was bound to take, become obvious.

Standing in *Johnson*'s pilothouse looking out into the darkness, Madeira became very conscious again of the quiet, forceful pounding of the ship's diesels as they drove her, rolling slightly, through the night and hopefully out of the path of the other ship.

Thump, thump, thump, he thought. It could pass for the ticking of a giant Doomsday clock.

William S. Schaill

In nine thousand, nine hundred, and ninety-nine out of every ten thousand situations like this, the ships pass clear of each other.

But what about *this* time? he wondered. Looking out into the hazy darkness, he had the sickening feeling this might be the ten-thousandth encounter, the statistical impossibility that somehow seems to happen with fatal frequency.

It's always worse at night, he reassured himself as he hurried out onto the bridge wing to get a better look at the approaching lights.

Nights when the wind, even if it's only the wind of passage, moans quietly as it passes over the decks and through the rigging.

Nights when your own ship, of which you can see little or nothing, races madly, blindly through black air and black water.

Nights when the other vessel exists only as a disembodied electronic blip on the radar or as multi-hued, will-of-the-wisp navigation lights: red, white, green, amber, blue, red over white, green over white, amber over white, a Christmas tree of greens. All float unsteadily in the mysterious air. All demand action, but none ever provide quite enough data for total comfort.

Madeira sighed. He damn well knew his unease was based on considerations considerably more solid than the terrors of the night.

The rules of the road were clear, but there always seemed to be a few cruds, clods, and smart-asses around who insisted on having their own way, rules or no rules.

Either that, or the other guy was drunk or asleep. Or the ship was on automatic pilot while the officers played cards.

Everything Hawkins had done up to now was correct.

Or was it? He could have stopped much earlier. Or turned away—180 degrees away.

Both were recommended in the classroom. Rarely were either actually done at sea.

Maybe he should tell Hawkins to stop after all.

No, not with the other guy headed right at them. And almost on top of them now! If they didn't dash out of his way the other ship would T-bone them, ram them amidships. It was too late for stopping!

There was really very little he could do but wait another minute, maybe less, to see if the other vessel responded, or if they were going to slip out of her path on their own. If not, he could alway try another, last-minute emergency turn and hope they received only a glancing blow.

Or he could just scream and run around in circles.

"I think you're right, Captain Madeira," Hawkins reported, joining him on the wing. "His bearing seems to be drifting aft and . . . Yes! Thank God! I can see only his red running light now."

After confirming for himself that the other ship was going to pass astern, not very far astern but far enough, Madeira exhaled the chestful of air he'd unwittingly been holding. He then followed Hawkins back into the pilothouse.

"Hawkins! What the fuck's that ship doing so close to us? Why didn't you call me sooner? How did she get there? What've you been doing?"

The young mate's relieved expression vanished as Bud Reilly, *Johnson*'s Master, stepped into the faint, red light of the otherwise darkened pilot house.

"No, Skip," answered Hawkins, a faint hint of uncertain defiance coloring his tone. "I was doing my job."

"Like when you almost ran that oil platform down yesterday?" The outrage in Reilly's voice was obvious. "Jesus Christ!"

Without waiting for a reply, Reilly stormed off to the port wing of the bridge to watch the other ship pass. Meanwhile, Bobby Bell, who disliked officers in general and especially those younger than he, sniggered quietly as he stood at the helm, waiting and hoping to be entertained further.

Madeira hadn't seen any oil rigs almost hit, and he'd already decided Hawkins'd handled the current crisis reasonably well. All the same, he didn't want to contradict or reprimand Reilly. Especially not in public.

While Madeira was the Operational Director, responsible for the whole MOHAB System—both *Johnson* and the mobile underwater habitat herself—the ship was Reilly's

Unless and until she failed to perform her mission.

"I'm afraid we won't get many star lines this morning," remarked Hawkins, attempting to change the subject and remove himself from the spotlight.

"You may be right," Madeira replied, trying to sound cheerful as he looked out into the on-again, off-again drizzle. "But we've still got at least an hour to get through this weather, and maybe more, before we lose 'em. Don't give up hope yet."

"I think we're past that guy," Hawkins remarked, primarily to himself. Then, after checking the automatic navigational plot generated by the ship's satellite-based Global Positioning System, he continued. "Bell. Left ten degrees rudder. Steer one-seven-five."

"One-seven-five," repeated Bell in a bored tone.

Once the ship had returned to her original course and the automatic pilot had been engaged, *Johnson*'s bow started to rise and fall gently, rythmically. It thrust forward purposefully, riding up and over, then slicing down. Astern she left a broad, slightly foamy path through the faintly visible Gulf swells.

Aside from the throaty, muted, roar of the ship's main engines and the continuous low-key static coming from the SSB radio, near-silence returned to the pilothouse.

Madeira walked toward the door to the starboard wing of the bridge and paused at the navigator's station. Hawkins returned to staring out the forward window into the dense pre-dawn darkness.

No matter what the kid did, thought Madeira, the Master found fault. Reilly had been on the boy's back ever since Madeira had arrived, and, he suspected, ever since Hawkins had came aboard. Hawkins was too timid when he maneuvered the ship, or he was rash. His paperwork was incomplete, or he was spending too much time on it. He wasn't getting enough work out of his people, or he was working them too hard. And Reilly never hesitated to deliver his judgments in public.

The criticism, Madeira felt, went well beyond what was necessary or desirable. Reilly was doing his damnedest to break the kid, and he was succeeding. Even during the few short weeks Madeira had been aboard, he noticed Hawkin's confidence ebbing, his enthusiasm collapsing. All replaced by a growing hint of loneliness and desolation.

As if aware of Madeira's thoughts, or maybe just on the alert for any new sources of attack, Hawkins turned away from the window and glanced quickly at Madeira, then turned away again.

Not sure what, if anything, to say to encourage

the mate, Madeira studied the navigational plot. The glowing, green-hued screen indicated they were about two hundred miles northwest of Key West, making eighteen knots through the Gulf of Mexico's warm, greenish-blue waters.

Steering a course slightly east of south, they were helped along their way by the Gulf's Loop Current, the counterclockwise rotating gyre that more or less follows the Gulf's shoreline from the Yucatan north and around until the Florida Peninsula forces it south toward Cuba.

Almost directly ahead, about sixty miles west of Key West, lay the Dry Tortugas, a small group of low, sandy atolls best known as the site of Fort Jefferson. It was in this brick fortress that the infamous, but possibly innocent, Dr. Mudd had been imprisoned after Lincoln's assassination. Roughly twenty-five miles southwest of the massive, lonely fortress was a dot, designated Waypoint A. Beyond that dot there appeared no Waypoint B. *Johnson*'s projected track seemed to end there, in the middle of nowhere.

Even though *Johnson* was steaming south, she was already enmeshed in a massive, interlocking system of ocean gyres or currents, each following its own counterclockwise path, which would eventually carry her far to the northeast. Almost without benefit of her diesel engines, she would soon be dumped into the Florida Current, which if allowed to do so, would transport her around the Keys and into the Florida Strait. There, the Gulf Stream would grab her and carry her away, up the East Coast.

Madeira glanced at the large paper chart spread out on the plotting table next to the automatic plot.

Good! Paul, as directed, had maintained a manual Dead Reackoning plot.

Madeira had full confidence in the GPS and its backup systems, but still found a regimen of pencil and paper plots and two celestial fixes per day comforting. There was always something that could go wrong, especially with electronics, which, any sailor will assure you, don't mix well with salt water.

Anyway, with the ship on automatic pilot most of the time, what else did the watch officers have to do?

"Lulu, Lulu, this is Betty Sue, ovah?" squawked the radio.

Madeira stared at the speaker as the callup was repeated a second, then a third time. Some fisherman, he thought. Bored to tears, wondering where the hell all the fish had gone, and looking for a friendly voice on a dark night.

"*This* is Betty Sue, Lulu. How y'all doing theya? Ovah."

Why the hell couldn't they learn to talk normally, he thought, still irritated with Reilly. Why do they always sound like they have a mouthful of bubblegum?

After turning to check the radar, which showed a few contacts but none close enough to be of concern, Madeira stepped through the door and out to the wing. He could feel the overcast, the solid cloud cover hovering not very high over his head, pressing down, hiding the stars from him. The air was both chill and sticky.

With a sudden, rattling roar, the drizzle turned into a thunderous downpour that reduced the visibility to zero and forced Madeira to scamper back into the protection of the pilothouse. The rain-drops—now huge, pregnant blobs that splattered substantially on the steel deck—confirmed that *Irving Johnson*'s almost invisible bow was cutting though a very weak front, a minor brawl between a small, intruding mass of dry, cool continental air and the warm, tropical damp of the Gulf.

Despite the rain, the wind was no more than a slight breeze and the seas, except for the modest, stately swell from the southeast, were almost non-existent. It was much too late in the year to have to worry about Northers, and still a little too early to worry much about hurricanes, although it *had* been an unusually warm spring.

Gulf weather being what it is, the sky would clear, at least in part, long before the gray dawn had advanced far enough to color and outshine the stars.

Or so Madeira hoped.

It was all a matter of waiting, he told himself as he tried to relax. Waiting for the sky to clear. Waiting to reach Waypoint A. Waiting for the engines, and the totally disinterested currents, to deliver them to the objective.

Three

Waiting. He'd spent so much of his life waiting, especially during those twenty three years in the navy. He was tired of waiting. He was getting old, he thought. Impatient.

A somber cloud settled over Madeira, one as thick as the downpour pounding on the pilot-house roof. With nothing else to do at the moment, he found himself thinking back to Cabot Station.

Once Cabot had been a living Naval undersea station. Now it was a cold, lifeless jumble of water-logged steel and concrete, a low-rise condo for codfish, resting under three hundred feet of storm-torn, bitterly cold North Atlantic water off Newfoundland.

When new, Cabot had been the ultimate in high tech. It had possessed the highest priority. By the time he'd arrived, however—a young officer with a reputation for tenacity if nothing else—Cabot had lost its youth and most of its glamor.

For over a year and a half he and his crew had managed to hold it all together. All the while, in the depths of his heart and mind, he had waited for the disaster he knew was bound to come, no matter how hard they worked.

When disaster did make its inevitable appearance, he, Cabot's Commanding Officer, had been ashore at a conference. One small electro-mechanical component had failed, triggering catastrophe. One old, screwed-up control that shouldn't have even been in service but was, because nobody'd send them a replacement.

Madeira shuddered briefly at the memory, then shoved the worst of it aside. It wasn't something he dwelled on—but it was always there, coiled, waiting to spring at him whenever he became a little too comfortable, a little too confident, a little too idle.

MOHAB represented a wonderful new adventure for him. It was a different approach to a world with which he was familiar, an opportunity to breathe fresh air without having to discard all his psychic baggage.

The habitat also represented the chance to reestablish his credentials, tarnished as they were by Cabot's loss and the string of okay, but not great, jobs the Navy'd given him in the years that followed.

"Christ, Al! You've got that shirt on again!" Reilly shouted out of the blue from across the bridge. "I thought we'd agreed you wouldn't wear it on the bridge at night. It's going to blind the watch."

Without thinking, Madeira tugged at the light windbreaker he was wearing over the brilliant, orchid-festooned shirt in question.

30

The son of a bitch must have bionic vision, he thought. How else could he see what I'm wearing?

"We've been through this before," Al replied in what he hoped was a light, jocular tone. "Think of it as a standby for the running lights. Just in case they crap out for some reason."

Madeira was already tiring of Reilly's snide little put-downs.

In fact, he was already tiring of Reilly himself.

The man appeared to be an excellent seaman when he wanted to be. He also struck Madeira as thoroughly arbitrary and capricious in the exercise of his own authority. Some days he was totally slack, the sailor's friend. Other day's—for no visible reason—he was a terror, even to those individual sailors who were normally his pampered favorites. He was, in short, just the sort of captain who keeps his ship constantly boiling and on edge.

Of equal importance, he was the sort of guy who couldn't seem to accept that just as the crew worked for him, he worked for somebody else. In this case, Al Madeira.

Unaware of Madeira's thoughts and seeming to have forgotten Hawkins for the moment, Reilly laughed a deep, rumbling, insincere chuckle that belied his long, sinewy frame and thin, almost pointy, face. He was dressed casually, as usual, in a moronic T-shirt under his windbreaker: Tonight's shirt proclaimed "SEX MACHINE" in large black and red letters.

As Reilly stood there, his long, thinning, sun-bleached hair floated in the breeze blowing through the pilothouse's open doors.

To Madeira, *Johnson*'s Master looked very much

like the aggressively hang-loose boat bum he'd undoubtedly always been.

On top of that, Reilly was a screamer, when he wasn't acting like everybody's pal. Madeira's first captain in the Navy, on a destroyer, had been a screamer, and he'd hated the type ever since. He'd also tried like hell to avoid being one himself.

"Think we'll get anything this morning, Al?" asked Reilly as he drew a cup of thick, steaming coffee from the percolator that burbled continuously under the chart table. "Looks kind of thick to me."

"It's thick, all right," Madeira replied, grabbing an unclaimed mug as he spoke, "but I think we'll get out from under it soon."

"What makes you think so?"

There it was again, Madeira thought. It wasn't just a question. There was more than a hint of belligerence, of challenge, in his tone.

"I don't know. Wishful thinking, I suppose. If it does break, I'll time for you and Paul. It's my turn."

"Okay," replied Reilly as he slurped at his coffee. "Paul needs some practice. Quite a bit, in fact."

"Skip!" the mate interjected, irritation showing in his tone, "I passed the exam. I've got my ticket."

"Yes, somehow you got a ticket, mate, but you've still got a lot to learn. Like keeping a civil tongue, to start."

The thought that Reilly might benefit from his own advice passed through Madeira's mind. At the same time, he had to agree that Hawkins might be a little better off if he kept his own mouth shut at times.

"As you say, Skip," answered the mate, the bitterness on his round, flat face all too clear even in the dim red illuminating the pilothouse.

All at once, the downpour ceased, as suddenly as it had started.

While Paul fumed sullenly in the pilothouse, Reilly and Madeira wandered back out to the starboard wing of the bridge to check the sky.

"They're still there," Reilly observed, pointing at the clouds as he spoke.

"I think I can see some thinning."

"Bullshit! You can't see any more than I can."

"We'll see."

"We'll also see about Paul. You will, that is. I already know he's not going to hack it. The owners hired him, I didn't. It was nepotism, and I don't like that kind of shit. I want to hire my own officers and I especially don't want somebody's incompetent nephew hung around my neck!"

"He'll be okay," replied Madeira, treading carefully. "He just needs a little time to settle in."

"And there's another thing I don't like! These secret orders we're sailing under. I'm sure you Navy guys're used to that sort of thing, but I'm not! My crew and I do everything together. I don't like not being able to tell them where we're going and what we're going to be doing."

"I don't like it either! I'm not as accustomed to them as you seem to imagine, but they're a condition of the charter. You, Bannerman, Peale, Higgins, and Gomez are the only ones who need to know until we reach Waypoint Alpha."

"I think it's all bullshit! Some sort of crypto-military bullshit!"

"I don't give a damn what you think! The charter party insisted on these terms and the owners, as you damn well know, need the charter, so they accepted them and we've got to observe them."

33

"Do *you* believe what they told us?"

"I assume we've been told the truth, but I'm keeping my eyes open. Frankly, I resent not being able to tell the crew as much as you do—*Johnson is* their ship—but they were told well ahead of time they'd have to wait."

"Damn right she is! *Our* ship! *My* ship! They're *my* crew and *Johnson's my* ship! And I don't like working for people like the ones who've hired us. I don't trust them. Do you?"

"Yes. I think I do."

"You're really making me feel much better about this. Do you think all this secrecy really makes sense?"

"Yes, if they're telling us the truth."

"Don't they understand we can't just steam off into the night and lose ourselves in the trackless oceans?"

"I don't think they're fools, although I've never met any of the principals in person. As far as I can tell, they want us to keep a low profile as long as possible. I think they're trying to avoid publicity as much as anything. They may be overdoing it a little, but they're paying the bills so we're going to do it their way—as long as it's legal and unless and until something drastic happens."

As he spoke, Madeira had the overwhelming desire to grab Reilly by his scraggly locks and pound his pointy face to a bloody pulp against the bulkhead in the hope it might improve his attitude. The man's treatment of Hawkins was both grossly unfair and insanely counter-productive. His attitude towards Madeira reeked of insubordination.

Catching his breath, Madeira was astounded at his own violent anger. It'd been so many, many years since he'd felt such personalized and intense fury. Anyway, Reilly was bigger than he was and he'd been with the owners for almost two years, while Madeira'd been there less than two months.

"I guess we'll just have to wait and see," said Reilly, his tone a mixture of resentment and ongoing challenge.

You're damn right, Madeira thought, struggling to control his own anger.

Madeira tried to shift his own thoughts to a more positive and constructive track. When it came to seamanship and shiphandling, he reminded himself, Reilly really was very competent. And up until a few months ago, he hadn't had an Operational Director over him to worry about. *Until I arrived, he had every reason to feel he was his own boss.*

"I'll be damned," Reilly exclaimed suddenly in a totally different tone, one of surprise and delight. "Look at that!"

"What?"

"A star!" he replied, his tone continuing to brighten. "There, to the southwest. Damn if you weren't right! It's clearing fast. We'll have plenty of time to shoot some stars."

Fifteen minutes later the horizon, first to the east and then in all directions, lightened sufficiently for the sky to separate itself from the sea. Reilly and Paul waited, sextants in hand, ready to shoot. Madeira, holding a pencil, clipboard, and stopwatch, stood behind them.

A temporary truce had descended as the three prepared for one of the sea's more solemn rituals. For over five hundred years the ceremony of shooting the stars had served to keep mariners from becoming hopelessly lost. To keep them from dying.

William S. Schaill

It had also served as a sort of cement that held together the the officers serving in countless thousands of ships.

Even today, when the satellites and little black boxes of the Global Positioning System will tell you where you are to within fifty feet, or even less, many still consider the ritual essential. They know that salt water and electronics don't mix. They know that the water will always, in the end, win. And they value the ceremony for its own sake.

"Sirius, Al," Reilly said suddenly, his voice alive with excitement, as if he were a hunter who'd just caught an unexpected glimpse of a prized and long-pursued quarry.

"I'm ready."

"Standby," the Master mumbled out of the side of his mouth as he squinted through the sextant's telescopic element and adjusted the arm, bringing the sparkling little dot that was Sirius down to the dark-silver horizon, now sharp and glimmering. "Mark!"

"Mark!" repeated Madeira as he made a note of the time. Reilly then turned the sextant on its side and pushed a small button, illuminating the micrometer from which he read the degrees, minutes, and seconds of Sirius's elevation in the night sky.

After Madeira had noted Reilly's data, it was Paul's turn.

"Procyon," he snapped in a tone that, while probably intended to be professionally brusque, failed to fully conceal the young mariner's excitement.

"I don't see Procyon, Paul," Reilly snapped back in a whiplash tone. "You sure it's not Capella?"

"Capella then!" replied Hawkins, his round face flushed.

Madeira winced. There are better ways to train, and to correct, junior officers. The truce seemed to be over.

"Stand by."

"Standing by."

Peering though the eyepiece, the mate made a delicate adjustment to the micrometer with his fingertips, then rocked the sextant slightly from side to side to make sure Capella was just kissing the edge of the black-silver sea.

"Mark!"

Each officer shot three more stars, Reilly snapping them confidently and rapidly, Paul working more carefully. The party then adjourned to the pilothouse, where each worked out his own solutions and plotted them on the paper chart.

When the mate finished plotting his lines of position and straightened up, Madeira leaned over and studied the chart. Seven of the eight lines crossed each other so closely they almost formed a dot. It was about the tightest fix he'd ever seen. As for the one maverick, not that it was off by much, he was surprised to note it was Reilly's. His irritation with Hawkins must have distracted him.

"Paul," Madeira remarked, "I think you're going to develop into a world-class navigator. This's an excellent fix, and with a little more practice, you'll develop more speed and confidence."

"Thank you," replied the young mate, smiling for the first time that morning. The smile, however, was a brief one, disappearing the instant he noticed Reilly's scowl.

With the tension securely back in place, the three walked out into the pastel dawn to watch in silence as the Gulf sun, huge and golden, rose shimmering out of the now-blue sea.

As the sun ascended, it split the few remaining clouds. In the process it illuminated the complex array of masts, girders, and the helo pad that grew like a jungle canopy over *Johnson*'s great, open bay.

Nestled in the bay sat MOHAB, her white paint already glowing in the sun's low rays. Now it was possible to see the clear, plastic hemisphere set into the habitat's bow, the day-glo-orange escape pod set into her deck, astern of the odd little conning tower, and the relatively large control surfaces that made MOHAB's stern look almost like the tail of an airplane.

It was Paul who first noticed the flash in the morning sky. "That sucker's coming in low!" he almost shouted, drawing Madeira's and Reilly's attention to the fast-approaching plane.

Madeira looked up just in time to see the twin-engine jet shriek overhead, the orange and black slash of the United States Coast Guard clearly visible on its fuselage. The plane then banked, returned for another look, turned again, and raced off into the rising sun.

Reilly, rolling his eyes, looked at Madeira and shook his head slightly. "All I can tell you, Al, is that the crew isn't happy about being kept in the dark. You'd damn well better come clean with them when we reach Waypoint Alpha. And make it clear it wasn't me who didn't trust them."

"I'll tell them everything I know and I'll get you off the hook. I promise."

"I intend to hold you to that promise, mate."

You can go to hell, "mate," Madeira thought.

Four

It's Goddamn hot down here, Madeira thought as
he stopped at the foot of the ladder leading down
from the top of the well wall to the well deck. Not
only was the afternoon sun beating down on him,
but the deck and walls were all radiating a fierce
heat.

Shading his eyes with the palm of his hand, he
looked aloft at the mast and the brilliant blue sky
around it. While *Johnson* hadn't altered course, the
wispy brown smoke snaking out of her funnel was no
longer tending aft. Thanks to the arrival of the Northeast Trades, it was now streaming out to starboard.

Unfortunately, while the Trades might be blowing
like hell up on deck, they seemed unable to reach
him down in the well.

Madeira turned back to MOHAB and studied her
a moment.

Blimp, he thought, was the operative word. A blimp with a day-glo orange beauty mark just aft of its stumpy little conning tower and two big runners, like those on a snow sled, which supported the blimp almost twelve feet above the deck.

Along the habitat's sides were several round airlocks and a number of hinged doors that opened into shallow, free-flooding lockers. Additional airlocks were also located on her back and bottom.

Madeira shook off the heat-induced sense of lethergy he felt descending on him, and started walking toward MOHAB.

"Freddie," he said when he saw the expedition's electronic technician's head pop briefly out of the main airlock, "is Carol in there?"

"Don't think so, Captain," replied Freddie Gomez, his round face dripping sweat, "but I'm not sure. I haven't seen her or Geoff for a while. They may have gone up on deck to take a break and get some fresh air. Or they could be in the office."

"Okay. Thanks."

Damn! he thought. She does manage to make herself scarce whenever I want to talk to her. Is it me or is it her?

He'd find Carol Bannerman, MOHAB's Chief Operator, later, he told himself as he strode over to the ladder that led up to the main airlock. For now he'd look around himself to see how the final preparations were going.

A dozen steps later and he was crawling into the habitat's Main Work Compartment, the largest by far of its four upper watertight compartments. It was at least as hot inside as it had been outside, although the two fans somebody had set up were at least moving the damp air around a little.

"How's it going?" he asked Gomez, who was lying

on the deck, soldering some wires that were hanging out of a large electronics console.

"Couldn't be better!" replied Gomez. "Everything but this one little circuit has tested okay, and I should be done fixing and testing it in another half hour."

"Excellent!" Madeira said as he looked around the compartment.

This is the heart of it, he thought. A large, self-propelled, one-atmosphere workspace into which custom-designed suites of electronics and other equipment can be installed to suit the needs of the project at hand. Everything else, including *Irving Johnson*, existed only to get this one space in place and keep it there.

"Can I do anything for you?" he asked Gomez. "Get you a soda, aim these fans better, or anything?"

"Not a thing. I'll be okay, but thanks for asking."

Madeira nodded, then walked forward, through the messing and berthing spaces, into the control station in MOHAB's bow. After looking idly out the plastic bubble, Madeira returned to the Main Work Compartment, and then continued aft through a small storeroom and into the motor room.

Everything appeared in order.

He returned yet again to the Work Compartment. "Okay, Freddie, keep up the good work."

"Roger," replied a voice from inside the electronics console.

Two hours later, *Johnson*'s high white bow was slicing into—then riding up and over—sparkling-blue eight-foot waves, each of which was capped with a frothy gold-and-white crown. Thanks to the building seas, the ship was beginning to pitch, rising and falling faster than before in short, elevator-like spurts. As the ship drove forward, she threw glistening clouds of spray back over her hunched shoulders.

Madeira stood in the pilothouse next to Frank Peale, *Johnson*'s small, weathered Chief Mate, and studied the nav plot. Twenty-five miles to the northeast lay Loggerhead Key, the westernmost of the Tortugas. A little over a hundred miles south lay Cuba, which, when seen on the display, made Madeira think of a twisty bacillus jammed into the mouth of the Gulf.

"As far as I'm concerned, we're there," he said to Peale as he looked up from the chart.

"You want me to assemble the crew then?" the Chief Mate asked in a voice with just enough singsong lilt to hint at an upbringing in Cajun Louisiana.

"Yes. Let's get it done before supper."

"Where?"

"Here, in the pilothouse. We'll all fit."

As he spoke, Madeira couldn't help wondering at the accuracy of his own statement. The combined crews of *Irving Johnson* and MOHAB totaled less than twenty, plus, of course, the three-man security group provided by the charter party. A Naval vessel of *Johnson*'s size and mission would have carried eighty to a hundred.

"Why not?" Peale asked. At fifty-one, the Chief Mate was the oldest person aboard, and also one of the few with whom Madeira felt at ease.

While Peale passed the word for the crew to assemble in the pilothouse, Madeira walked out to the wing and leaned on the rail. He stared intently at the creamy bow wave as it erupted quietly just aft of the prow, then rolled and slipped rapidly along the ship's vibrating side, pulsating slightly as it went, until it merged with the wake.

The strengthening, spray-laden wind, a combination of the Trades and the ship's own motion, snatched at his shirt and burrowed into his light, unzipped jacket. *Johnson* rolled stiffly, with a stuffy reluctance, inclining far to one side and suspending him out over the heaving froth. It was as if he were floating, gliding, hanging in the wind.

His attention shifted from the passing froth to the richly darkening blue waters themselves. They were the sort of blue he'd tried, and failed, for years to capture on film. They were the sort of blue that could never be captured on film because its essence is a factor of the mind rather than one of wavelengths. It was a blue one might ache to embrace, or to be embraced by.

All he had to was let go, he thought, relax his grip, and he would slip smoothly over the rail and down into that entrancingly deep, deep blue. There, in that divine blue, he would frolic briefly, freed finally and forever from the tedious weight of gravity, guilt, and responsibility. Then, at peace, he would be effortlessly and painlessly reabsorbed.

Christ! he thought with a start, backing away from the rail as he did. Where the hell had *that* impulse come from?

"We're all here, Al," Reilly said with what Madeira felt certain was false cheer.

"Thanks, Bud," replied Madeira, turning to examine the assembled crew.

His eyes settled on Carol Bannerman, MOHAB's Chief Operator. She lounged there, leaning against the rail, tall and fluid, her coveralls just tight enough to tantalize every man in the ship. A curl of amusement, a snicker maybe, adorned her smooth, full lips. In all, she radiated an aura of maddening desirability, icy, distant, and even contemptuous of all that surrounded her.

How had Frank Peale described her a day or two before? The sexiest damn woman he'd ever laid eyes on—except his wife?

Was her contempt an act? he wondered. A pose she'd found necessary to survive in what was still largely a man's field? Or was it a reflection of her true feelings?

She moistened her lips slightly.

The wind must be drying them, Madeira thought. Then she suddenly returned his glance, catching him by surprise.

Everything about her is so smooth and full, he thought. Everything but her eyes, whose laser-like intensity so belied the casual sneer on her lips.

He'd heard through the grapevine that NOAA hadn't killed itself trying to keep her when *Johnson*'s owners were recruiting. But nobody'd been able, or willing, to tell him exactly why.

Was it the sneer that had done her in? Or had her mere presence, an element over which she had absolutely no control, made it impossible for too many to concentrate on their jobs?

Either possibility seemed very likely, and either way, he would have to deal with it.

"All right. Listen up," he managed to utter, struggling to tear his eyes from Bannerman's. "I know you all want to know where we're going and what we're going to be doing, and I know you're all a little unhappy that you haven't been told until now."

"Damn right!" somebody shouted in a tone Madeira found extremely irritating.

"I'm sorry you couldn't be told, but the charter party insisted on it.

"Anyway, we're going on an archaeological expedition. Something of a treasure hunt. We've been hired by a private syndicate which is working with the Cuban-American Museum in Miami. They've located a Spanish treasure ship in twenty-four hundred feet of water on the Blake Plateau, about two hundred miles off South Carolina."

He noticed Reilly whispering something to Bobby Bell and several other seamen. The Master turned and looked at him, while the seamen smiled knowingly at each other.

"In a few minutes we're going to turn east and run through the Florida Strait. Then we'll head north until we rendezvous with *El Dorado*, the syndicate's ship."

"This wreck have a lot of gold in it?" asked that same irritating, unidentifiable voice.

"There may be some, but they seem to feel if we find anything of much value, it'll be silver. Their major objectives are scientific and historical."

"Right! What sort of numbers we talking here, Cap?"

I wish I knew who the hell that is, Madeira thought.

"They estimate up to a quarter of a billion," he admitted reluctantly.

"A quarter billion? You mean two hundred and fifty million?"

"Yes," Madeira said. Then he tried to move on quickly. "They've done a rough survey using their own ROVs from *El Dorado*, and they want us to do a detailed one and then to excavate. They have a staff archaeologist, a Dr. de Navarre, who will be supervising that part of the project."

"Gold! Shit, gold!" He heard the undercurrent, the murmuring amongst the assembled crew.

Where, he wondered, had Reilly managed to dredge up this gang? He knew they weren't typical merchant seaman. The hippy captain had somehow managed to create a whole crew in his own loud, smart-ass image.

"Let me repeat that they've played down the treasure aspect. They admit it's there, but they're more interested in the history. That's why they've hired us. If it were just a matter of treasure, they could grab it from the surface. They're spending millions of dollars to hire us, and MOHAB, because they want to excavate this wreck just they way they would a site on land."

For a moment there was silence, broken only by the sounds of the wind and the sea and the rumble of *Johnson*'s engines. Madeira's eyes settled briefly on Bannerman's. The expression of distant, uninvolved amusement had returned, along, perhaps, with even greater contempt for those around her.

"How long's this going to take?" asked one of the seamen sitting with Bell and Reilly.

"We've been chartered for a minimum of three weeks. I'm hoping we can get it done in that time. We'd *better* be able to because most of our sales pitch to them was that using MOHAB would speed up the recovery process greatly and, of course, improve the accuracy of the archaeological work and lessen the damage to any artifacts."

"We'll be at sea all that time?"

"Most of it. Why? You have something else to do?"

"No."

"Who's this syndicate? We allowed to know that?" It was another of Bell's companions.

"It's a syndicate of Cuban-American businessmen from Miami."

"Oh!" the seaman responded, a knowing look on his face. "Bang! Bang!" He used his right thumb and forefinger to simulate a pistol.

Madeira glowered at the man, angry that Reilly was doing nothing to rein in the childish distractions.

"What about souvenirs, Al?" It was Reilly himself this time, his face covered by a big, innocent grin.

Madeira's eyes hardened, reflecting his irritation with the question itself and with Reilly's behavior. Especially his present expression.

"There won't be any, not for us anyway. The charter party is paying well over a hundred thousand dollars per day for the efforts of this ship and this crew. You are all being paid roughly twice what you'd get on any other ship . . . and you will all be receiving a bonus if the job is completed on time. If anyone is caught trying to keep anything, anything at all, he'll be placed in confinement until the ship next reaches port and there he'll be charged with whatever the owners' attorneys think they can make stick!"

Goddamnit! thought Madeira in the silence that followed. Reilly just set me up! Conned me into overreacting!

He could feel his face flushing as he looked over the crew.

When his glance settled on the Security Director, Jake Smith, who was dressed as usual in splotchy camouflaged fatigues and floppy sun hat, his irritation grew.

It wasn't the uniform that bothered him, even though it was designed for use in the desert, or the side arm strapped around Smith's waist, or the automatic rifle slung over his shoulder. It was that big, shiny pigsticker strapped to his leg!

Actually, he scolded himself, it was all of it. It all made him nervous because he knew that the walking armory might yet prove to be indispensable and he wasn't totally confident of his own abilities in the security area.

His gaze returned to Reilly, and his anger reflashed. There was to be no peace with Reilly, he told himself. Reilly didn't want peace. He wanted Madeira's job—even though he had absolutely no qualifications for supervising underwater operations.

And what, Madeira wondered, did Carol Bannerman really want?

As he wondered what was really going on inside Bannerman's head, Frank Peale turned *Irving Johnson* east. Although she spread not one sail, the path she cut through the Florida Strait would soon be almost identical to that followed by the Spanish *nao Nuesta Senora de la Misericordia* over four hundred years before.

Five

"I wasn't totally satisfied with that all-hands meeting of yours this afternoon, Al," Reilly said. "And I doubt the crew was either. I'm sure they think you're trying to put something over on them. Or taking them for granted. I'm afraid you've still got a morale problem."

As the ship pitched and rolled, so did the small officers' and technicians' dining room. Madeira struggled to extinguish the slow-burning rage that continued to smolder within him as he watched a ray of the low-lying sun creep back and forth across the gimbaled table. He then looked up from his cream of chicken soup and across the dinner table towards *Johnson*'s Master.

"You may be right, Bud," he replied. "In fact, I'm afraid you *are* right. Fortunately, this vessel has an excellent set of senior techs and officers."

Madeira looked around the table. Hawkins,

Freddie Gomez, and the Chief Engineer were looking directly at him. The two assistant engineers and Geoff Higgins, MOHAB's Assistant Operator, were staring intently at their food. Carol Bannerman seemed to be looking out the porthole at the setting sun.

"I'm confident that with your leadership they'll recognize their duties. I'm sure we'll all get the job done, get it done right, and earn the very good pay we're all receiving.

"And for my part," he added, tasting bile as he spoke, "I'm going to work on being a little more diplomatic.

"How does that sound to you, Bud? As a plan, a starting point?"

"Of course," mumbled Reilly, irritated that he'd been so easily outmaneuvered.

"If you'll excuse me," Hawkins said quietly, "I'll relieve Frank now so he can get some supper."

Madeira nodded while Reilly continued to scowl.

An hour later Madeira was dead to the world, lying on his back and snoring loudly in the simple, but relatively roomy, stateroom-with-office set aside for the Operational Director.

Within a few minutes of his dropping off, Jake Smith banged on the door to Madeira's stateroom. Receiving no reply, the security chief opened the door to the room and shook Madeira on the shoulder.

"Captain Madeira! Captain Madeira!"

Torn from the dark, dreamless pit into which he'd fled from his frustrations, Madeira turned suddenly and eyed his visitor. He then glanced around the almost dark room, as if to orient himself. His mind spun briefly in confusion a second or two before the habits of so many years at sea snapped into place.

"Yes, Jake? What's up?" he asked, now wide awake and noting, as he spoke, that the ship was pitching and rolling with much greater violence than she had been when he'd collapsed into his bunk.

"We just received a message from the Director of Customs at Miami. She's sending two agents out by helo."

"Why? When're they supposed to arrive?" asked Madeira as he glanced out at the gathering dusk through one of the two big portholes that graced the stateroom.

"I don't know. Nineteen-thirty hours."

Madeira turned and looked at his little wind-up travel alarm—which had originally belonged to his grandfather, the immigrant, Portuguese cod fisherman, and which he'd been carrying around with him for almost thirty years.

The clock was, he reflected, just about the only material possession he'd acquired, or held on to, as an adult. In fact, just about all he had to show for all those years, many of them at sea, were a pension and a lot of memories, not all of them happy.

And maybe, a few friends here and there.

The clock's little hands, glowing a faint radium-green in the dim light, indicated it was well past seven.

"When did the message arrive?"

"About ten minutes ago."

"They sure as hell aren't giving us much warning."

"That may be the idea, sir."

"Has Captain Reilly been notified?"

"And Mr. Peale, sir. I notified them immediately so they can prepare to receive the helo."

Groaning inwardly, Madeira levered himself out of his bunk. He asked himself what the hell Customs wanted, and scented trouble as he did. Then, without turning on any light other than the small red light next to his bunk, he groped around for shirt, trousers, socks, and shoes.

"Tell me, Jake, do you like your work?" Madeira said, wondering the same about himself as he asked.

"More or less. Not as much as I used to, but there're still times," replied the Security Director, echoing Madeira's answer to himself.

"Do you have any idea what you might do if you weren't doing this?"

"Nope. I'm really not qualified to do much of anything else. Except maybe mow lawns."

Madeira, smiling skeptically, stood up and scrambled into his trousers. Not only was he beginning to like Rambo—outrageous mustache, pigsticker and all—but he was starting to suspect the security officer might be a great deal brighter than he'd originally assumed.

"I'll see you, Reilly, and Peale at the helo pad in five minutes."

"Roger."

Alone again, Madeira braced his hip against the sink and stared hard into the mirror as he washed his face in the dim red glow of his night-light.

He needed a shave. Even in the faint light he could see the stubble. And he could feel it too. But then he always looked as if he needed a shave.

Was it possible, he wondered, that once again he was about to discover he'd underestimated the situation? That once again he was in way over his head?

Not only did he have serious personnel problems, starting with an out-of-control captain, but he also had a nasty feeling somebody—somebody including him—had political problems too. And politics had never been his strong point.

Had the syndicate, he wondered with the casual cynicism of the times, backed the wrong person in the last elections? Or was Reilly right? Was it the syndicate itself that was up to no good?

When Madeira arrived at the helo pad five minutes later, he found *Johnson*, riding high with her ballast tanks pumped dry, charging through the Florida Strait's increasingly choppy seas. To the north, invisible in the near-darkness, lay the Keys. To the south, and equally invisible, smoldered Cuba. Ahead, to the east, stood rank upon rank of dense black line squalls, the offspring of a low-pressure trough located to the northeast of the Bahamas. It was the same trough whose dispersal had been repeatedly, and inaccurately, predicted all day.

At almost precisely nineteen-thirty hours a Coast Guard helicopter, its lights blinking in the murk, its rotors creating all the sound and pounding fury of a full gale, settled on *Johnson*'s helo pad.

The instant its wheels touched the pad's canted, side-slipping white deck, two figures, dressed in blue coveralls and nylon windbreakers, oozed out the door and moved rapidly away from it. The helo, now thrashing the air with even greater fury than before, immediately began to rise again, back to the relative safety of the unsettled, black air.

"Drake. U.S. Customs," said the first figure to reach Madeira, who was standing with Reilly and

Smith on a small catwalk running slightly below, and outboard of, the pad.

Madeira stiffled a yawn, not of boredom or disdain but of lingering fatigue, as he studied the badge and ID offered by the beefy, red-haired Customs officer.

Having never seen a Customs Service badge before, he had absolutely no idea what one should look like. For that matter, he thought, even if this is what they're supposed to look like, how hard would it be today to run off a thousand or so counterfeit ones? And as for the ID card, it looked more or less like every one of the thousands of government IDs he'd seen over the past quarter century. Those, he knew, *were* counterfeited in vast numbers.

"Al Madeira, MOHAB's Operational Director," he finally replied, offering his hand to Drake. "This is Captain Reilly, *Johnson*'s Master," he continued, "and this is Mr. Smith, our Security Director."

As he spoke, the thought occurred to Madeira that Smith might not really be Jake's last name. In his line of work a flexible identify might be very convenient. Even comforting.

"Howard. INS," said the second figure, a middle-aged, almost scholarly black man with grayish hair, a dapper mustache, and a slight smile, while Drake was shaking hands with Reilly and Smith.

"INS?" Madeira said.

"Immigation and Naturalization Service," replied Howard.

"Yes. Thank you," Madeira said. "I know what the INS is. What I want to know is why you're here? We were told two Customs officers would be arriving."

"We decided to team up," said the INS agent. "To work together."

"We have our orders, Al," interjected Drake of Customs.

"Yes, of course. What can we do for you? What are you here to do?"

"We'd like to keep an eye on things for a day or two," explained Drake. "Look into a few matters. Those're our orders and you know how *that* is, Al. Orders, I mean."

"I'm familiar with the problem. Now tell me, is it you people who have the Coast Guard buzzing us twice a day?"

"Not as far as I know, but they don't tell me everything. The Coast Guard may have its own reasons."

I wonder, Madeira thought, if I was as damn evasive and condescending as this guy when I worked for the government.

"Very well. Is there anything we can do for you now? Where do we start?"

"I'll start by taking a look at some of your voids," replied Drake, referring to the multitude of odd, enclosed spaces—generally too small or inconvenient for any practical use—found throughout every ship. As he spoke he smiled and pulled out a marked-up copy of the ship's plans. "If you don't mind."

"Not at all! I'll have the Chief Engineer give you a guided tour."

As he spoke, a gust of cold, damp wind punched out of the night and rumbled past, only to die away again.

"That's fine, Al. The Chief'll be fine, though I may want you and Captain Reilly with me from time to time."

You son of a bitch, thought Madeira as he nodded in agreement.

"And you, Agent Howard. What can we do for you?"

"I'll start with your personnel records. Then I'll probably want to interview a few of your crew members. And please make sure they all have all their papers before they come to see me."

"Of course! When do you want to start?"

"Right now, if you don't mind."

"Certainly," Madeira said.

"I'd like to start with your papers, Captain. And Captain Reilly's also," said Howard of the INS.

Madeira and Reilly spent the next four and a half hours scampering all over the ship. Explaining to Drake why certain recent alterations to the ship didn't appear on Drake's copy of her plans, even though the Chief Engineer had already explained it all once. Crawling through the bilges with the Customs officer. Rounding up sailors, even those in their racks, to be interrogated by Howard.

Howard finished shortly before midnight. Drake, although still prowling, seemed satisfied for the time being with the Chief Engineer's company.

Madeira and Reilly, both seething but, for once, not at each other, trudged up to the bridge for a final look-see before retiring.

"The Feds all settled in?" asked Frank Peale, who had the watch.

"Yeah, Frank," Reilly answered. "It looks to me like they're settled in for a long time. It's that damn syndicate. I told you they're trouble!"

"Is it true the IRS arrives tomorrow?" Peale asked, looking out the window at the latest volley of raindrops as they slammed into the pilothouse window.

"I wouldn't be a bit surprised, Frank!" replied

Reilly, looking at the navigational plot. "Where the hell are we?"

"We're moving right along, Captain. We're well past Cay Sal and about to turn north."

"What's the traffic been like?" Madeira asked, his head now pounding almost in concert with the ship's engines.

"Pretty light. Couple tankers. A big container ship blitzed by an hour or so ago, and a couple fishing boats. There were a bunch of yachts, sport fishermen, but they've all pretty much disappeared, except for one lunatic who's running up fast from the south. He must be beating his brains out at the moment."

Madeira and Reilly grunted in unison. And then the phone buzzed and Madeira answered.

"This is the Chief, Captain," the Chief Engineer said. "I think you and Reilly better get down here to the starboard steering room pronto."

"What's the problem?" asked Madeira as his stomach started to churn.

"Agent Drake found a couple ounces of grass in one of the voids."

"Oh, Goddamnit! We'll be right there."

"What?" Reilly demanded.

"Marijuana. Drake found some in the starboard steering room."

"Shit!" Reilly mumbled as he stepped around the control console with its rows of red, green, and orange lights. He followed Madeira down the first of several ladders and companionways that led from the bridge to the starboard steering room, the small room in the very stern where the electric motor that controlled the starboard rudder was located.

When they arrived they found the Chief, his bald

head glistening slightly and his customary smile absent, and Agent Drake standing in silence. The Customs officer was bracing himself with one hand against the steel bulkhead as the deck rose and fell. The Chief was posed, legs spread slightly apart in the middle of the space. In his free hand Drake was holding a small plastic bag containing the brown vegetable matter.

"You gentlemen know anything about this?" Drake demanded.

"Looks like somebody's personal stash," Reilly said with a hint of relief in his voice. "It's obviously been opened and closed a few times and half of it's gone." The steering motor whirred briefly in the background.

"And?" said Drake.

"And so it's not a case of big-time smuggling."

"That remains to be seen. As I always say, where there's smoke there's fire."

Then, without giving Reilly time to respond, Drake turned to Madeira. "We're going to have to go into Miami to take a closer look at all this, Cap."

"I thought the Zero Tolerance Program was over," Madeira replied, his alarm all too clear.

"We're not talking about seizing the vessel or anything like that. At least not yet. And that program is discretionary now. Like I said, I want to take a closer look at everything, make sure I've got a handle on it all."

The satisfaction in Drake's smile was impossible to miss.

The phone buzzed. "I think you and Reilly had better get back up here," Peale said when Madeira answered.

"What's the problem?"

"That speed demon to the south. He's headed right for us and he's got me spooked."

"We're on our way," Madeira said.

"There's a problem on the bridge, Drake," he said after hanging up. "You mind if Captain Reilly and I go do something about it?"

"No, that's fine. And be sure to change course to Miami. I'll be up in a few minutes, after I look around a little more."

Four minutes later Madeira and Reilly were back on the bridge. Both were puffing slightly from having sprinted up far too many ladders.

"This's him," said Peale, pointing at a glowing dot on the radar screen. "I don't understand what the *hell* he's doing. He must be making fifty knots in this shit, and he doesn't seem headed anywhere in particular. Unless he's steering an intercept for us!"

Making fifty knots along the edge of a tropical storm of some sort, Madeira thought, his mental alarms starting to scream. And making no effort to run for cover.

"You sure it's a boat, Frank?"

"Could be another helo, I suppose, but it looks to me like a boat. The blip's too small for a ship."

It looked like a boat to Madeira too.

"Did you notice where he came from?"

"No."

"Could it have been from Cuba?"

"We're eighty or ninety miles north of their territorial waters!"

"It's that Goddamn syndicate!" Reilly said.

"Maybe it's nothing," Madeira replied, "but in the past I've found assuming that has been a mistake."

He then walked over to the navigational plot.

"The choices are Key West or Miami. Miami's the

closest and . . . we don't have a choice, do we? Drake's already made the decision for us."

"Miami it is, then," Reilly said.

"Very well. Frank, all ahead flank. We're going to make a run for Miami and hope it's all just our imagination."

"It'd better be," replied Peale. "It's seventy miles to Miami and that boat'll be here in about twenty minutes the rate he's going."

"I know," Madeira said, picking up the telephone.

Six

"Smith speaking, sir," said the man with the bushy blond mustache at the other end of the line.

"This is Madeira, Jake," Madeira replied quietly but firmly. "Did you remount the fifty on the helo pad?"

"Affirmative! Why?"

"Get your two deputies back there and rig it for firing! There's something heading for us at about fifty knots and I don't like the feel of it."

"Why would anybody be after us now? We haven't recovered anything yet!"

"You'd know better than me. A competitor maybe?"

"Wait one . . . "

Wait one what? thought Madeira.

"I'm on my way to the pad, Captain Madeira."

"Roger. And step on it!"

"I'm on my way, sir."

Madeira paused, catching his breath and attempting to sort through the multiple, contradictory impulses racing through his mind.

"Frank!" he shouted to the Chief Mate.

"Yes, Al?"

"Get Drake up here!"

"Roger. Where is he?"

"Probably still in the starboard steering room. With the Chief."

In all likelihood, Madeira told himself, it was just some hot dog, some stock-and-bond hotshot with too much money for his own good out getting his thrills by tempting fate. Any minute now the moron would turn and head home, wherever that was. Before his engines failed or his hull cracked. Before he caught a wave the wrong way or the wind grabbed his bottom and flipped him.

Three and a half hours to Miami, Madeira thought, feeling the increased vibration and the louder, throatier roar issuing from the funnel as *Johnson*'s engines were pushed to the limit.

He had no good, logical reason to assume this vessel, approaching so fast, represented any threat at all. No good reason except a knot in his stomach, a knot he'd learned, the hard way, not to disregard.

"What the hell you people up to?" demanded Drake as he burst, panting, into the pilothouse.

Damnit! Madeira thought, he still thinks we're trying to pull something on him.

"We're not up to anything, Drake. That target on the radar . . . here . . . may be up to something."

Drake studied the blip, now about five minutes away and still maintaining the intercept, then picked up the phone.

"How do I get Howard?" he demanded over his shoulder.

"Here," Reilly said, pushing the appropriate button.

"Howard?" Drake said into the phone.

After a pause, he continued. "Yes. This's Drake. I don't know what the hell's going on up here, it may be nothing, but there's a boat approaching at very high speed. You stay down there and keep an eye on things, and don't let any of their people get behind you. I'll stay on the bridge."

While Drake was speaking, another phone buzzed. Reilly grabbed it and listened a moment. "It's Jake Smith, Al. He wants you."

"You set back there, Jake?" asked Madeira, looking out the aft window of the pilothouse as he spoke. Four blobs of denser gray-black, Smith, his two deputies and the fifty-caliber machine gun—were all faintly visible on the helo pad.

"Yes, sir, we're almost ready. We're just going to throw up a little protection for ourselves, some shoring timber and steel piping. Not enough to stop a cannon, but it'll keep any small-arms fire down.

What's the plan?"

"You're to make sure they don't get aboard from astern. As long as we keep moving fast, and keep twisting and turning, I don't think they can get aboard over the sides, they're too high. But I think it *is* possible for them to run up our wake and jump aboard aft."

"What about grapnels?"

"You mean if they come alongside and use them? It's possible, I guess. We're going to have to make it as difficult as we can for them."

"Gotcha!"

"But I don't want any firing unless and until I tell you to! Understood?"

"Understood."

"I see 'em now," reported Peale, a pair of big night glasses jammed into his eyes. "Looks to me like one of those damn Cigarettes, a big one! Fifty, sixty feet. Maybe its a drug boat. Headed right for us and moving!"

"Very well," Madeira replied automatically. "Bud, did you hear what I told Jake? I'm going to want you to handle the ship."

"Yes. You want to keep moving and keep twisting?"

The feral, snarling roar of the approaching boat's huge engines was now clearly audible as the Cigarette pounded toward them, slapping the black waves and tossing up high curtains of spray. The Cigarette's engines were soon totally outshouting the purposeful rumbling of *Johnson*'s considerably more powerful yet infinitely more domesticated diesels.

"Yes, if it comes to that. Wait for me to tell you to take evasive action."

"I'm going to disengage Mike and put Rollins here on, just to be ready."

"Good," answered Madeira, as he watched Rollins, one of the ship's more dependable seamen, step over to the steering console and disengage the automatic pilot.

"Zero Two Two, Rollins," Reilly ordered.

"Zero Two Two, Skipper."

"*Johnson*, this is U.S. Customs. Heave to!" squawked the radio, with what sounded to Madeira like a slight accent.

"What the hell!" he mumbled, stunned. Grabbing a pair of night glasses, he raced Reilly to the wing of the bridge.

"I say again, *Johnson*. Heave to! This is Customs."

Madeira and Reilly stood side by side in the salty

rain, binoculars raised, studying the Cigarette. Now about fifty yards to port, the big speedboat had slowed and turned to parallel *Johnson*'s course.

"They look like Customs," Madeira remarked skeptically. "They do use that kind of boat." And, he added to himself, a lot of Customs officers speak with a slight accent.

"Horsehit!" Reilly spat. "Any thug can buy a blue jacket—I think those jackets are blue—and stencil 'U.S. Customs' on it."

"Drake," said Madeira as he turned toward the Customs agent, who was looking at Reilly with an expression of intense distaste, "what do you know about this? Is this more of you?"

The Cigarette, her immense engines thundering and rumbling despite having been throttled way back, pounded wildly in the short, dark seas. *Johnson*, now in full flight, rose and fell and rolled with considerably more decorum.

"I'll take a look," Drake said as he hung over the bridge rail, studying their pursuers. "I don't know anything about this. Nobody told me a fucking thing about it. They could be Customs, but—"

"Don't you people have some sort of recognition signal or something you can use to identify yourselves?"

"Yes, more or less."

Drake rushed back into the pilothouse and picked up the radio mike, "This is *Johnson*. One Customs Officer is already aboard this vessel. Alpha Two Seven. Over."

"*Johnson*, this is Customs. Heave to and prepare for boarding."

"This is *Johnson*. I say again, Alpha Two Seven."

"Why the hell don't they respond?" demanded Reilly.

"I don't know," Drake said. "They may be operating out of Key West, or Tampa, or even Jax."

Before Drake could finish, Madeira heard a rapid, muffled thwacking sound behind him, almost as if someone were sucking loudly on something.

Turning, he was astonished to discover a line of jagged holes punched through the aluminum bulkhead and on up into the shatterproof glass of the pilothouse windows.

"Everybody in the pilothouse down!" he shouted. "And keep down! Drake's buddies are shooting at us."

"Ain't no buddies of mine," Drake snarled as the three of them, crouching all the way, retreated to the starboard side of the pilothouse and, they hoped, out of the line of fire.

"Okay, Bud," Madeira said, "commence evasive maneuvers. Ram 'em if they give you the chance. Otherwise, try to keep 'em on the quarter where Smith can get a clean shot."

"Right full rudder!" Reilly responded. "Steady on Zero Nine Zero."

While Reilly turned the ship east, Madeira turned on the PA system. "The ship is under attack. All hands, except for security personnel, are to stay belowdecks, under cover. I say again, all hands are to stay belowdecks."

Then, while his announcement was still echoing through the ship, he grabbed the telephone and punched the button for the helo pad.

"Jake, commence fire whenever you think you can get a good shot at them."

"Understood!"

With that, the fifty started barking sharply and rapidly, its muzzle blast faintly visible from the bridge as a flickering blue-yellow glow in the damp, heaving darkness.

"Where's Gomez?" Madeira asked into the darkness.

"Right here, sir," replied Freddie as Madeira leaned over to study the nav plot.

"Patch me into a voice-distress frequency!"

"Roger. You've got it!"

"Mayday . . . Mayday . . . Mayday," Madeira said as clearly as he could into the radio mike. "This is the research vessel *Irving Johnson*. I am under attack, receiving automatic-weapon fire from an unidentified vessel. My position twenty-four degrees, thirty minutes north, eighty degrees, twenty-one minutes west. Am maneuvering on various courses at one nine knots in an effort to evade attack. Mayday . . . Mayday . . . Mayday."

After two tries, he received a response. "*Irving Johnson, Irving Johnson*, this is Coast Guard Group Miami. I understand you are under attack. Do you require assistance?"

"Coast Guard Miami, this is *Johnson*. Affirmative. We require assistance."

"Roger, *Johnson*. Do you have any information concerning identity of attacking vessel?"

"This is *Johnson*. Vessel initially identified itself as U.S. Customs, but the Customs agent embarked on *Johnson* does not believe vessel is his."

"*Johnson*, this is Coast Guard Miami. We will confirm with Customs. Stand by."

While Madeira stood by, *Johnson*, her engines straining to drive her at almost twenty-two knots, twisted and turned, slicing through the rising seas and cold drizzle, desperate to evade her attacker.

Aft, the fifty-caliber machine gun fell silent.

"Where is he?" asked Madeira.

"Don't know," replied Reilly. "He's fallen back into the dark."

"Here he comes again," Peale shouted, standing over the radar screen. "Looks like he's trying to come alongside on our starboard bow."

"My ass!" Reilly said. "Keep me posted. I can't see a fucking thing."

"About a hundred yards now. He's almost abeam, coming in at right angles."

"Fifty yards now."

Madeira braced for the sharp turn he was sure Reilly was about to make.

"*Johnson*, this is Coast Guard Group Miami. How long has the Customs Officer been aboard you?"

"Twenty-five yards now," called out Peale.

"Right full rudder," Reilly shouted. "I can see him now!"

"Heave to, *Johnson*!"

"I think we're going to get him! I think we're going to nail the fucker amidships!"

"*Johnson*, this is Coast Guard Group Miami. I say again, how long have the Customs Officer been aboard you?"

"Damnit, Rollins! You all the way over? Do you have the rudder all the way over to the stops?"

"Coast Guard Miami, this is *Johnson*. The Customs Officer has—"

"Shit! We're going to miss him. The bastard's goosed it and turned inside us. He's headed aft along the starboard side."

The fifty exploded to life again just as the ship, now beam to the massive, pounding seas and still turning hard, lurched sharply over on her starboard side. Everybody in the pilothouse was forced to grab something, anything, to maintain their footing.

Christ! thought Madeira when he realized the gun had fallen silent. I hope that didn't pitch Jake and his crew over the side! Almost as if to reassure him, the fifty commenced barking purposefully again.

And then he thought of MOHAB, all two hundred plus tons of her, and shuddered. Cradled and braced for heavy weather though she was, it was always possible that she might break lose as *Johnson* twisted, turned, and rolled.

That would be the end, if it happened. The end for MOHAB herself. The end for *Johnson* if MOHAB battered her way through the ship's sides, and the end for Al Madeira, assuming he survived the wreck.

Seconds later the solid wall of water generated by an intense squall slammed into the ship. The thunderous drumming on the roof of the pilothouse immediately drowned out all other sounds, including that of their attackers' bullets punching additional holes in the windows.

"Come around to Zero Three One if you can, Bud," Madeira shouted, returning to the most immediate threat. "We're being herded away from Miami."

"*Johnson*, this is Coast Guard Group Miami. We did not read your last transmission," squawked the radio. "Repeat your last transmission."

The fifty fell silent, but not the storm.

"Okay."

"Coast Guard Miami, this is *Johnson*. The Customs Officer has been aboard since about seventeen-thirty hours. He arrived in one of your helos."

"Where are they, Frank," Reilly shouted. "I've lost 'em again."

"Roger, *Johnson*."

"So have I. All the radar's showing is sea return. I won't be able to see a thing until this rain lets up."

"Shit!" Reilly replied as Rollins, the helmsman, steadied on course Zero Three One.

"Jake," Madeira said into the telephone, using the lull to check on the security group, "are you all okay back there? I was afraid we'd dumped you overboard on that last turn."

"Yeah, we're okay, sir. We've rigged some hand-holds but if this keeps up, we're going to drown right where we are."

"Hang on then! Can you see him? We've lost him."

"I think so. I think I can see him coming right up our wake, it's sort of glowing, you know, phosphorescent, just like you thought he might try."

"How close is he?"

"It's hard to judge in this crap. I'd guess a hundred yards and closing. I'm waiting to see the whites of his eyes before opening fire again."

"Just don't wait so long you find he's stuffed something between your ribs."

"No chance of that."

"*Johnson*, this is Coast Guard Miami. We have confirmed with Customs that one of their officers is aboard you. We have also confirmed that Customs knows nothing about the vessel attacking you. We are dispatching a cutter and a helo to investigate."

"Roger, Coast Guard Miami," Madeira replied, glancing at the Global Positioning System plot again. "Be advised my present position is twenty-four degrees, twenty-eight minutes north, eighty degrees, twenty-two minutes west. Am coming to course Zero Three One, speed one-nine. Will maintain this course and speed if possible. Be further advised I am in the middle of an intense line squall and more appear to be headed my way."

"Roger, *Johnson,* I understand two-four degrees, two-eight minutes north, eight-zero degrees, two-two minutes west, course Zero Three One, speed one-nine and intense line squalls."

A succession of rapid, muted concussions assaulted Madeira's free ear. Smith had finally seen the whites of their eyes.

"Roger, Coast Guard Miami."

Dropping the radio mike, Madeira slammed his opened hands onto either side of his head, trying to hold it together, or at least to drive away the pain. It felt as if all the fury of the battle and of the storm had been concentrated and pounded into his skull.

Recognizing the futility of his efforts, he picked up the phone and called back to the helo pad.

"What's the situation back there now?"

"They're still coming up our wake and we have them under fire," Smith shouted above the continuous thundering crack of the gun and the equally thunderous hammering of the rain.

Madeira, looking aft, could see nothing at all. Not even the helo pad and the gun crew. "What's their range now?"

"Twenty-five yards maybe."

"I don't think they're trying to board us, Bud."

"Well, then, what the hell *do* you think they're trying to do?"

"Shoot us up! Sink us! In these seas they've got to get close just to hit us."

"That why they tried that Customs bit?"

71

"That's my guess. To keep us from doing what we're doing until they could hit us."

Still looking aft, Madeira spotted a bright flash astern of the gun, and off to one side. It started small and seemed to grow.

"Congratulations!" he shouted into the phone, the awful pounding in his head momentarily forgotten. "Wasn't that a hit you just got?"

"Say again?"

"I just observed a big flash aft."

"Yes, I saw it too but I'm not sure. . . . Oh, shit! No!"

"What?"

"That wasn't a hit. They just fired a Goddamn missile at us!"

Seven

Madeira was stunned briefly by Smith's warning. He barely had time to press his nose against the aft window before a sharp, hard, blindingly white ball of flame erupted in the canopy of cranes and beams that covered the bay. The blast's flash sliced through the rain and dark like a laser, instantly vaporizing whatever fluids happened to fall within its sway.

Even before the glowing ball had expanded to its fullest glory, a chest-crushing boom rolled forward and filled the pilothouse with its thunder, causing everything not welded into place to rattle violently.

"Jesus Christ!"

"Shit!"

"Definitely not Customs," shouted Drake, who'd been largely silent during the enagagement. "We don't use missiles anymore, not since we shot one at a drug plane and wiped out a whole family of taxpayers having dinner in a farmhouse."

"I'm glad that's been cleared up," Madeira replied, his ears still ringing and his mind still so stunned by the missile, he was barely aware of the inanity of Drake's remark. Or of his own reply.

"Jake," he shouted into the phone, "can you still see him? Can you see any more on the way?"

"Not any more. I can't see him anymore. I think he's dropped back. We were damn lucky! I bet that was a heat-seeker. Probably headed for the stack and ran into a crane on the way."

"Any casualties?"

"No, but there's been a shitload of hot metal zinging around back here. From the explosion, I mean. It's been falling on us."

"Very well. Keep under cover as much as possible and keep your eyes open. We still can't see a damn thing on the radar."

"Roger."

Twenty-three years in the Navy, thought Madeira, and I was never once involved in ship-to-ship combat. Now that I'm a civilian . . .

He paused a moment, rubbing his head. The ship, now running across the seas, was rolling and jerking. Suddenly, he turned to Reilly. "Did you feel that?"

"What?"

"A sort of grinding."

Before Reilly could answer, Madeira had the phone in his hand. "Jake."

"Yes, Captain?"

"Take a look down into the bay. Is anything going on there?"

While Madeira waited for Smith's reply, the ship

rolled to port again, and again he thought he felt the grinding.

"We got real trouble, Captain!" the Security Chief reported a few minutes later. "It looks like some of MOHAB's shoring has worked loose or snapped. I think the damn thing's moving!"

"Is anybody down there?"

"All I can see is Bannerman. She's trying to shove a brace back in place."

"Goddamnit!" growled Madeira in frustration as the ship rolled yet again.

"Turn north!" he snapped to Reilly. "Turn into the seas and slow to bare steerageway."

"Roger," replied Reilly, who then repeated the order to Rollins, the man at the helm.

"Where's Hawkins supposed to be?" Madeira asked Peale.

"Amidships. Checking for damage."

Madeira grabbed the PA mike. "Mr. Hawkins! You are to collect a party of seamen and get back to the bay immediately. MOHAB is breaking loose!"

He glanced around the pilothouse, eerie in the dim red light, and studied the drawn faces around him.

Reilly and Peale could handle the situation there for a few minutes, he decided. Until MOHAB was resecured, the ship's ability to manouver would be very limited. So getting the habitat tied down again, before the attacker reappeared, should be his top priority.

"I'm going to see what I can do about MOHAB."

With that, he sprinted out the door, into the heavy rain, and down three ladders to *Johnson's* weather deck. He continued running over the slick deck until he arrived at the rail along the forward end of the bay. He looked down into the great open space, now lighted with cargo lights. There was Bannerman, soaked to the skin with her long brown hair all scraggly, struggling to jolly a ten-by-ten timber into one of the reinforced sockets built into the bay wall.

The ship rolled heavily to port again as Reilly turned into the messy seas. As the ship rolled, Madeira felt the grinding sensation again, only stronger now since he was closer to the problem. He could also hear the deep screech that went with the grind. And he could see MOHAB's great white mass, glistening in the damp light, as it hopped toward Bannerman.

Christ! he thought. She was trapped between the two-hundred-ton blimp and the wall.

His breath catching, Madeira charged down the ladder into the bay. He could feel the ship beginning to pitch as her bows started to meet the waves head-on. He could also feel her slowing.

Just as he reached the bay's deck, Madeira saw Bannerman scamper out from behind MOHAB and into the clear. Then he spotted Hawkins, his blond hair plastered by the rain to the top of his head, followed by the Bos'n and half-a-dozen seamen. They were all charging down the ladder on the other side of the bay.

Headed as she was into the seas, *Johnson* was already beginning to behave much more reasonably—rolling very little and generally much less lively.

Madeira hurried over to Bannerman. "Are you okay, Carol?"

"Yes, Goddamnit!"

She was clearly angry. And maybe more than a little scared. Madeira started to tell her she should have called for help the instant she'd realized there was a problem, but caught himself. Now wasn't the time.

"Okay. Why don't you, Hawkins, and the Bos'n put this thing back to bed."

"Okay."

He watched as the work party scrambled across the slick deck to replace shores, blocks, and tie-downs. Bannerman, he decided, was okay and MOHAB seemed quiet. For the moment. There really wasn't much he could contribute to the process except maybe shouting a little unnecessary and unwanted advice.

If the attacker held off for a while, gave them enough time to get MOHAB back to bed, they could continue to hold off the Cigarette all the way to Miami.

If not? If they attacked again in thirty seconds or twenty minutes?

He didn't know.

His proper place, he decided, was back on the bridge again.

"Anything new?" he asked as he puffed his way into the pilothouse.

"Nope," Peale replied in his customary Cajun lilt.

Madeira reached for the phone and buzzed the main engine room.

"Chief," he said a moment later, "I want you to inspect all your spaces for damage."

"We're already doing that. So far, nothing."

"Good! Keep at it."

The phone buzzed again. "This is Hawkins, sir."

"How are you doing?"

"Making progress, although it'll take at least another hour to get her completely snugged down."

"As soon as you do ask Bannerman to check MOHAB for damage."

"She's already started."

"Oh. Is there any?" Madeira asked.

"Not that she's found so far, sir."

"Good. Then we'll get Freddie in there to start checking the electronics in a few minutes."

"Roger."

"Very well," Madeira concluded.

That's such a useful phrase, he added to himself. You can mumble it whenever you don't know what the hell else to say.

"*Johnson*, this is Coast Guard Group Miami. What is your status?"

The radio, which had been mumbling quietly in the background, had suddenly burst into life.

"Coast Guard Miami, this is *Johnson*. Several minutes ago attacker fired what appeared to be a heat-seeking missile at us. Missile detonated among our top hamper. No casualties. No serious damage. We are currently in the middle of an intense squall. Unable to see attacker. Unable to detect anything on radar."

"Did you say 'missile,' *Johnson*?"

"Affirmative, Coast Guard Miami. Mike. India. Sierra. Sierra. India. Lima. Echo."

"Roger, *Johnson*. Keep us posted."

"Roger, Coast Guard."

Silence again returned to the pilothouse as both Madeira and Reilly started pacing in small circles, each on his own side of the control console.

"Where the hell is he!" Reilly snarled a few minutes later. Both he and Madeira stopped and looked at Peale.

"Still nothing but sea return here."

"No news is good news, I suppose," said Madeira.

"Jake," he said into the phone, "you see anything back there?"

"Negative."

"If it'd just clear up a little, we could see something on the radar."

"Then something could see us, too," Madeira replied.

"Freddie," Peale asked, turning to the electronics specialist, "is there some sort of magic you can work on this radar?"

"I'm afraid not, Mr. Peale. I'm afraid we're just going to have to wait for the rain to let up."

"I knew you were going to say that!"

Thirty tense, silent minutes later, after Freddie Gomez had headed aft to check MOHAB's electronics, the radio came to life again. *"Johnson, this is Coast Guard One Four Seven Six, Over."*

One Four Seven Six? Must be the helo, Madeira finally realized, surprised that he was unable to hear or see it.

"Roger Coast Guard One Four Seven Six. This is *Johnson.*"

"Johnson, we believe we have located you but are unable, due to the extreme weather, to hold position. Be advised we believe we have detected at least two other vessels within ten miles of you but are unable to further identify."

"Roger One Four Seven Six," replied Madeira, imagining the bouncing, banging, crashing hell the helo crew must be experiencing. "What are your intentions?"

"We'll cover you the best we can, *Johnson.*"

"Roger." Madeira guessed that the heaviest weapon aboard the helo was an automatic rifle of some sort.

Where the hell are they? Madeira thought over

and over during the next hour as *Johnson* pounded her way north through squall after unbroken squall, guarded, or so he hoped, by the unseen angel.

"It's starting to let up a little," Peale finally reported. "I think I've got the coastline, some of the northern Keys, but there's still a lot of crap on the screen."

The phone buzzed. It was Jake Smith. "I think I hear a chopper someplace."

"Roger, Jake," answered Madeira, "that should be the Coast Guard."

Madeira walked over beside Peale and looked down at the radar display.

Yes! Reception *had* improved.

"What do you think this is?" he asked Reilly, who was now also standing beside him.

Johnson's Master studied the blip a moment. "It's big, too big for that boat. Tanker maybe, or a containership. Maybe a cruise ship headed for Everglades City or Lauderdale."

"Coast Guard One Four Seven Six, this is *Johnson*."

"Roger, *Johnson*. This is One Four Seven Six."

"One Four Seven Six, can you identify contact bearing Zero Eight Seven, range One Seven miles from me?"

"Be advised, *Johnson*, we now have approximately fifteen contacts within fifteen miles of you. None appear to threaten you at this time."

"Roger."

He stepped over to the window and looked out. The rain was definitely slacking off somewhat. He'd just have to be patient, and pray.

"Al," Peale broke in, "it's beginning to clear up. Fast! I've got half-a-dozen contacts including a fairly small one to the northwest on our intercept. There's another about eighteen miles to the west."

"The one coming at us must be the cutter," Madeira said, hoping he was right. "What's the one to the west doing?"

"Not much. He's about ten miles offshore and is either hove to or following the coastline slowly."

"Which direction?"

"The one to the west? West, I think. If he's moving at all."

"How far's the cutter?"

"About twenty-five miles."

"Anything to the south?"

"Nothing! I don't see a damn thing there except rain shadows!"

Was the contact to the west the Cigarette? Madeira wondered. Idling along? Watching? Waiting?

Or was it a fishing boat? Or a yacht?

And, Madeira asked himself, how realistic was it to expect the helo to be able to make positive IDs of so many different vessels under the prevailing conditions?

Presumably the cutter would have noticed their attacker if he'd blitzed into Miami, but there were half-a-dozen inlets to the north or west he could have reached by now. And once the big racing machine had slipped into any one of those inlets, he'd be lost. It'd be almost impossible to find him among the coral and mangroves and Cigarette-filled marinas.

Hell! Maybe the vessel closing them from the north wasn't the cutter! Maybe it was the Cigarette!

Could he possibly be fast enough to have repositioned himself that quickly?

Could the helo really do much if it was the Cigarette?

"Research Vessel *Johnson*, Research Vessel *Johnson*, this is the Coast Guard Cutter *Point Refuge*."

"Roger, *Point Refuge*. This is *Johnson*. Over."

"*Johnson*, this is *Point Refuge*. I hold you twenty-three miles due south of me. Is this correct?"

Madeira walked over to the navigational plot, and after examining it, raised the radio mike to his lips. "*Point Refuge*, this is *Johnson*. Your last transmission correct. We have second contact, about five miles southeast of you. Do you know the identity of this contact?"

"Negative, *Johnson*. Do you have any reason to believe contact is attacker?"

"Negative, *Point Refuge*."

"Be advised my orders are to escort you to Miami. Accordingly, am unable to investigate contact."

"Roger."

"Be further advised I have harbor pilot aboard. You are directed to stop abeam of Miami Seabuoy. I will come alongside at that time and transfer pilot."

"Roger, *Point Refuge*."

The phone buzzed. "This is Hawkins, sir. MOHAB's all secure again. Do you want the Bos'n and me to inspect the rest of the ship?"

"Affirmative, Paul. And good work on MOHAB."

Madeira sweated through the next forty-five minutes, alternating between studying the radar display, which showed the mystery contact still hovering far to the north, and examining the bullet holes in the bulkheads and windows.

"Here's the cutter now," Reilly said at last from the port bridge wing.

Madeira and Peale joined him just in time to watch the ghostly form of the white ninety-five-foot cutter slide past in the drizzle. It then turned and took station about fifty yards abeam to starboard, between *Johnson* and the unidentified contact to the north.

Although Madeira was under no illusions about the cutter's ability to defend them, or even herself, against missiles, he felt a great deal calmer now that she'd arrived.

Returning to the pilothouse, he picked up the radio mike: "*Point Refuge*, this is *Johnson*. We are very pleased to have you with us."

"Our pleasure, *Johnson*. Wish we could have reached you sooner."

"Ship's in good shape," reported Hawkins, who'd suddenly appeared on the bridge, "except for the starboard quarter crane, which the missile hit and is now useless, and some holes in the superstructure."

"We can operate without the crane," Madeira remarked, thinking aloud, "and we can patch the holes for now. Very well, Paul. Thank you. The Chief reports his spaces have received little or no damage, so we're okay."

Just under two hours later they were abeam the Miami Seabuoy. Reilly immediately turned into the messy seas, and stopped while Peale lowered a Jacob's ladder and a number of fenders. As he did, Madeira let out a shuddering sigh of relief.

Within seconds, the cutter had slipped alongside, bumping just once. A figure wrapped in orange day-glo raingear immediately sprang from her heaving deck onto the swaying rope ladder. The climber, the harbor pilot, made the trip up the ship's high, rolling side seem effortless. He climbed calmly and steadily, hoisting himself clear of the foaming, breaking mass of waves that were slapping and pounding between the two steel hulls. When he reached the top of the ladder he paused briefly, then hauled himself over the rail.

"I'm Peale," Frank said. "The Chief Mate."

"Barlow," replied the pilot. "Quite a night," he added after looking around a minute.

"Captain Madeira, Captain Reilly, this is Captain Barlow," said Peale, performing the introductions after he and the pilot had reached the bridge.

"Pleased to meet you, sir."

"It's a pleasure, Captain."

"How do you do."

"I understand you've had quite an adventure," Barlow said. "I want to hear all about it on the way in."

"Certainly," replied Madeira, "though I haven't figured it out for myself yet."

"The Coast Guard wants me to take you in to the port and moor you there so they can talk to you and look the ship over."

"So does Customs," Madeira said glumly, wondering where the hell Drake and Howard had disappeared to. Now that he thought about it, he hadn't seen either since the cutter had slipped alongside.

"You seem to have a lot of friends," Barlow said.

"Just as well," answered Madeira. "I want to talk to the owners and take a good look at the ship myself."

As Maderia started to describe the past few hours, Captain Barlow got *Johnson* under way again.

"Now, you were saying this boat first appeared to the south and she was making fifty knots?"

In between restrained expressions of wonder at the tale Madeira was telling him, Captain Barlow piloted *Johnson* effortlessly through Government Cut, between brightly lit Miami Beach and the white stucco and red tiles of opulent Fisher Island to the south. He then continued on into the arrow-straight, man-made Main Channel of Port Miami.

So routine did it all seem, so matter of fact, that by the time the ship was moored to the rain-soaked quay, which glistened in the buzzing floodlights, Madeira was beginning to wonder if the tale he'd just told Barlow might not be a figment of his imagination.

But if so, what were the holes in the windows and bulkheads?

Eight

Even before the last mooring line was dropped over the bollard on the wharf and Captain Barlow had signaled "Finished with Engines," a tall Coast Guard commander with a very large Adam's apple had boarded *Johnson*. The commander was immediately escorted to the ship's small conference room. After accepting a cup of coffee, he got right to the point by asking Madeira to describe the encounter.

"You're absolutely sure you have no idea who the attacker was?" he asked skeptically after Madeira had completed his account.

"None," Madeira answered, "although I think it's obvious they weren't there to rob us."

"What were they trying to do then? Stop you?"

Madeira looked at him a moment. "It doesn't make much sense to me. I was told there are several other salvage operations to keep an eye out for, but at the same time I was also told our charter party has clear title to the wreck."

"That doesn't always mean much in the treasure-hunting business," replied the commander, leaning back in his chair. "Never did. We see a lot of claim jumping. I'll do some checking. In the meantime, I'm going to need a full written account of this whole affair from you. I want it before you leave Miami."

"I was hoping to leave at dawn."

"You plan to continue?"

"Yes, although I still have to talk with the owners."

"Then you'd better get writing!"

"May I ask a question or two?"

"Certainly," replied the Coast Guard officer, looking slightly uncomfortable at the role reversal.

"I don't want to sound unappreciative, but it took you a little longer to respond to our Mayday than I would have expected."

"Yes. It was the possibility that Customs might be involved that caused the problem. There was also some suspicion, especially after you reported the missile attack, that your Mayday was a hoax. Some good ol' boys amusing themselves. Or kids."

"You must have known we were in the area! One of your planes has been checking on us twice a day ever since we left Houston!"

"That's not something I'd know anything about. But let me warn you of something I do know and I'm not sure you understand: You guys would never win any popularity contests in Washington."

The commander paused, sipping his coffee, then continued. "How many did you say you had in?"

"Twenty-three," replied Madeira. "Twenty-three years active duty."

"I've got over twenty myself. I suppose you deserve something more than I've given you."

As he spoke, the Coast Guard officer's Adam's apple bobbed up and down and he glanced around quickly, almost furtively.

"The truth is that you treasure guys, especially Cuban-American treasure guys, make the government nervous. The IRS is always certain you're trying to cheat them. The State Department is always afraid you're really putting together a private war with Castro. Customs is positive that it's all a cover for some big drug operation. And as for us, you guys always mean lots of trouble and extra work. Just like tonight."

"Why the hell don't you just arrest us?" Madeira demanded. "There's always something you can get anybody for."

"Because, for better or for worse, your employers seem to have some sort of pull themselves. As far as I can tell, you're to be kept on a short leash but to be allowed to go your way. Anyway, I don't think they can make up their minds exactly what to do about you."

What is life if not trouble? thought Madeira, finding himself smiling grimly as he did.

There was a knock at the door and Howard of the INS walked in.

"I'm heading back to my office now, Captain," he said with a smile. "I'm sure you'll be pleased to know that everything appears in order, immigration-wise."

"I am, thank you," replied Madeira as he stood to shake Howard's hand.

"I appreciate what you've done," Madeira said to the Coast Guard commander after seeing Howard to the door. "I'll keep what you've told me in mind and make sure none of the government's worst fears come true."

"If you're attacked again we'll come running," said the commander. "That's the best I can promise. Remember, this isn't a local decision. Personally, I'd love to be invited on a treasure hunt someday. After I've retired."

A few minutes later, while Madeira was sitting at his desk struggling to get the night's events down on paper in a coherent manner, there was a knock in his door and Drake walked in.

"I'll be seeing you, Cap," the Customs officer said upon entering the office.

"Where do we go from here about that bag of marijuana?"

"I've been instructed to interpret it the way your Captain Reilly did; as somebody's personal stash."

"I assume you can determine whose from finger-prints?"

"We probably could if we were going to follow up on it, but we're not." Madeira couldn't fail to note the tinge of frustration in Drake's voice. "It looks to me like your owners, or your charter party, have some important friends."

"Al! I want a word with you."

Madeira paused, his hand on the door to his stateroom, then turned to face Reilly.

"Yes, Bud?"

"About tonight . . . "

"Your shiphandling was magnificent. I thought the whole ship performed very well." As he spoke, Madeira thought how was very tired he was. It had been a very long night and he desperately wanted a few hours rest before getting under way.

"You may have been satisfied, Al, but the crew and I are very unhappy about the whole affair. If we wanted to take part in naval battles, we would all have joined the Navy."

A wave of fury surged up within Madeira. "Bud. We all had more than enough warning that something like this might happen and everybody's being paid a great deal more than the usual War Zone Bonus. This isn't the first time a merchant vessel has been attacked and it certainly won't the last. However, if anybody wants to leave the ship here, in Miami, he can do it with my blessing. Is that what you want to hear from me?"

"That's not quite it, Cap."

Startled, Madeira spun to find himself facing Bobby Bell. Between them, Bell and Reilly had Madeira boxed in the narrow corridor.

"What the hell do you want, Bell? What are you doing here?"

"I'm here to speak for the crew."

"I thought that was Captain Reilly's job."

"He's an officer."

"So you're the new union steward?"

"No. That's still Rollins. But he don't do his job."

"So what is it you want?"

"We want the ship to stay in Miami until the union sends somebody to investigate the whole business."

"You're free to leave the ship if you think this project is too dangerous or that you're not being paid enough for the risks. In fact, I'll see you get a month's pay, including bonus, if you do leave."

"That still ain't it, Cap. We want vindication for what you put us through tonight. We want the ship tied up here and the crew all drawing what we're

The Wreck of Misericordia

getting now while the union finds out what you and the owners and that damn syndicate are really up to."

"File a grievance. That's what the union's for."

"I already did, but Rollins said it would take him a while to process it. That son of a bitch simply don't get it. He ain't going to keep that job for long."

Madeira began to relax slightly, although he didn't allow the fact to show. Rollins was a very level-headed guy, and Madeira was almost certain that the union steward understood full well how most of the crew felt. If Bell had to go around him, then Bell was speaking only for himself and a few of his worthless friends.

"Okay, Bell. You've delivered your message, so now you have no more reason to be in this corridor."

Bell glowered at Madeira a moment while his right fist clenched. He glanced at Reilly, snarled "Shit," and stormed off.

"Al, I'm afraid you personally have a serious problem with employee relations. You appear to me to be totally unable to relate to them. To see it from their side."

Madeira laughed suddenly. At the effort Reilly had so obviously made to stage the skirmish.

"You mean I don't hug them and feel their pain? I'll leave that to you."

He then opened the door to his stateroom, stepped in, and quietly closed the door behind him.

Some three hours later *Johnson* got under way again. None of the crew had left the ship, and both the owners and the charter party, while very concerned about the attack, had directed that the project continue if at all possible. As Madeira had reminded Reilly, the possibility of trouble had been discussed repeatedly—and by everybody involved—in Houston before the ship had sailed.

After *Johnson* had worked her way down the channel and dropped the pilot at the sea buoy, Madeira wandered aft, to the forward bay wall.

Still exhausted from the long night and uneasy about what was to come, he leaned on the rail and looked out over the blue Atlantic.

The air was sharp and clear, as were the hot, acrid exhaust fumes, shimmering and fluid, that streaked like a yellow-brown ribbon past his head and over the side. There wasn't a cloud in the sky. Nor an attacker in sight.

And the steady beat of the engines, their low, tactile roar, made it all the harder to stay awake.

Madeira continued to lean on the rail, studying MOHAB as she rested in the bay, braced again and shimmering in the diamond-hard, all-revealing, late-morning sun.

So powerful was the sun, he could feel the ultraviolet rays slamming into his body. The sensation was more one of grating than of burning. It was as if a dull knife was being drawn across his bones.

His eyes began to close and his muscles to relax as he watched the shadows of the derricks, booms, and lifts that formed a loosely woven canopy over the bay. Driven by the ship's slow rolls, the shadows marched and countermarched like The Devil's Own Regiment—exploding and shrinking, stretching and bending—back and forth across the bay's light-gray deck. In that harsh light, however, there was no gray deck, and no penumbras. Under that sun, only jet black and burning white could exist.

There were more than shadows moving in the bay. Carol Bannerman, Freddie Gomez, and Geoff

Higgins, the Assistant Operator, were all had at work checking MOHAB over one more time. Prepping her for the upcoming mission.

The ship was again hitching a ride on the fast-moving Florida Current, galloping north through the Florida Strait. Off the starboard quarter, and well below the horizon, slumbered the Bahamas, a maze of low, sandy islands; a centuries-old haven for pirates, smugglers, drug-dealers, big-game fishermen, and romantics.

Rolling and occasionally pitching fitfully, *Johnson* followed a course sailed by countless thousands of ships during the past five hundred years. It was a course that, with painful frequency, had resulted in death and destruction either on the deceptively inviting Florida shore or among the countless shoals and sandbars of the Bahamas.

Just like *Johnson*, thought Madeira, the ship whose remains they were bound to exhume had undoubtedly been attempting to use this very same exit. She had been riding the escalator north and then hoping to hitchhike east, to Spain, on the back of the Gulf Stream.

While the Spanish *nao* had clearly made it farther than many others—those whose bones were mixed in with the coral and sand, resting under the clear, shallow waters that lay all around him—she still hadn't made it all the way.

Something had happened, Madeira thought, his imagination beginning to spark. A storm? Pirates? What else could it have been?

The gates now opened, his tired mind filled with imagined details of the most fantastic sort: chests of gold and silver, gems of every imaginable color; shadowy galleons driven before the storm, forced over almost on their beam's ends, the remains of their sails streaming away in the dark, water-filled air; great seas curling, breaking, and pounding; lightning flashing and reflashing; long-gone mariners struggling, praying, and dying.

Madeira shuddered, forcing his thoughts away from death and destruction. The visions were all too realistic, all too familiar.

All the same, the fascination remained: The gold continued to glitter and the gems to sing, luring him just as a flashing spoon will lure the cruising marlin.

Realizing he was on the verge of falling asleep, Madeira turned. He pressed the small of his back against the steel railing and looked out at the surrounding blue seas, teased and whipped now into a steep chop by the fresh breeze. It was another of those scenes he'd tried, a thousand times, to capture on film, only to fail repeatedly.

The only way to see it was to live it.

He turned and looked down again into the bay. His eyes settled on Bannerman. She was, without doubt, the most magnificent woman he'd ever seen. She was tall, perfectly proportioned, fluid, and her every motion demanded his total attention and shortened his breath.

"Oh, hell!" he mumbled to himself. She was also a subordinate with whom he had to talk about last night.

He started down the ladder into the bay reluctantly. By the time he reached the deck he'd lost all benefit of the wind. The air was at least twenty degrees hotter than up above and the sun just as harsh as ever.

"*Hola*, Captain Madeira," said Freddie Gomez when he caught sight of Madeira.

"*Hola*, Freddie," Madeira replied. "Find any damage from last night?"

"Nope. Not a bit. The electronics suite is great. Bannerman hasn't found anything either."

"Good. You know where she is?"

"Right here," said Bannerman from behind the lift that was built into the bottom of the habitat, between the sled-like runners.

"I gather we're in good shape, that everything's go?" said Madeira as Freddie disappeared through the hatch into MOHAB.

"That's affirmative," Bannerman said in one of those deep, almost husky Southern accents that seem to originate well below the speaker's neck.

"It's good we caught her in time last night."

Bannerman's face clouded as she studied him for a moment. "You're saying I should have called for help . . . sooner! You're hinting that if any damage had resulted it was all my fault!"

Madeira took a very deep breath, hoping he didn't blow it.

"Carol, up until now you've been a diver and a worksub operator. This is the first job you've had which involves real supervisory responsibilities—"

"That's right," she said before he could finish. "They said I wasn't ready for it."

"We're betting they were wrong! You're alert and hardworking and you've got well more than your share of guts. All you need is a little guidance, and I plan to provide as much as I can."

As she continued to stare at him, her expression seemed to change from anger to skepticism.

"The lesson for today is that when a supervisor sees a problem he—or she—can't solve with one hand, then he bellows for the Bos'n to round up some strong backs and do something about it."

"Okay," she finally replied, her expression now incomprehensible to Madeira. He suspected she might be toying with the idea that he'd either just lost his mind or been born a fool.

A deep sense of disappointment and loss settled over him as he studied her reaction and discovered that he was no longer viewing her as the sexiest woman in the world.

He could see that she was still beautiful, of course, but he also found himself forced to think of her as just one more junior officer who needed a little squaring away.

Like Hawkins.

Only he suspected that, unlike Hawkins, she wasn't particularly interested in being squared away.

Nine

"Eduardo is dead," said the voice over the telephone.

"I'm very sorry to hear that," Cesar Rivera replied. "How did it happen?"

"He was driving up the Turnpike very early this morning from Tavernier, and seems to have stopped along the side of the road—north of Homestead—to take a piss. Or maybe just to rest—nobody seems sure. The police believe he was mugged and killed. He was shot in the head and his watch and wallet were gone."

Rivera could imagine the scene clearly. The night was dark. The Turnpike long and empty, bordered by broad, low fields of ripening vegetables. Eduardo racing north in his white Mercedes, possibly a little drunk and without doubt jubilant at the telephoned congratulations Cesar himself had expressed just an hour or so before.

There, just ahead, was the overpass, the one

under which he was to rendezvous with Sandra. They were, or so he thought, going to have a little celebration, just the two of them, before he continued on home to his family.

Eduardo would have undoubtedly braked, and probably down-shifted, before pulling off the Turnpike under the overpass. Then he would have stopped next to Sandra's convertible.

Cesar Rivera doubted Sandra was waiting in her car. He could guess she would be standing back under the overpass, partially in the shadows.

"I'm over here, Eduardo," she would have said. Or something like that.

Eduardo would have slid out of his car and walked toward her, a smile of anticipation on his face. Then she would have raised the pistol.

But she probably didn't shoot him right away. She would have played with him as long as she thought it was safe to do so. She would have made sure he fully understood that he had no hope whatsoever. Then she would have fired.

Without doubt, thought Rivera a little uneasily, Sandra had enjoyed every second. As far as he could tell she killed neither for money nor for power, but because killing and maiming seemed to give her a visceral pleasure. That was a truth about her that he could never afford to forget.

At the moment her fetish made her useful to him. He was certain, however, that she would derive just as much pleasure from killing *him* as she did from anybody else.

"Do they have any suspects?" Rivera asked.

"Nobody in particular, or so they say. They believe it fits in with several other attacks during the past six months."

Eduardo had proven to be much more competent

than he would have ever guessed, Cesar thought as he looked out over the Gulf's blue-green waters from the window of his ninth floor condo. Too competent, in fact.

Havana was convinced the treasure was going to be used against Fidel. Or his successors. Accordingly, Cesar had been instructed to harrass *Johnson*, to discourage the expedition. Cesar, in turn, had assigned the job to Eduardo, confident that the latter's efforts would be credible yet halfhearted.

But something had gotten into Eduardo. Suddenly, he had decided to prove to the world that his *cajones* were bigger than anybody else's.

Bigger even than Cesar Rivera's.

It was even possible, he thought with almost distaste, that Sandra had provided the inspiration.

Whatever its source, Eduardo's furious attack on the ship had come very close to succeeding. And if allowed to try again, he might very well finish the job.

"Tell Barbara how sorry I am to hear about this. And tell her not to worry. I'm confident something can be done for her and the children. I'll drive up to Miami myself tomorrow."

"I'm sure she'll find your sympathy a comfort, Cesar. And your efforts on her behalf."

"It's the least I can do," replied Rivera to the woman who had just executed Eduardo.

After hanging up, Cesar leaned back in his chair and looked up at the ceiling. Short, plump, and bald, he looked very much the retired soda-pop salesman, a job he had had for the past ten years.

Years before, however, he'd been slender and blessed with a full head of hair. He'd also answered to the name Agustin Ramirez. He was the same Agustin Ramirez who was widely believed to have died so valiantly in Angola, a member of the army Fidel had rented to the Russians to fight the Fascists.

He went to the refrigerator to get himself a root beer.

He sipped the soda a moment, then turned and walked into his study. There he sat down at his little computer and typed out a brief report of Eduardo's death. He zapped the report to the e-mail address of an automobile dealership in Cleveland. Within a few minutes, after forwarding through a chain of a half-dozen addresses, it would find its way to Havana.

He returned to the kitchen and looked over the breakfast bar into the living room. The condo was comfortable but uninspiring. Worst of all, it could not possibly be made secure. He would have to leave it soon. Very soon.

Cesar Rivera hoped that Eduardo's death would serve to contain the damage and give him a little more time to arrange for his own survival.

With the exception of Eduardo's fit of efficiency—and he both assumed and hoped that Sandra had cleared that up—everything seemed to be going very well. Especially Antonio's part of it.

There had been others besides Antonio Perez whom Ramirez had taken apart and rebuilt to his own specifications. But Perez, in Ramirez's opinion, was the greatest of them. Indeed, he had come to love him as he might a son.

He had taken a piece of garbage and recycled it into something useful. He had guided and supported it for over thirty years until it had become a tool fit for a god.

In the beginning Ramirez had dedicated Antonio to the Revolution. It had been his plan to use him for some mighty stroke that would awe and astound the world.

But the years had passed and the right opportunity had never appeared.

Along the way the world had changed. Once, only the Soviet Union had been willing to be Cuba's friend. Now, everybody wanted to get chummy, just as soon as the Americans backed off. Under those conditions the Revolution couldn't possibly survive. Sooner or later the Revolutionary Ship would tear its bottom out on the reef of reality.

He looked out the window and thought about time. He was getting older now and so was Antonio, although the latter was the younger by a few years. How much time did they have left?

He was sure Fidel himself still supported him, but Ramirez had accumulated an army of high-level enemies over the years. Some of them, he knew, were already preparing to move against him.

And then there were *los jovenes*, the young up-and-comers. The world was changing so very rapidly, everybody over forty now seemed obsolete, and *los jovenes* seemed more willing than ever to dispose of their elders.

In his own case, Cesar thought glumly, the prospect was especially discouraging. He had never considered obsolete spies as elder statesmen. Rather, he considered them to be embarrassments that should be eliminated as rapidly as possible. And he suspected that his successors would hold much the same opinion.

At least he'd never made the mistake of acquiring a wife and children.

He wondered how much more time Fidel had. He then decided Fidel's future meant little now to him.

He was totally on his own at this point. As he always had been.

Cesar Rivera figured he had a few weeks, maybe a month or two, to arrange for his own salvation. To survive he would need every one of the two hundred million dollars he hoped to gain. His path was clear.

He would leave for Miami immediately. Not tonight, right now! And he would never again return to this condo.

He would keep in touch with Havana, but from now on they wouldn't know precisely where he was.

Or so he hoped.

Ten

Looking like a child's toy bobbing quietly in the bathtub, *El Dorado* rolled gently in the distance, rising and falling on the sparkling, wind-textured swells that had replaced the sharp chop of the previous evening.

"*Irving Johnson, Irving Johnson*, this is *El Dorado*," drawled the speaker of the bridge-to-bridge radio.

Reilly sauntered into the pilothouse while Madeira, Hawkins, and Peale all remained standing on the wing of the bridge. Each had his binoculars pinned on the small, dark-green research vessel that rode the swells with such an air of stuffy dignity.

"This is *Irving Johnson, El Dorado*," Reilly said into the microphone. "Do you wish us to come alongside?"

"Negative, *Johnson*. You are to stop one hundred yards upwind of us. We will come alongside you to transfer our party. There will be three individuals and approximately twenty parcels."

"How large are the boxes?"

"They're all manageable. None over about fifty pounds."

"Roger, *El Dorado*," Reilly replied with a scowl, as if he interpreted the instructions as criticism of his shiphanding ability. He then turned to Peale.

"Frank. Prepare to receive them to port. And rig out the waist davit to handle their gear."

"Aye, aye, Skip," the wiry Chief Mate said with that slight Cajun lilt to his voice. "You've got it. To port." He headed for the ladder leading from the bridge to the main deck.

Reilly nodded in acknowledgment. He then walked over to the steering console, disengaged the automatic pilot, and edged the wheel around, causing the ship to turn to starboard. He waited, watching the compass as numbers of increasing size marched past the lubber's line. Suddenly, with a snappy flourish, he shifted the rudder, turning it briefly to port. He then put it amidships, reengaged the Iron Mike, and moved the two throttle levers to "Stop."

"That'll do it," he remarked to himself, with a note of satisfaction in his voice, as he sauntered back out to the bridge wing.

"*She*'s sure as hell seen better days," remarked *Johnson*'s Master to Madeira, gesturing towards *El Dorado* as he spoke.

"Yes, she has," Madeira replied quietly.

Just looking at *El Dorado*, he felt he could recite her history. Ninety feet of thin steel plate with raised focs'l and small deckhouse forward and a large, open deck aft. She'd obviously been built originally as an oil-rig-crew or supply boat. Then, in the eighties, when the offshore drilling business collapsed, she'd undoubtedly been tied up to a dock for some time, like so many hundreds of her sisters, while her owner's creditors tried to sell her.

What came next was not so obvious. Perhaps her current owners had purchased her then and immediately put her into service as a treasure hunter. Perhaps she'd had some other, intermediate, incarnation: as a fishing boat, a crab or lobster boat, a dive boat, or a whale watcher.

Whatever the details of her past, it was clear she wasn't far from her end. Great rust streaks showed though the green paint on her sides. Her plates were deeply rippled, forced inwards over the years by the sea's constant pounding to reveal her skeleton-like frames.

Over time, stress and corrosion would gnaw their way through her never-thick skin, pitting and eventually puncturing it. Her machinery would become increasingly expensive to maintain as part after part was worn out of tolerance and her engine mountings were slowly but surely smashed and twisted out of position by the sea's relentless battering.

Finally, at the same time her repair bills ballooned, her insurance premiums would skyrocket and she would find herself making that one last voyage, to the scrap yard.

Her ultimate fate, like that of all living things, was so obvious and unremarkable that Madeira wondered why he suddenly found it so compelling. It must be the proximity, he decided. I'm not that young either.

"*El Dorado*, this is *Johnson*," said Reilly, who'd returned to the steering console. "I have stopped and am ready for you to come along my port, I say again, port side."

"Roger, *Johnson*," the radio mumbled. "I'm heading for your port side."

Johnson rolled and bobbed in the long blue Atlantic swells while her small, worn consort approached, her bow plowing bravely into and over the swells. Despite his having kept his glasses on *El Dorado* almost continuously, it wasn't until the treasure hunter was within a hundred yards that Madeira could see two figures emerge from the deckhouse and take positions on the weather deck. One then indicated with a wave of his arms that they were ready to receive *Johnson*'s lines.

"It is my intention," boomed *El Dorado* over the radio, "to come alongside only long enough to transfer my passengers and their luggage."

"Roger," Reilly replied.

Madeira continued to observe the approaching vessel with a certain detachment. While the success or failure of the entire project did rest on his squat shoulders, the details of this particular maneuver were not his concern. Much as he'd grown to dislike Reilly, he knew him to be an excellent seaman and felt no discomfort at leaving him to attend to his responsibilities.

"We'd better get down there to welcome them, Bud," he finally remarked.

Reilly shook his head, looking at Hawkins as he did. "I think I'd better stay here. I'm not sure Hawkins can handle it without fucking it up, and I don't want the sides all dinged up!"

"Skipper!" Hawkins said, an anguished look on his face. "I can keep her head into the seas!"

"Can you do it without letting the ship creep forward? Can you guarantee you won't pound that little green turd to pieces?"

Hawkins, red-faced, stood mute.

"As you wish, Bud," Madeira said. Paul might very well benefit from a little coaching, but Madeira was almost certain Reilly would never give the young mate the chance to even try his hand. "They'll just have to settle for Frank and me as the welcoming party."

Without waiting for a reply, Madeira trotted down the three sets of ladders that led from the bridge to the main deck. He then continued aft along the bay wall deck to the point where Peale had lowered a mass of fenders, and a Jacob's Ladder, down *Johnson*'s high sides.

"We're all set, Al," Peale reported, his broad grin reflecting the pleasure with which he greeted practically any maneuver or opportunity to exercise and demonstrate his seamanship.

Madeira accepted the report with a nod and a polite smile, then joined the Chief Mate at the rail.

Looked at in the distance, the long, smooth swells might appear of little consequence. In reality, they greatly complicated the process of getting the two vessels together. Thanks to those innocent-looking mounds of water, the exercise was transformed from one that involved only course and speed to one that also involved altitude.

"She's starting her final approach," remarked Peale, staring across the flashing waters at the other vessel's dark, all-too-obviously scarred and dented flanks.

"He'd damn well better not mess up my nice white sides," continued the Mate. "That green'll stand out ten miles away if she slams us hard."

As he spoke, *Johnson*, whose sides would tower over *El Dorado* in just about any circumstances, rose yet higher as she climbed the next swell and teetered on its crest. Far below, her toy-like suitor struggled through the adjoining trough.

"Don't worry, Frank," Madeira replied with a sly glance. "That's why she's got those big black truck tires hanging along her rail."

"Very funny! The black will be even more obvious!"

Whatever doubts either Peale or Madeira may have held were soon put to rest as *El Dorado* turned smartly, slowed, and slipped alongside. The one-time crew boat backed hard, spitting out a puff of black smoke in the process, and settled precisely on station beside the fenders Peale had lowered for her.

"Get those lines over!" the Chief Mate shouted to the two line handlers he'd stationed fore and aft. Even before the lines were secured, the first of the transferees had jumped at the swaying ladder and started to climb. At the same instant, the two steel hulls slammed together, screeching and grinding despite the multitude of fenders and black tarry truck tires.

I'll be damned, thought Madeira as he looked down at the bobbing orb of short-cropped brunette hair, hair that burned with a deep, red-gold fire visible even through his sunglasses. *She's a lot more athletic than I'd have imagined*.

It was Cristina de Navarre, the expedition's archaeologist, whom he'd met briefly six weeks before at a hurried meeting in Houston.

The object of Madeira's wonder was a tall, skinny, young-looking woman dressed in dungarees and a chambray shirt. The archaeologist dragged herself up and over the side and paused a moment, bestowing a dazzling, if lopsided, smile on **Madeira** and Peale.

She's not as young as she looks, thought Madeira as he studied the very real lines etched into the otherwise-smooth skin around her eyes and strikingly firm jaw. *And her head's a little too big for the rest of her.*

Without even catching her breath, the object of Madeira's attention draped herself back over the rail and waved down at the large, dark-haired individual following her.

"Climb! Rafael, climb!" she shouted down, laughing as she did.

The man paused and leaned back, looking up at her so that Madeira could see his face clearly. As he did, there was another thump and further screeching as the two hulls rolled and ground against each other, almost as if in a frenzy of lust. The sound caused both Peale and Madeira to wince in unison.

It was an elegantly Latin face they were gazing down at. Long and narrow, alert, highlighted by a prominant, aquiline nose almost as substantial as Madeira's, and crowned by straight, black, slicked-down hair. It was also the face of a man struggling against age—Madeira guessed a few years greater than his own—and lack of physical conditioning.

Rafael Cienfuegos was not scrambling up the ladder with the same gusto as Cristina de Navarre had shown. Yet despite the obvious pain that accompanied every breath he drew, he was able to present a magnificent, broad smile. His teeth sparkled and showed from ear to ear. He acted as if he were having the time of his life.

"Upwards, Tina! *Siempre arriba!*" he shouted as he thrust his right arm up to the next rung and

109

recommenced his climb. It was clear from his hurried glances down that he was uncomfortably aware of the boiling maelstrom foaming and surging directly beneath him as the two ships continued to thrust themselves against each other.

"Bravo!" she replied with an even more enthusiastic smile.

Apparently satisfied with his progress, she raised her right arm, the gold bracelet on her wrist glowing in the sunlight, and signaled two deckhands on *El Dorado*. After waving back, they moved to the pile of bags and boxes packed into cargo nets and stacked on the rolling deck.

"They're ready for you to swing our gear aboard," she said to Peale, continuing to smile, yet studying him intently, as she spoke.

My God! thought Madeira as he watched her hopping around. She looks like a flake but she knows exactly what she's doing.

Continuing to follow her every motion, he found himself chuckling, not in derision but rather delight at her enthusiasm and unlikely but very powerful grace.

"Christ!" the Chief Mate snarled, turning to the men at the davit. "Get that damn whip over the side and down there and get that damn luggage up here before she beats a hole through our side."

"Dr. de Navarre," said Madeira, "it's good to see you again. Welcome aboard."

"I'm very glad you finally got here, Captain," she replied. "And please call me Tina. I asked you to do that in Houston."

Before he could reply, she continued. "At last we're ready to start.

"This is Rafael Cienfuegos," she added, gesturing in the direction of the large man, who had just struggled over the rail and was still clearly out of breath.

"Rafael Cienfuegos," he said, offering Madeira his hand.

"Rafael's a member of the syndicate financing this operation," explained Tina. "He's their on-scene representative. And this, Rafi," she said, gesturing toward Madeira, "is Captain Madeira, MOHAB's Operational Director."

"A great pleasure, Captain Madeira," wheezed Cienfuegos. "We have been looking forward to your arrival."

"We're very glad to be participating in this project," said Madeira.

"Yes, so are we," said Cienfuegos, beaming. "Your reputation precedes you."

"Thank you," Madeira replied. Not sure how to respond further, he fell silent, his eyes drifting in the direction of Tina de Navarre.

She's really very pretty, he thought, continuing to smile. Almost beautiful, in fact, in a skinny way. But what's the story on her left eye?

She's cross-eyed, he suddenly realized. Every now and then that left eye drifts in toward her nose!

"Captain Madeira," Tina said, "I can't tell you how much I'm looking forward to working with you and MOHAB. This is an opportunity few will have, I think." As she spoke her eyes, crossed or not, radiated a manic energy.

"I certainly hope you're wrong," Madeira said. "We hope a great many people will make use of MOHAB over the next ten to fifteen years."

"Yes, of course," said Cienfeugos, clearing his throat. "I must also tell you, Captain, that we were very worried when we heard of the attack made on this ship."

"No more than we were, I can assure you," Madeira replied, now fully alert and on edge. "Do you have any idea who it may have been and why?"

An expression of concern crossed Cienfuegos's face. "We can only guess that it is some other salvage group interested, perhaps, in taking the treasure for itself. Although, of course, it is ours! This sort of thing has happened to us before, on other projects, and I was told that your owners were told such things might happen. We are very gratified that no one was injured or killed, of course."

"So am I," said Madeira, thinking that he'd probably placed too much emphasis on the Naval aspect of his experience when applying for the job. "What about the current Cuban Government?"

The Cuban looked at him a moment. "That is, of course, very possible. Some in the government there consider many members of our group to be enemies."

Cienfuegos's eyes glanced quickly over Madeira's shoulder.

"Perhaps Mr. Smith has reached some sort of conclusion," Cienfuegos continued as Madeira realized that the Security Director had just materialized on the scene.

"I'm afraid I haven't, sir," Smith mumbled, the movement of his lips barely visible under his mustache. "I can make a couple guesses, but they are of no more value than your own."

"Very well then," Cienfuegos said. "We must all remain alert! Tina, is all our luggage and equipment aboard?"

"This is the last of it, Rafael," replied Tina, who apparently had been watching the transfer out of the side of her eye and keeping count.

"Good," Cienfuegos said. "Now that we all know each other, perhaps we should get to work."

"I couldn't agree more," Madeira said. "You and your partners are paying dearly for every minute of our time. I gather you have some videocassettes from your initial survey?"

"And some chart diskettes we have also prepared," added Tina.

"Very well. The best place to examine them and plan the next step is our Operations Center."

"To the Operations Center then," Cienfuegos replied with vigor. "We will look into our accommodations later."

"Where's Dale?" Tina asked, a note of concern in her voice, just as Peale was about to signal *El Dorado* to cast off.

"Dale?" Cienfuegos said in a perplexed tone, as if he'd never heard the name before.

Who the hell's Dale, wondered both Madeira and Peale.

"Right here, Tina," replied a voice from over the ship's side.

"*Bueno!*" Tina replied, hurrying over to the rail and looking down.

"You scared me, Dale. I was afraid I was so busy talking I'd lost you."

With Tina's continuing, although perhaps unnecessary, encouragement, Dale Anderson, her young assistant, dragged himself over the rail and was introduced.

"Is everybody, and everything aboard now," Peale asked, clearly frantic to get rid of *El Dorado* and her big black truck tires.

Tina looked around, counted the boxes, then nodded.

"All passengers and luggage aboard and secure," Peale mumbled into the walkie-talkie he was carrying.

"Roger," responded a voice through its speaker.

"Which of these are personal items?" Peale continued to Tina and Cienfuegos. "And which are equipment? I'll have the personal gear taken to your quarters."

"These are personal," replied Tina, pointing at the four canvas bags. "These are gear to be used in MOHAB, and those over there are gear we'll probably want to keep aboard the *Johnson*."

"I'll take care of it."

"BARUUP!"

"Mr. Peale," shouted one of the deckhands, "*El Dorado*'s casting off. They're getting underway now."

"Thank God!" the Chief Mate replied under his breath, turning from the piles of gear and luggage. "Get those lines in, pronto, and get the fenders in as soon's she's clear. Then we'll stow this gear."

With Madeira and Cienfuegos leading, they headed forward toward the Operations Center, which was located in the superstructure, aft of Madeira's and Reilly's cabins and under the pilothouse. Jake Smith fell in behind everybody else and looked suspiciously around as he followed them forward.

"You seem fascinated by MOHAB," Madeira observed to Tina after noticing that she couldn't seem to take her eyes off the white blimp as they walked past.

"Believe it or not, Captain, that's an understatement. Do you really appreciate what an opportunity it represents for me? For fifty years now, ever since SCUBA was invented, we've been talking about conducting underwater excavations with the same detail and accuracy we achieve ashore. I think MOHAB's going to finally make that possible, especially for deeper wrecks, and I'm going to be the first to do it!"

"We're hoping, of course, that others will do so too."

A smile formed and a gentle laugh emerged from beneath her glowing, smoldering, ember-like hair. "I understand. But think of it!"

Then she laughed again. "You have undoubtedly thought about it many times."

"I have," Madeira said, his enthusiasm rekindled by hers. "It's a first for us too."

She turned away from MOHAB and looked at him, her eyes sparkling, a few faint freckles only now becoming noticeable on her cheeks. "You're in for the adventure, aren't you? You're not a stockholder?

"A few minutes ago," she continued before he could answer, "you looked a little defensive when Rafael mentioned your reputation preceding you. Are you?"

"Defensive about my reputation? A little, I suppose. I've made a few mistakes."

"You mean Cabot Station?"

"Yes, Cabot," he replied, taken aback by her straightforwardness. "A lot of people died there. Needlessly."

"I don't think you have anything to be ashamed of. You went back and saved most of them. That's what Rafael was talking about."

Why the hell, he wondered, had he allowed himself to get involved in this discussion?

It's because of her eyes, he decided. So intensely demanding.

His past and what he thought of it were none of her business, but he felt no desire to kill the discussion.

"Do you dwell on it?" she asked.

"No, but it's always there."

"You shouldn't dwell on it. It is past and done and the most important thing is you went back. That was *muy hombre*! Do you know what that means?"

"Yes. Thank you," Madeira said, deciding to stop letting her eyes bully him. "Now, shouldn't we get to the briefing? You're the star performer."

"I suppose so."

How do you describe them? he wondered as he guided her up the ladder to the Operations Center. Her eyes.

They weren't brown, weren't blue, weren't anything he could put into words, but he found them infinitely more compelling than any pile of jewels, real or imagined, glinting coldly on the ocean floor.

Be careful with her! he warned himself. There's a madness in those eyes, an energy that goes far beyond mere enthusiasm.

He had to keep up his guard, he concluded. Not get carried away. Madness is often contagious.

Eleven

"As you can see," Tina said, "our wreck is located close to the eastern boundary of the Blake Plateau, in slightly more than four hundred fathoms." She nodded toward the first computer-generated chart.

Madeira forced himself to look away from her lightly tanned face to the chart.

"So what sort of currents are we talking about?" asked Carol Bannerman as she leaned forward to study the bathymetric chart of the waters off the southeast coast of the United States.

"So far we've observed surface currents up to one and a half knots, maybe a little more at times. The bottom currents have been pretty much the same, for the most part, although there have been some fluctuations. Will there be any problem with them?"

"Naw," drawled Bannerman, "I think we can

handle them. I'll just have to be a little careful when we bottom. MOHAB can be a little clumsy at times."

That's an understatement! Madeira thought, surprised at the positive note in her voice, a note in total contrast to her normal sourness.

"And you two gentlemen?" Tina asked, looking at Crown and Savage, the expedition's two saturation divers. "Will currents like these cause you trouble?"

"No, not really," Crown replied, the shorter of the two short, slender divers. "It may make us work a little harder, but we can deal with it."

"Right," echoed Savage. "No problem."

"Good! Now here," Tina continued, nodding at Freddie Gomez to display the next visual, "is a much-larger-scale chart of the area almost immediately below us."

She paused a moment to give the visual time to appear.

"This chart," she explained, "covers an area about half a mile by half a mile and represents all the work we've done so far. This is the main pile of ballast stones. And around its edges you can see a number of wooden ribs and some planking. Most of the hull has been carried away by the current over the centuries. If it weren't for the current, I might add, most of the hull would still be here—the water's cold enough to do a good preservation job.

"Here, here, and here are what we think are piles of ingots of some sort, almost certainly silver, and these, all along here and here, are cannons.

"Oh, yes! And these appear to be masses of corroded silver coins. Pieces of eight, for you romantics."

"So we're going to get the gold and silver for

you?" asked Reilly, a hint of something—Madeira wasn't quite sure what—in his tone.

"If we were just after the bullion and the coinage, Captain, we'd probably recover it from the surface using ROVs. But we're after more than just the goodies. We want to do a thorough excavation, something which has never before been possible at this depth. I'm confident there're literally thousands of artifacts mixed in with the ballast stones, and more sprinkled off to the northeast."

"Are we working for the museum or this syndicate?"

"Both," Tina replied. "The syndicate's financing the expedition and the museum gets the historically or scientifically significant artifacts. Along with zillions of megabytes of data—and that's the real treasure."

"If I may, I'd like to know more about the syndicate," Reilly persisted.

"May I explain that, Tina?" Cienfuegos asked, smiling, his gold-capped inciser glinting even in the harsh mortuary light of the compartment's fluorescent bulbs.

"Why not, Rafael?" she responded, also smiling.

A sizzling, and totally unexpected, bolt of anger—a thrust initially hot and sharp, then icy cold and breath-stopping—raced through Madeira's chest.

Was there a hint of something special between them?

How special?

That smile of hers! She seemed ready to bestow it on practically everybody. But did it have a special sparkle when she looked in Cienfuegos's direction?

Stick to business! Madeira told himself with growing irritation.

119

William S. Schaill

"Captain Reilly," intoned the object of Madeira's envy with a vaguely professorial air, "my partners and I are all Cuban. Although *my* family is of no great significance—I am only a syndicate member because of the modest commercial success I have enjoyed since coming to the United States—those of my partners have been very prominent in Cuba for many hundreds of years. Some even arrived while the Great Colon, the Admiral of the Ocean Sea himself, was still alive. In fact, the families of several of us, one in particular, were closely involved with the ship whose wreckage we are about to explore. Not only did they have cargo aboard her, but some had relatives aboard. Thus, it is part of their heritage, our heritage, and we wish to learn all we can about it.

"You are here," he continued, "because Tina feels that the only way a thorough excavation can be done is from your MOHAB. Yes, we have located what appears to be a large amount of silver, and probably gold, but we are very interested in much more than that. We want historical items, items which might be personal in nature. Tina feels we need you to do a thorough job, and if MOHAB is able to do what we have been told it can, I agree with her."

"So your syndicate was formed to trace your heritage?" concluded Reilly with a lingering air of very faint sarcasm.

"Of course! In part!" Cienfuegos laughed, his smile just as broad and friendly as ever. "We are businessmen! We expect the syndicate to make money, just like any other business, but we also are looking for a little adventure and, yes, the opportunity to pursue our heritage."

The Wreck of Misericordia

"Can we expect more members to show up for a little 'adventure'?" Reilly asked.

"I very much doubt it. For most of our members, just being part of the syndicate is adventure enough. They have no desire to go to sea, or to go under it either. None of us is particularly young."

Tiring of Reilly's efforts to conduct an inquisition, Madeira changed the subject to one of more interest to him. "Can you tell me more about the ship?"

"I'd love to," Tina replied. "As I'm sure you know, for many hundreds of years the Spanish Plate Fleets, the treasure fleets, would assemble in Havana. After consolidating, documenting, and sealing all their cargos, especially the gold, silver, and gems from the mainland, they sailed north through the Florida Strait. Then, usually at some point near our present position, they turned east towards Spain, carried along all the while by the Gulf Stream."

"Yes. That rings a bell."

"Okay! Most, if not all, of the treasure ships which have been found and excavated up to now were located in fairly shallow water. Most were driven onto reefs or rocks by bad weather, and many had survivors who were able to report where and how they were lost."

She paused, smiling a slightly lopsided little smile at Madeira, then continued. "A great many other ships were lost in the Atlantic, in deep water, after they had made it north, beyond the Bahamas."

"So you think this may be the first deep Spanish wreck to be excavated?"

"Yes," she almost shouted, as if about to break into applause, "and not only that, we're almost certain of her identity. It's a *nao*—a big ship—named *Nuestra Senora de la Misericordia*, and she sank within a few minutes of noon on November 13, 1562."

"What was it? A late-season hurricane?"

"No," replied Tina, starting to laugh even harder as her eyes sparkled in total appreciation of the irony. "It's really quite funny, in a painful way. It seems her bottom just fell out.

"According to the records, it was a beautiful autumn day with light winds. The *flota*'s pilots had just completed comparing their noon positions— and amazingly, they were within ten or twenty miles of each other—when *Misericordia* started taking water. An hour later she was gone."

"How many were lost?" Madeira asked.

"None! All they lost was the treasure. And a lot of face, I suppose. That's why I feel free to laugh about the whole thing."

So much for howling winds driving them to their deaths, thought Madeira, remembering his earlier visions of the wreck's origins.

"What was wrong with her?" asked Reilly, who was obviously fascinated, despite his better judgment.

"Worms and old age. In many ways, the Spanish were astoundingly inconsistent, almost careless. They had very strict rules about who could send ships in the *flotas* and very strict requrements concerning the seaworthiness of the ships to be sent. Some years they enforced the rules vigorously while others, everybody, from the King down, seemed to look the other way."

"To save a few bucks they loaded all the treasure into an old piece of crap and her bottom fell out a few weeks later?"

"I'm afraid that's it. They could be incredibly stupid at times, although it's worth remembering that the Spanish Empire was the first world empire and that it's been around longer than the British one."

"How'd ya find this wreck?" Bannerman asked, a hint of suspicion creeping into her tone. "Even if the *flota's* pilots agreed within a few miles, and their position was correct, it's still damn hard to find a wreck twenty-four hundred feet down!"

"It was an accident, a very fortunate accident." Tina beamed. "The wreck was located about ten months ago by two geologists who were conducting a survey of the Blake Plateau's surface using a combination of Magnetic Anomaly Detectors, side-scanning Sonar, and video-equipped ROVs. When we heard that they had come across a pile of ballast stones and cannons at this location, we thought it might just be the *Misericordia*. Naturally, both scientists and the natural-resources firm for which they work are now minority partners in the venture.

"Would anybody like to look at the videos we made from the ROVs?" she asked quickly, before Reilly had a chance to ask what percentage the geologists and their employer were in for.

"I certainly would," Madeira said, now as totally captivated by the project as by the speaker. "This is my first real treasure hunt."

"You're going to love it, Boss," Savage said.

Tina and Cienfuegos laughed, while Reilly responded with a forced smile, inwardly rolling his eyes. Jake Smith, the security specialist, continued to sit silently in the corner, half hidden behind his huge blond mustache. The expression of ferociously serious suspicion never left his large face.

Freddie Gomez rolled the video, a gloomy, greenish, grayish, and whitish production, and Tina pointed out each of the features she'd previously noted on the chart.

"I gather," Madeira said at the conclusion of the video tour, "you feel this vessel went down all in one piece. All the heavy wreckage, the ballast stones, the ingots, the ordnance are grouped together."

"Yes, that's our assumption. We also assume that many of the smaller, lighter artifacts have been carried to the north and northeast by the current. That's one of the main things we hope you can do for us; conduct a detailed search and survey over a much larger area than we've been able to. We *have* identified a few objects we believe to be smaller artifacts, but I'm hoping there'll be many more."

"At least," Madeira observed, "the Stream's swept the bottom nice and clean there. It's sure going to make it easier for us to recover what you want recovered."

"That's true but it'd be much nicer, from my point of view, if there were a thick layer of mud and silt to protect the artifacts. As it is, many will have been swept away or dissolved over the centuries, and most of those that're left are probably badly scoured. Our big hope is that some are trapped and hidden among the ballast stones, where they're at least partly protected."

"On to another matter," Madeira said. "I'm not sure I fully understand the legal situation concerning this wreck. Your group does have some sort of legal title to it, don't you?"

"I'll defer to Rafael on that."

"We have legal title to it," the Cuban said smoothly. "The wreck is in International Waters, although just within the U.S. Exclusive Economic Zone. While they have been trying to agree on an

International Seabed Regime for many years now, there is none at this time."

"Okay."

"However, a number of nations, including the United States, do have various laws which will apply when we attempt to bring our recoveries into the country. We have, for this reason, petitioned the U.S. District Court and been granted title to the wreck. I must mention, however, that the government is not going to do anything to help us protect that title until the artifacts enter U.S. territory."

"So we've learned. Is there anybody in particular who we should be looking out for?"

"There is one group, the *Fortune Hunter* syndicate—I believe they were mentioned to your owners—and then there are others. There are always others. As you well know, the seas are filled with sharks."

"If you have title, how would they get the treasure ashore?"

"That would be no problem for them. They will simply take it ashore in another country. *Fortune Hunter*, for example, is not only of Panamanian registry but is also home-ported in Panama. There are many who are more than pleased to look the other way at times."

"Yes, of course," Madeira replied, wondering where his head had been the past twenty-three years.

Twelve

"*Johnson,* this is MOHAB."

Despite the distortions generated by radio transmission and amplification, Carol Bannerman's throaty twang was still clearly discernable. "All hatches and thru-hulls secured. All systems go."

"Roger, MOHAB," Reilly said into the microphone. "Stand by for flood-down."

Reilly looked up and around to make sure *Johnson*'s bows remained headed into the lazy, sapphire swells. He then examined a display that showed the opened or closed status of every door, vent, or other opening into the bay. Satisfied, he picked up a second mike and spoke into it.

"Stand by to flood-down," his voice boomed over the ship's loudspeakers.

"Commence flood-down, Frank," he continued, turning to Peale, who was now standing at the flooding controls, "and keep an eye on those starboard tanks."

Peale, who was well aware of the ship's irritating and so-far-inexplicable tendency to list to starboard during flood-down, nodded. He punched a row of buttons, which opened ten valves and permitted the Atlantic's clean blue water to flow into the ballast tanks located along her sides and bottom.

There was, at first, no noticeable response to his efforts. Within a few minutes, however, the ship seemed to shrink. Her freeboard aft disappeared, each long, slow swell oozing and sloshing higher than its predecessor. Paradoxically, the lower the ship's stern settled, the higher her bow rose. With every passing second it seemed to occupy an increasingly large portion of the horizon.

"Flood the bay," Reilly directed.

Peale twisted another set of knobs, and frothy blue-white water jetted into the bay.

As the water level rose, the Chief Mate glanced at the clinometer and noted the slight list to starboard. To correct it, he cut the flow of seawater into two of the starboard tanks.

"Ten feet of water in the bay," Reilly reported to MOHAB.

"Roger," responded Bannerman.

Half a mile to the east, *El Dorado* maneuvered to keep clear. Her crew watched in fascination as *Johnson* continued to settle into the waters, barely responding now to the swells that continued to roll past, and at times over, her still-sparkling but much decreased sides.

"Stand by on the gate, Frank." As he spoke, Reilly scanned the wall of the bay, insuring that the two deckhands Peale had stationed aft with the drogue

127

were safe on the side bay wall, well clear of the soon-to-be-opened gate.

"Standing by."

"Drop the gate." Then, into the radio, he repeated, "MOHAB, we're dropping the gate."

"Roger."

Peale punched another button on his console, retracting the great, tapered steel pins that protruded from the ends of the gate into holes in the bay walls. When the green "Gate Locked" light on the console was replaced by the red "Gate Free" one, Peale punched yet another button.

With a grinding rumble that could be felt, although not heard, throughout the ship, the bay's aft wall—two great, hollow, slab-like steel doors hinged to the deck—started to lean slowly forward. The hydraulic arms that controlled the gate continued to retract into the deck, and the slabs continued to tilt until the ocean's blue water surged over them and thundered into the well.

From the very start of the sequence, Madeira— who was seated in the Second Operator's chair next to Bannerman—was entranced by the swirling, thrusting interplay of brilliant, all-revealing whites and increasingly cool, absorbent blues.

The drama commenced with the first surge of foamy water across the light gray deck. Those first jets raced this way and that as the ship rolled slightly, reminded him of a bull just released into the ring. Snorting, sniffing the air, pausing, exploring. As Madeira watched, the individual streams soon joined into a solid, churning sheet, one whose color grew increasingly deep as its surface rose swiftly up MOHAB's runners.

Within minutes, the foam-covered surface— roiled and bumpy here, smooth and slick there from the fast-moving artificial currents—was lapping at the bottom of the plastic bubble. Then it was at eye level, allowing him to study the contrast in perfect cross-section: the white light above, the deepening blue below, and the thrashing, boiling interface.

Even when the water level had risen far above his head, the action continued. It was as if he were in a swimming pool on a sunny, windy afternoon. Strange shadows, pale and elusive, played tag with equally insubstantial blobs of bright blue-white refracted sunlight. The shadows raced back and forth and around each other on the well's deck and walls, reflecting the continuing turmoil on the surface.

"Fifteen feet of water in the bay, MOHAB," Reilly reported.

"You should be afloat very soon."

"Roger, *Johnson*."

Madeira felt a bumping, grating sensation as the habitat rose slightly, then settled back onto the deck, its runners grinding against the steel below it. He looked down at the three schematic views of MOHAB displayed on the control console—one from overhead, one profile from port, and one from starboard. Shown on the views were all of MOHAB's hatches, ballast tanks, thrusters, and her main motor. All were still a steady green.

"Stand by for launching, MOHAB."

Before Bannerman could reply, Reilly was snapping out orders to Peale and the helmsman on the bridge. "Ahead dead slow. And mind your helm. Steer straight for a change! Frank, keep a careful eye on the trim. Stand by to slack off on their nose line. Keep a light strain on the lateral guy lines!"

By now, with over eighteen feet of water in the

bay, MOHAB was well afloat and becoming increasingly lively.

"Stand by to launch drogue," Reilly said into the radio.

"Roger, *Johnson*," replied Bannerman. "Launch drogue when ready."

"Launch drogue!" Reilly snapped into the PA. Then, into the radio, "Launching drogue, MOHAB."

"Roger, *Johnson*."

Taking great care to keep it clear of the propellers, the two seamen slid the drogue, a cone-shaped sea anchor ten feet in diameter, down a small ramp protruding over the fantail into *Johnson*'s wake. They then slowly paid out the line connecting it to MOHAB's stern.

"Drogue's stable," reported one of the seaman after the day-glo-red buoy that floated above the device was well astern.

Reilly repeated the report to Bannerman.

"Slack the nose line," Bannerman replied.

After a nod from Reilly, Peale started slacking MOHAB's nose line, and the habitat immediately started to edge aft and out of the bay, pulled by the the drogue.

Madeira glanced at the two video-displays, generated by cameras mounted below the radar on MOHAB's infrequently used conning tower. He watched the well's sun-drenched sides as they slid slowly past. He then glanced out the thick plastic hemisphere and could see, through the surging, bubble-streaked water, the lower portions of those same walls. They were white with a faint tinge of blue from this perspective, and also moving slowly by him. Just like the walls on the video monitors.

He was keenly aware of MOHAB's motion, and of his own. Of the walls' slow progression. Of the habitat's gentle rising and falling. Of his life moving—ahead he hoped.

This wasn't just another drill, another training launch. This was the real thing. This was MOHAB's first paying job. And it was a treasure hunt to boot.

He allowed himself to drift briefly, to savor an almost childlike sense of anticipation, a dream-like trance, free for those few seconds from his perpetual preoccupation with ever-threatening reality.

"Tripping the first pair of lateral guys," Bannerman reported to Reilly.

"Roger."

"How're ya'll back there?" Bannerman asked into the intercom.

"All secure here," replied Higgins, MOHAB's assistant operator. Just like Tina, Cienfuegos, Dale, and the habitat's two saturation drivers, he was strapped into a seat in the main work compartment.

Bannerman gently moved a lever, activating the port aft thruster and thereby keeping MOHAB on a straight, smooth course out of the bay. As she powered up the real thruster, the little green one on the schematic display began to blink, slowly at first and then faster as power was added.

Back now from his dreams and in real world, Madeira tensed. Now seemed an especially likely time for a screwup of some sort.

"Tripping the second pair of lateral guys," Bannerman reported to Reilly as she adjusted the thrusters again.

MOHAB had now slid out and completely clear of *Johnson*.

"Tripping drogue now!"

Madeira watched on the video display as the two buoys, one connected to the sea anchor and the other to the end of the line that had been secured to

MOHAB, both drifted aft to await recovery by *Johnson*'s crew.

"Tripping nose line. . . . ..Now!" Bannerman said when both buoys were well astern.

"Going ahead slowly." She advanced the rheostat, which controlled MOHAB's small but adequate main propulsion motor, and the little green motor on the schematic started to pulse.

"Roger."

With the last line securing her to the mother ship released, MOHAB, now under her own power, turned with blimp-like agility to starboard. The schematic was now a symphony flashing green symbols as Bannerman made heavy use of the thrusters to control the ungainly vessel. Once clear of *Johnson*'s stern, she turned slightly to port, into the long slow swells.

"Check all fittings and secure hatches," Bannman ordered over the intercom. "Prepare to dive."

There was a pause as Higgins worked his way through the habitat's relatively large spaces making one final predive check for leaks or other problems.

While Bannerman prepared MOHAB for diving, Madeira had little to do but wait, worry, and resist the temptation to try his hand at backseat driving. He glanced at the video display, which showed *Johnson*, which was abeam and about a hundred yards to port, to be almost as much a submarine as MOHAB itself. A thousand yards upwind *El Dorado* bobbed cheerfully in the bright sun.

"All secure back here, Bannerman," reported Higgins.

"Roger. We're going down."

Then, to Reilly. "*Johnson*, we're commencing our dive."

"Roger, MOHAB."

Bannerman flooded MOHAB's ballast tanks, and splashes of red appeared immediately in the schematic's ballast tanks. Superimposed on the red-green mix was a number that indicated the percentage of the tank's volume that was now occupied by seawater.

MOHAB, now possessing a slightly negative buoyancy, began her elephantine, spiraling descent through the deep waters.

As the ocean's saphire blue darkened to an onyx black and Bannerman switched on MOHAB's floodlights, Madeira shivered and glanced at the thermometer. The bubble, which had been so hot in the mid-afternoon sun, had cooled rapidly. He wondered if the thermostat or the heaters themselves were malfunctioning, and decided not. The temperature was still within the acceptable range. The heaters would soon snap on.

"Shouldn't we be picking up that Sonar beacon they say they placed on the ballast stones by now?" Bannerman asked as they passed one thousand feet.

Madeira glanced at the navigational display, which indicated they were within a half mile of the ballast stones' location, not counting the fifteen hundred feet they were above them.

"Anytime now," he replied, staring out into the floodlit blue-dark that had swallowed them.

Why, he wondered idly, did he now feel so at home with the dense, dark, infinitely heavy waters that surrounded them? It wasn't that he felt comfortable or at ease—he was all too aware of the risks for that—but he did feel as if he belonged. What was it the depths offered him?

"Ditditdit . . . Ditditdit . . . " The signal was faint, but it was there.

"Okay, Carol. Sierra. That's the bouy!"

"I've got it now. I'm homing on it."

MOHAB continued her corkscrew path to the ocean's bottom, following the invisible stream of dits, her operator compensating for the ever-present set to the northeast. Then, with a suddenness that never failed to surprise Madeira, mottled shadows appeared on the lower edge of the illuminated blue-black ball that surrounded them. An instant later the shadows resolved themselves into shapes, ghostly at first, but then solid.

"We're seventy-five feet off the bottom," Bannerman reported.

"Perfect, Carol! You've done a magnificent job! Unless I'm way off, those blobs below us are the ballast stones. You're right on target." As he spoke, Madeira leaned forward, as if to reach out and touch the bottom.

Bannerman nodded silently in acceptance of the compliment.

"Tina. Rafael. Can you see the bottom back there?"

"Yes, very well, thank you," Tina replied. "With these three videos, we can probably see better than you can."

But you can't reach out and touch it, thought Madeira.

"We aim to please," he replied.

"Before we settle down and get to work," he continued, "I want to scout the area a little."

Not getting any objections, he turned to Bannerman. "Carol, using this pile of ballast stones as a center, would you please execute a slow, circular search pattern at two knots with fifty-yard intervals between each ring."

"Roger."

"And stay about seventy-five feet off the bottom."

"Roger."

"*Johnson*, this is MOHAB," he said into the digital encoder.

"Roger, MOHAB."

"We have located the wreck and are about to commence a brief survey of the area prior to bottoming."

"Roger."

While MOHAB made the first pass of her search pattern by ponderously circling the pile of stones— and the "picket fence" of ribs that poked up around it—Madeira studied them intently. Thanks to the swift, constant current, the bottom appeared to be composed almost completely of very coarse sand and gravel or exposed, hardened, rock-like sediments. With the silt, ooze, and other fine sediments continuously carried away and not permitted to settle, the stones, highlighted by the harsh shadows created by MOHAB's moving floodlights, stood in high relief and sharp detail.

Jesus! he thought. It's all there. A whole ship, a whole era concentrated in that one, compact mound.

For the next half hour, MOHAB moved slowly around the wreckage in ever-larger circles, its floodlights creating a tiny, glowing ball of light in the immense darkness of the great ocean.

While Bannerman attended to the driving, Madeira sat, almost transfixed, staring at the wonders laid out before his eyes on the current-swept bottom. Aft of them, in the main work compartment, Tina, Dale, and Higgins directed and monitored various sensors and plotters. All the while, as the data poured in, the two archaeologists carefully compared the sensors' reports with what they could see on the videos.

It was almost exactly as the child within Madeira would have imagined a treasure wreck. Except, of course, for the lack of a massive, listing hull and spars all festooned with seaweed streaming out in the current. There were the two, and possibly three, piles of astoundingly well-defined bars, presumably silver. Laid out in two reasonably precise rows, one on top of the stones and one off to one side, were the cannons. About twenty seemed visible, most still pointing out at right angles to *Misericordia*'s centerline.

Spread among the stones and trailing off to the northeast were other shapes. Non-natural shapes, familiar but not quite recognizable shapes, all mixed in with the naturally occurring nodules. Some were hiding among the constantly shifting shadows, while others stood boldly exposed.

These tantalizing forms were the most fascinating part of it all, he decided. The gold and silver weren't his, and never would be, but the pleasure and adventure of discovering the blobs' identity were all his.

"All right," he said at last, tearing his fascinated eyes off the littered sea floor when MOHAB was about two hundred yards out from the stones. "I think we've all got a good feel for the wreck. The bathy charts show a canyon of some sort about a mile to the east. We're going to take a quick look at that."

"Roger," Tina replied enthusiastically.

"Roger," echoed Bannerman in her flat drawl, glancing at the navigational plot as she did.

"MOHAB, this is *Johnson*," the digital encoder

boomed just as Madeira reached for the mike to report the expansion of their survey area.

"Roger, *Johnson*," Madeira replied.

"What's your status, MOHAB?"

"Have just completed initial survey of wreck. Am headed for brief examination of canyon located approximately one mile to the east of our current position."

"We have a visitor. There's a ship that's been loitering about twenty-five miles out. We have her on radar, but have not been able to see her or to establish radio contact."

"How long's she been there, *Johnson*?"

"About two hours. Since shortly after you left."

Goddamnit to hell! thought Madeira. I'd forgotten about them, whoever "they" are. I've let myself become all too wrapped up in what's going on down here.

Which competitor, which threat, was it? Was it *Fortune Hunter* or one of the other sharks Cienfuegos had mentioned? Could it be the syndicate itself? Maybe it was the United States. Maybe it was just some misguided whale-watching boat looking for right whales at the wrong time and in the wrong place.

Of greatest importance, what where their intentions?

"Very well, *Johnson*. Be alert, but Jake's not to do anything rash. We will proceed to canyon, then return, bottom, and get on with our work."

"Roger, MOHAB."

Thirteen

Rafael Cienfuegos, his perpetual smile locked in place despite the terror he felt, kept his eyes on Tina as she worked at the electronics console. His breathing was ragged as he struggled desperately to concentrate on her smile and to identify the tune she was humming quietly when not talking shop with Higgins.

How could she remain so calm? he asked himself, flexing his hands, trying to relax his deathgrip on the chair's arms. Didn't she feel it? Didn't they all feel it? The tightness? The unbearable compression that made every inhalation an act of will? The ache of his near-bursting heart straining to cram tar-like blood through his arteries and out his ears? Didn't they hear it? The horrible throbbing that filled the hot; choking air, threatening to pulp his brain?

Tearing his eyes off the impossibly, and gloriously, cheerful archaeologist, he looked around the compartment. Curving, light gray walls wrapped around him, hugging him, and embracing each other over his head. Exposed pipes and wiring. Morgue-like worktables. Sinks. Drains. Cameras. A chain hoist dangling overhead like a hangman's noose. In one corner, the big, L-shaped electronics console under a number of video monitors.

It could have been an altar.

Cold! he thought. The room was as cold and cheerless as the ocean that surrounded it. Thank God the lights were on. If it were dark, he didn't know what he'd do.

Maybe they did feel it. Maybe they were all as terrified as he was. Maybe they'd all been forced to become good actors. To conceal fear. To conceal everything. Just as he had.

But if that was true, how could they bear to talk to each other? How could they bear to make any noise at all when they should be listening, alert to pick out the song of death from the thundering throbbing that filled his head.

He had no idea what death would sound like, not here anyway. Would it be a snap? A groan? A rumble? A pop? A thump? A sigh?

And once it gave voice to its arrival, what was to be done?

Nothing! He knew that much. There was nothing to be done. And yet, despite the obvious futility of it, he continued to listen with almost total concentration.

Shit! he thought to himself. What shit! None of them, not Tina, not any of the others, was hiding anything. None of them was the slightest bit uncomfortable about being squeezed into a tiny steel can under almost half a mile of impossibly heavy seawater.

He was all alone in his terror, he thought with

disgust, which made it all the more awful, and infuriating.

"You okay, Rafael?"

Tina's question startled him. He'd been staring at
her, yet he hadn't seen her lips move.

Could she be telepathic? he wondered.

"Of course," he lied. "I'm fine."

Tina looked at him with a skeptical expression.
"You're not fine, Rafi," she said very quietly, "but I
don't know what to do about it."

Despite his fear, Cienfuegos couldn't help but delight in her concern for him. "Don't worry about
me, Tina. You have important work to do."

Truly, he thought, she's an absolute marvel. Now
he was too old to be of any romantic interest to her.
But thirty years ago? If only he'd met her, or one
like her, thirty, no, forty years ago.

You pig! he screamed silently at himself. 'You
can't even admit the truth to yourself'. The truth, he
reminded himself, was that forty years ago all that
would have interested young Antonio Perez about
Tina was the promise that blossomed between her
legs.

He tried to convince himself that he'd come far in
those forty years and changed in the process.
Today's Rafael was a very different person from the
Antonito of then. Rafael could understand and ap-
preciate. Rafael could admire. Rafael could love.
Rafael also had a great deal more to lose than did
Antonito, and damn well knew it.

Cienfuegos swollowed painfully and looked
around the work compartment again. It's getting
darker, he thought. Something's wrong! The lights
are dimming. We'll soon be in the dark.

His breath caught as he waited for confirmation.
But nothing happened. The lighting seemed to

keep getting dimmer and dimmer, but it never went out.

Exhausted by the unsatisfied wait for darkness, his thoughts returned to the ocean's pitiless, indifferent weight. Would its application be a slow, grinding, crushing process as each organ, each bone, each cell was shattered? Or would it be no more than a moment of blinding agony?

Sweating heavily, he tried to escape to other times and places, only to run head-on into the past.

He was trapped, as much imprisoned now as he ever had been. The past was still there—hidden, restrained, controlled—but always capable of breaking out and dragging him back to what had been. To that to which he could never bear to return.

The past. The past had started in Havana. Not the Fidelista Havana of yesterday morning, but the infinitely more varied and schizophrenic Havana of before. The glittering, squalid, classically Latin capital of the dictator Fulgencio Batista.

"Diablito."

When he was small, they used to call Antonito "little devil." In no way was it intended as a term of endearment.

By the time he was seven, his mother, an unmarried maid at one of the grand resort hotels, had already given up trying to control him. Yet like most mothers, the unfortunate woman continued to gush with love for him right up to her untimely death from TB four years later.

At twelve the urchin Antonio was a veteran criminal. One of many working the streets and alleys of Batista's pleasure capital.

By his sixteenth birthday, around when Cuba took its first steps towards becoming a workers' paradise, he was a local "somebody." A strutting, uneducated punk greatly feared by the very young and the very old of the neighborhood.

Then Fidel Castro had stormed down from the mountains and found—as he might well have anticipated, but the rest of the world had not—that there was nothing left to fight. That behind the glitter there was nothing but tropical rot.

A few months later Antonio Perez's life took a crucial, and very painful, turn.

It was a hot, utterly windless afternoon. Forty years later Cienfuegos could still smell the stench of sunbaked urine; of rotten vegetables and sizzling coconut oil; of diesel exhaust; of life in the tropics.

At least he thought he could remember all that, along with the dust and the drooping trees planted to shade the benches at the bus stop—the benches with the advertising for somebody or other's mortuary painted on the back—but he couldn't be sure. He couldn't be totally sure if those were his own memories or somebody else's. He felt a strange vagueness at times, an unwillingness to accept those visions as the reality of his own past.

Despite the squalor through which Antonio swaggered, swinging his shoulders and snapping his fingers, Cienfuegos was certain he remembered that Antonio felt good that afternoon. He was young and strong. He was a man. He had a little money in his pocket and the girls liked him.

As for the latest revolution, he hadn't known know what to make of it. The new *caudillo* didn't look all that different to him from the old one. Both claimed to speak for the people. Both would, in the end, do what they pleased. He doubted it would make much difference one way or another. Not to him anyway. He certainly didn't need its promises; only the weak would look to them for succor. The strong, like him, always took what they needed and wanted. The strong needed no one but themselves.

One day, he thought, a smile spreading across his face, he might be a *caudillo* himself.

If he should decide that was what he wanted.

He stopped to admire a small portable radio displayed in the soiled, almost empty, window of a tiny shop. He had a radio, but it was big and old. It had to be plugged in and sometimes didn't work. This was a little battery-powered one, one he could carry with him and listen to anywhere.

"Put it down!" the old man said when Antonio entered and picked up the radio.

He studied the shopkeeper a moment, his anger growing. The man was old and shaking. He was afraid of Antonio. So why, wondered Antonio, was he so stupid as to try to order me to do anything?

He'd noticed the old buzzard before. He'd marked him as a troublesome, disrespectful old shit in the past. That must be the explanation.

"Fuck yourself, old man,!" he snarled as he started to walk out of the store, the radio still in his hand.

"Give it back, you whoreson! Give me the radio, you thief!" shouted the old man in a high, thin voice as he grabbed Antonio's arm with his own shaking, claw-like hands.

Antonio, now enraged, spun and, instead of returning the radio, slammed his clenched fist into the side of the man's shriveled, sweat-beaded head. Before the stunned shopkeeper could crumple to the floor, Antonio had dropped the radio and delivered another half-dozen blows using both hands and feet.

Antonio's victim, already terribly frail, was dead by sunset, and Antonio, badly bruised, bleeding from half-a-dozen open cuts and still very much surprised, found himself lying in a police cell. Whatever the new *caudillo*'s position concerning private property may have been, it was clear he would not permit Antonio to beat old shopkeepers to death.

The trial was rapid. There was no question about the facts and, since Antonio lacked any defenders, influential or otherwise, there were no political factors to consider. Within ten days of his offense he was sitting, chained, in the back of an open truck along with twenty other criminals.

The instant Antonio Perez caught his first glimpse of *Angel del Llano*—a cluster of unpainted, concrete-block buildings surrounded by barbed wire and set in a harsh, sunbaked plain in which a few cacti provided the only visible suggestion of life—Antonio recognized the prison for what it was.

"*Amigo*," he whispered to the prisoner chained next to him, "does anybody ever leave this place alive?"

"*Silencio!*" shouted the guard, lovingly fingering his trunchion.

An hour later, Antonio was thrust into a large, common cell with eight other prisoners and two buckets, one filled with foul water and the other with shit.

The lights in MOHAB's work compartment blinked. This time, thought Cienfuegos, it isn't my imagination!

The lights blinked again and the deck lurched underneath him, tilting, falling, beginning to spin, threatening to dump him out of his chair and onto his face.

"Hang on!" thundered Bannerman's voice over

MOHAB's public-address system. "Stand by for violent turbulence!"

Rafael Cienfuegos, in a state of near-total shock, half of him still enmeshed in the past, was only vaguely aware of the warning, even though it was repeated twice. Only when MOHAB pitchpoled and corkscrewed simultaneously did all of him return to the hideous present.

"Rafi!" Tina shouted as the stern rose and the deck continued pitching forward, twisting, dropping sickeningly, suddenly, ponderously, as if it would never stop. "Grab your chair! We're going to get bounced around."

Still disoriented, the Cuban obediently and unthinkingly grabbed the arms of the seat. As he remembered where he was, and as where he was continued to pitch and spin, his eyes grew with explosive force and speed.

Oblivious now to all but his own fears and to the need to conceal them, Cienfuegos fell into himself. In the process, all thoughts of *Angel del Llano* were driven away, replaced by a vast mass of despair.

Everything he'd ever feared might happen was happening.

Everything!

Fourteen

"Jesus Christ!" Bannerman growled. "I can't hold this whore's nose up. . . . She won't do a damn thing I want her to."

As she cursed and sweated, she continued to pull back hard on MOHAB's control stick.

Madeira, who'd been studying the Sonar plot while they approached the canyon, glanced up just as MOHAB started a violent, counterclockwise spin. His breath momentarily stalled as he tried to look forward, out through the plastic bubble.

According to the Sonar image the canyon was a broad, shallow valley, cut into the sediments of the relatively steep rise that bounded the Blake Plateau to the east.

Instead of seeing what he expected—the canyon's off-white, clean-swept bottom emerging from the surrounding darkness into MOHAB's lights—he found himself staring into a black hole. It was a void, or a mass—he couldn't be sure—as densely dark as its celestial namesakes. Only after the habitat had almost entered the darkness did he realize the phenomenon was infused by a myriad of tiny, sparkling microstars.

He felt as if he was falling, or being shoved, down into the great density before his eyes. It was as if they were going over Niagara Falls in a barrel.

"Nose's down forty-five degrees," Bannerman reported through gritted teeth. "Fifty now, and we've descending fast. I'm going to back full."

"Roger," Madeira answered as he lurched forward and down, nearly flying out of his chair. Only the seat belt that now held him suspended in midair, nearly cutting him in half, prevented him from falling into the plastic bubble.

"Fifty-five degrees and still descending. We're headed for the bottom!"

"Blow all tanks!" gasped Madeira, his eyes wide, his head spinning, his hands scrambling to grip the fear-slick armrests. "See if we can lift ourselves out of this."

"Roger."

There was nothing more he could think of to do but wait, and nothing he could think of to suggest. As he watched, the schematic of the habitat became an almost solid mass of madly blinking reds and greens. No matter what Bannerman did, MOHAB continued to pitchpole, her down angle increasing by the second. Like a corkscrew, they were being driven deeper by the invisibly swirling waters, bound for the rock-hard surface of the canyon floor—unless they slammed into one of its sides on the way down.

"Sixty degrees!"

God Almighty! he thought. MOHAB was never

built for this sort of acrobatics. She's a low-powered, underwater houseboat. A blimp, not a high-performance submarine.

It wasn't the depth that was the danger, it was the attitude. Even a Naval attack sub would come out much the worse if forced to stand on its nose for any length of time, and MOHAB was designed to sit quietly on the bottom after the most sedate of descents. They way she was going now, something, something big and fatally damaging, was bound to break loose.

Damnit! he thought with disgust. He'd just made another giant mistake. He should never have used MOHAB to explore the canyon. That was what ROVs and worksubs were for.

"Sixty-two degrees."

He could feel the habitat shudder as her energy-efficient but pitifully low-powered electric motors backed full. In the background he could hear the metallic hiss of compressed air being forced into the ballast tanks along with the unnerving moans and groans of the habitat's steel body as it was forced into an increasingly unnatural and painful stance. It was as if a house were picked up and stood on its end.

"MOHAB, this is *Johnson*," squawked the digital encoder. "Sonar indicates you're engaging in very erratic maneuvers. Are you in trouble?"

"Shit sure are!" Bannerman mumbled as Madeira replied to *Johnson*.

"*Johnson*, this is MOHAB. We're caught in some sort of eddy. May be caused by a turbidity current cutting into the Stream."

He paused a moment to check the trim indicator. "We currently have a sixty-three-degree down-bubble and are diving."

The moanings and groanings were becoming

more tortured as they were joined by the low-pitched screech of metal being stressed, maybe even torn.

"We're backing full, blowing all tanks, and operating all thrusters, but are unable to regain control at this time."

Madeira felt blood rushing to his head as he continued to hang, doubled over and suspended by his seat belt. Gasping to draw a breath, he watched as a book and a pen dropped past him and landed, with a thunk, in the bubble.

"Gonna flood aft," Bannerman grunted. "Need weight aft . . . get the stern down . . . use the motors to drive up . . . we're headed for the bottom."

"No, Carol. Don't add weight anywhere. Keep backing and maintain full power on the thrusters. The motors are too weak to do anything. The angle seems to have stabilized and . . ." He glanced at the fathometer. "I don't think we're diving anymore. The worst is probably over."

"Bull*shit*!" The second syllable positively exploded as she struggled to force air in and out of her deformed body. "We're totally out of control . . . gotta get the stern down."

Books, coffee cups, pens, and other small items continued to tumble or fly past him, crashing into the clear bowl below and providing a counterpoint to the continuing chorus of anguished steel.

"This thing's going to weaken soon and drop us. If we've got too much weight aft, we'll flip and slam into the bottom. That'll be the end of the screw and probably of the pressure hull too."

What the hell?

There, beyond the layer of junk collecting in the bubble!

Was that the bottom? Had it been there the last

time he'd looked or had it just become visible? He looked again at the fathometer, unintentionally holding his breath as he did.

No change.

"Stand by to flood aft," Bannerman barked, using a carefully husbanded lungful of air. "I'm the Chief Operator of this pig!"

"You won't be for long if you touch that flooding control."

Was he wrong? Was he being stubborn?

He could well understand her actions. All her training and experience, except for two short familiarization dives in MOHAB, had been in small, highly maneuverable worksubs. Subs that were almost infinitely more maneuverable and powerful than the habitat.

Everything she wanted to do would have been correct—in a worksub.

Bannerman turned and looked hard at him, her hand hovering over the flooding control.

"I say again, MOHAB. Do you require assistance?"

Something large and heavy enough to create a slight breeze whizzed by Madeira and crashed into the bubble with a sickeningly substantial crack.

Yes, he thought, we do need help but there's nothing *you* can do for us. Then he held his breath as he waited for the deadly jet of water to erupt, flowerlike, from the presumably damaged bubble.

No, he decided as the seconds passed and the flower of death failed to blossom, he wasn't wrong. The original plan—to try to ascend, to lighten the habitat as much as possible—was the correct one, the one to stick with.

He studied the scene beyond the bubble. There was no sign of the bottom, although Sonar showed it about 150 feet away. Once again, all he could see was the night sky—an intense black filled with a million little sparkles of white fire.

How long had it been anyway? How long had this nightware been going on? How long had those pens and cups been rolling around in the bubble?

Couldn't have been more than five minutes.

He'd ridden a roller coaster once as a kid.

Once!

It was an immense red, white, and blue monster covered with grease and rust streaks. He'd hated every second of the mad rush down the ancient, squeaky tracks. For what seemed a time without end, he'd hung face-down, while the car, shaking, rattling, and swaying from side to side, had hurtled toward the ground. He'd also hated every second of the long, slow climbs to the next peak, knowing what was to follow. He felt the same way now, only worse.

"*Johnson*, this is MOHAB. We're experiencing severe difficulties but there's nothing you can do at this time except stand by."

He added to himself, you might be kind enough to send down some ROVs to collect our corpses.

"Okay!" Bannerman finally spat out. "We'll do it your way.

"God!" she mumbled under her breath, "I hate this Goddamn pig."

"Workroom," snapped Madeira suddenly into the intercom. "What's your status?"

There was no immediate reply.

"Workroom, what is your status?" he repeated, tension now evident in his voice.

"This is the workroom." It was Geoff Higgins, the Assistant Operator, and it was clear from the labored, gasping pace of his words that he was in great discomfort. "No casualties so far, but we're all hanging by our seat belts."

"Is there any damage back there?"

"Nothing that I can see, sir. Nothing significant."

"Roger." Madeira paused a second. "For your information, we have been caught by some sort of eddy or turbidity current and are being carried down into the canyon. We have blown all ballast tanks and are backing full. Our attitude seems to have stabilized for the moment, and I hope and expect that we will soon rise up and out of this mess."

"Roger," Higgins grunted.

A stony, sweaty silence settled over the entire habitat. In the bubble, Bannerman and Madeira both stared out at the still-visible ocean floor while MOHAB continued spinning out of control in an easterly direction. In the work compartment, two closed and dogged watertight doors aft of Madeira, the balance of the crew just stared at each other, or inwardly, into their souls.

And there, on the inside of the bubble, thought Madeira in a daze, mixed with the pens, pencils, and paper, is water. A small, splashing pool of water.

Water!

His heart stopped briefly as he watched the water splashing before his eyes, turning the cluttered bubble into a stew pot. Turning left, he discovered a thin stream of water cascading past and between him and Bannerman.

This is it! he thought with an almost overpowering sense of sadness. The hull's been breached and it will soon be crushed.

He reached out to touch the stream, expecting to feel the ocean's eternal cold and the rock-like force of water under a thousand pounds per square inch of pressure. Instead, he scalded himself.

"Where the hell's this hot water coming from?" he asked, his fear now turning to a burning irritation.

Carole Bannerman turned toward him, then looked between them.

"There's a big thermos pitcher of hot water on the shelf behind us. I put it there before we secured the watertight door so I could have something hot on the way down. It must have fallen over."

Madeira cursed quietly, then tried again to concentrate on thinking of something to do, something to bring MOHAB under control.

He could find nothing new to try. Everything that might be done was being done. In fact, he found himself thinking, at this moment MOHAB's fate was an act of history. Whether or not the habitat would survive was based on the decisions made long ago by the men and women who had designed and built her as well as the actions he and Bannerman had already taken.

All the same, he forced himself to be alert, alert for anything that might offer new options and call for new decisions. If the circumstances did change, history, and fate, would be reopened.

Suddenly he felt a particularly alarming screech, followed by a very substantial rumble and thump. Something big had shifted. Something below them, on the lower level.

Madeira turned and looked at Bannerman, who was already looking at him.

"That sounded like a fuel cell shifting. Or one of the Pfeifer Units," he said.

Both scanned the console, looking for evidence

of trouble in the electrical generation and storage systems, and finding none.

"It must have been a Pfeifer Unit," said Bannerman, referring to the high-capacity capacitors MOHAB used to store electricity in place of storage batteries. "It sounded as if it was right below our feet."

Madeira thought a minute, waiting as he did for more evidence to make itself known. The Pfeifer Units were located on the lower level forward, under the conning and living spaces. The fuel cells, which provided the habitat's power, were located on the lower level aft. In between on the lower level was located the hyperbaric suite used by the divers for decompression. "Workroom," he finally said into the intercom.

"Workroom, aye."

"Did you hear or feel something big shifting below you—something like a fuel cell?"

There was a pause as, Madeira assumed, they discussed his question.

"Negative," came the reply.

"You're probably right," he said to Bannerman. "Let's just hope it doesn't break completely loose."

Fifteen

While Bannerman and Madeira concentrated on identifying the alarming noises coming from below their feet, a very basic change in their circumstances was occurring, unnoticed, before their eyes. Only after they had decided it was a Pfeifer Unit that had broken loose did Madeira glance down into the bubble—and then the fact took another second or two to register. The soggy stew that had been in the bubble's center had moved. It had slumped down toward what was normally the bubble's lower edge, toward the control console.

Glancing at the trim indicator, he confirmed the observation.

"Fifty-nine degrees, Carol," he said in what he hoped was a more relaxed tone. "I think we've seen the worst of it."

As he made the prediction, he crossed his fingers

that the runaway 250-pound Pfeifer Unit didn't make a liar of him.

"Roger," she replied tersely, not looking at him.

He checked the depthmeter, and discovered they were beginning to rise.

"I'm going to flood a little in a minute or so," declared Bannerman before Madeira could say anything. "As soon as I'm sure we're out of this and as soon as I have trim back under control."

"Workroom," Madeira said into the intercom. "What's your status now?"

"That was fabulous!" Tina replied. As she spoke, Madeira could hear Crown and Savage hooting something in the background.

"*Estupendo!*" the archaeologist continued. "You know, people pay real money for rides like that. Do you charge extra for it? What happened anyway?"

Madeira, the tension within him beginning to ebb, burst into laughter. "Some fools may pay for that," he replied, thinking primarily of the two divers, "but I'm sure as hell not one of them—and I doubt Carol is either.

"Is everybody okay back there?" he asked.

"Yes, Captain. Rafael's white as a sheet but we're all okay. I'm afraid we didn't do a very good job of stowing some of our gear. We'll clean it up as soon as possible."

"Any serious damage to the gear?" Madeira persisted, no longer laughing. He and Bannerman were both responsible for the failure to insure the habitat's total readiness for sea. While they'd been lucky this time, they might not be the next time. If the bubble really had cracked or if too much weight had accumulated forward, it would've been all over.

"No serious damage," Higgins replied.

"Very well."

"Forty-seven degrees," murmured Bannerman.

"Carol," Madeira said, "as soon as you feel you've regained control, I want to bottom so we can make a complete inspection of the vessel."

"Roger."

"Crown and Savage!" he added into the intercom, "If you two can stop yucking it up for a while, I want you to get down to the hyperbaric suite as soon as we level off and suit up. After we bottom, I want you out to check for external damage."

"Roger!" came their enthusiastic reply.

Madeira had turned to examine the navigational plot, feeling that the situation was finally well under control, when a high-pitched alarm shrieked to life.

"Shit!" he snarled as he turned to the Sonar plot.

"What is it?" Bannerman asked.

"A hill, or maybe just a huge boulder, sticking up from the lip of the canyon. Whatever it is, it's right on our projected track. How much control do you have now?"

"A little. Very little. The control planes on this hog are so damn small!"

"Come right! Can you come right at all?"

"Roger."

Once again blood rushed to his head and his muscles tensed painfully, even though the habitat was now almost horizontal.

"Three hundred yards," he reported to Bannerman.

"I'm doing everything I can!"

"Two hundred . . . I think we're drifting right a little."

"I sure as hell hope so!"

"We might miss it; I simply can't tell."

Slightly less than a minute later, MOHAB's port

runner struck a glancing blow to the boulder. The habitat shuddered and bounced out of the turmoil and back into the constant, almost gentle set of the Stream.

While Bannerman struggled to regain control of the ponderous vessel, Madeira continued to hold his breath, waiting for the flooding alarm to sound.

After almost a minute of bone-cracking silence he exhaled explosively, then leaned forward and spoke into the intercom.

"Higgins, I want you to check the points where the port runner is secured to the hull and frame. You're looking for any evidence of leakage, cracking, or distortion."

"Roger. I'm on my way."

"Don't try to bottom until we've finished checking the runner out," he added unnecessarily to Bannerman.

Still leaning forward, and still sweating heavily, he trained one of the external video cameras, number eight, mounted under MOHAB's belly, in the direction of the port runner.

"Damn!"

"Is it serious?" Bannerman asked, her eyes flitting nerviously in his direction as she concentrated on regaining steering and trim control.

"Still don't know. Camera eight's either gone or damaged. I'm trying ten now."

Camera ten was mounted portside, forward, and also under the habitat. By using it Madeira was able to get a clear view of a portion of the ghostly, almost disembodied runner, which seemed to float in the surrounding gloom.

"Okay. From what I can see, the forward part of the runner is okay. Now let's see if I can train seven around to look at the aft section."

Again, Madeira succeeded in conjuring up a view of MOHAB's exterior, only this time the runner was much more distant, almost merging into the shapeless background.

"I'm not sure what I'm looking at. It looks like it might be bent, the part I can see anyway. There's a lot I can't see, though, and I don't think any of the other cameras are in position to help."

After studying the video another minute, Madeira spoke into the intercom. "Crown. Are you two suited up yet?"

" 'Nother fifteen minutes, Captain. We just got down here."

"Roger," replied Madeira, very aware now that his unease was showing. "As soon as you're ready I want the two of you to go out and inspect the port runner. And take a minicam with you."

"Roger."

"Carol," Madeira said as he looked at the fathometer, "do you have enough control to hover for half an hour while they go out and check the runner?"

"Yes. We might drift a little down-current, but I can keep us level."

"Good," he replied.

"Crown," he continued into the intercom.

"Roger."

"When you go out, I want one of you to stay just outside the lock and tend the other."

"Roger."

"And the one who goes exploring maintains physical contact with MOHAB at all times. No swimming. No jumping. I don't want anybody ending up back near the screw."

"Roger."

While they waited for the divers to complete suiting up, Bannerman concentrated on fine-tuning her control over the habitat. Madeira reached for the microphone attached to the digital encoder.

"*Johnson*, this is MOHAB."

"Roger, MOHAB, this is *Johnson*. What's your status?"

"We've escaped the eddy and are under control again, but have sustained damage to our port runner and possibly the hull from hitting a large boulder. It's also possible that one of the Pfeifer Units has broken loose, although it doesn't seem to have affected the power system.

"We may also have damaged our bubble," he added, looking forward. "We are currently assessing the damage. What's the weather like up there? Can you recover us if we have to surface immediately?"

There was a long, unpromising pause before Reilly replied.

"If it's an emergency, we can do it, but it'll be a nightmare. We're currently caught in a severe line squall. Heavy rain, very high winds, zero visibility—and I mean zero, I can't see the bow right at the moment—choppy, nasty seas. As Peale might say, it's as dark as a shortchanged whore's mood!

"If at all possible, I'd like to wait until dawn. Radar shows another half-dozen squall lines moving in on us."

"Captain Madeira," interjected the intercom, "I think we're okay for now. The hull appears dimpled in one place, near one of the struts, and one internal support may have a crack, but there's no evidence of a leak."

"Roger, Geoff. Now I want you to get forward and down into the lower level. It felt like one of the Pfeifer Units may have broken loose. And be damn careful while you're crawling around down there."

"Roger."

Madeira leaned back in his chair, imagining the chaos above, the possible damage below, and the heavy, heavy waters in between. Any effort to pack MOHAB back into *Johnson*'s bay under the conditions Reilly described—sheet-solid rain, wind-maddened seas, and almost absolute blackness—was an invitation to disaster.

The options, however, were no more appetizing. Every additional instant spent underwater provided that much more opportunity for any hidden damage to show itself. On the other hand, ascending and rolling the balance of the night away on the surface would subject the hull to tremendous stress. So, for that matter, would hovering submerged but clear of the bottom.

Bottoming was the most, and least, desirable choice. If the port runner and hull held up, things might be fine. If not . . .

"*Johnson*, this is MOHAB," he said into the encoder. "We'll complete our damage assessment, then decide what to do next."

"Roger, MOHAB."

"We're go down here, Captain!" squawked the intercom.

Madeira glanced at Bannerman, who nodded.

"Roger, Crown. Lock yourselves out when ready."

"Roger."

Madeira sat back and watched, via the video camera mounted in the access trunk, as the divers closed the inner hatch—which thereupon changed from red to green on the schematic display—and bled high-pressure air into the trunk. Three minutes later the lower hatch dropped open.

"We're on our way," Crown reported "I'll do the inspection and Savage will tend me."

"Roger," Madeira replied as he shifted his attention to the images being generated by MOHAB's external video cameras.

Almost immediately the two suited and tethered figures floated into sight. One, as he had instructed, remained clinging to the ladder that descended from the trunk. The other—that would be Crown—worked his way over the the port runner and then slowly along it.

"I've found the problem." It was Higgins, reporting from the lower level almost directly below Madeira's feet. "You were right. Pfeifer Unit Starboard Three has broken loose—as far as I can tell one of the frames holding it in place was only secured with one bolt." As he spoke the Assistant Operator sounded winded, as well he might after crawling through the lower level's very cramped passageways.

"Is the unit damaged?" asked Madeira, silently cursing the undoubtedly-never-to-be-known shipyard worker who had botched the unit's installation.

"No, I don't think so," Higgins reported. "It's shifted a few inches, but it doesn't appear damaged."

"Can you resecure it?"

"Affirmative! I'm sure I can jolly it back into place and get the bracing back into place and bolted."

"Very well."

"Captain Madeira, this is Crown."

"Roger, Crown."

"The port runner is bent a little, I don't think enough to cause a problem, and other than that I can't find any external damage."

"Show me the bend."

"Rogcr."

Almost instantly the bent runner, as seen by the

minicam clipped to Crown's left arm, appeared on one of the monitors.

"Okay," Madeira said after studying the damage a moment. "Crown, you and Savage come on back."

Even before Crown could respond, Madeira was calling the surface. "*Johnson*, this is MOHAB. Our port runner is slightly bent—not enough to cause any problems—and one of the Pfeifer Units shifted a few inches and is now being moved back into place and resecured. We're going to bottom and wait for dawn."

"Roger, MOHAB. Good luck."

Five minutes later the divers were back inside and Bannerman had MOHAB hovering, one hundred feet off the bottom, bow into the current, about two miles to the southwest of the canyon.

"This position looks good," Madeira remarked. "Bottom whenever you're ready."

Working with thrusters, ballast controls, and dive planes, Bannerman guided the habitat down through the continuously flowing waters toward the unmoving bottom.

While Bannerman struggled with MOHAB, Madeira tried not to clutch the sweat-soaked armrests of his chair as a wave of renewed anxiety suddenly hit him. The runner was undoubtedly okay, he reassured himself, as was the Pfeifer Unit.

But there were a million other things that might fail.

Hoping to appear calm, he waited for the anguished shriek of twisting metal and horrified shouts of those in the work compartment when they caught their first sight of the rock-hard water slicing its way in.

Just as it had at Cabot Station.

Then, when he first felt the runners settle lightly but uneasily on the bottom, every muscle in his body snapped to an even more painful attention.

Once that first, tenuous contact was made, Bannerman twisted the ballast controls with an almost vicious force. The surrounding waters, so very heavy from the weight of the immense water column pressing down on them, tore into the partially filled tanks. The ocean's added weight pinned the habitat down and prevented the powerful current from dragging its metal hide across the rocky ocean floor.

There was no grinding, gnashing, or shuddering. MOHAB had settled evenly on her runners and no murderous streams of water were forcing their way through her pressure hull.

At least not yet.

Madeira sighed quietly and forced himself to relax. "Well done," he said to Bannerman, hoping to dissipate whatever residue might remain of their earlier conflict. "I think you handled this whole thing very well."

Bannerman merely grunted.

He considered going on, telling her he thought he understood her frustrations at NOAA, reminding her that MOHAB was a new start for both of them, but decided against it. Carol Bannerman was in no mood for a pep talk. He also doubted she considered her current position as MOHAB's Chief Operator to be a career-enhancing one. At least not at the moment.

"Six and a half hours until dawn," he finally said, loosening his seat-belt and leaning forward. As he spoke he leaned forward to examine the gouge in the plastic bubble.

"As soon as everybody's had a chance to hit the head—I can't be the only person who has to—you, Higgins, and I're going to do another complete inspection of the vessel, especially of the lower level. Meanwhile, the others are to clean up and secure all the gear that's broken loose. Then I want everybody—and especially you, because you're going to need all your wits to get us back into *Johnson*—to get some rest. And something to eat."

"Sorry about that fight I gave you," she said suddenly, catching Madeira totally by surprise.

He looked at her, confused and bothered. He was still very much aware of her sexuality, but at the same time had come to think of her as a charge, a trainee entrusted to him.

"You responded in accordance with your training and past experience. The truth is that neither of us appreciated just how limited MOHAD's maneuverability is. Now we both understand that she's really a self-propelled office building and sane people don't use office buildings to explore underwater canyons."

"Roger," she replied impatiently as she rose from her seat and joined the general dash aft in the direction of the heads.

Three hours later, believing everybody else to be resting in their bunks, Madeira took one more tour around MOHAB. "Just a quick final check," he told himself, looking for whatever might have been missed during his last inspection and pessimistically expecting to find dangers totally new and unexpected.

Upon entering the main work compartment, he was astounded to find Tina sitting there, humming to herself as she studied printouts of the wreckage and proposed survey plans.

"*Hola! Capitan. Que tal?*"

"Pardon me?"

She laughed. "Hello, Captain. What's up?"

"We're still alive."

"I never doubted we would be. I told you, your reputation preceded you."

"It might be a good idea for you to turn in for a while."

"Oh, I will, I suppose, but I really feel fine. You and Bannerman did all the work today. I've been playing with the console, familiarizing myself with it, and going over the survey plan again."

"I'm sorry about today," he replied, wondering if her insomnia might really be a mask for nervousness or fear.

"Don't give it another thought!" As she spoke, a slightly drained expression replaced her smile. "I'm quite used to the idea of death."

"Oh?"

"I'm Colombian, you know. I was raised in the United States, but I was born Colombian and I'm still a Colombian citizen."

Exhausted and, he suspected, even more stupid than usual from the day of near-disaster, Madeira stared blankly at her.

"Drugs?" he asked. "You mean the drug business?"

"The *narcotraficantes* are just the latest manifestation. The brutality, the banditry, the vendettas. Especially the vendettas! Some are hundreds of years old. Whole towns have died in one night of blood! Hundreds of people massacred. And not just once, but time and time again! We've have been dancing with death for almost five hundred years, and it all started long before that: long before Colon

166

and the *Conquistadores* came to the New World; long before the *Reconquista*, for that matter, the bloody centuries the Christians spent reconquering Spain from the Moors.

"To die by someone else's hand," she concluded, "to die violently, is an almost classically Colombian thing to do." She slammed her fist—and in the process, her glimmering gold bracelet—on the console.

Madeira, his experience with personal, premeditated violence limited, was stunned by the vehemence and enormity of her words.

He knew there were dark corners of the earth—strange, foreign, distant places—where interminable violence and brutality seemed almost as common as breathing. Places where terror was a way of life. But those corners had always seemed far, far away.

Now, face-to-face with the fury that filled Tina's eyes, he felt with chilling certainty that his isolation was over, that the universe was closing in on him.

Whatever it was he was now involved in was going to broaden his horizons. Perhaps far beyond anything for which he might wish.

"But you always seem so cheerful, so optimistic!" he stammered, sitting down as he did.

"Because I am," replied Tina, a slight smile creeping back onto her face. "I have to be. It started as an act, but over the years I've come to believe it myself.

"It's not hard, you know. They are very few of us, Colombians or otherwise, who are where we are, doing what we are because we really want to. And I'm one of those few."

"Having a worthy cause must help, I suppose," Madeira mumbled.

"Please don't talk to me about worthy causes. The bloodier the revolution, the worthier the cause in whose name it was launched. Anyway, there's nothing particularly worthy about what I do. I do it because I enjoy doing it. I love it, in fact. It's part treasure hunt and part puzzle. Some archaeologists are into buried treasure and some are into sunken treasure, but we're all really treasure hunters at heart."

"Curiouser and curiouser." The phrase emerged from his childhood and echoed in Madeira's mind.

Sitting quietly, he savored the open, slightly manic smile that filled her elegantly lopsided face.

What was it, he wondered, that made him want to be with her? That made it essential that he be with her and join in her madness?

It was life, he decided. Her madness was life and he wanted life more than anything he could imagine.

He leaned forward and kissed her on the cheek.

"Thank you," she said softly, still smiling and showing not the slightest surprise. "I think we'd better each get some sleep now. Once we're back aboard the *Johnson* you've got to fix whatever has to be fixed so we can get back to our treasure hunt."

Sixteen

"Prepare to surface!" Bannerman drawled into the intercom.

"Roger," replied Higgin's voice over the intercom.

When the Chief Operator turned slightly in his direction, Madeira nodded his agreement. Then he leaned back in his chair and tried to look like a passenger.

Despite his worst fears, the remainder of the night had passed quietly. The liftoff and ascent had been equally without incident, as, he assured himself in retrospect, they were bound to be. If there were cracks in the runner or its struts, or if one of the shock absorbers had been damaged, the problem would only become obvious later, during the final stages of docking, when MOHAB started bouncing on *Johnson*'s deck.

As he watched, the TV camera mounted on MOHAB's conning tower broke through the surface, revealing the sullen, soggy morning to which they were returning. Although the sun should have been up, it was nowhere to be seen, hidden behind the one-hundred-percent cloud cover.

Ahead, with the swells surging around her focs'l and forward superstructure, then foaming up and over her already flooded after section, lay *Johnson*. Her white paint seemed to almost glow against the universal background of textured, heaving gray.

"You have any objection," asked Bannerman as the habitat's rotund form wallowed in the long gray swells, "to my handling the docking from here? That conning tower's as useful as balls on a cow!"

The conning tower had looked great on paper, but in practice, it turned out to be of little value, especially when any sort of sea was running.

"No, that's fine."

Rising and falling sluggishly in the long, slow seas, MOHAB crept up to *Johnson*'s flooded, almost invisible, stern.

When the habitat was about fifty yards from the mother ship, an inflatable boat, its outboard snarling, roared through the opened gate dragging a bundle of warping lines. Once clear of the bay, the inflatable charged up the humped back of each swell, then skidded down the front, chased all the way by the not-quite-breaking crests, pounding madly every inch of the way.

"Stand by for hookup," *Johnson* warned.

"Whenever you're ready," replied Bannerman.

The inflatable slowed, then nuzzled up to MOHAB, which was now about twenty-five yards astern of *Johnson*. At the very first opportunity, one of the inflatable's wet-suited crew jumped onto the habitat's wave-swept deck. He quickly secured the nose line and the two forward lateral guys, then allowed the swells to nudge him aft, where he secured the remaining two lateral guys.

"Hookup complete," *Johnson* advised as the soggy line-handler was dragged back aboard the Zodiak. "Stop your motor and use thrusters at your discretion. We are commencing to heave around now."

Almost immediately, Madeira could feel a slight jolt as a strain was taken on the bow line.

While *Johnson*'s warping winches drew MOHAB towards and into her, Bannerman twitched the thruster controls from time to time to keep the habitat centered and parallel with the bay. As she did, the little green thruster icons on the schematics of MOHAB burst into frenzied fits of pulsing.

Madeira, sitting silently, continued to watch, his attention a mixture of fascination and edgy alertness. By keeping his eyes on the video monitors, he could get a surprisingly clear view of the surface. Once they'd closed to within ten to twenty yards of *Johnson*, however, his attention was drawn to the plastic bubble, and the ghostly gray form of a ship that rose and fell gently below them.

He wondered what Tina, seated about ten feet from him, with only a bulkhead between them, was looking at and thinking about at the moment.

Within a few minutes, the habitat had entered *Johnson*'s flooded bay and come to a jerky, bobbing halt.

"Discharging ballast," *Johnson* reported.

Bannerman, her work for now completed, settled back in her chair with what sounded to Madeira like a sigh to wait for the deck to rise up under MOHAB.

Although still subject to the influence of the swells, MOHAB's motion—now that she was surrounded by the bay's walls—was much less than it had been in the open ocean.

Madeira tensed. This would be the test!

Thunk!

The port runner thudded onto *Johnson*'s heavily reinforced deck, the shock absorbers dissipating most, but not all, of the concussion.

Thunk! Thunk! Thunk!

The habitat continued to roll, the runners slamming into the thick, reinforced steel, finally settling securely onto the deck as the water level continued to drop.

"I think," Madeira said to Bannerman once the habitat seemed securely parked, "this is about the roughest weather we're ever going to want to do this in."

"Yes," Bannerman said, a scowl having returned to her face. "This must have been the max for this hog!"

An hour later, Madeira, Peale, and Reilly were standing on the still-damp deck below MOHAB watching while Bannerman, Higgins, and Freddie Gomez slowly rolled a portable X-ray machine along the slightly bent port runner. As they watched, they all kept a good grip on the habitat since *Johnson* continued to roll and pitch fitfully in the steepening seas.

"Que tal?"

Madeira turned, a foolish grin spreading across his face, to find Tina and Cienfuegos standing behind them.

"So far, so good. The shocks're fine and we haven't found any significant cracks, so keep your fingers crossed. As long as we don't find any cracks, that bend doesn't really matter."

"What about the Pfeifer Units and the fuel cells?"

"They're all okay, although a second one was loose. Somebody in the yard really screwed up."

"Then we're going back down again today?" Tina asked in a tone that demanded a yes.

"Definitely! The sooner the better! The weather appears to be deteriorating. We're at the edge of a trough that's moving up from the Bahamas. By late afternoon it'll be much too rough to launch or recover MOHAB. We're going to be pushing it as it is."

"Good!" she replied. "Then you'll get a chance to prove we can keep operating when a surface expedition would have to stop."

"Tell me, Captain." It was Cienfuegos, who appeared to have recovered completely. "This trough? Is there any chance it may develop into a *huracan*?"

"I doubt it," Reilly replied before Madeira could open his mouth. "It's already headed north. Usually they have to hang around in the tropics for a while to gather their strength. Anyway, it's too early."

"Doesn't mean a damn thing!" Peale mumbled. "I've seen May hurricanes and a dozen other spring storms just as bad."

When he realized Tina was still waiting for him to answer, Madeira smiled and shrugged his shoulders. "Whether or not it turns into a hurricane will make a big difference to Reilly and Peale—and to our friends out there." He pointed in the direction of the still-unidentified ship hoving at the horizon. "But it won't mean much to us."

Twenty minutes later, when the inspection was completed, Madeira stepped back. Looking around, he noticed Tina standing off by herself, on the catwalk surrounding the bay, staring out to sea.

"We're in good shape," he said to her, smiling and

panting from running up the ladder. How delicate her face looked in profile, set against the storm-darkening horizon. "We couldn't find anything except that one bent runner. What Higgins thought was a dimple in the hull wasn't, so we'll be ready to get under way again in about an hour."

"Good," she replied, without turning.

"Is Rafael Cienfuegos okay? He really doesn't have to come with us. I don't think he enjoyed the last trip much."

"I don't think any of us enjoyed the last trip very much! Did you?"

"Ha!"

"He still plans to come. I told him he didn't have to, but he takes his duties as the on-scene member of the syndicate very seriously."

"Is he, are they, afraid we're going to steal the loot?"

"No, not really. It's mostly in Rafi's mind. I'm sure his partners don't care if he goes down in MOHAB."

Rafi! thought Madeira, a thousand volts of jealousy zapping through his chest. There it is again, that slight intonation, that hint of something special.

"They trust me," Tina continued, "at least I think they do, and I think they're also counting on you, based on your past record. As long as Rafi's here, aboard *Johnson*, to keep an eye on the artifacts and to remind everybody who's paying the bills, they'll be very happy."

"Tina," Madeira said, staring out to sea, unable to look at her, "do you trust them? Are they really interested in the history, or is it the treasure they're after?"

"Do you mean is Tina de Navarre really just window dressing? No, I don't think so—and this is the third project I've done with them, although the others were much smaller."

"Then it's not an effort to raise money for something political? For some new Bay of Pigs operation or something like that?"

"Good pun."

"What?"

"Raise money."

"Oh."

"You have to remember, Al, they're refugees. All of them. But they've lived in the United States for most of their lives, so maybe they're not sure whether they're Cubans or Americans. It can be confusing, you know!"

"I guess I can imagine," replied Madeira, discovering, to his combined surprise and dismay, that he really could. All too easily.

"And I'm sure most, if not all, were once active in the anti-Castro movement, or at least very sympathetic to it. But now I think most of them have decided that Fidel will leave soon enough without their help. The man can't live forever! And most of the syndicate members are pretty busy making money.

"To answer your question, I think they want the history *and* they want the money. I don't know if they want it for a specific purpose or not."

"Excuse me, Al."

Startled, Madeira turned to find Reilly standing behind him, a strange expression on his face. How much of the conversation had Reilly heard? he wondered.

"Yes, Bud?"

"*El Dorado* reports she's getting low on fuel and would like to go into Charleston to refuel."

Madeira turned and looked out over the heaving waters at the little green treasure hunter laboring heavily, half obscured by spray.

"Definitely! I'm sure they're overdue."

"I'll send them on in now then?"

"Roger."

As he watched Reilly walk forward toward the superstructure, Madeira noticed Jake Smith. The unsmiling Security Director was standing on the opposite bay wall looking down into the bay. And for a little variety, thought Madeira, he was wearing starched and creased jungle greens instead of his usual desert outfit.

Rambo had sure as hell proved himself, he thought. While Madeira had no illusions about Smith's invincibility, he was coming to find his presence, and his perpetual skeptical frown, almost comforting.

By noon, MOHAB and her crew had disappeared again into the depths. Two hours later she was resting on the bottom, a thousand yards to the east of the boulder they'd clobbered, in a position well clear, Madeira hoped, of any turbulence.

"Higgins," Madeira said into the intercom as he looked out the bubble.

"Yes, Captain," replied the Assistant Operator from the ROV control console in the main work compartment.

"After we launch, I want you to take it west, parallel to the canyon edge but well north of it, and then go in from the side when you're about two miles west of the mouth. Keep it at least two hundred feet off the bottom—you saw what that eddy did to us—and we'll see what happens."

"This may be hard on the ROV."

"Better it than us," Madeira replied, trying not to think about the ROV's $250,000 replacement cost. "In the meantime, patch the video display through so my monitor shows what yours does."

"Roger. Launching the ROV . . . now!"

As Higgins spoke, one of the Remote Operated Vehicles—robot submarines composed of two side-by-side, torpedo-like cylinders with a streamlined, rectangular box mounted above and runners mounted—lifted out of its cradle between MOHAB's runners and swam off into the darkness.

Since neither was convinced that all the surprises scheduled for the day had occurred, Madeira and Bannerman remained at the conning station and followed the progress of the ROV, both on the Sonar plot and on the video monitor.

"So far," Madeira mumbled when the plot showed the ROV located about a mile and a half from the boulder and still well to the north of the canyon, "the only current seems to be the Stream."

"Two miles, Captain Madeira. You want me to turn now?"

"Roger, Higgins."

Obeying Higgins's orders, which were transmitted to it by modulated sound-wave pulses similar to those used in Sonar, the ROV turned to the left and headed down into the canyon. Madeira held his breath, expecting whatever had cut the canyon, and grabbed them, to grab the robot. As he waited, he noticed that the black-hole effect was absent; that the water in the canyon now looked no different from that all around him.

"My instruments still show about one and a half knots setting to the northeast."

"Very well," Madeira said, feeling almost disappointed that the ROV wasn't already rocketing down the chute, "but keep your eyes on it."

All hands kept their eyes on the ROV's track and watched it swim steadily down the canyon, subject only to the consistent drift of the Stream. Even the canyon itself, a black-and-white world as seen through the ROV's eyes, one which remained black and white even when viewed in color, was predictable.

After studying the dim scene for some time. Madeira had to admit to himself that, except for the noticeable steepness of the wall on the left, it was all remarkably unremarkable. Naked gray rock, for the most part, with patches here and there of gravel and sand.

"Whether or not this channel was formed by turbidity currents," he remarked to Bannerman, "I'm sure they roll down it from time to time. And I'm still sure that's what happened to us. We got caught in a localized eddy created when a turbidity current slammed into the side of the Gulf Stream. I just wish it were still happening so we could learn something about it."

"You sure you aren't just trying to prove to yourself that you didn't imagine it all?" Bannerman asked.

"No, I'm not sure of that at all," replied Madeira, surprised at Bannerman's sudden attack of humor and irritated that he couldn't come up with a humorous reply. "Let's get on to the job site."

Some five hours after leaving *Johnson*, MOHAB turned clumsily and headed back for the wreck site. There, it settled onto the hard face of the Blake Plateau, down-current from the rock pile and roughly in the middle of the artifact field.

Meanwhile, on the surface, *Johnson* was now battling gale-force winds and steep, nasty seas of the sort that would have inevitably brought all surface operations to a complete halt.

Madeira stared out the bubble at the bottom, at the piles of stone, silver, gold, at the occasional speck of detritus as it was carried past him by the current.

"Captain Madeira." It was Higgins calling him on the intercom.

"Yes, Higgins?" he replied, still thinking about currents and eddies.

"We're ready to launch an ROV and start placing the transponders whenever you are."

"Roger, Higgins. You may start whenever you're ready."

The sooner the nine navigational transponders—small Sonar beacons used to aid in the precise navigation and location of the ROVs—were placed on the ocean floor, the sooner the wreck survey could commence.

"MOHAB, this is *Johnson*," squawked the digital encoder.

"Roger, *Johnson*."

"We have identified the vessel which has been hovering at extreme radar range. She's definitely *Fortune Hunter*. As soon as *El Dorado* left for Charleston, she closed us."

Madeira's back snapped straight as his mind slammed back into the here and now. "Where is she now, *Johnson*? What's she doing?"

"She's about fifteen hundred yards to the east of us. She doesn't seem to be doing anything but hanging out, watching us. It's almost as if she's waiting for something."

Hell! thought Madeira. So much for having title to a wreck two hundred miles out at sea.

"Rafael," he said into the intercom, almost as an afterthought, "would you mind coming to the work compartment, please. It seems *Fortune Hunter* has finally shown herself up top."

"With great pleasure," replied Cienfuegos's voice almost immediately.

Seventeen

"Tina," asked Madeira as he sat down next to her at one of the worktables in MOHAB's work compartment, "how much do you know about *Fortune Hunter*? Do you know any of her owners or personnel? How about her archaeologist?"

As he spoke, he noticed the faint but fresh scent of whatever perfume or cologne she was wearing. Flowers, he thought. And some sort of light spice.

Tina looked up from the fuzzy photomosaic of the wreck, which had been assembled from photographs taken by *El Dorado*'s ROV before *Johnson*'s arrival. Even before her eyes met his, the smile on her face had started to slip.

"I'm afraid not, Al. I don't know any of them, except by reputation. They're supposed to be a rough crowd. As for their archaeologist, they use freelances, like me. In fact, they often work without one."

"Then you can't guess what they'll do next?"

181

"Nope, not for sure. They may not know yet themselves. I assume they'll hang around, looking for an opportunity to put their ROVs over and grab whatever they can."

That's what I was afraid of! Madeira thought, imagining a running gun battle between the salvage vessels.

His eyes settled briefly on Higgins, who was sitting behind Tina and off to one side at the ROV control console. The Assistant Operator was hunched forward, totally absorbed in positioning one of the navigational transponders on the rocky bottom, and appeared to be oblivious to their conversation.

Not that there was any reason to hide it from him.

"How much do you think they know about the wreck?" Madeira asked.

"Probably a great deal. They may be rough but they're not fools, and they've been in the business a long time. The wreck's identity, at least what we think it is, is part of the public record, from the court proceedings. It's fairly easy for an experienced researcher to locate a known wreck's manifest in Spain."

"What about the unregistered valuables you mentioned, the gold, silver, and jewelry being smuggled back into Spain?"

"They're bound to know about some of it because we had to reveal the Velazquez *memoria* in court, but they probably don't know all the details."

"The Velazquez *memoria*?"

"That's the document I mentioned before, the memorandum written by one of Senor Velazquez's ancestors shortly before he died. It's really a brief autobiography and it includes a detailed description of what they put in the *Misericordia* and what happened. By the time he was an old man, he seemed to consider the whole affair somewhat amusing."

"Was there really a lot of contraband?"

"I think so. Disregarding the stuff only an anthropologist could love, the value of the contraband, mostly gold and emeralds, probably far exceeds that of the registered cargo."

Madeira sat in silence for several minutes, tapping the table with a pencil.

"What did you tell Reilly to do?" she asked.

"I told him to be alert but not to do anything rash, unless they launch ROVs. As far as I'm concerned, somebody else's ROVs stumbling around here are a very definite threat to MOHAB. And to us."

"What's he supposed to do then?"

"Bump them! Run up alongside them and bump side to side."

"I was afraid you were going to have Jake shoot at them."

"No. Unless they try to shoot at us. All I want to do is keep them from launching ROVs. The sooner we can recover the valuables, the better then. If we can show them we've got most of the loot aboard *Johnson* . . ."

He paused, his brow furrowing.

"If we do recover the most valuable part of the treasure first, will the syndicate let you finish your work?"

"You need not worry about that, Captain."

It was Rafael Cienfuegos, responding to Madeira's summons. "We have contracted for your services for a specified minimum period, and I doubt your owners will let us out of that commitment. Furthermore, should Tina be progressing well, and request additional time, I'm sure we will provide what we can, within reason."

"Did you hear what I told Tina about *Fortune Hunter*?"

"Yes. I have been here for several minutes."

"Can you tell me anything more about her?"

"No more than what I am sure Tina has told you. We are aware of her, along with a number of other treasure syndicates, but I am sure Tina knows them better than any of us. She, after all, is in the business full-time."

"Alllright!" shouted Higgins in self-congratulation, his Southern accent resonating the triumph. "Alllright! Thaat's it! They're all in place."

"*Estupendo!* Higgins, *estupendo!*" cheered Tina, turning away from Madeira and Cienfuegos. "Now, would you please test the whole system? Program it to make the ROV run along the eastern edge of the pile of ballast stones and see what happens."

"Sure thing. But it'll take a few minutes."

"Okay."

Then turning back to Madeira and Cienfuegos, she continued. "It wouldn't be hard to strip most of the silver off quite quickly—it's sitting there, right on top of the stones, where it was probably stowed originally—but doing so might screw up the archaeological part of this project."

"Which is the most important part!" Cienfuegos interjected, with a concerned look on his face.

"But then again, it may not be that much of a problem. It may turn out that the silver has to be treated more as overburden than as artifacts. If so, we'll want to get it out of the way as quickly as possible. I won't know for sure until we've done the survey and dug a couple trenches through the rock pile.

"Higgins," she continued, turning as she did towards the assistant operator, "are we ready to run that test yet?"

"Very close! It's all programmed. As soon as the ROV reaches the down-current end of the pile, we'll start."

While Higgins guided the ROV the last few yards and turned it into the current, the other three gathered around his console, and the one next to it. There they could watch the navigational plot along with a bank of video monitors. Some of the monitors exhibited the view from the ROV, while others offered one of several floodlit views from the cameras mounted on MOHAB's exterior.

"Commencing run . . . now!" Higgins reported.

The spectators all nodded, continuing to watch intently as the large robot began to creep slowly upstream. Its track ran along, and ten feet above, the eastern edge of the eight-foot-high mound.

Thanks to the ROV's new and very expensive stereoscopic cameras, Madeira now found the wreck totally real, totally touchable. Each ballast stone was astoundingly sharp and immediate. Each gray-black ingot of silver was obviously the work of human hands.

And what was that, between the stones, under the silver, peeking out of the shadows? What were they? All those different shapes, shapes whose precise identity he couldn't quite pin down at the moment, but which would be obvious after only a little thought?

As Madeira stood, mesmerized by the slow-moving drama, a small voice in his head pestered him to check the other monitors, and especially the navigational plot. He wasn't there to study the wreck. That was Tina's job. He was the bus driver and chief mechanic. His job was to get her to the wreck and keep all the machinery running so she could do hers.

It was only by the greatest act of will that he was able to force his eyes to move from the image of the wreck to the monitor of one of the MOHAB-mounted cameras. There he could now see the ROV's shadowy, boxy-cylindrical shape moving past in the distance. After sneaking a quick glance at Tina, he then turned to the dry, graphic display showing the ROV's track moving. It was precisely as it was supposed to be. Right along the edge of the wreckage.

"*Ay! Dios mio!*" Tina murmured.

"What?" asked Cienfuegos, concern again showing on his normally smiling face.

"One moment," Tina said as she frantically pushed buttons, rewinding and freezing the video-tape to show what she'd seen seconds before.

"Look! Look at this!" she said finally, pointing at a shape on the frozen frame.

"What is it?" Cienfuegos persisted.

To Madeira the shape to which she was pointing looked like a large ingot of silver that had been bent in the middle—or maybe it was several ingots all fused together—with some sort of odd encrustations at each end. The more he studied it, though, the more he doubted it was metallic.

"I'm not sure, but . . . "

"End of run," reported Higgins, who apparently hadn't been listening to the conversation. "That looked right on. What's next?"

"Tina," asked Madeira, "do you want to send the ROV back to pick up that whatever-it-is?"

"No. Not now. After we complete the survey. I

can't stop everything every time I think I see something. It's been there for four hundred years, so another day or two won't hurt. We've got it in the computer now so we can always go back and get it."

"Okay, Higgins," Madeira said, "try a downstream run."

"I thought you decided that wouldn't work."

"I did but we may have even more of a time problem than we did, so I want to make sure."

"Roger."

Higgins reprogrammed the computer, turned the ROV around, and sent it hurtling downstream, toward the northeast. By the end of that very fast run, Madeira's suspicions were confirmed. In order to get the detail they were looking for, the ROV would have to back continuously into the current. But the computer was unable to control the unit, when backing, well enough to keep it on track.

"Okay, Higgins. We were right," Madeira remarked. Turning to Tina, he asked "What's next?"

"We get on with the survey."

"Are you sure you don't want to pick up that whatever-it-is?"

"Please don't tempt me. Time is of the essence, no? So let's get the survey done."

For the next twenty hours, the ROV swam slowly through the dark waters, its floodlights illuminating and its paired cameras imaging a narrow path of bottom, some two meters wide. First it ran along the wreck's long axis. Then across the rock pile, on the short axis. Then it crisscrossed, from northeast to southwest. Then from northwest to southeast.

If life were perfect they would have also surveyed from the southern quarters north, but due to the current, such was not possible. It was difficult enough keeping the vehicle on track and under control when it ran across the current, let alone down it.

Once the rock pile that'd once been a ship had been imaged from every possible angle, the survey was extended to the surrounding bottom—fifty meters to each side and up-current and five hundred meters down-current.

Madeira, Higgins, and Tina's assistant, Dale, each spent four-hour watches at the console, manually correcting the vehicle's course when necessary.

Tina spent the entire twenty hours, with the exception of four very brief visits to the head and galley, at the neighboring console, studying the images in real time, locating, identifying, and cataloging targets for recovery. Occasionally, she generated three-dimensional images that revealed the presence of countless other details that would have been totally invisible in less sophisticated images.

During that twenty-hour period, an immense amount of data was generated by the ROV's cameras and sensors. Thanks to some very expensive custom software—paid for by the syndicate—this data was immediately cataloged, evaluated, and annotated by Tina, and by the computer itself, and stored in the computer's memory.

Almost simultaneously, just in case the unthinkable happened to MOHAB and its crew, the digitalized data, including video images, was transmitted to *Johnson* via pulses of encoded, multi-frequency sound waves. The surface ship, in turn, retransmitted the data to the museum in Miami by radio.

Finally, near the very end of the survey, shortly after Madeira had come on for his second watch,

Tina dozed off. She awoke with a start a few minutes later.

"I'm sorry, Al. I guess I'm not as tough as I thought. Did I miss anything?"

"Not much, except the guy in the big hat and football pants who popped out of the rock pile waving a sword and shouting something in Spanish."

"Did he happen to mention his name?"

"Velazquez. I think he said Velazquez."

She laughed, then groaned.

"What's wrong?"

"I'm afraid I've been sitting here too long. I'm all cramped up. I can't even straighten my head up."

Except for the faint rustling of artificially circulating air, and the inaudible, but easily imagined, rubbing and scraping of the passing current against the habitat's skin, MOHAB was silent. For all intents and purposes—the others being asleep up forward in their bunks—he and Tina were alone. They were cut off from everything else by 2,400 feet of dense, black water.

Be careful! he warned himself. He wasn't in the Navy anymore, but there were still rules. He couldn't permit his own self indulgence, or anybody else's, to screw up, or slow down, the program. No stupidities, no misunderstandings, no private passions could be permitted to interfere.

Alert to the dangers, he walked over and stood behind her. "Here, let me see if I can help."

She smiled at him but said nothing as he placed his hands at the base of her neck. The computer guided the ROV along the tracks of its last few slow passes over the survey area and recorded the raw data, while Madeira kneaded the small, quivering walnuts he found buried at the base of Tina's neck.

In the process, he confirmed what he already suspected. Slender though she appeared, her muscles were extremely well developed. She must have dug too many ditches over the years, he decided.

"Uggggg," she said starting to swing her head in slow circles. "I can move it a little now. Thank you."

Madeira smiled, his hands coming to a rest.

"Oh, no. Don't stop yet. Please. Do my shoulders a little. Once I can hold my head up straight, then I'll stand up and get some blood to my feet. They're asleep too."

Five minutes later, Tina was pacing around the workroom with all the grace of Frankenstein's monster, grimacing, trying to restore the circulation to her legs and feet.

"Al," she half grunted through clenched teeth, "MOHAB's a miracle! This survey by itself is worth the entire trip. Do you realize just how much data it provides? Years could be spent just analyzing it, without doing any excavating at all, although, of course, we will. We'll start digging just as soon as I get a little sleep and get another hour or two to study the data."

"I'm very pleased to hear you feel you're getting your money's worth."

"And then some!"

"And what about that little item you were so excited about a few hours ago?"

"Twenty-seven-fourteen," she replied, smiling with a mixture of anticipation and self-satisfaction as she rattled off the coordinates of the meter-square space of ocean bottom in which the object rested. "Can the ROV pick it up on the way back after its last pass?"

"You have but to ask."

Several minutes later, as Madeira took manual

control of the ROV to guide it the last few yards to its target, he decided the object didn't look like a bent ingot after all. Viewed from the angle he now had on it, it looked almost like the Greek letter sigma, although it wasn't really bent enough in the middle.

The closer the ROV edged to it, the clearer the video image became, until Madeira heard Tina, standing next to him, gasp and felt her body tense.

"We've got it, Al! This pile of rubble was definitely *Nuestra Senora de la Misericordia*! And old Velazquez and his buddies really did have guts!"

"What?"

"You'll see. I may still be wrong, but I don't think so."

Using only the most gentle finger movements, Madeira guided the ROV down to the object. Then, having balanced the ROV's forward motion with the current's efforts to push it back, he used the mechanical arm that projected forward from the tool platform to push the object into the pouch-like structure rigged between the ROV's runners.

"*Estupendo,* Al. You've got it!"

The ROV rose from the bottom and plodded back to MOHAB. Like a loyal dog, it then gently dropped the pouch on a large, flat tray that was suspended on an elevator below the habitat, directly under the main recovery airlock.

"Up, Al. *Up!*"

Madeira raised the elevator until the tray disappeared into the habitat's hull, and then sealed the lock through which it had passed. As he de-watered the lock, the surrounding water pressure forced the external door tighter against its gaskets, creating an even more secure seal.

Madeira and Tina opened the hatch into the now-dry recovery lock.

"Is that it?" asked Dale, who'd just walked into the compartment having been awakened by the sound of de-watering. "Twenty-seven-fourteen?"

By the time he'd finished speaking, Tina had the hatch completely open and was reaching down in the lock.

"Please help me get this out," she called.

They lifted the filled pouch out of the lock and gently slid it onto a wheeled table, much like a hospital gurney. Then, with equal care, they removed the object from the pouch.

To Madeira's eye it remained, at first, just an odd-shaped rock, partially covered with blotchy growths or encrustations. Tina, however, immediately spotted the jade eye staring out at her, the unconcealed corner of the cat's mouth, the unnatural line of its legs, and let out a whoop.

"It *is* a *chac mool*, Al. A *chac mool*! Old Velazquez and his friends really must have been out of their minds if they were trying to smuggle three of these back to Spain."

Madeira wanted to join in the excitement, but couldn't. All he could do was look blank.

Tina studied Madeira's expression a moment, then smiled.

"Sorry. A *chac mool* is a kind of Mayan idol to which offerings were sometimes made. As you'll see when we clean it up, it's one of the rain god Chac's helpers. He's lying on his back, resting on his elbows, with his knees bent up and a dish resting on his stomach. The dish is supposed to catch the rain—and the offerings."

"Okay," he replied, trying to understand. "So they were sending a souvenir home."

"It's a little more complicated than that. When the *conquistadores* first conquered Mexico, the

192

chief bishop in charge immediately set out to destroy all the symbols of the Maya religion—the *chac mools*, the *codices*—those were their books—everything! And, I'm afraid, he was very successful.

"Some survived, but not many. A few *codices*, for example, were sent back to Spain for the King and the Church to examine, and various other religious articles were smuggled in. But it was a very dangerous thing to do.

"The penalties for something simple, like smuggling a few tons of gold or silver, were pretty severe, but if you were well connected or clever you could often fix it.

"Pagan idols were another matter. They weren't just innocent souvenirs. They were something that could get you an invitation to chat with the Holy Office—that was the Inquisition. And even the King himself didn't mess with them."

"Couldn't they just have been using it as ballast?" asked Madeira.

"That's the point! Old Velazquez listed three *chac mools* in his *memoria*, along with some gold Chibcha masks from Colombia. He and his pals sent them back, to friends, along with all the loot. He never explained how he planned to get them past the Customs officals at Sevilla. Bribe them, I suppose.

"Anyway, if the statue were broken or defaced, then it might be possible it was being used as ballast.

"But this guy is perfect! Which makes this wreck the *Misericordia*!

"And as far as I know, this is the first *chac mool* ever found in a Spanish wreck. And *we* found it!"

Madeira, finding he couldn't help but share her delight, had all he could do to keep from hugging her.

Eighteen

"You ready, Lead Diver?" Bannerman's voice boomed with a force and presence that filled Madeira's head and seemed to echo endlessly, forcing him to turn down the volume.

"Roger, MOHAB. We're ready," replied Madeira after glancing across the airlock and receiving nods from Crown and Savage, the habitat's two saturation divers.

"Roger. Flooding the lock . . . now!"

Madeira, who was seated on one of the benches in the lock, glanced again at his dive buddies, then squirmed a little.

The tethered, semi-armored deep-sea systems they were wearing were incredibly uncomfortable. They were, in fact, even more uncomfortable than the ancient and long-gone Mark 5 systems, the huge copper helmet and rubberized canvas dress. They were hot and heavy and usually stank of somebody else's sweat. They were also inclined to chafe any number of places.

In his opinion, while they provided vastly greater performance, they represented no progress whatso- ever in terms of comfort. Once you were in the water, they were okay. But until then . . .

Oh what the hell! he thought. The Great Treasure Hunt, for he could think of it in no other terms, had begun in earnest. Tina, half-mad with joy, had cat- aloged the telltale *chac mool*. Then she'd carefully packed it into a "sarcophagus," a climate-con- trolled storage capsule, and stowed the capsule away in the habitat's storage spaces. Now it was his turn. The hour had arrived to prove MOHAB's spe- cial capabilities.

Anyway, he didn't anticipate having to make many more dives. That was what Crown and Sav- age were for. He had to make this one only because he knew what The Crab and its framework were supposed to look like when assembled and they didn't.

Madeira looked down at his heavily weighted boots—essential in the relentless current to which they would soon be subjected—and watched as the first jet of dark, high-pressure water shot onto the deck beneath his feet. These, he decided, weren't bulls, but a pack of feral dogs. Angry, foaming, they raced around the perimeter of the lock, snapping and snarling, then seemed to turn and attack his boots the very first instant they could reach them.

Over one thousand pounds per square inch, he thought with a sense of clinical detachment. That was the ambient pressure outside MOHAB. That was the pressure that would, in another few min- utes, exist within the lock. One thousand psi. Roughly twenty-four tons pressing on the back of each glove. And twenty-four more pressing on the palm. More than enough to squeeze and deform his joints, for example, or if things went really wrong, turn his body into blood-red jelly.

Thanks, however, to the smelly, uncomfortable semi-armored suit, his body would probably not turn to jelly. Not today anyway. Instead of being subjected to the impossible pressure of 2,400 feet under water, his middle-aged body would only suffer the rigors of a three-hundred-foot dive. In fact, even before they left the lock they'd have been exposed to sufficient pressure long enough to require decompression before returning to MOHAB's one-atmosphere environment. By the end of the day, by the time they'd finished the task at hand, they'd be totally saturated and would require several days of decompression.

The only other alternative was a fully armored suit, which would keep him at one atmosphere. Unfortunately, the fully armored systems were bulky and offered only limited maneuverability.

"How're we doing, gents?" Madeira asked when the lock was about half filled with water, thrusting thoughts of pain and mortality behind him.

"I'm all go, Boss," Savage replied.

"Roger," reported Crown.

"Good."

During those last few moments of silence and inaction, Madeira listened to the sound of his heliox breathing mixture circulating around and through him. It echoed in his ears, whistled through his nose, rasped down his throat, and in and out of the spongy bellows in his chest. His mouth was already dry, his throat rough. Sitting there, listening, he let his thoughts drift back briefly to the current that surrounded and tugged at them.

"Lock flooded," Bannerman advised. "Opening hatch . . . now!"

The instant the hatch dropped open, the water around him seemed to come to life. He could sense eddies, strange little disturbances, all creatures of the surrounding flow whose smooth progression their presence was disrupting.

"Let's go."

"Roger."

"Tally-ho!"

"Say again?"

"Tally-ho!"

"Oh! And hang on. This current'll carry you well past the wreck in no time. Hell, it'll take you to England before you know what's happening."

"Why not? It's a nice place."

"Roger."

"Very funny!"

"Gentlemen . . . " It was Tina's voice, recognizable despite the digital decoder's best efforts to distort it beyond recognition. "Would you all please remember to be very gentle with this wonderful wreck?"

"Kid gloves, lady. Kid gloves!" Madeira replied, wondering at the concept of treating a large pile of rocks gently and at the even-more-disturbing idea that Tina could be in love with such a mound. What the hell! There was hope for him yet!

Even before Madeira's whole body was out the hatch, while only his legs were dangling in the flow, he was pressed hard against the ladder. By the time he'd climbed down the dozen rungs and set his feet on the Blake Plateau's hard, almost broom-clean surface, he knew they were in for a tiring struggle.

It wasn't that walking into the current was in any way impossible. It was certainly no more impossible than walking hour after hour in molasses. It was the constant pressure of the Stream that would tire them. The continuous need to hold on. The fight to just stay where you were. That was what would wear them down. That and the discomfort of their armor; the physiological stresses imposed by the elevated, though still relatively low, pressure inside the suits and the infinitely more debilitating psychological stresses, the demons that thrived on cold, darkness, fear, and fatigue.

"Okay," Madeira said as he moved out of the way, "Next!"

He decided this would be his last deep project. And his last cold-water project. After this, after he'd helped Tina have her wreck, it'd be tropical seas and tourist dives for him.

While Crown descended the ladder, Madeira looked around him. In the distance, all remained a dense, eternal black. Closer at hand, thanks to MOHAB's powerful floodlights, a large portion of the rock pile was visible. Shadowy and indistinct but visible.

Despite everything he'd just said to himself about being sick of cold, deep dives, he felt the wreck's attraction, and heard the call of its treasure. There, rising in high relief from the Plateau's flat, light-colored bottom, was the mound of darkish rocks and ribs. Even at this distance he could discern the cannons and other, yet more tantalizing shapes, shapes he knew would soon resolve themselves into treasure of one sort or another. It was all so close and so real. He could just walk over and touch it, pick it up, and look at it.

And he was about to!

"Onward!" he almost shouted as Savage joined Crown. As he said it, he was both aware and amused that he was beginning to sound like Tina.

"Let's get this Tinkertoy Pic N Pak set up so we can see what's really under all that rubble."

And, he added to himself, if we do this right the first time, I won't have to come out again until its time to leave.

Giving him the thumbs-up sign, Crown and Savage turned toward the nearest of MOHAB's thirty external cargo bays: shallow, reinforced, free-flooding niches set into the habitat's weather deck and sides.

Savage unlatched and lifted the bay's door-like, hinged fairwater, which maintained the habitat's smooth, curving lines. Inside the bay lay a bundle of foot-wide aluminum trusses, each twenty feet long, and each with teeth cut along one side. Laid neatly along the top of the four-foot-diameter bundle was a long brown snake, a collapsed, sausage-shaped flotation bag.

"Stand back," Madeira warned as he reached into the external bay and jerked a lever. The bundle of trusses slid out and down, its descent controlled by three wire whips that were each slowly paying out.

"Ready to inflate?" Crown asked after the bundle had landed on the bottom and they'd cast off the whips.

"Wait till I finish securing this," Savage replied, shackling a safety wire that ran from a winch mounted on MOHAB's side to one of the straps holding the bundle together. "Okay, you can start inflating now."

Using a high-pressure air hose that, like the wire, issued from MOHAB, Crown soon had the long brown sausage filled sufficiently to give the whole bundle a small amount of positive buoyancy. It was enough to lift the bundle off the bottom, but not so much that one of them couldn't keep it from breaking free and shooting madly toward the surface.

"Bay twelve next," Madeira directed. "We'll try taking two bundles per trip."

"Roger."

"Roger."

The procedure was repeated at bay twelve, only this time the new bundle was wired to the first, then a small additional amount of air was bled into the sausage.

As Crown completed restowing the hose, Madeira raised a remote-control wand, aimed it at the safety wire winch, and pushed the "Slow Payout" button. The three divers then half walked, half floated downstream though the thick, chill fluid. As they went, their boots raised small clouds of sand that were quickly swept into oblivion by the passing current. The two long bundles, with their slowly unreeling safety line, drifted with them.

Twenty yards later the bundles were floating, tugging gently on the safety line, a few feet above the near end of the rock pile. Holding the beams with one hand, Madeira stared down at the jumbled mass now directly beneath his boots. For a moment he was unable to take his eyes off the heavy, dull-gray, metallic forms—unmistakable despite the blotches of discoloration and soft coral—that were mixed in with the stones.

As he watched, a long thin thing, a fish of some sort, glided unexpectedly out from among the stones. Hugging the bottom, bobbing and weaving, it then darted off into the surrounding dark.

That shadowy, sinuous form was, he realized, the first living thing, the first mobile animal anyway, he'd seen since emerging from MOHAB. Of course, he hadn't been looking for animals. If he had, he might have seen more, though not that many since complex life was far from prolific on the cold, dark, deep, current-swept Plateau.

The eel, or whatever it was, disappeared, and he returned his attention to the fascinating shapes and shadows mixed in with the stones.

Forgetting himself for the moment, he knelt and picked up an ingot of silver, about eight inches long. Lying near it, he noticed with sense of almost childish wonder, were the scabrous remains of a rapidly deteriorating iron cannon ball.

He really was on a treasure hunt and this was real sunken treasure!

"Addictive, isn't it!" said a voice, softly musical in Madeira's ears despite technology's best efforts to homogenize and standardize it. "Tons of silver, millions of dollars worth, and who knows what else might also be there, mixed in with the silver and the stones and the cannonballs."

"Just remember," continued the voice, "it's not real. The fun, the thrills are in the doing. The finding. The figuring out. Once it's in a locked bank vault, or stored away and forgotten in the basement of some museum, it's nothing. You can't eat it. It won't make your sore muscles feel any better. Most of it's not even very pretty."

"Well . . . okay," Madeira mumbled, his sense of purpose returning. "I've had my fun, I guess. Let's get this Tinkertoy laid out and assembled."

"Roger."

"Dig we must . . . "

"The fun is just beginning, *Capitan*."

They worked as rapidly as they could, making a major effort to maintain near-neutral buoyancy so as not to damage any of Tina's artifacts by crunching on them. As they worked, the three divers maintained their almost ethereal gait, drifting down the rock pile's long axis, leaving a trail of toothed trusses behind them.

Once they reached the down-current end of the rockpile, they collapsed the sausage and reduced their own buoyancy to the point where their boots could achieve traction on the bottom.

"One hour. Your bottom time is now one hour," Bannerman reported over the digital encoder.

"Roger," replied Madeira, not paying a great deal of attention to the data as he aimed the control wand and signaled the winch to heave around on the safety wire.

Keeping a strain on the wire, and allowing it to assist them, they began the up-current trudge, past the mound of stone and silver, back to the brightly lit habitat. Once there, they paused a moment, then extracted two more bundles of trusses and pipes. They then attached and inflated the sausage, secured the safety wire, and once again allowed the current to carry them down on the wreck. There they deposited pipes and trusses at predetermined points along its length.

"Two hours. You've been out two hours now," Bannerman said as they started down-current with a third load.

Okay, Madeira thought, panting. We're pretty much on schedule. I wonder what the hell *Fortune Hunter*'s up to.

"Damn!" he mumbled suddenly through gritted teeth as a sharp bolt of pain zapped up his leg.

"What's wrong, Lead Diver?" asked Crown and Savage in unison.

"My foot just slipped into a hole between the stones," replied Madeira, lying on his collapsed left leg, his right leg up to the hip no longer visible.

"Can you get it out?" Savage asked, turning and heading for him, followed by Crown.

"No," Madeira grunted as he tried to push himself up. "The current's got me pinned against the side of the hole and it feels as if some of the stones have shifted."

Strangely, he thought in a slight daze, while he could feel the pain of his twisted knee, he couldn't feel any of the heavy stones that he could see pressing against his suit.

Well. Maybe it wasn't so strange after all.

"Hang on," Savage said, grabbing Madeira as he spoke and holding him against the current. "Crown. You dig!"

"Yes, Crown, you dig!" echoed a softer voice, all musicality now gone.

"Don't worry about the artifacts," added the voice unnecessarily.

While Crown dug, Madeira wondered what, if anything, lived in the hole his leg was occupying.

"Try it now," Crown said after a few minutes.

"Roger," Madeira replied as he and Savage pulled on the offending leg, which, in due course, reappeared.

"How's it feel?" Savage asked as Madeira flexed the leg.

"Okay. It's okay. How's my suit look to you?"

Savage knelt and examined the leg of Madeira's suit. "I don't see any problems. Your pressure okay?"

"Affirmative. Let's get back to work."

"Goddamnit!"

"What's the problem, Crown?"

"Savage's tether's wrapped around my waist."

"How the hell'd that happen?"

"I don't know."

"Well, clear it!"

Crown yanked on the tether, to get enough slack to untangle himself, and Madeira toppled toward him.

"That's *my* tether you just yanked!"

"Sorry. But if you've seen one, you've seen 'em all."

By the four-hour point all the elements had been put in place and the divers were busy pinning and snapping them together. The row of four-legged A-frames rising over the mound, anchored with thick studs fired into the Plateau's stone surface. The transverse members running across the A's. The upper longitudinals running between the peaks of the A's and the lower longitudinals—the toothed trusses—which were locked into each other and suspended below the transverse members.

Despite the current's determined efforts to knock the structure over and despite the divers' growing fatigue, the assembly had gone almost exactly as Madeira had done it in a Houston warehouse six weeks before.

"You two hungry?" Madeira asked at the six-hour point.

"About to faint," Crown replied as he secured the last pin in the framework, his efforts illuminated by the miner's light mounted on his helmet.

"Okay, let's take a break and get some food. Then we'll finish up."

"Roger!"

They trudged slowly back into the Gulf Stream, sweaty and tired, their bodies chafed by the semi-armored suits. When they reached MOHAB's main diving lock, Madeira paused and turned, looking back at the treasure mound and the dim metallic spine and ribs that they'd assembled over it.

"We do good work."

"Yes, don't we."

"I couldn't agree more!" Tina added.

After savoring each other's congratulations, they struggled up the ladder and closed the airlock's lower hatch.

"De-watering lock," Bannerman boomed. "Will maintain at ten A's."

"Roger," Madeira replied.

Twenty minutes later, the lock was substantially dry, and the air pressure had been reduced to the equivalent of three hundred feet below the surface. The divers helped each other remove the helmets. They then settled back on the hard, damp benches to eat the peanut butter sandwiches that had been sent in to them via the small medical lock.

"So far," Madeira observed in a tired voice, "everything's gone like clockwork."

"Except for your leg and a few tether tangles," Crown replied as he chewed on a sandwich.

"From now on we have to be especially careful."

"Damn! I'm bushed."

"That's exactly why—"

"Yes. We know."

They sat in silence, trying to digest the sandwiches and sipping orange juice.

"Ready?"

"Okay, let's get it done."

"Roger."

Once back out in the cold, dark world of the Blake Plateau, they climbed to MOHAB's weather deck, opened yet another external cargo bay, and carefully extracted The Crab, the heart of the Pic N Pak system and one of MOHAB's main power-guzzlers.

A large, box-like object, The Crab had two hydraulic, articulated arms. One of the arms ended in two thick, strong pincers, while the other ended in two basket-like claws similar to the *cestas* used in jai alai. In addition to the arms, two video eyes poked out of the box along with a long vacuum hose some six inches in diameter.

An hour later The Crab was hanging from the toothed truss. Its power and video cable had been strung along the upper longitudinal beam. Its drive gear now meshed with the truss's teeth and its two formidable arms dangled, reaching greedily down towards the treasure.

"Ready to test The Crab," Madeira reported, stepping back from the mound and hoping the mechanism didn't explode or go crazy and attack one of them.

"Roger," responded MOHAB.

At first, nothing happened. Then, with a shudder, the crustacean-like box started moving slowly along the connected trusses. It scuttled first to the far end of the mound and then back to the near end. As it moved, its power cable rolled and unrolled smoothly from the spring-loaded reel on its top.

No sooner had The Crab come to a stop than its arms, first one, then the other, began to reach down toward the mixture of stones and silver. The claws snapped, wildly at first, then with growing delicacy. Finally, the nastier-looking of the two claws grabbed the nozzle at the end of the vacuum hose and thrust it down towards the barren ocean bottom off to one side of the mound. Almost immediately, a column of gravel and water leapt upward from the bottom and into the hose.

"That's wonderful!" MOHAB said. It could only be Tina, thought Madeira. Nobody else there would have phrased it that way.

A second test was run after they rigged the long conveyer system alongside The Crab's track.

"I'll be damned," Madeira mumbled to himself as he watched The Crab pick up a ballast stone and gracefully place it on the conveyer. The moving rubber belt then carried the stone beyond the far end of the mound, then dropped it on the naked bottom.

Never in his career had things gone so smoothly. Something must be wrong! Something must be about to happen!

And then, as if to confirm his unease, he thought he spotted something. Something big. Something hovering, skulking at the very edge of vision, at the very limit of MOHAB's lighting.

He turned slightly and looked more closely, relocating the motion first, then focusing on the object itself. It looked like a large shark, or the misshapen caricature of one. It had a shark's face and tail, but its middle was all wrong—all skinny and twisted!

It must be one of the abyssal varieties, he decided. Some sort of chimaera, one of the species not often seen by human eyes, or at least not by his eyes before.

As far as he's concerned, thought Madeira, this must be the shallows. I wonder what he's doing all the way up here.

"Anything new on *Fortune Hunter*?" he demanded, conscious again of the millions of dollars worth of treasure resting right there in front of him. Treasure for whose protection and safe delivery he would soon be responsible.

"No," Bannerman replied. "*Johnson* reports she's just standing off, more or less occupying the position *El Dorado* did when she was there."

Why the hell hasn't she made her move yet? he

asked himself. Was she waiting for them to recover the treasure and get it aboard *Johnson*? Was it really blatant, outright piracy they had in mind?

No! That was stupid! They couldn't be *that* hungry! They were waiting for whatever opportunity might present itself to sneak in, to root around and grab what they could. Later—well after the fact—they'd say they didn't understand the situation. Or weren't sure of their position. Or they wouldn't bother to say anything at all!

"Before you gentlemen come back, please don't forget the baskets."

The baskets!

That musical voice!

He had work to do.

Almost twelve hours after first leaving MOHAB, Madeira, Crown, and Savage, all totally exhausted, returned to the airlock.

Once the lock was de-watered, Crown and Savage crawled up one of the two side trunks, the one running from the lock to the hyperbaric suite. There they'd remain, except when outside, under pressure for the duration.

Madeira crawled up the other side trunk, into the habitat's decompression chamber. There he would spend the next two days degassing—waiting for the excess gasses that had infused throughout his body to percolate slowly and gently out of his blood and organs. And while he waited, the gasses would also be waiting patiently—for a radical drop in pressure and the resulting opportunity to burst forth in a painful, maiming-if-not-fatal froth.

While Madeira played a waiting game with the nitrogen in his body, Tina began excavating her first survey trench. It was roughly two meters wide and ran from one end of the mound to the other.

Hour after hour The Crab picked up ballast stones, one by one, and deposited them on the conveyer belt to be carried away.

Its arms moved slowly and carefully as the mechanical crustacean also grabbed silver bars and selected specimen stones and an increasing flood of other artifacts. Mixed in with the flood was a trickle of gold—a cross, a chalice, and three small gold bars.

Everything that Tina wanted to save was picked or scooped up and deposited into one of the big wire-mesh baskets that the divers had placed as their last act before returning to MOHAB. Each was numbered to correspond to a one-meter-long section of the trench.

Every now and then one of the arms grabbed the end of the vacuum hose and inserted it into the trench, where it sucked up and bagged smaller artifacts. Only the very largest items, cannons and the like, were left for later recovery.

As the excavation continued, every meter of the trench was photographed repeatedly and the location of every significant find carefully plotted. The images, along with Tina or Dale's notations, were fed into the computer, then transmitted to backup storage in Miami.

Round the clock The Crab advanced slowly along its track, removing everything below it. At the console, Dale relieved Tina, who relieved Dale, who relieved Tina.

Nineteen

"We just got some bad news," Tina said into the decompression chamber intercom, her tone reflecting a mixture of fatigue and resignation.

Madeira snapped up to a sitting position and looked at the video monitor. He'd been chafing and dozing his way through the last few hours of the extended, very conservative decompression schedule made necessary by his age and record of having been bent repeatedly in the past. Now he had to struggle to clear the mist from his mind.

He knew it! The minute he'd entered the pot, something was bound to happen. It always did! Everything had been going much too smoothly.

"What's wrong? The Crab acting up?"

"Nothing that simple, I'm afraid. The syndicate's ordering us to go to Charleston."

"Why? Are they worried about *Fortune Hunter*?"

"No. Not directly anyway. The IAA and the Cuban

government have teamed up to try to get an emergency injunction, a court order, to keep us from finishing up."

"What's the IAA?"

"The International Antiquities Agency. It's part of UNESCO."

"So where does *Fortune Hunter* fit in?"

"They don't. Except they'll probably slip in and grab what they can while we're gone!"

"Never a dull moment!"

"Not in this business! Anyway, the hearing is going to be at the Federal Court in Miami. The syndicate's sending a chartered jet to pick us up. The lawyers want us there to explain what we're doing, to prove we're serious about the science."

"When do we have to be there?"

"We have to be at the Courthouse on the twenty-first, at nine A.M."

"Okay. Do they realize they'll have to pay our normal day rate all that time?"

"Yes. They're not happy about it, but they're prepared to do it. In fact, several of them will probably be there, so you'll get a chance to meet them."

"Very well," Madeira mumbled. "How long do these things take, I wonder?"

"I've only been involved with one other," Tina replied. "Everybody talked all morning and we were back on the job that night. Of course, that was an easy one. The two sleazebags making the trouble didn't have any claim at all. Somehow, this one sounds more serious. Otherwise, I doubt the syndicate would call us in since, as you mentioned, it's going to cost them hundreds of thousands of dollars. In addition to whatever they have to pay the lawyers."

"What does Rafael say?"

"A very bad word. Other than that, he knows nothing more than we do."

"Whatever happens, happens. In the meantime, let's get as much done as we can," Madeira concluded.

"Carol, what sort of conditions is *Johnson* reporting?" he asked.

"The same as it's been the last few days, choppy but nothing we can't handle. And they don't expect it to change much the next few days."

"Okay. Tell Reilly to get *El Dorado* back here ASAP! I want her on station before we leave. In the meantime, Tina, keep excavating until Carol lets me out of here. Then, we'll recover and stow what you've collected so far while Carol and Higgins prep MOHAB to surface.

"Anybody see any problems?"

"Yes," Tina said, nibbling gently at her thumbnail as she spoke. "I don't know how long we'll be gone and we may never be allowed back. I've got to back-fill the trench to protect the exposed edges. It'll take me at least four or five hours to retrieve and replace enough stones to do the job, even with Crown and Savage out there helping."

"If that's the right way to do it. Do you think they're going to expect them in court too? If so, we're going to have to start decompressing them right now."

"I doubt it. I think you and I will be more than enough. If *we* can't convince them, then they can't be convinced."

"Okay."

"And I'm going to scream if some damn lawyer makes us stop or takes it away from us!"

"Why would they? You're doing a very careful job."

"Dale and I are freelances, Al, and in this business freelances are suspect. No reputable scholar is going to stand up in public and say we're doing a good job unless we're associated with him or her, or with some other big name."

"How about you, Carol?" Madeira continued, his bones resonating to Tina's anguish, at a loss about how to respond constructively to it.

"No problem. It won't take much to prep MOHAB. What about The Crab?"

"We're going to have to leave it, and pray. It wasn't designed to be disassembled and reassembled repeatedly."

"Roger," Bannerman replied.

"Tina, I'll let you be the one to break the news to Crown and Savage."

"I already have. They're suiting up now."

"Okay! That's it! You're a free man," Higgins finally announced. He had relieved Bannerman at the decompression-chamber control console.

Within less than a minute, Madeira was crawling out the circular hatch of the chamber. A few minutes later, after a quick stop at the head, he walked into the main work compartment, where Tina was sitting at the ROV console.

As he could see from a quick glance at the monitors, the two saturation divers were working alongside the ROVs, or at least more or less in tandem with them. One was replacing still more stones, while the other collected baskets of artifacts that had been collected by The Crab and moved them clear of the backfilling operation.

"Almost done?" he asked hopefully.

Tina turned with a start. Concentrating as she

213

was on the video monitor while she maneuvered the ROV, she had been unaware of Madeira's arrival.

"No," she replied with a cross between a sigh and a growl. "We've still got another hour or two, and even then I'm afraid there's really no good way to backfill an excavation like this. These stones'll provide some protection, but I'm sure something'll be lost."

"You're undoubtedly right, though I'm sure they'll provide almost as much protection as they did before we arrived. What more can you do?"

"Nothing. Why don't you, Rafi, and Dale—he can rough-sort the artifacts as well as I can—start recovering while we finish this."

"Sure. I'm sure I'll find it fascinating."

"I always do."

"We'd better use one of the divers to help load the elevator."

"Do you care which?"

"No."

There was a pause while Tina spoke with the divers. Savage volunteered, over Crown's noisy objections.

"I simply can't understand you gentlemen," Tina said into the digital communicator. "I thought you loved working with me."

"You're a slave driver, Tina."

Madeira couldn't tell which troll had spoken.

"He's all yours," Tina said with a big smile.

"Thanks."

"Which do you want us to start with?"

"The baskets. The most important goodies are in them. After we have all the baskets, we'll pick up the silver bars and wedges. Then, if we have time, we'll get the cannons and anchors."

"What about the gold?"

"It's all in baskets."

Turning away from the console, Madeira found Dale bent over a vat filled with an oily, viscous liquid. Beside him was one of the coffin-shaped, reinforced fiberglass boxes mounted on a knee-high dolly. Behind the assistant archaeologist, and looking almost like a normal watertight door set into the deck in the center of the vault-like space, was a very large, rectangular airlock. Beside the airlock were a sorting table and two more coffin-like boxes, one of which Cienfuegos was in the process of pushing into place. Yet more coffins, twenty-one in all, stored two up, slumbered quietly in special shelves that ran along each side of the hold, located just aft of the work compartment.

"Tina wants to finish backfilling," Madeira said to Dale, "so we'll sort and pack while Savage loads the elevator. You're going to have to tell me what to do once we get the baskets in."

"Sure thing! There's really not much to it," Dale replied as he straightened up. "You'll get it in no time at all."

"Do we start by wheeling this sarcophagus over to the workbench?"

"I knew you'd be a natural at this kind of work!"

"At the lock!" Savage's voice boomed over the encoder, interrupting Madeira's efforts to come up with a suitable retort. "I'm ready to start recovering. Lower the elevator."

"Roger," replied Madeira, glancing at Dale, who was nodding affirmatively, as he did.

After checking to make sure the visible, inner hatch was secured, Madeira flooded the lock, using the cold, hard deep-ocean water to drive the air in

215

the lock back into MOHAB's air banks. With the
"Lock Flooded" light now flashing, he pushed another button and watched an external TV monitor
as the lock's outer hatch swung down and back
from the habitat's hull. Once the hatch was safely
out of the way, yet another button started the elevator itself, a large rectangular tray with two-foot-
high sides and a dense pattern of drain holes. As it
ground its way slowly down, the tray was prevented
from flapping in the strong current by a surrounding framework that was braced on each side to the
longitudinal runners on which the habitat rested.

"On the bottom," Savage reported just as
Madeira noticed small clouds of white exploding
along the elevator's edges and pushed the "Stop"
button.

"Whenever you're ready," Madeira said.

"Roger. I've got two baskets in hand now. I'll drop
them off and get two more."

"We're going to start out lifting only two at a
time, until I'm a little more confident about this
process. I'd much rather dump two baskets than
four."

"Roger," replied the diver.

Madeira watched on the monitor as Savage deposited the two baskets on the elevator.

"They're all snuggles," he reported after twisting
one of the baskets and then clamping both in place.
"Have around whenever you're ready."

"Roger," Madeira said. "Stand clear. And make
sure your umbilical doesn't get caught on the elevator!"

"Roger-roger," replied the diver with a note of as-
perity. He already had one mother, he thought, and
didn't need the Operational Director as another!

His eyes glued to the video monitor, Madeira pushed the "Up" button and watched, ready to punch "Stop" the instant disaster struck. The lift wires, one running to each corner, tightened and the elevator, along with its priceless cargo, rose, swinging slightly, threatening to jam against the downstream guide. Before it could drift too far, a gloved hand was thrust out from beyond the edge of the video screen and leveled the load.

"Well done, Savage," Madeira said, now breathing more easily. "I'm glad you didn't stand *too* clear."

"Roger," was Savage's laconic reply.

A moment later, Madeira felt a very slight thump through his soles as the elevator rose into place. He closed the outer hatch and activated the de-watering pump. Within a few seconds a green light blinked on. The outer hatch, pressed in now by the force of the surrounding depths, had been securely seated.

For the next six minutes seawater was slowly pumped from the lock and the pressure of the air introduced in its place gradually reduced. In this way the artifacts, just like humans, were slowly decompressed. The precaution was necessary to protect against the slight, but still real, possibility that gas bubbles trapped within any pottery or other porous items might burst, damaging the artifacts.

Madeira finally opened the inner hatch and hooked a small overhead chain hoist to one of the two dripping baskets.

"You want both on the table?" he asked Dale.

"No. I don't think I can handle more than one at a time. Put the second basket on the deck. Mr. Cienfuegos can help me with it when I finish the first."

"Sounds good. I just don't want Savage standing around with nothing to do, not at twenty-four hundred feet anyway."

With that, he helped Dale lay the basket gently on its side on the table, then turned and hoisted the second one out of the lock and set it on the deck.

While Madeira attended to securing the inner hatch, flooding the lock and lowering the outer hatch, Dale rapidly sorted the dripping mass of absolutely priceless rubbish. Some of the treasure literally quivered with life as various exotic invertebrates—slinky, star-like beasts with long, narrow, twisty arms; tiny shrimp; worms of all descriptions; bugs and crabs—all crawled out of the mass of slime and soft coral, scrambling and hopping around in outrage.

"Wow!" exclaimed the assistant archaeologist as he held up an encrusted blob that was totally unidentifiable to Madeira. "You don't run across these all that often."

"What is it?"

"Some sort of personal seal, I think. Tina's going to lose her mind, especially if we can identify the owner."

"Oh," replied the retired Naval officer, now concentrating on lowering the elevator.

"How many this time?" Savage asked.

"Let's go for bust," Madeira replied after noting the amazing mixture of speed and gentleness with which Dale was sorting. "We'll lift four baskets at a time from now on."

"Al!" barked the intercom.

"Yes, Carol."

"*Johnson* reports that *El Dorado*'s getting under way now and is headed back."

"Thank you."

218

After raising the elevator and closing the outer hatch, and while waiting for the lock to de-water, Madeira had another opportunity to watch Dale as he finished sorting the first basket. In place of the pulsing mass that had emerged from the basket, the artifacts—some heavily corroded or encrusted; others quite recognizable as nails, buttons, pottery fragments, several cups and bottles, and two forks—were now in a number of separate piles.

"These," Dale explained, pointing at the pile that included what appeared to Madeira to be spikes or nails and, possibly, an almost totally corroded knife blade of some sort, "are all iron or steel.

"Those," he continued, pointing at another pile, "are copper and brass, I hope. Silver and possibly lead or pewter—we'll have to be sure to fine-sort this as soon as possible—are behind the copper. Glass and pottery over here, and organic stuff, wood and leather, here. Would you please hand me some of those baggies while I make a final check?"

"What about these?" Madeira asked, pointing to a small pile off to one side."

"The gold?" Dale replied, picking up a clump from the pile and rubbing off the soft growths that bound it together, revealing the unmistakable yellow hue of a heavy gold chain. "That doesn't require any special treatment at this point. Unless it has inlays of some sort, we'll just rinse it in fresh water and stow it."

"Okay," mumbled Madeira, handing the archaeologist the baggies.

"Thanks," Dale said as he accepted the baggies with one hand while he used his other hand to pass a large magnet over several of the piles.

"Ha! Look at that!" he remarked with a mixture

of irritation and amusement as he pulled the magnet away from the pile of copper and brass. He pointed at the blackish whatever that had jumped up and attached itself to the magnet. "I missed one."

While Madeira opened and unloaded the airlock, Dale carefully placed the artifacts in baggies, then added either a wet sponge, or solid salt water, to each partially filled baggie. "We're going to want to dehydrate them under controlled conditions," he explained as he worked. "Sometimes, in fact, we can electrolytically reduce some of the corrosion back to its metallic form, so we don't want the corrosion to dry and fall off."

After all the non-organic artifacts had been bagged and sealed, Dale noted the date and basket number on each baggie. Then, with Cienfuegos's help, he loaded them carefully into one of the coffins and surrounded them with padding.

"I'm a little surprised we've found any of this," Dale remarked as he gently attacked the remaining, and smallest, pile of organic artifacts.

"For much organic stuff to survive, you usually need a thick, heavy load of silty mud to protect it," he continued, gently placing what might have been a piece of badly discolored leather in a baggie.

"Fortunately for us, small pockets of silt have built up between the ballast stones. And the icy water helps too."

Finally, before sealing and labeling the baggie, he filled it with some of the oily fluid in the vat.

"A mixture of fresh water and a polymer," explained the archaeologist. "The water starts leaching the salt out and the polymer leaches in, replacing the natural oils that washed out centuries ago and holding it all together, we hope."

"Estupendo!" Tina chirped, walking towards them from the console just as Madeira was unloading the thirty-second basket. "You two are doing great!"

"We're doing our best. All done backfilling?"

"Yes. The ROVs are all home and secured and Crown is locking The Crab in place and checking the framework one more time. Then he's going to help Savage."

"Outstanding!"

"Now it's my turn to have some fun!"

"You mean running the elevator?"

"No. We've already got an excellent elevator operator. I'm going to sort through the treasure with Dale."

"I thought that's what you meant."

"Don't worry. You'll get your chance. I want to teach you as much about this as I can."

By very early morning all the filled baskets had been recovered and their contents—including several small gold crosses, a gold chalice inlaid with emeralds, a tiny gold statuette, and a variety of gold chains—had been sorted, bagged, and stowed in sarcophagi. The larger artifacts—sixty silver bars, ten wedge-shaped pieces of silver that, when placed side by side, formed a wheel, and five cannon—were carefully stacked and secured to the hold's deck.

Madeira and Bannerman, neither wanting a repeat of the canyon adventure, made a very careful inspection of the habitat, checking especially that the dense and slippery cargo, its weight already calculated and carefully distributed, was securely lashed in place.

"Prepare to lift off," Bannerman snapped into the intercom after strapping herself into the command chair.

Madeira, seated next to her, had one last twinge about leaving The Crab and its framework behind, exposed to whatever mischief nature or *Fortune Hunter* might succeed in committing. He then forced that particular worry from his mind.

He was exhausted, and so was everybody else. He didn't have to be an archaeologist to be certain they'd accomplished a fabulous amount, that MOHAB had more than proven her worth. Neither did he have to be an antiques dealer to know what they'd already recovered was worth millions. All the same, the strain on the habitat's crew had been unsustainable. From now on he'd have to cut the pace, to insure that everybody got more rest.

"Lifting off!" Bannerman warned immediately upon receiving reports from the work compartment and the hyperbaric suite that all hands were strapped in.

Madeira felt more than heard the high-pressure air entering the ballast tanks, driving out the heavy water that had pinned them to the flat, hard bottom.

There was a noticeable jolt as the habitat rose suddenly. Bannerman, as if caught off guard and unprepared, shoved the throttle forward, desperate to prevent the current from wresting control of MOHAB away from her.

Once clear of the bottom, they reported their departure to *Johnson* and commenced a slow, spiral ascent.

"I see them," Bannerman said as they passed the one-thousand-foot point, "but which is *Johnson*?"

Madeira glanced down at the Sonar plot. She was right! It showed three ships in the vicinity, presumably *Johnson*, *El Dorado*, and *Fortune Hunter*. But which was which?

"*Johnson*, this is MOHAB," Madeira snapped,

now both tired and irritated, into the encoder. "We're passing one thousand feet. Activate your damn Sonar beacon!"

There was an extended pause, a pause so long that Madeira began to wonder if the watch officer, whoever he might be, was asleep; then one of the blips on the plot started pulsing.

"Beacon activated, MOHAB. Can you find us?"

"Roger, *Johnson*," Madeira, answered suspecting it was Reilly on the other end. "We can find you."

Ten minutes later, MOHAB's upper works burst through the none-too-slick interface into the predawn dark.

Studying the video monitor as he turned the camera mounted on the habitat's conning tower, Madeira quickly spotted *Johnson*'s running lights rising and falling a hundred yards or so to the east. Turning to the radar, he identified a smaller target, presumably *El Dorado*, another half mile to the east, and what could only be *Fortune Hunter* about two miles to the west.

"What do you think of these seas, Carol?" he asked.

Bannerman studied the monitor a moment. "Ten feet if they're an inch."

"And breaking, damnit. What did Reilly report before we surfaced?"

"A short chop."

"I'd never call this that," Madeira replied, thinking that Reilly could be incredibly unhelpful when in one of his moods. "Can you do it in these seas?"

"I can do anything," Bannerman said with a grin.

Twenty

A few minutes later, MOHAB's strange, almost useless, little conning tower again rose from the depths. Madeira found himself returning to an ugly mean-spirited world filled with nasty gray seas—humpbacked, darkly furry trolls dancing brutishly under a low gray sky.

Johnson, now flooded down and waiting for the habitat's return, was clearly visible to windward. With much of her length submerged, and with the canopy of cranes and beams aft blending into the overcast, the research ship's tall superstructure resembled more a buoy than a ship as it rose and fell sullenly in the passing seas.

A mile or so further east, *El Dorado* pitched and rolled bravely, holding station as instructed.

"MOHAB, this is *Johnson*." It was Frank Peale, standing at the glass-enclosed docking control station that grew out of the aft face of the superstructure, overlooking the bay. "I have you in sight two-three-five yards astern of me. Commence your approach when ready."

"Roger, *Johnson*, Bannerman replied as she leaned forward to study the monitor. "Commencing approach now."

Using main motor and rudder, Bannerman turned the two-hundred-ton blimp and headed right up *Johnson's* barely perceptible wake.

Madeira, still irritated with Reilly and less than comfortable with the conditions, forced himself to sit back in his chair. He struggled to not highlight his anxiety and tension by leaning forward as he shifted his glance between Bannerman and the video display.

Any number of unfortunate occurrences, or miscalculations, even an unusually potent knuckle—the eddy formed when *Johnson's* rudder was moved—could cause problems for the clumsy, underpowered habitat.

When he noticed the sheen beginning to form on Bannerman's face, he felt no surprise. They both knew it wouldn't take much of a collision to incapacitate MOHAB, the massive pneumatic fenders running along the inner bay walls notwithstanding. Even if they survived, their reputations wouldn't.

Especially his.

"MOHAB, this is *Johnson*. Stand by for Zodiak."

Madeira glanced again at the video display, shocked to see they'd approached to less than fifty yards from *Johnson* without his being aware of it.

The bay walls, which had been barely visible from the distance, now towered over him like a pair of storm-lashed harbor breakwaters, the waves surging against, and even bursting over, them.

"Roger, *Johnson*," Bannerman said as she cut

power to the main motor and prepared to use the thrusters to maintain heading.

The black rubber boat shot out of the bay trailing a bundle of deceptively thin, super-strong synthetic lines. As it came, its immense outboard bellowing and belching great clouds of bluish fumes, it skipped lightly over the short ribbon of slick water that trailed out behind *Johnson*.

Within seconds the speeding boat raced out of the relative tranquility afforded by *Johnson*'s slick wake and found itself fully exposed to the rolling seas. Half-bouncing, half-flying, it continued its passage, leaping from crest to crest and pounding the three-man crew's livers to pate.

By turning the video cameras, Madeira was able to follow the boat as it slammed its way toward them. When it reached the habitat's bow, the coxswain trottled down and spun the engine. Almost instantly, the inflatable itself spun, then came to a dead stop, perched on the crest of a wave. So sudden was the stop that it seemed to Madeira as if the boat had been caught in a still photograph.

During that very brief pause, lasting no longer than a few heart beats, one of the boat's survival-suited crew snapped the remote-release hook on one of the lines to the large ring set into MOHAB's nose.

The instant the Zodiak had maneuvered itself clear of the line, Peale started to winch the habitat into the ship, causing MOHAB to shudder with a sudden jolt.

As they were slowly drawn forward and in, Bannerman played the thrusters, maintaining a nearly equal distance between MOHAB and each of the walls, and the schematic came to pulsing life.

Still bouncing madly, the rubber boat was soon alongside to starboard, where its crew snapped on two lateral guys. Following one more organ-bashing trip by the boat, they repeated the process to port.

"Twenty yards to gate," Peale reported. "You're doing great, Bannerman!"

"Roger," Bannerman replied, making an effort to prevent a slight smile from disfiguring her professional intensity.

She really is good, thought Madeira as he continued to eye the slowly approaching, lock-like bay ahead and the unruly gray waters that surrounded them. She may be a real tough customer at times but she seems to have finally developed a feel for MOHAB.

Not that everything's going perfectly! he thought as MOHAB bobbed, then snap-rolled to port. One of the nasty, not-so-little ones that Reilly seemed to consider nothing more than a mild chop had just slammed into the habitat's conning tower.

"Ten yards to gate."

Looking down through the plastic bubble, Madeira could now see *Johnson*'s shadowy-dense stern below him. To all appearances it was a sunken wreck, its details, normally above water, distorted by the ten feet of intervening sea.

"Over gate."

There was the gate, now in its down position. Two pale-gray dominoes lying face-down.

The air in the bubble felt hot to Madeira. He knew it was his imagination.

"In position," Peale said, exhaling a very private sigh of relief as he used the aft pair of lateral guys to check MOHAB's forward creep and hold her in position. "Raising gate. Stand by for pumpout."

"Roger," replied Bannerman, tentatively lifting her hands off the thruster controls, ready to grab them again at the first sign of trouble.

Madeira looked out the bubble at the water-filled bay. It was cold, gray, and lifeless, in perfect tune with the sky and the sea. He couldn't help but contrast it with the sparkling blue lagoon, filled with sun and shadow, from which they'd departed.

Did the change mean anything? Anything important, that is?

"Gate up and secured. Pumping out."

"Roger."

Standing high over the bay in his glass room, Peale punched a series of buttons, and twelve big stripping pumps burst to life. Almost instantaneously, twelve jets of solid water, six per side, each almost two feet in diameter, shot out just above *Johnson*'s waterline.

Of course it did!

Of course the change meant something. He just didn't know what. Except that the weather had changed for the worse.

And then he noticed the beer can race by the bubble, twisting and turning as it went, sucked toward one of the pumps.

Then there was another. And another. And another.

For a minute or two it looked as if a gigantic school of red-and-gold fish—beer-can fish—was whirling past.

There was a thump, and a shudder, as MOHAB's runners pounded down on *Johnson*'s deck, then lifted off again.

"Hooray!" chirped Tina's voice over the intercom, just after MOHAB struck the deck again and, after several rapid efforts to leap to freedom, relaxed and accepted the situation. "We're home!"

Even before the bay was totally freed of water,

the Bos'n and four seamen were sloshing around the habitat, clamping its runners to the deck and installing special shoring beams between MOHAB's hull and reinforced points in the bay walls. By the time the water level was down to an inconsequential inch or two, the main hatch was open.

The chill wind, that very same nor'easter that was causing the short, nasty seas, was now free to whistle in, snaking its way from compartment to compartment.

"I guess you had a good dive," Reilly said as Madeira emerged from the main hatch and stepped onto the still-soaking gray deck.

"We sure as hell did, Bud. As far as I can tell, it was a roaring success. And I gather you had a fine time yourselves."

"What do you mean by that!"

"The beer cans in the bay. There must have been five hundred of them."

Reilly laughed. "I decided we needed a little R&R. You know what that is, Al. R&R? They even have that in the Navy."

"So I hear. Did you run any emergency drills while I was gone?"

"In my opinion, none were necessary. The crew doesn't like them. They're bad for morale."

"Captain Madeira?"

Madeira turned and looked at Jake Smith, noting in the process that the security specialist had abandoned, for the moment, his automatic rifle, leaving him with only a knife and a pistol.

"Yes, Jake?"

"You still want the artifacts moved to Laboratory Bravo?"

Madeira hesitated a moment, changing mental gears. Thanks to Tina, he too now tended to think of the treasure as little more than a collection of marvelous, almost mystical toys. He had come to view it with the same innocent delight a child might feel contemplating a sparkling speck of pink quartz. He had to force himself to remember that MOHAB's cargo also represented very real, very portable wealth—many millions of dollars worth—and it was his responsibility to protect it.

"Yes. I still think that's best. Bravo's about the easiest-to-secure space we have and Tina and Dale want to do some more work on them."

"I'll take care of it."

"Okay, but check with Tina, she's the final authority."

As he spoke, Madeira shivered slightly in the cold gray wind.

"MOHAB's secured, Captain," reported the Bos'n to Reilly.

"Okay, Boats. Is Ms. Bannerman satisfied?"

"Yes," affirmed Bannerman's voice from under the habitat. "It'll do."

"Who's monitoring Crown and Savage?" asked Madeira, remembering that the two divers were still imprisoned in MOHAB's hyperbaric suite, and would be until well after he'd left for Miami.

"I've taken care of that," Bannerman shouted, a note of irritation in her voice. "Higgins's on the console now and I'll relieve him."

"Let's get under way and head in then," Reilly interjected.

"In a couple minutes, Bud," said Madeira, looking out at *El Dorado*'s dark-green hull pitching and pounding in the chop. "I want to prepare some brief written instructions for them."

"Okay. I'll tell them to stand by to come alongside," answered Reilly, thinking that written instructions were a foolproof way to get your cock chopped off if something goes wrong.

Twenty minutes later, just as another Coast Guard patrol plane disappeared into the overcast, Madeira rejoined Reilly on the drizzle-soaked upper deck of the starboard bay wall. Fifty yards away, *El Dorado* held station, pounding her way into the short, wet seas on a course parallel to *Johnson's*.

"Those guys are getting to be like clockwork," he observed to *Johnson's* Master.

"Your instructions all ready?"

"Yes," Madeira said, holding up a sealed envelope.

"Okay," said Reilly, raising a walkie-talkie to his mouth. "*El Dorado*, this is *Johnson*. We are ready to pass you a message. Come alongside our starboard transfer station."

"Roger, *Johnson*. Coming alongside now."

Even before the diaphragm in the walkie-talkie's speaker had stopped vibrating, a puff of dense black smoke burst from *El Dorado's* tiny funnel and her spray-shrouded bow spun toward them.

"What're you telling them? If I'm allowed to know," asked Reilly, watching Madeira stuff the envelope into a plastic cylinder.

"I'm telling them," replied Madeira as he screwed the watertight end on the cylinder, "that their job is to prevent anybody, and especially *Fortune Hunter*, from messing with the wreck. Or with The Crab! If anybody arrives, they're to stay as close as possible and watch carefully. If anyone starts to root around, they're to be stopped."

"How?"

"Cut their ROV tethers. Bump 'em. I don't want any personal injuries, no shooting, but it's our wreck!"

"You're the boss!"

They stood in silence, watching *El Dorado* approach, Madeira carefully coiling the retrieving line attached to the cylinder.

"Tell them to stand by," he said when the smaller vessel was about ten yards away.

After hearing Reilly repeat the message into the walkie-talkie, Madeira swung the cylinder once in a four-foot circle and with an underarm snap, pitched it up and out into the wet air. The cylinder, trailing its light line, seemed to rise, and float, just hanging in the grayness. Then it drifted down and bounced once on *El Dorado*'s deck before one of her hands grabbed it.

Five minutes later, while Madeira was coiling the retrieval line around the cylinder and wondering if *El Dorado*'s skipper really did possess the judgment necessary to execute his orders, the walkie-talkie screeched to life: "*Johnson*, this is *El Dorado*. Your instructions read and understood. We will do our best to carry them out."

Without stopping coiling, Madeira nodded to Reilly. At this point, all he could do was cross his fingers.

"Roger, *El Dorado*. We're headed in now."

"Bon voyage."

"Bud, I need a shower."

"I've been meaning to mention that, Al."

"And a nap," Madeira continued, trying to overlook Reilly's interruption.

"See you this afternoon."

After pausing to check on Jake Smith's activities, and determining that Tina had the situation well in hand, Madeira showered, snacked, and with a groan, stretched out on his bunk, convinced that before long he was going to need every scrap of energy he could muster.

Twenty-one

It was early evening by the time *Johnson* stopped next to the Charleston Sea Buoy to pick up the harbor pilot. The thick overcast and drizzle had deteriorated into heavy rain. The air, the sea, the sky, and the future were all a uniform, opaque gray such that very little was visible to the unaided eye.

The pilot boat was waiting at the buoy and the pilot, a short, bearded man, lost no time climbing aboard *Johnson*. After the usual introductions and pleasantries, he got the ship under way again and headed in between the two long stone jetties that curved out from the low shore into the shallow, near-shore waters, forming a funnel almost three miles long.

"How well to these really work?" Madeira asked, pointing at one of the long, thin rock piles between which the pilot was threading his way.

"Quite well," replied the pilot. "They do a good

job of helping keep the channel scoured out. Remember, we've got two good-sized rivers here, the Ashley and the Cooper, both emptying into the Lower Harbor. Come the ebb tide and it really rips."

Within a few minutes, they were between the low gray shadows that were Morris and Sullivan's Islands, at the very entrance to the Lower Harbor. And within another minute or two, the pilot had ordered the engines stopped. "Stand by to anchor, Captain," he said to Reilly.

Reilly repeated the command to Peale, who was up forward at the anchor windlass on the focs'l.

"Let go!" the pilot said quietly.

The order was repeated, the anchor splashed down into the dark water, and *Johnson* was moored in Charleston's Commercial Anchorage A.

Commercial Anchorage A was located right at the mouth of the harbor, almost out in the Atlantic. It was over four miles from the city, and almost six to the boat landing they would be using at the Municipal Marina.

It was not the anchorage Madeira would have chosen.

But nobody had asked his opinion.

Even before the pilot had disappeared over the side, a police boat came along. Aboard was a police captain. And before the police captain had even reached the main deck, yet another boat arrived, this one delivering two attorneys who represented the syndicate. With them was their paralegal aide.

Fifteen minutes of maddening confusion followed on the floodlit and rain-drenched main deck before Madeira finally succeeded in convincing the two attorneys to go with Tina while he and Reilly attended to matters of interest to the police.

"About that fifty-caliber machine gun," the police captain said, getting right to the point after they had moved into the limited cover provided by the overhang of the boat deck.

"Yes?" responded Madeira, expecting to be asked to see their federal permit for it.

"I don't want it used while you're here. No matter what! It carries too far."

"Yes, sir, I understand."

"Good!" concluded the police officer as Reilly and Jake Smith led him off for a tour of the ship and her defenses.

With a sigh, Madeira headed off to join Tina and the lawyers.

Tina and the Lawyers. It sounded to him like the name of a rock group.

By the next morning the weather hadn't improved one bit.

Madeira stood in the clammy, quiet pilothouse, drinking his second cup of coffee, and looked out over the Lower Harbor. He squinted into the steady gray downpour, which was threatening to turn first light into an all-day affair.

Off to port, and almost abeam, he could make out the squat blob that must be Fort Sumter, floating in the middle of the harbor. To starboard, a shadowy, denser line of gray hinted at the Mount Pleasant shore. But forward, to the north, the city itself was totally obscured by the early morning gloom.

Sipping the hot brew carefully, he studied the current-slick surface that flowed past, fascinated by the tussling and tumbling of the water and by its fierce efforts to drag the ship out to sea with it.

"Buenos dias!"

Madeira shoved aside all his gloomy thoughts and turned to find Tina standing next to him. She was even more radiant than usual, and all it seemed to take was earrings, a touch of makeup, a dress, and her usual broad smile.

"Good morning," Madeira responded, surprised at the sudden surge of cheer he felt. "This is one of the most romantic cities in the country, although you'd never know it in this weather."

"So they say. I'm sure we'll find out. Did you get any sleep after the lawyers left?"

"Very little, I'm afraid."

"It doesn't show. You look very handsome in that suit. It looks very good on you."

"I keep hoping the pinstripes will make me look a little taller and thinner."

Laughing, she placed one hand gently on his shoulder and kissed his cheek. "You are more than satisfactory just as you are."

"Ready?"

"Yes. Are we late?"

"No. We're supposed to meet the lawyers at the airport at six, but it's a chartered plane, so they're not going to leave without us."

"Chartered airplanes. Two lawyers *and* somebody to do their work for them. We're going big-time today, no?"

"I'm never sure how to answer those questions you insist on ending with 'no.' "

"All you have to say is, 'As always, Tina, you are totally correct.' It's really very simple, no?"

Chuckling, Madeira strode out to the wing and looked aft. The launch had been brought in from the boat boom and secured to the landing stage. Rafael Cienfuegos, the Boatswain, and two seamen were standing at the head of the ladder, in the rain, looking up at him.

"We'd better get going," he said as he finished the coffee and walked back into the pilothouse.

"Let's do it then!" she responded, picking up her thick briefcase.

Immediately upon their arrival at Miami International Airport Rafael Cienfuegos, whose presence at court was considered unnecessary, hopped into a cab. He was very apologetic that he would be unable to attend the hearing and provide moral support. There were, however, certain pressing business matters that he had been unable to straighten out in the numerous telephone calls he'd made from the ship.

At nine-forty-five, Madeira, Tina, the two lawyers, and the paralegal were all sprinting into the Federal District Court House, oblivious to the overcast that reigned over the entire Southeast Coast. Five minutes later, with all but Tina puffing slightly, they entered a large conference room.

"Tina!" cried a small, balding man. "I was afraid you would be late."

"I'm sorry, Diego. We did cut it a little close. I hope it hasn't caused a problem?"

"No. No, you have arrived just in time," he replied, now smiling.

"Diego. I don't think you've met Al Madeira, MOHAB's Operational Director?"

"*Mucho gusto*, Captain. I can not tell you how pleased we all are with the work you have done so far."

"Al, this is Diego Velazquez, the chairman of the syndicate. And the owner of the *memoria* I'm so fond of quoting."

"It's a great pleasure, sir."

"We'd better all take our places," said one of the attorneys quietly. "The judge is on his way."

"Ah!" Velazquez responded, throwing his head back. "Where are our places?"

"Along this side of the table. The plaintiffs are on the other."

"Of course!" exclaimed the Cuban-American, just as the court reporter entered the room and set up a tape recorder and several microphones.

With all parties standing, Judge Weaver entered and seated himself at the head of the table. Walking beside him was an older man whom Tina recognized as Professor Richard Standish, one of the grand old men of marine archaeology. The professor remained standing.

"I apologize," said Judge Weaver as the opposing forces took their seats, "for having to conduct these proceedings in a conference room. There will be no courtrooms available for another week and, in view of the emergency nature of Plaintiff's petition, this seemed the best solution. Is there any objection?"

"I can't say that I am thrilled with the informal setting, Your Honor," said Mr. Alfaneque, the plaintiffs' lead attorney, "nor your limiting us to one expert witness."

"It is you, Mr. Alfaneque, who has insisted this is an emergency situation," replied the judge, "and I'm treating it as such. As to limiting each side to one expert witness, I am more than willing to accept Dr. Hammerly's testimony as highly competent by itself."

As he spoke the judge nodded toward Hammerly, who was sitting alongside Alfaneque.

"I seriously doubt," Judge Weaver continued, "that a week of testimony by two armies of experts will make anything clearer to me than will the testimony of the two experts we have here and now."

"Yes, Your Honor," Alfaneque said, still obviously less than happy.

"Mr. Lawrence?"

"We have no objections to your arrangements, Your Honor."

"Then allow me to introduce Professor Robert Standish to those of you who don't know him. I have asked him to serve as a Special Technical Advisor to me in this matter. Again, is there any objection? Do either of you object to my making use of Professor Standish's counsel? Naturally, any advice or opinions upon which I base my decisions will be documented should you wish to challenge them in any appeals."

This time nobody objected, so Professor Standish sat down beside the judge.

"On May twenty-first of this year," said Judge Weaver, "I granted Grupo Hispano-Americano title to a wreck tentatively identified as that of the vessel *Nuestra Senora de la Misericordia*.

"That decision was based on my determination that the wreck was abandoned; that the wreck is located in international waters and not in the territorial waters of any nation or state; that the law of maritime salvage and finds applies; that Grupo Hispano-Americano has, in fact, discovered the property in question and reduced it to their possession through preliminary exploration and the recovery of certain artifacts which were presented at the May hearing and that Grupo Hispano-Americano was in the process of expending considerable effort in launching an expedition to complete the recovery of the vessel and its cargo.

"I now have before me two petitions. In one,

Plaintiff argues that the vessel and its cargo were never abandoned but rather were lost and that they are, in fact, the property of the Republic of Cuba. In this petition, Plaintiff asks that I restrain Defendant from further recovery operations and award title to the vessel and its cargo to either the Republic of Cuba or the International Antiquities Agency. In the second petition, Plaintiff argues that Defendant is using untested and unproven technology to conduct its excavation of the wreck and that the use of such technology represents a grave risk to the wreck and its contents. In this second petition, Plaintiff requests an emergency restraining order to prevent Defendant from damaging the wreck before the first petition is decided and, if necessary, appealed.

"Mr. Lawrence, have you had adequate opportunity to study both of Plaintiff's petitions?"

"We have, Your Honor," the syndicate's senior attorney replied.

"You are prepared then to respond?"

"We are, Your Honor."

"Before proceeding I am going to administer an oath to Doctors Hammerly and de Navarre," Judge Weaver said, "as well as to Captain Madeira. I want you all to understand that any statement of fact you may make in front of me constitutes testimony and will be made under this oath."

"This is a somewhat irregular method for handling testimony, Your Honor," huffed Alfaneque.

"But not without precedent. Your objection is noted."

Then, after administering the oath, the judge indicated that Lawrence was free to start.

"Thank you, Your Honor. I would like to start by examining Plaintiff's assertation that the vessel was never abandoned."

"Yes?"

"There is a huge amount of case law which establishes that the passage of over four hundred years is sufficient to establish abandonment whether or not it is possible to prove that the owners actually intended to abandon it. I have here a list of the citations, Your Honor."

"Thank you," Judge Weaver responded as he leaned forward to receive the paper. Alfaneque scowled as he accepted the copy Lawrence passed across to him.

"Furthermore," Lawrence continued, "even if the vessel was merely lost, rather than abandoned, the only possible claimants would be the Spanish Crown along with the heirs of the vessel's and cargo's private owners— several of whom we can now prove definitively are principals of my client. The Republic of Cuba has no possible claim."

"Your Honor!" Alfaneque snapped, "we contend that the Republic of Cuba is heir to the interests of the Spanish Crown. We also contend that any heirs of the private owners currently resident in Cuba have, or will have, assigned their interests to the Republic of Cuba under the terms of the Republic's laws concerning personal property."

"Gentlemen," the judge said firmly before Alfaneque could catch his breath, "interesting although all this is—and it really is—we are getting ahead of ourselves. The first question I must decide is whether or not the vessel was abandoned. Do either of you have anything more to say on that subject?"

William S. Schaill

Neither did, although it appeared for a second as if Alfaneque was about to say something.

"Very well then," said Weaver. "I'm familiar with all the cases mentioned by Mr. Lawrence, and taking into account what has been said today, I see no reason to change my original ruling that the vessel was abandoned."

"Your Honor," Alfaneque thundered, pounding the table as he spoke, "this case involves the heritage of all mankind. The *Nuestra Senora de Misericordia* is a precious, irreplacable time capsule! It is the scientific knowledge that is of greatest importance here, not the artifacts themselves, and it is our belief that Defendant is unqualified and unsuited to protect this heritage."

"That, Mr. Alfaneque," Judge Weaver said, "is one of the reasons we are moving right along to your second petition. I am well aware that both the artifacts and the data we are dealing with here are quite fragile. It is also clear that my award of title may be overturned on appeal. I must make an effort to insure that the property in question is not damaged until title has been fully established."

"Thank you, Your Honor." Alfaneque beamed. "As stated in our petition, we have serious doubts about the technology being employed. It is new and untested. It's very likely we'd be better off if this wreck were left for another fifty years, until new systems are developed and fully tested and until appropriate and responsible international regimes are better able to control the process."

"In another fifty years," Tina snarled, "there'll be very little left worth excavating!"

The judge looked over the top of his glasses at her, but said nothing.

"In addition to our concerns about the technology being used, we are also concerned about Defendant's qualifications to conduct an excavation of this size."

As Alfaneque spoke, Madeira noticed Tina's back stiffen. Glancing then at her face, he was shocked to see the rigid expression that had come to dominate it.

"Dr. de Navarre appears to have an adequate educational background, but she is much too junior to conduct a project of this size. Of equal importance, she totally lacks any current, meaningful academic affiliation. An excavation of this importance requires the participation of a number of experts and simply must be controlled by a senior, internationally recognized scholar."

Madeira's eyes remained on Tina throughout the assault, recognizing there was nothing he could do at the moment to help.

"Your Honor!" Lawrence shouted. "I must object to these personal attacks on my clients!"

"Have you completed your argument, Mr. Alfaneque?"

"Yes, Your Honor, for the moment."

"Mr. Lawrence?"

Before responding, Lawrence whispered first to Tina, who nodded, then to Diego Velazquez, who also appeared to agree.

"Your Honor," he finally said, "Mr. Alfaneque has stated that the data is what interests his clients most. My clients will be more than pleased to provide a copy of all raw data, on a daily basis, to the IAA with the only condition—and this is a very common one in the exchange of data between scientists—that it not be published without specific permission."

"Totally unacceptable!" Alfaneque rumbled. "We

can accept no such conditions. Anyway, there would be no way to guarantee the purity of the data unless a responsible international organization is doing the excavating."

"Mr. Lawrence," said the judge. "I think the best way I can reach any conclusion concerning the methods your clients are using and their competence is to have the operation to date, and the systems used, explained to me in detail. Although I am only a layman, I will have Professor Standish at my side. I understand Dr. de Navarre has brought photographs and other materials with her to show me?"

"Yes, she has, Your Honor."

"Very well. I will ask her to make a presentation and then I will ask Dr. Hammerly to critique Dr. de Navarre's plans."

Both attorneys nodded their agreement.

"I think we could all use a short recess," said the judge. "We'll start my education in fifteen minutes."

For the next three and a half hours—with no recess for lunch, which was brought into the room—Tina made her case. Using photographs, diagrams, a blizzard of printouts, and two videos, she explained MOHAB, The Crab, the computer systems, and the results to date to an increasingly fascinated Judge Weaver.

Only twice did the judge turn to Professor Standish for advice. In both cases his questions concerned exactly what constituted "traditional standards" as recognized by most archaeologists.

Much to everybody's surprise—perhaps even his own—Dr. Hammerly, Plaintiff's expert witness, seemed to end up even more fascinated by the operation than was the judge. While Madeira watched him, the archaeologist leaned forward and watched intently as Tina's video showed The Crab creeping forward and reaching down delicately to pick up first a clay wine jug and then the meager remains of a sword. Impressed as he appeared to be by Tina's light touch, he was positively delighted when he examined the computer-enhanced visuals that showed the position and catalog number of each artifact before the Crab plucked it.

After Tina's presentation was completed, and very much to Mr. Alfaneque's irritation, the only objection Hammerly chose to raise was concerning the small number of archaeologists involved in the dig itself.

In response, Tina pointed out that the excavation was only the first step, that all the data and artifacts would examined by a number of experts once they had made it ashore. She then reviewed her earlier demonstration of the computer system's stunning ability to map and catalog the artifacts and visuals.

From the expression on Hammerly's face as he listened to Tina's rebuttal, Madeira suspected that Plaintiff's expert witness was considering asking to join the expedition.

With the hearing clearly coming to an end, Judge Weaver turned to Madeira.

"Captain Madeira, so far you have played no part in these proceedings."

"No, Your Honor."

"All the same, Mr. Lawrence's materials include an outline of your background."

"Yes, sir?"

"Do you feel you understand Dr. de Navarre's activities well enough to spot any embezzlement, should it occur?"

"Yes, sir," Madeira replied, suspecting as he did that he was making a mistake by agreeing.

"Thank you all. Mr. Alfaneque, I understand the

historical interest of this wreck and your client's concern about it. Mr. Lawrence, I also understand the very great financial costs to your clients of every minute spent in these proceedings. I will retire to my chambers and announce my decision within an hour or two."

Twenty-two

"Isn't this a wonderful country, Captain Madeira?" Diego Velazquez asked excitedly, tiny beads of water adorning the narrow fringe of hair that almost surrounded his shiny bald head.

"Yes!" he continued as they marched out of the Federal Court Building, through the dying drizzle, toward his own white Mercedes. "Where else would a high judge protect the honest and well-earned interests of a few small people against the demands of the whole world?

"Yes!" he said yet again, practically shouting, slamming his right fist into the rain-soaked palm of his left hand. The blow generated a slight, soggy, squishy slurp, and provided Madeira with no opportunity to reply. "Not merely against the unjust demands of their own government, but against those of the entire world! Against the avarice of all the uncounted billions of people there are!"

William S. Schaill

"Don Diego," Tina said, skipping over a puddle with a grace made especially surprising by the high heels she was wearing, "we all know the judicial system isn't always as reasonable as it seemed today. And the judge *did* make you increase the bond to ten million dollars. Mr. Lawrence is certain they will appeal some of the advice Dr. Standish gave him. On top of that, I now have to give my raw data to those jerks at the IAA even before I get to study it. Worst of all, we're all going to be back in court in August."

"Of course, my dear, but today it acquitted itself with great honor. *Viva* Judge Weaver!"

Velazquez paused when they reached the car. Then, after opening a rear door and motioning grandly to Tina to enter, he continued. "For almost fifty years, you know, many of us have waited to return to Cuba but the truth is—please, Al, make yourself comfortable . . . "

As he paused, Velazquez opened the right front door and motioned for Madeira to get in. He then continued, barely missing a beat, as he closed the door. "Many of us will never return. We are comfortable here now. We have come to feel this is home. And a whole generation—two generations have been born to know no other. That is why we feel we would like to greatly expand our little museum, so the younger ones may know something of the fire, the splendor, of their heritage. In that way they will gain the confidence to create their own children's great heritage."

With a final wave of his hand, Velazquez seated himself next to Tina, closing the door behind him.

"Home, Filipe," he said to the chauffeur.

"At your service, sir," replied Filipe, a hint of a smile showing below his aviator sunglasses.

Madeira settled back in his seat, marveling at how cool and dry its leather surface remained despite the stiffling heat and humidity outside the car.

"But as to going back?"

With a start, Madeira realized Velazquez had started speaking again.

"I, for example, I doubt I will ever return, except perhaps as a tourist. In truth, I have no wish to return. And one of the most important reasons I feel as I do is my belief that here one may at least *hope* for justice. In so much of the world, one is not even permitted to hope for such a thing; one is only allowed to hope for what one is permitted to hope for. Where else could we get the deal we get here?

"How very extraordinary, *no*?"

"I don't know if it's extraordinary or not," Tina replied, a troubled look on her face. "I'm still not sure where I'll want to go when it's time to die. I envy you your certainty, Diego."

"There is nothing for you to envy, *nina*. Mine is the certainty of old age, nothing more. When you are my age, that is all you have—certainty. On the contrary, it is I who envy you the exciting life I see ahead for you. But let us not talk of death and philosophy now. We have won a great victory and it is my desire that we have a little celebration."

My Lord! thought Madeira, looking at his watch. The diminutive millionaire was as crazy as Tina was.

Or was he just a more-skillful-than-average con man?

"It's almost four now," Madeira finally said, "and I still feel it's very important we get back to the wreck before the weather improves too much and *Fortune Hunter* does something unfortunate."

"Clearly! replied Velazquez. "I couldn't agree with you more. But it *is* Friday night and we *have* won a great victory. We will all go to my *casita*, where you can freshen up. Then we will go to El Mandril, a little club I am very fond of, for drinks and a very early dinner. The airplane will wait for you and we can get you back on the ship well before midnight. You don't intend to sail before dawn, do you?"

Madeira looked at Tina, at the slight, tempting, impossibly provocative smile she was wearing. In a minor, but startling, flash of comprehension, he understood that she was promising something wonderful if only he would be reasonable and agree to this one tiny-to-the-point-of-insignificance proposal.

She's nuts! he told himself again. She's worried sick about what *Fortune Hunter* might do, yet now all she can seem to think about is going out to dinner!

Then his own logic reappeared and, grasping the realities of the situation, he surrendered. Totally.

"Of course, Diego. There're a couple things I want to check on, but the ship's ready to sail and of course I didn't plan to leave until morning."

"Splendid! Use the telephone at my house. With luck, Rafi will be able to join us."

"Diego," Tina said, "if we're going to the Mandril, I'm going to have to buy a dress. I can't wear this one!"

"Of course, *nina*. As soon as he drops me off, Filipe will take the two of you shopping . . . eh, Filipe?"

"With pleasure, Don Diego."

Half an hour later, the afternoon sun had finally cut its way through the clouds and haze, and Filipe had done the same through the dense early evening traffic. The Mercedes turned through a pair of wrought-iron gates into Velazquez's *"casita,"* which was an immense, rambling white stucco affair with still-brilliant red tiles, all surrounded by a carefully cultivated near-jungle of plantings.

"You had better hurry," Velazquez observed as he got out. "Many of the stores now close at five-thirty.

"I shall see the two of you shortly?" he concluded rhetorically as he closed the door behind him.

"Filipe," Tina asked, "do you know La Poquitita?"

"Yes I do, *doctor*. The boutique on Biscayne Boulevard?"

"Yes. Will you take us there, please?"

"As you wish."

"Don't worry, Al," Tina said, leaning forward and gently touching his shoulder as Filipe pulled out the gate and turned into the almost-solid traffic, "you're not going to spend the whole afternoon watching me look at dresses. I know exactly what I want and I'm very quick. I'm really not mad about shopping myself."

True to her word, it took Tina less than twenty minutes to select the dress and accessories she wanted.

Once he'd recovered from the shock he felt after glancing discreetly at the price tag on the dress, it took Madeira no more than an additional five minutes to walk next door and buy a new shirt, socks, tie, and set of underwear.

At seven, as Madeira was knotting his new tie in one of Diego's bedrooms, there was a knock at the door.

"There is a phone call for you, sir," said the houseboy when Madeira opened the door. "Please take it here." As he spoke, he pointed to a phone next to the bed.

251

"Thank you," Madeira said as he picked up the receiver.

"Captain, this is Jake Smith."

"Thanks for getting back to me so quickly," said Madeira, staring in the mirror as he did, wondering if the phone was tapped and deciding he didn't really care. "How'd you do?"

"They're on their way. Four of them. Shoulder-launched. They'll arrive about ten tonight at the airport. They're obsolete, but they're a kind I know how to use."

"What'd they cost?"

"Twenty . . . plus the plane charter. As I told you, it's a buyer's market these days and it's not just surplus like we're getting. There are a dozen small countries with their own industries and they'll sell their stuff, brand-new, even built to order, to anybody with ready cash. I don't trust some of their stuff, though, and the new ones cost *so* much more. I'm more comfortable with what I've used before."

"You and your people going to be able to get it all aboard by yourselves?"

"No problem."

"Okay. We're not going to get back until early morning. Make sure there's a boat left at the marina for us to take out. I don't think we'll need a crew. I have some idea how to drive one."

Smith laughed dutifully.

After hanging up, Madeira continued to stare at himself in the mirror.

His stomach was starting to feel a little queasy. It was much the same feeling he'd had that night not long ago in the Gulf when he'd watched the big container ship's lights approaching and agonized over whether he, and Hawkins, were doing the right thing.

Was he going a little overboard now? Was he getting too involved in something he didn't totally understand?

It wasn't the weapons themselves that bothered him; similar devices had been his business for all of his adult life. But he wasn't a Naval officer anymore, and it was illegal for civilians to own missiles, no matter how sincere their need for them.

They weren't supposed to need them anyway.

Damnit! he thought, almost uttering the curse aloud. He had no choice! Somebody was willing to kill them to prevent the completion of the job, and nobody in authority seemed interested in doing much about it!

He looked around the airy, cheerful, guest room. At its opulent furnishings of rubbed woods and brightly printed fabrics. At the old silver, crystal, and stone, all seemingly unrelated, yet combined in a most wonderful harmony. The room and its furnishings made him feel both uneasy and, paradoxically, totally at home.

He glanced out the window and spotted two gardeners taking advantage of the slight cooling of the evening to weed, primp, and trim the riotous plantings.

It was Madeira's first experience with great wealth, and he was suffering from a form of culture shock.

Would he really like to live this way?

He thought so, but couldn't be sure.

What was it, he wondered, that was bothering him so?

The sense of quiet power? The muted glitter? The servants?

Maybe the lifestyle had nothing to do with his discomfort.

Maybe it was the wreck, and the circumstances around it. The attack on *Johnson*. The cold darkness of the ocean's great depths. The shadows, the unanswered doubts, which continued to surround the syndicate and its true purposes.

He had already grown to like Diego Velazquez and Rafi Cienfuegos, but he was less sure than ever that he could trust them. He'd known Cienfuegos a week or so, and Velazquez less than a day. Each had lived a half century at least. Each possessed a past—a full quota of dreams, terrors, ambitions, and objectives—about which Madeira could know nothing.

And he really knew no more about Tina than he did about Velazquez and Cienfuegos.

They all spoke Spanish. They all had known each other for some time. And Al Madeira was odd man out.

Or was there more to it than even that? Was his problem that he was beginning to suspect he didn't even understand himself?

Why was he now willing to do things he'd never have guessed he'd ever agree to do? The missiles represented a major escalation, the breaching of a boundary he still wasn't sure he was prepared to breach. Yet it was his idea and his alone.

It was as if he were being driven far off any course he'd ever intended to follow. He felt as if incomprehensible currents were dragging him to the very edge of the earth.

There was a knock at his door.

"Al, are you decent?"

"Yes, unfortunately. Come on in."

The woman who entered his room was the most glamorous, elegant being he'd ever met. His breathing uneven, he stared at her a moment, and realized she was everything he'd always suspected he was missing during all those long years.

And then an alarm bell, the loudest he could ever remember hearing, sounded in his mind:

Who was this glorious, electrifying vision? Why did she seem to fit in so perfectly with—as if born to—the highly buffed floor tiles, the obviously costly yet understated furniture, the art, the servants, the almost overwhelming aura of centuries-old wealth?

Why was fate offering her to him? Tempting him to sail to the very edge of the earth?

What had happened to the pretty, slightly obsessed flake in the coveralls? The one with the drifty eye, who liked to laugh and seemed most happy when she was up to her elbows in muck, sorting through the trash of the ages?

How could she have afforded to pay over two thousand dollars for that dress? Almost, it seemed, on a whim?

Freelance archaeologists couldn't possibly be paid that well!

Could they?

Twenty-three

"You take my breath away," Madeira stammered as she glided toward him, a mischievous smile playing across her face.

"Good!" replied Tina. "I'm working very hard at it."

"I'll be ready in a minute. Am I holding up the show?"

"No, not at all. Diego and Elana usually don't eat until about nine or ten. In fact, he normally wouldn't think of showing up at El Mandril before then, so I'm sure he's not worried. You don't have to hurry."

"I'm afraid I do."

"Yes?"

"I'm hungry, and we *do* have to get back to the ship."

"I'm hungry too. I've spent too many years living like an American."

256

Twenty minutes later, with Diego, Elena, and Tina in the back seat and Madeira riding shotgun, Velazquez's Mercedes glided through the *casita*'s gate and turned right into the passing stream. Slipping effortlessly from lane to lane, Filipe swept them up Bayshore Drive and into South Miami. The trip seemed to Madeira like no time at all, occupied as he was in listening to Diego's enthusiastic and detailed description of the future of Dade County.

"This is it!" Velazquez remarked with a satisfied tone as Filipe slowed down in front of El Mandril.

"Hideous, isn't it?" Elena Velazquez asked when she noticed Madeira staring at the night club's neon sign, which portrayed a grotesque red-and-blue caricature of a baboon. "I'm very embarrased to say Diego dreamed up the design himself. He's one of the owners of this place, which is why we come here so unfortunately often."

Velazquez himself, after listening politely to his wife, burst into fits of laughter. "That's exactly why I like it. It's so dreadful. I must be permitted my own little joke, and even Elana will admit that the food and music are excellent."

Elana admitted nothing, but failed to deny it either.

The hour being preposterously early by Latin standards, El Mandrill was, at best, a quarter filled. The band hadn't even appeared, much less warmed up.

"Al," Velazquez said after a round of drinks had been delivered, "I must ask if you really wish to continue this project."

"I certainly don't like getting shot at, if that's what you mean, Diego, but I understood something like that might happen. We all did. And I like to see jobs through to their conclusion."

"And what about the United States Government?" As the Cuban spoke, Madeira thought he detected a hint of unease in his glance.

Madeira leaned back in his chair and looked Velazquez straight in the eye. "As soon as they can prove you people are violating federal law, I'll stop. As long as you're legal, we keep working!"

Madeira asked himself again why he was so eager to continue. Was it the project itself? Was it pride? Was it Tina? Whatever it was, it was very interesting.

"Thank you. Your loyalty will be rewarded, I assure you. Now tell me, is there anything we can do to help you defend yourselves in case something more happens?"

"Short of chartering a destroyer from the Navy, I doubt it. Jake Smith has arranged to get some additional weapons we both feel will help, but other than that, there's not much else to be done at this point."

"Bueno!"

"Diego," Madeira said, leaning forward after taking a sip of his drink, "does the United States Government have any good reason to believe you and your associates are attempting to overthrow the current Cuban Government?"

"I and most of the others have been very active in the past, yes, but now, now that it is only a matter of time until Fidel is gone, I am prepared to allow politics a chance.

"Anyway," he continued, extending his arms out and up, as if granting a benediction, "as I have said, I consider myself almost as much American now as Cuban. I am old, I am settled where I am. Let those who have to live with it shape the new government in Cuba."

"Who attacked us? Do you know?"

"We have sources that make us think it was the Cuban Government. They would be most interested in stopping the project."

"What about *Fortune Hunter*?"

"A crew of pirates to be sure, but—"

"If you are no threat to the Cuban Government . . ."

"You must understand, Al, that Fidel and his thugs have thought of Rafi, me, and many of our friends as enemies for over thirty years. Suspicions like that do not die easily.

"We are not what they believe, but they still believe it. Just imagine what we could do with, say, two hundred million dollars of virtually untraceable gold and silver if it was our intention to overthrow the government!"

"But it won't be untraceable," Madeira replied. "We're keeping very detailed records, and our government will inventory it when we land it."

"You know that and I know that, Al, but they cannot be sure. It is entirely possible we might be planning to land it somewhere else, Panama perhaps."

A knot developed in Madeira's gut. A very large, hard one. Everything Velazquez said could well be true, or equally well not be.

"You still have doubts?" Velazquez asked.

"Yes. A great many, I'm afraid."

"And you have no way of being sure, until it is all over!"

"If then."

"Yes, that is all true."

"You know," said Madeira, moving on to another

subject that was also bothering him a great deal, "Rafael Cienfuegos is almost paralyzed by his claustrophobia. How was he chosen to be your on-scene rep?"

"He was the only member of the syndicate who could take the time."

"What's his background? If I may ask."

"Of course you may! Considering the position we have put you in, you should be permitted to ask just about any question."

"Thank you."

"Think nothing of it. About Rafi. I have known him, oh, over thirty years now. He escaped from Fidel early in the sixties. Like so many, Rafi arrived with nothing, nothing but a willingness to work and to learn.

"He was in prison, you know. Yes! They rounded him up in one of the big sweeps of student trouble-makers. It was very difficult for him. He doesn't like to talk about it. In fact, there are things that he will not talk about at all. Very bad things, I think.

"Then they let him out and he came here, to Miami, in a water-filled rowboat. That was another terrible experience.

"By the greatest of good luck," Velazquez continued, "Rafi found a job working in a dry-cleaning store. After several years, the owner decided to retire and offered to sell the business to him. Rafi had saved some money, but not nearly enough, and having heard that I was looking for investment opportunities, came to me. I listened and investigated and decided he was a good risk, so I loaned him some money. I have never, for a moment, regretted having done so.

"Rafi is a very bright fellow and he applied himself. Within two years, three less than the term of the loan, he came to me and paid it off. During those years I had come to know him quite well, to like and respect him. Once the loan was paid off and he was well established, we were free to be friends, which we have remained these many years."

"He's still in the dry-cleaning business?"

"Yes, of course! He has about fifteen stores now, but that is not where he has made most of his money. You see, in addition to learning the importance of solving people's problems for them—that is why one goes to a dry-cleaning store, no? to have a problem solved—in addition to learning this valuable lesson, Rafi also developed a very strong feel for location, for where to put his stores. In time, he found himself in real estate, buying and selling properties and building small shopping centers. Thanks to his feel for location, he is now a very, very wealthy and successful fellow."

"Rafi has been very successful in every respect except one," interjected Elena. "He has never been successful in love. He has never enjoyed the comfort of a family and that, I have always believed, is the source of that air of sadness that he so often wears."

"That's true," agreed Diego. "On one or two occasions we have all thought that Rafi has finally found the right woman, but our hopes never came to fruition."

"Yes," Madeira replied, "I've noticed that sadness, but I'm most concerned about the claustrophobia."

"Is it causing you a problem? If so, then we naturally must do something about it."

"No, I can't say it's causing us a problem. He works very hard to make himself useful despite it. What worries me is what it's doing to him. To tell the truth, I've grown to like him."

"I am glad to hear that, but I must tell you that, unless his fears are causing a problem, we must do nothing. Once Rafi agreed to take on this responsibility, it became a point of honor for him to fufill it. Do you understand? We can do nothing! We must do nothing! We must permit Rafi to do as he sees fit."

"Very well," Madeira said, looking around and noticing the band had arrived and started to play and a number of couples had already taken to the dance floor.

He could, he was confident, insist on Cienfuegos's remaining aboard *Johnson*, but why bother? Velazquez was right; as long as Rafi was a problem only to himself, why prevent him from doing what he felt he must do?

Taking a deep breath, Madeira was surprised to discover how totally his concerns seemed to have evaporated, how relaxed and at home he felt. The dangers and uncertainties remained, but tonight, tonight it was Diego and Elana, Al and Tina. He'd just have to take it on faith that Velazquez wasn't lying through his teeth, setting him up for something awful, because he had no way at the moment of learning anything for sure.

"It's been years since I danced," he remarked, turning towards Tina, "but I really feel like it tonight."

"Before eating? I thought you were starving."

"I was. We'll do just one number, then come back and order."

"No rush," Tina said, the smile on her face spreading. "Let's make this a real night on the town! It'll be a while before we get the chance again."

"Estupendo!" replied Madeira, pushing his chair back from the table.

"Estupendo?" Tina said, looking slightly startled and laughing almost as hard as Velazquez while Madeira drew her chair back for her.

"You know," he added, whispering in her ear as they walked toward the dance floor, "I think I can remember how to tango, but you may have to help me a little."

"To begin, *mi amor*, this is a mambo. But don't worry, I'll have you bumping and strutting with the best of them in just a few short minutes."

"We should perhaps join them, Elana. No?" Velazquez said.

"We should perhaps go out with them more often, Diego, if that's what it takes to get you on the dance floor these days."

That one number stretched into an entire set during which Al and Tina strutted and bumped, slid and spun. They held each other in an intimate embrace, when not with their arms, then with their eyes, as they flew across the floor, through time and space, alone in the Universe. While the music thumped and stuttered and soared, they laughed together, nearly oblivious to Madeira's occasional missteps, and said little.

Only when the band, sweating profusely, laid down their instruments and quietly left for wherever it is that bands go during their breaks, did Al and Tina return to the table and order the dinners they finally returned to eat two sets later.

"Thank you, Al," Tina said, her head resting on Madeira's shoulder, as the jet took off from Miami. "I had a wonderful evening."

"I think we both should thank Diego and Elana for that." As he replied, Madeira's mind drifted back, despite his best efforts, to the problems ahead and the nagging, seemingly unshakable doubts that continued to cloud his thoughts.

"How well do you know Diego?"

"I've known him about four years, I guess," Tina replied, sitting up. "What's wrong?"

"You know Rafael, Diego, and, I gather, the rest of the syndicate reasonably well. You know where they come from; you understand them. I still know very little about any of you. Should I be sleeping with a pistol under my pillow?"

"I'll swear before God that Diego and Rafael are good guys," said Tina, "but that won't solve your problem, will it? You're not sure about me, are you?"

"Insane, isn't it? I'm madly in love with you and have been since the day I watched you climb aboard *Johnson*."

"Yes?"

"I was astounded how well you fit into Diego's house, into his lifestyle. I'd never pictured you in a setting like that before, and only now do I appreciate how much like them you are."

"I thought you enjoyed our night on the town."

"Of course I did, and I love you whether you're in a two-thousand-dollar dress or coveralls, but it takes some getting used to."

"You do like it, don't you?"

"The dress? I think it looks fabulous on you."

"But you don't understand how I can afford it on my paltry income?"

"I suppose so, although it's not really my business."

"But it is, for several reasons, including the fact that you have to decide who to trust."

"Okay?"

"Okay! My family's been in the New World as long as Diego's has. I had direct ancestors present at the founding of Bogota. As fortune would have it, I am a member of one of the more prosperous branches of the family."

"Oh."

"Once or twice, when things have been going really badly, I've written home for a little cash—it's mine, you see, my uncle takes care of it for me—but as long as I stay in the U.S. I intend to live by the sweat of my brow. If, someday, I return to Colombia to stay, maybe then I'll feel freer to spend my inheritance, but as long as I'm here having fun, I'll make do with what I can earn. If anybody's trying to steal the treasure, it's not me!"

"It doesn't seem likely, does it?"

"But I don't want you to worry about the money, or the dress," she continued, kissing him on the cheek as she did. "Sorting and collecting garbage is my sport, not shopping. I bought this dress because I wanted to be especially pretty. For you."

"I can't tell you how well you succeeded!"

At three-thirty in the morning, when they arrived at the Charleston Municipal Marina, the sky had totally cleared, revealing an almost solid field of stars, each sparkling in its own cold glory. Beneath this celestial brilliance, the city itself and its port were wrapped in a chill, low-lying fog.

Shivering in their lightweight raincoats, Madeira and Tina spent almost half an hour wandering around the Municipal Marina, trudging down ramps and along dew-slick finger piers, looking for the workboat that had supposedly been left for them. As they searched, the dark waters of the Ashley River flowed by, almost totally invisible except for the occasional wavering reflection they provided of the marina's lights.

"Damn!" Madeira growled when they had finally found the small, open boat. He looked up from the boat a moment to watch the fibrous globs of vapor drift by under the marina's yellowish floodlights. "They left us the one without radar!"

"I wish I'd had the wits to stuff a pair of sneakers in my briefcase this morning," Tina replied as she tripped on the uneven dock. "Do you know the bearings to get back, or are we going to have to wander all over trying to find the buoys?"

"Fortunately, I do, although I hope we can find a buoy or two along the way so I can correct for whatever the currents are doing tonight."

"If we can't find any?"

"Then who knows where we'll end up."

"Sounds sort of romantic," she stuttered between chattering teeth. "You did say this is one of the most romantic cities on earth, didn't you?"

"Ha!" Madeira said as he started the boat's twin diesels. "We're both freezing to death and I really can't guarantee we won't get lost. If you'd like to wait until dawn, I won't accuse you of being chicken."

"Where'll we go at this hour to get warm?"

"Find a hotel."

"We might never leave."

"Good point! We can't salvage your wreck from a hotel room. Hop in."

"As you wish, *mi capitan*!"

"*Johnson*, this is *Johnson* workboat," Madeira said into the radio as he waited for the engines to warm up and, at the same time, wondered if the ship's anchor watch was awake.

"'This is *Johnson,* workboat."

"*Johnson,* we're about to head back to you. This is Madeira and Dr. de Navarre. Is there anybody else still ashore who we should wait for?"

"Negative. Mr. Cienfucgos returned several hours ago. You're the last."

"We're on our way then."

"Roger."

"Cast off forward."

"Casting off forward," Tina shouted, grateful for any excuse to move around, any activity that might help her forget just how cold she was.

Standing at the dimly lit control console, Madeira backed away from the pier and maneuvered the heavy thirty-foot aluminum vessel almost blindly out of the marina. Despite having tried to think out the maneuvers ahead of time, he was repeatedly caught by surprise by the river's willfullness, forcing him to use full power to maintain control of the boat.

Once well clear of the marina's piers and break-waters, he throttled back and turned left, coming to a more or less southeasterly course. Within a few minutes, and very much to Madeira's relief, Tina spotted a flashing greenish-whitish glow almost directly ahead.

"Outstanding," mumbled Madeira, turning a few degrees to the left. "I'm pretty sure which marker that is. We're in good shape."

Riding on the Ashley's smooth, powerful back, they continued toward the intersection of the river and the harbor's South Channel.

"Tina," Madeira said after several minutes of silence, "I've pretty much decided this is going to be my last deep job. I've been down too long. I think there's something I've been missing."

"You don't have to apologize to me. It's a grim business. As far as I'm concerned, the deep ocean's about as appealing as Bogota on a rainy winter day. If it weren't for *Misericordia*, I'd never set foot in MOHAB again."

"You know the story about the sailor who retires and heads inland with an oar on his shoulder?"

"Yes. He keeps going until somebody asks him what he's doing with that funny-looking fence post."

"I'm surprised you know it."

"You shouldn't be. I've had to work with a lot of sailor types over the years, and you guys all eventually tell that story. Is that what you want to do? Head for the mountains?"

"The mountains? No, except maybe for vacations . . . but I'm not going deep again either."

A few minutes later they noticed a rapidly flashing green light peeking through the dense gray darkness to starboard. "We're almost at the intersection," remarked Madeira.

"How much farther?"

"A mile or less."

"Then how much more back to the ship?"

"Two miles. Maybe a little more."

"Did you memorize the whole chart?"

"No, but I tried to memorize the track from the ship to the marina."

"Are you going to need me to get the ship under way?"

"No. I think you should sleep through it. Reilly can do it without me, for that matter."

"I'm sure he'll be more than happy to."

"That's why I'd better be there."

"I'm afraid you're—"

"Shush." As he held his finger to his lips, Madeira listened intently. There, mixed in with the rumble of the workboat's diesels, was another sound, a snarling, gurgling growl that made the fog itself pulse. It was a sound he'd heard many times. It was a pair of powerful gas engines, engines built strictly for speed, throttled back and slightly out of sync.

"There's somebody else out here, and fairly close."

As he spoke he tensed, sweat forming on his chilled forehead. Somewhere out there, hidden among the pulsing gray cotton that surrounded and isolated them, not so very far away and showing no lights he could see, was a powerful speedboat of some sort.

A Cigarette perhaps?

Should he sound fog signals, assuming the other vessel to be innocent, or should he try to slip by, hoping their radar was crapped out?

Fat chance!

"Can you see anything?" he said quietly to Tina, who was still standing forward of him. "A light? A shadow? Motion? Anything?"

Twenty-four

Agustin has aged greatly since I last saw him, thought Rafael Cienfuegos as he studied his Creator. It had been a year, a year at least, since they'd last been face-to-face. In the meantime, the long decades devoted to a life of manipulation and deception had finally caught up with the hitherto immortal Ramirez. Not only was his face finally beginning to sag, but there was a certain hesitation about his eyes. It was the self-doubt of a man who has just accepted that he is truly no longer young.

While Madeira and Tina danced across El Mandril's dance floor and through outer space, Cienfuegos shared a table at a clean but nondescript restaurant in Hialeah with Agustin Ramirez—best known in Miami as Cesar Rivera—and Sandra Argento.

"The plan to stop them in court was an utter failure," explained Ramirez, speaking quietly in the near-empty restaurant. "Alfaneque did the best he could with what we gave him. I'm sure the effort will satisfy Havana that we are still trying."

As he listened, Cienfuegos couldn't help but smile slightly, despite the growing ache in his head. From Ramirez's current point of view, the worst thing Alfaneque could have done was succeed.

Throughout his life, Rafael had viewed Ramirez with very mixed emotions. He had always understood, both intellectually and emotionally, that Ramirez had created him. And for this he had no choice but to honor him as one might honor a father.

But if Ramirez was to be viewed as his father, he had to be recognized as a very harsh and demanding one. A father who had always made it clear that the son had been created only to serve.

And for that, Cienfuegos had never been able to love him as a real son might love his father.

It was all as clear to Cienfuegos now as it had been when it happened. Ramirez had taken a strutting punk named Antonio Perez, a nobody who would do almost anything to be a somebody, and had made him just that.

At least in the new somebody's mind.

The Cuban intelligence officer had crafted his creation, Rafael Cienfuegos, into an elite tool of the revolution and convinced the tool that he was one of the chosen.

Ramirez had then shaped and guided Cienfuegos's rise to prominence among the Miami Cubans. He had told him who to know and how to get to know them. He had provided valuable commercial and personal intelligence. He had even financed him during one or two bad spells.

But, Cienfuegos reminded himself, he too had played a role in his own success. He had worked hard and made intelligent use of what Ramirez had given him.

Even Christianity permitted the Created to believe, at least a little, in his or her own individuality and free will.

For many years, Cienfuegos had been proud to be in the vanguard of the revolution. At the same time he had also been proud to be a financial and social success.

But during the past few years, ever since the Russians had decided to replace the Americans as the world's premier capitalists, the revolution had begun to look a little foolish. All of a sudden, much of the world seemed to consider it, and Fidel, some sort of joke.

As the world had turned to reengineering itself, Cienfuegos had begun to lose confidence in the cause. And in himself. And even in his Creator.

Ironically, Ramirez himself seemed also to have lost most, if not all, of his own faith. Assuming, of course, it's even possible to discuss a possession so mortal as faith when speaking of a god.

"So we are now free to get on with this business?" asked Cienfuegos, rubbing his forehead as he spoke and wondering how it would all turn out.

"Yes," Ramirez said. "Sandra has the work submarine in Nassau."

Cienfuegos glanced at Sandra. So she's now his chief assistant, he thought. He must really feel his back is up against the wall!

"She will load it aboard *Fortune Hunter*," Ramirez continued, "and I will join her there in a few days. We will wait for your signal, Rafael. And then, when all is done, the treasure, Sandra, and I will disappear from the face of the earth. Only you will be left in place, and we will look forward to your joining us in a year or two."

"Are you sure the crew of *Fortune Hunter* can be trusted?" Cienfuegos asked, certain that in time Sandra would insure Agustin really did disappear from the face of the earth.

"They will receive a large share of the treasure. And to whom would they complain? If they say anything, they will be admitting to piracy."

"Havana?"

"We will have kept Velazquez and his friends from getting the treasure, and Havana has many other things to worry about these days. They may care, but not much."

"The United States?"

"Will believe Havana did it, but will have absolutely no proof."

Despite the holes in it, thought Cienfuegos, it was a plan that probably would work. Unfortunately, as often seemed the case with Ramirez's plans, it would be Rafael Cienfuegos who was left behind. But, as Ramirez had pointed out several times, if all went well, Rafael would be viewed as one of the victims.

It didn't really matter, of course. As always, he would do all that was required of him. Even though he knew Ramirez would be more than happy to abandon him.

It was true that he had never felt any real affection for Ramirez. It was also true that he was coming to view him more as a frightened old man and less as a deity. All the same, he still felt bound by a special loyalty.

Just because your Creator changes sides—or develops feet of clay—doesn't mean that you're permitted to abandon him.

By now Cienfuegos's head was pounding horribly. He couldn't remember ever suffering so much! Not even in MOHAB. Not since *Angel del Llano*.

Agustin had created him, but it was Tina's mad enthusiasm that had become the fire that sustained him.

How was he to remain loyal to Ramirez without destroying Tina?

He had been placed in an impossible position!

Twenty-five

"I think he's ahead of us," Tina whispered as they crept through the dense night.

"This is idiotic," Madeira replied, only now realizing just how badly the Cigarette's attack had spooked him. "He must have radar. He must know we're here. And the chances are nine hundred ninety-nine to one he's no threat to us. Whoever he is."

"And if he is a threat?"

"I'm not sure what to do. I doubt he'd try ramming us, these workboats are too well built, but he could shoot us up easily enough. Or toss a granade."

"Then what do we do?"

"Jump overboard, I guess."

"We could run back to the marina."

"If it's the Cigarette, he'd get us long before we got there."

Unseen by Madeira, Tina shrugged as the workboat continued its passage through the fog.

"Boat ahoy!" thundered an artificially enhanced voice shortly after Madeira noticed, but did not recognize, a pulsing whiteness in the fog ahead. "This is the Charleston Marine Police. Stop your engine and stand by."

"Thank God!" Tina sighed.

Damnit! thought Madeira. Are they really the police?

Unintentionally holding his breath, he listened to the intimidating rumble of the other boat's twin engines, now growling slightly louder as they were revved up to approach the workboat.

What options did he have now? From the sound, from his own seaman's instincts, he knew the other boat was bigger, faster, more powerful than the workboat. And from the sound and the flashing strobe, it wasn't far off their starboard bow.

There did exist the tiniest of chances that he and Tina might, by running, make it to *Johnson*. On the other hand, running would almost certainly result in their being attacked, whoever the other boat was.

Statistically, he decided, they were better off stopping.

"I'm going to stop, Tina," he reported as he throttled down and put the engine in neutral. "Please come over here, behind the steering console, and if I shout 'jump,' or if they make any threatening move, get over the side immediately."

"Okay, Al," she answered quietly, moving to his side.

"And if we have to leave the boat, don't try to fight the current. Try to swim across it, to the right. Try for James Island—that's the closest land, I think."

Madeira checked to insure that the radio was still

on. Then, in the unseen distance, carried by the gentle easterly that might, in time, dispel the impenetrable haze, he heard the faint, low roar of elephants trumpeting.

Blow down, he thought. They're ramming compressed air through *Johnson*'s main engines to make sure none of the cylinders have cracked and are leaking cooling water.

Within another half hour or so, assuming all was well, the engineers would light off the engines and warm them up. On deck, the Bos'n and his men were already stowing and securing anything that even hinted at being able to move once the ship started to pitch and roll.

This had to be the police! he thought, furious with himself for giving into his own paranoia. Why would anybody bother attacking the workboat when the gold and silver were aboard *Johnson*?

Unless there were others already aboard the ship.

A spotlight snapped on ahead, cutting a sword-like path through the milky, all-too-substantial night air as it swung toward them.

Stand by! he thought as he moved to place himself between Marina and the fog-solid, glowing beam that was skipping quickly over the dark waters. Within an instant it found them, almost drowning him in its glare. Rigid, silent, waiting for the blow, of whatever nature it might be, to be landed, he felt as if he'd been stripped naked.

They could see everything. He could see nothing but the glare of the light.

"Good evening, sir," boomed the loud-hailer as the beam swung off to one side and was then extinguished, leaving only the pulsing strobe. "You may proceed."

As the voice spoke, a vague, almost amorphous

277

shape under the flashing light seemed to absorb much of the surrounding darkness, thereby becoming infinitely darker and better defined.

"Kind of far out, aren't you?" Madeira shouted.

"Perhaps under normal circumstances, sir, but our captain decided to keep an eye on your ship. For your own protection."

"He didn't mention it to me."

"The captain likes to play things close to his vest sometimes, sir."

"I appreciate the thought," Madeira said to the now-visible, but still-dark, patrol boat, "even if he didn't trust me. We'll be gone soon."

"Yes, sir. And we can go home."

"Captain Madeira," bellowed the Bos'n through the hazy light that encased *Johnson* as they approached her. "Don't bother to put the boat on the boom. We're going to hoist her right aboard. One of my men is waiting for you on the landing stage."

Madeira looked up the ship's towering sides, and after spotting the speaker, waved in response, then turned toward the landing stage and slowed as he approached it.

"Welcome back," Frank Peale said as Madeira and Tina reached the top of the gangway. "How was Miami? Are we still legal?"

"We're still legal," Madeira replied, his fatigue now almost overpowering. "The judge reaffirmed the title to the wreck and refused to order us to stop, but he also increased the bond the syndicate's had to post. He said he expected the other side to appeal, and he didn't want to see all the artifacts disappear in the meantime."

"*Cucarachas!*" Tina snarled as the Bos'n, in the background, shouted "Heave around!"

"And?" asked Madeira, his fatigue-stiffened face forming itself into a smile.

"And what?"

"Is that all you're going to say?"

"Yes. That's my final comment on the whole matter."

"As long as we're legal," mumbled Peale, trying not to laugh outright at her outburst.

There was a quiet whirring sound as the work-boat was winched up and swung aboard *Johnson*.

"Are you two gentlemen sure you can get this ship under way without my supervision?"

"Yes, thank you, Tina," Madeira said. "Between us, Frank, Reilly, and I can somehow manage."

"Good night then."

After Tina had disappeared, Peale looked at Madeira. "Al, you know between Reilly, me, and the pilot, we can probably do it without you too."

"Any one of you could, Frank, but I think it'll be best if I'm there. Will you call me twenty minutes beforehand?"

"You've got it!"

Madeira's body and mind were both numb as he turned and headed toward his stateroom. He was too tired, he decided, to bother turning back and telling Peale about the judge's having taken him aside and sworn him as a bailiff or marshal or something.

Whatever the precise title had been, Judge Weaver had made it all too clear that Madeira would be held personally responsible if any of the treasure disappeared.

But that was his problem, not Peale's.

An hour and a half later, when Madeira arrived on the bridge, the sun was already huge, golden and pulsing. It was well above the horizon and directly over the harbor entrance, rapidly burning away what remained of the haze.

"Gunnuh to be 'nutha beautiful day," the pilot remarked when he caught sight of Madeira. "Y'all gunnuh have some fine wetha ta finish yuh work in."

"Yes, I hope so," Madeira replied, debating with himself whether or not to have a cup of coffee. Feeling the vibration of the main engines through the soles of his shoes, breathing the fresh air of dawn, he decided the prospect of going to sea and finishing the project was a more than sufficient stimulant.

"Glad you could make it, Al! I thought you might be a little too pooped."

"Wouldn't miss it for the world, Bud," Madeira said, feeling trapped again in one of Reilly's catty little games.

"Stage and gangway aboard and secured," Peale reported.

"We all ready, Captain?" the pilot asked.

"Yes, sir," replied Reilly. "Mr. Peale can heave around on the anchor anytime you want."

"Very well. Let's do it! If yuh would, please, Mr. Peale."

And that was all it took. Without Madeira's raising a hand, without his saying a word, the ship got under way and steamed out of Charleston, out beyond the shallow, turgid coastal waters, out into the deep, impossibly blue ocean.

Back to Tina's wreck, the wreck of *Misericordia*.

Twenty-six

Fifteen minutes after *Johnson* stopped abeam the Charleston seabuoy to drop off the pilot, Madeira was back in his rack, seemingly dead to the world. In fact, his subconcious was undoubtedly reliving every wonderful moment of the preceding evening.

Almost eight hours later, the ship had passed out of the green-brown coastal waters into the glorious blue of the deep ocean. The golden sun was now advancing toward the western horizon and Madeira was up again, fed and refreshed, standing on the starboard bay wall with Frank Peale, shooting the breeze.

"What the hell's that?" Madeira snapped as he momentarily glanced aft along the slick, swirling, partially healed scar slashed by the ship's passage through the blue waters. "Somebody's thrown a bag of bag of garbage overboard!

"Hell! That's not garbage! That's a man!"

"Man overboard! Port side!" bellowed Peale.

"You get that man-overboard pole over the side," Madeira ordered, already in motion toward one of the phone boxes mounted along the bay wall, "and keep your eyes on him while I call the bridge."

"Will do," replied Peale, turning towards the flag-tipped pole-and-life-ring combination mounted on a stanchion.

After tearing open the weatherproof door on the phone box, Madeira put the instrument to his ear and punched the "Bridge" button, then waited for what seemed an eternity.

"Bridge," he finally heard as he watched the pole tumble over the side, its strobe light already flashing.

"This is Madeira. Man overboard, port side. This is no drill!"

He heard his message repeated to Hawkins, and almost immediately, the ship's whistle exploded to life, shrieking hoarsely and hysterically as the bow started to swing rapidly to starboard.

"Man overboard, port side," boomed the ship's PA system between the whistle blasts.

"Man overboard, port side!" it repeated. "This is no drill! Prepare to launch the Zodiak!"

"I'm going to the bridge," Madeira shouted. "You take the phone and keep him in sight."

"I've lost him already," Peale snarled in anguish. "I can still see the pole but not him. This glare's impossible!"

"Shit! Shit! Shit! Shit!" Madeira cursed. *He* couldn't even see the pole anymore.

While Madeira foamed, *Johnson,* her course now some sixty degrees to the right of her original one, stopped turning to starboard and, after a brief pause, began turning rapidly to port.

"Okay, take this phone and keep your eyes on the

pole. Once we get back to it we should be able to find him!"

The instant the phone was in Peale's hand, Madeira sprinted forward, his middle-aged heart and lungs already protesting. Glancing down into the well, he noticed Bannerman and Higgins man-handling a dull black rubber boat, with outboard, aft along the bay's wide deck. They were headed to-ward a hinged opening in the steel gate that stood between them and *Johnson*'s ramped stern.

He paused, aware that the bridge had called for the use of the inflatable, and wondered if it had been the right choice? Or should one of the much larger workboats be swung out on its davits?

Hawkins, he decided, had chosen the best recov-ery vehicle. In fact, the kid'd handled the whole emergency very well so far. By the time he reached the bridge, the Williamson Turn that Hawkins had been executing was almost completed. *Johnson* was now headed slightly west of south, steaming right down the center of her still-visible wake.

"I want all hands on deck to look for him," Madeira gasped to Reilly, who, upon hearing the whistle, had galloped to the bridge.

"That's what we're doing right now," replied the research vessel's Master, his tone trumpeting his ir-ritation at Madeira's intrusion into his sphere of responsibility.

Madeira, recognizing his error, nodded in ac-knowledgment.

"Okay, Hawkins," Reilly snapped, offering not the slightest hint of approval, not the least recognition for what Madeira considered a very skilled perfor-mance, "I've got it now."

"Aye, aye, Skip," replied Hawkins, whose flushed, excited face told Madeira that, whether or not

Reilly ever acknowledged it, the young mate knew he'd done well.

"Do we know who it is, yet?" Madeira asked.

"We think it's Forbes," Reilly answered without turning to look at him.

"The assistant engineer?"

"Yes. He was supposed to be working in the Generator Room. The Chief doesn't know what the hell he was doing on deck."

"He may have been looking for me," said Freddie Gomez, who'd just arrived on the bridge, puffing slightly. "I was supposed to help him find out what was wrong with the automatic fire-extinguishing system."

By the time *Johnson* had returned to the man-overboard pole, there were thirty pairs of eyes scanning the surrounding surface, which now appeared even more limitless to Madeira than ever in the past.

After steaming south a mile or so beyond the pole, *Johnson* commenced a box search, following a path that carved ever larger boxes, each centered on Forbes's estimated position.

Nothing. Absolutely nothing but gorgeous blue water in all directions.

"Okay," Madeira sighed, his guts now twisted into a tangled mass of pain, "call the Coast Guard. Ask them to get some helos out here ASAP!"

"Roger," Reilly replied unhappily, as he drafted the request for assistance and handed it to Freddie for transmission.

Madeira stepped through the door to the port wing and looked out over the great blue expanse of the Atlantic.

He'd fallen overboard once, during the summer

he'd worked for his Uncle Carlos. He could still remember the shock of hitting the water; still taste the salt of the boat's foamy wake; still smell the stench of the exhaust hanging low over the water and sinking into the troughs; still feel the terror of watching the transom disappear behind the first wave, bobbing and shrinking as it went.

He knew what it was like to suddenly find yourself, totally without warning, in the water, watching your only hope for survival steam away, oblivious to your absence.

But he'd been missed immediately.

Even before the boat's transom had had time to rise on the wave and then slip down again behind the next, Carlos had known he was overboard. The old cod fisherman had twisted around, hanging out over the boat's side, and locked his eyes on Al's receding figure. At the same time he'd slammed the rudder quadrant against the stops as he forced he boat around in a sharp, rolling turn.

What if Carlos *hadn't* realized he'd gone over? What if it'd been him who'd fallen from *Johnson* on a beautiful, sunny afternoon like this one?

What do you do, assuming you're conscious and not badly injured? Do you wave? Shout?

Of course!

And what if the ship continues on, getting smaller with every passing second? Do you give up?

No! You assure yourself somebody's seen you, or is about to, and the ship will turn back. You try to save your energy by kicking off your shoes, bobbing, or trying to knot the cuffs of your trousers and, after inflating them, using them as a flotation bladder.

And then what? Do your arms get tired, do they

start to feel as if they're being torn from your shoulders? Or do you find yourself swallowing salt water first?

When do you start to feel the bitter flames of thirst? Before or after the ship's steamed over the horizon? Before or after night falls? Before or after you start worrying about sharks?

And what could it possibly be like to watch the ship turn, head back . . . and steam right by you? Looking but not seeing!

How long do you last?

Without flotation gear, a day at most. Almost certainly less.

With a life vest, the wait could last forever, much longer than any sane person would want it to.

And it would all happen in almost total silence.

He'd much prefer, Madeira decided, to die surrounded by the fury of a storm than to slip quietly away on a day like today.

Where the hell was he!

Why couldn't they find him!

How could he possibly have gone down so Goddamn quickly!

Rafael Cienfuegos stood on the boat deck and, like everybody else aboard the ship, scanned the horizon, looking for what he alone knew would never be found. Only he knew for sure that Forbes's reappearance was no more likely than that of the Stilson wrench that had killed the assistant engineer.

This ocean, thought Cienfuegos, goes on forever. The sight of limitless, burning blue plain took him back to a shattered plywood scow, a shoebox of soggy rice, five gallons of rusty water, and Pepito.

It had been fifteen days. A voyage of fifteen endless days—days of relentless summer sun hammering down from all directions, hacking at their crusted, tearless eyes, ricocheting back at them from the very blue sea itself.

Somewhere between each of those endless days had been an equally awful night—fourteen nights spent sitting in the waterlogged scow. They were unable to lie down because to do so meant to drown. They were unable to sleep, to escape the thirst and hunger. They shivered uncontrollably in the bitter, salty cold.

It had all been too much for Pepito. The price of survival had been too high.

Pepito had been a legitimate refugee: not one of Ramirez's creations. The revolutionary need to survive had not been programmed into him, and the biological need had proven insufficient. In the end, the sea and the sun had driven him past his limit. Shortly after midnight of the fourteenth night, Pepito had disappeared into the surrounding blackness with a splash and a great shout of joy.

Six hours after Pepito's triumphant escape, the sun, that Grandest of Inquisitors, returned to start another day's work and revealed the end of Cienfuegos's first ocean voyage.

There, not five hundred yards from the scow, a battered coastal freighter was plodding south through the gentle seas, fighting both the Stream's northerly flow and that of time.

It was a genuine stroke of fortune. Had the sun's arrival been delayed by a thick overcast, or had the tramp been capable of any greater speed, the scow's terrible voyage would undoubtedly have extended all the way to eternity.

The tramp's captain tried at first to not see Cienfuegos. He had, in the past, made the mistake of picking up Cuban refugees. His reward had invariably been to become enmeshed in the bureaucratic suspicion and abuse that attend all such acts of charity.

Then, fearing perhaps that on some not-too-distant morning *he* might be the one adrift in a waterlogged small boat, the captain relented. Sighing through his long, curly gray beard, he turned toward the near-derelict and stopped his ancient engines.

I have survived so much, thought Cienfuegos as his thoughts returned to *Johnson* and the memory of Forbes's death.

He had liked Pepito, and always felt a little sorry when he thought about his suicide.

But Pepito had died for a purpose. Ramirez had maneuvered him into going with Cienfuegos in order to strengthen Cienfuegos's cover; to enable Cienfuegos to work more effectively for the revolution.

He had liked Forbes too. Not that he knew him very well, but he seemed like a decent young fellow. And looking back on it, Cienfuegos now felt certain that the assistant engineer had died for no meaningful purpose. Pepito had died for the good of the revolution. Cienfuegos had killed Forbes not for the revolution, but rather for the good of Agustin Ramirez.

If only his head didn't hurt so!

Twenty-seven

Some eighty long hours after Madeira had first spotted the "sack of garbage" tossing in the wake, *Johnson* was back on station over the wreck.

To the west, the great golden sun shimmered, low in the sky and about to disappear beyond the unseen land. To the East, *El Dorado*, despite her age and unbecoming dress, glowed in the sun's almost horizontal beams. The little green former crew boat seemed to glide over the sparkling wavelets, barely touching them as she danced in attendance on her larger consort.

For over three days, one full day more than the Coast Guard had considered worthwhile, *Johnson* had steamed back and forth, in square and criss-cross patterns, looking fruitlessly for the missing engineer. For most of the search Madeira, obsessed with the need to recover Forbes, had remained on the bridge, wearing a grimly preoccupied expression. Not even Tina had been able to distract him, although, feeling it was not her place to do so, she hadn't tried very hard.

Finally, during the afternoon of the third day, he'd forced himself to accept the reality of Forbes's loss, and had reluctantly ordered the return to the wreck.

"Everything ready, Bud?" he asked in a tone that made it clear that all had better be!

Madeira continued to scan the horizon. At least, he thought, *Fortune Hunter* had made herself scarce. Then again, maybe it would be better if she *were* here, so he could see what she was doing.

"We're ready, and Bannerman reports she'll be set in fifteen minutes."

"Good."

Half an hour later, the sun now gone, MOHAB's crew was strapped into their seats and all hatches were secured.

"All secure," Bannerman reported to *Johnson*. "Commence flooding when ready."

"Roger," replied Peale. "Commencing flooding now."

Tons of seawater, oily slick in the artificial light, dark and foreboding, oozed furiously into the shadowy, floodlit bay.

God! thought Madeira, his stomach tightening as he watched Bannerman finger the joystick nervously. He was no longer looking forward to getting back to Tina's wreck. The only thing he wanted to do was complete the job and get himself and Tina the hell out.

He looked out through the bubble. There were no cheerful little shadows this time, skating and skipping around the bay. They'd all grown up and become a mature, menacing blackness.

This was his last deep job, he reassured himself.

From now on he'd stay where the sun shone, where he could see who and what might be trying to get him. Where the water was warm and gentle.

There was a thump as the habitat rose slightly off the deck, then bumped down again.

"We're light," Bannerman reported to Peale.

"Roger."

Madeira examined MOHAB's operator out of the corner of his eye. She was tense too. Too tense for what should by now be a routine evolution. For a fleeting moment he felt a sort of kinship with her.

"Lowering the gate," Peale advised a few minutes later, after MOHAB was well afloat. "Launching drogue."

Madeira happened to glance up at the top of the starboard bay wall. There, clearly visible in the harsh glare of the floodlights, stood Bobby Bell. The seaman appeared to be staring at Madeira and otherwise doing nothing, not that there was much for him to be doing at the moment. On further reflection, Madeira realized that Bell hadn't done much of anything, good or bad, ever since the confrontation in the passageway outside Madeira's stateroom.

Madeira had wanted to discharge the troublemaker in Charleston, but Reilly had moaned and groaned about it causing union trouble, so Madeira had let it slide, even though he doubted the union would have cared. It was, he felt, more about Reilly's ego than about the union.

Somehow, he thought as MOHAB slipped aft in the bay, it was not a good omen for Bobby Bell to be the last person he saw aboard *Johnson*.

Not many minutes later, MOHAB was floating free, well astern of *Johnson*, drifting slowly northeast with the Stream.

"All secure," Bannerman reported. "Preparing to dive."

"Roger, MOHAB."

Madeira glanced down at the pulsing green representation of MOHAB on the control panel, and then back out the bubble. As was so often the case, he was very conscious that only two thin inches of plastic separated him from the entire Atlantic Ocean. His thoughts turned to Tina, who was strapped in with the others in the main work compartment. He wished he was sitting next to her rather than with Bannerman. It was truly amazing, he thought with a glow, just how exciting, or at least interesting, even the most mundane items seemed to be when seen through her eyes.

Yet, he realized, even she now seemed gripped by the same tension that was squeezing the rest of them. It was as if she were looking over her shoulder, interested only in completing the excavation, unable to concentrate on and enjoy the pleasures of the process, the excitement of discovery.

Then Rafael Cienfuegos popped into his mind.

The distinguished, and highly self-disciplined, Cuban had never made it to the party at El Mandril, pleading the press of business. He then had returned to Charleston by himself on a commercial flight.

Since then, he'd said very little to anybody. He wasn't, it seemed clear, being rude or unpleasant. He appeared to have just totally withdrawn, to be considering matters so weighty that he had no attention to spare for any one else.

The balance of the dive was as routine as had been the launch, causing Madeira's tension, paradoxically, to mount. He sat stiffly, alert for that wandering, totally unexpected eddy that might throw the habitat out of control. Or the crazed whale that might appear from nowhere and ram them.

Down MOHAB spiraled, describing small red circles on the navigational plot, circles whose common center was the red dot that represented the wreck.

"I see it now!" It was Tina's voice, animated by a hint of renewed excitement, coming over the intercom. "I can see the ballast. And the frame. And The Crab. It all looks just like we left it."

Madeira leaned forward and stared out the bubble as Bannerman turned MOHAB directly toward their target. The wreck, he thought, wrapped as it was in The Crab's rib-like framework, was really a giant cadaver, the remains of a long-drowned monster.

"Before we settle down, Carol," he said, "let's make a couple passes over it, as close to the frame as you can get without ramming it."

"Roger."

After half-a-dozen passes, Madeira was ready to agree with Tina's initial impression that all was as they'd left it.

"Okay, Carol, let's settle down and get to work."

"Roger."

"Mi amor," Tina whispered into Madeira's ear after sneaking up on him, "you are a very good student. You are getting very good at that."

Madeira, who'd been sorting soggy artifacts into fluid-filled baggies while Cienfuegos wheeled stacks of silver ingots around in silence, straightened up. Groaning from the ache low on his spine, he swung his arm up and back and wrapped it gently around her neck. "You think I'm good enough to get a paying job doing it?"

"There aren't any. Anyway, I like you better as a sea dog. You keep the artifact business as a hobby."

Madeira laughed. Since their return to the wreck, nothing bad, or even discouraging, had occurred, and despite the hard labor and long hours, MOHAB's morale was vastly improved over that of four days before.

Then, remembering they weren't alone, Madeira relaxed his grip on Tina, glancing at Cienfuegos as he did. The obviously fatigued Cuban just smiled back with what Madeira thought was a distant, almost wistful expression.

"I'm afraid I'm going to have to get glasses soon," Tina said. "My eyes are so tired."

"You shouldn't look at so much television."

The intense, nonstop labor had commenced within minutes of MOHAB's bottoming. Even before control was reestablished over The Crab, Crown and Savage were out, working with the ROVs to inspect the framework and insure nothing had come loose, to position wire baskets at key locations, and to help The Crab remove the overburden Tina had placed to protect the excavation. Only then, after all the instruments had been returned, did the concert begin in earnest.

MOHAB's complement was divided into two sections, each of which worked at least eight hours out of every sixteen. Then the action started—many hundreds of ballast stones were shuffled around the ocean floor, and a thick, steady stream of artifacts flowed into the habitat.

All the while, using video and computer-controlled plotting and positioning systems, every item, its location in three dimensions, and the conditions surrounding its recovery were all carefully documented. This steady, almost overpowering torrent of data was poured into MOHAB's computers and simultaneously, in real time, also transmitted up to *Johnson*, where Freddie Gomez insured that it was retransmitted ashore.

"Diego's ancestors were unbelievable," Tina continued laughing as she rubbed her already red eyes. "Do you realize we've recovered over ten times as much gold as was shown on the official manifest? And we haven't finished yet! I just hope we find the other *chac mools*. That would be truly *estupendo!*"

"*Claro!*" Madeira replied, hoping he was pronouncing it right.

While many of the sarcophagi were satisfying full of cultural artifacts—pottery shards, wood samples, scraps of leather and bone, and bits and pieces of what the uninitiated would call trash—the most obvious fruits of their efforts were the stacks of grayish-black bulk silver being stowed below in the main hold on the lower level.

Of undoubtedly greater monetary value, but less obvious since they were now stored in several locked sarcophagi, was the horde of gold chains, plates and platters, candlesticks, medallions and crosses, several inlaid with jewels.

Strangely, Madeira thought as he looked at the assembled treasure, he still felt no lust for it. It was not his to spend and never would be. It was merely a product he was paid to process.

Of all that surrounded him, only Tina seemed to possess value.

"If they'd been caught, they'd have been drawn and quartered, right?" Madeira said.

"I'm not so sure now. If they'd been small-time operators caught smuggling a few pounds of silver, they'd undoubtedly suffer all the tortures of Hell. But this operation was big-time and the Spanish respected gall as much as anybody. More so, in fact!

"I'm sure the King and his officials—those who weren't involved somehow—would have been furious. But they'd also be terribly impressed. If they suspected treason, if they felt threatened by it, they would have made Velazquez eat his own intestines. Otherwise, they might very well have confiscated most of it and then toasted the perpetrators' good health. Velazquez would have lost most of the loot, but he'd have kept his head. And even his social standing."

Tina and Madeira both paused and turned as Higgins rocketed toward them through the hatch from the bubble.

"We've got big trouble," he shouted. "*Johnson* reports she's had an explosion in the Generator Room and she's on fire. It's already burned through the bulkhead into the bay, and Peale's afraid it's going to go through the outer hull next.

"He doesn't sound like he thinks they can get it under control."

Twenty-eight

The day was a mild and gentle one, no more threatening than that on which *Nuestra Senora de la Misericordia* had foundered so many hundreds of years before. There was no way, short of blind luck, that Frank Peale might have received any hint of approaching disaster.

Peale, who had the afternoon watch, was steaming slowly in a square pattern over the flat, sunhardened waters. While the Mate was high on the bridge, battling boredom, the first phase of catastrophe occurred deep within the ship's hull, in the unmanned Generator Room.

The Mate could not possibly have heard the popping detonation of two small shaped charges placed by Rafi Cienfuegos. Neither could he have been expected to hear the sound of diesel fuel jetting out of the sheared fuel line onto the generator's red-hot head. Nor the explosive whoosh when the fuel flashed and instantly transformed the small space into an inferno that almost rivaled that of the sun.

He could, of course, have been expected to respond to the automatic fire alarm, but he never heard it because it never sounded, just as the Halon extinguishing system failed to snap into action and suffocate the fire. While the sensors did all twitch in response to the heat and smoke, their frantic electrical warnings led to nothing, thanks to Rafi.

The first Peale learned of the fire was the wailing of the alarm as the gyrocompass realized it was receiving no power. Glancing around, he discovered the electronics had all gone as dark as the radios had gone silent.

"Shit!" he mumbled.

Then, to the seaman on watch with him, he said, "Take the helm, disengage the automatic pilot, and steer Zero Nine Zero Magnetic."

"Yes, sir."

Waiting for the emergency system to cut in—it should have been almost instantaneous but wasn't—Peale glanced aft to check on *El Dorado*'s location. He was startled to see great, black waves of smoke vomiting out a blower vent on the starboard bay wall and sinking through the hot, lifeless air, filling the bay with a near-solid, heaving mass.

"Shit!" he said again, his voice even higher than usual. "We're on fire! There's a fire in the Generator Room! Stop engines!"

While the helmsman moved the throttles, linked mechanically to the engines, Peale's hand slammed down on the general alarm.

Nothing happened!

Of course! It needed electrical power just like everything else; everything else but the whistle. As long as there was compressed air in the flasks, the whistle would sound.

Continuing to curse, Peale reached for the lever that controlled the whistle. Just as his hand closed on it, the gyro alarm went silent and the radio returned to static life as the emergency batteries cut in. He slammed the general alarm again, and was rewarded with its loud shrieks. He then moved to his right and examined the Halon console. It was showing no lights, no lights at all! Either the power failure had screwed up the indicators, or the automatic system wasn't working.

After pulling out the safety lock, he shoved down the toggle switch and prayed. The only way he'd know if he'd succeeded in manually triggering the system was to watch the smoke and see if it changed.

Peale had no intention, however, of waiting for anything. He lunged toward to the PA system and picked up the mike: "Fire! Fire in the Generator Room. Fire party muster on the boat deck aft of the superstructure, starboard side."

The smoke, he noticed as he spoke, was just as thick and gooey as ever, if not more so.

The fuel supply! The automatic shutoff must not be working better than any of the other automatic systems!

He grabbed the phone and buzzed the normally unmanned Engine Room, which was located just forward of the bay, between the Generator Room to starboard and the Compressor and Watermaker Room to port. He hoped to catch one of the engineers there doing maintenance work.

"Engine Room. What the hell's going on?"

"Fire in the Generator Room! I want you to secure the generator fuel supply at the bunker and keep an eye on the firewall."

"What about the automatic system?"

"It's not working! Now get your ass in gear!"

"I'm on my way!"

Looking aft, the Mate watched as the fire party assembled on the boat deck, well forward of the smoking vent. Several of them, he realized, had only a very limited idea of how to put on their oxygen gear, and even those who did seem to know what they were doing were doing it in a very slow, hesitant manner.

He'd begged Reilly to run more drills!

Speaking of Reilly, Peale thought, where the hell was he? He's supposed to take command here so I can get that fire party moving.

"You want me up here or back aft, Mr. Peale?"

Peale turned and looked at Freddie Gomez. "Up here, Gomez. I'm afraid I'm going to need you here to help me."

"Yes, sir."

"First, I want you to notify MOHAB that we have a fire in the Generator Room. Then notify *El Dorado*."

The phone buzzed.

"This damn deck's getting hot, Mr. Peale." It was the Bos'n, leading the fire party. "I was hoping to pump foam down the scuttle in the deck, but we can't get near it."

Goddamnit! thought *Johnson*'s Chief Mate. The deck's too hot and the fire's under the deck so there's no way they're going to be able to cool it down. "Can you get at it from the bay? How about that vent the smoke's coming out?"

"We can try, but the wall's hotter'n hell too, so we'll have to try to shoot the shit in from the distance."

Fat chance! thought Peale. The smoke, he realized, the oily, acrid, deadly airborne goo, was fast filling the bay. It was rolling thickly, in great waves, from side to side.

Just like filthy black water!

Now some was splashing up and over the sides, then spreading out slowly across the sparkling, sun-drenched sea.

He tried to imagine what it was, or would soon be, like for the Bos'n and his party, and decided he was glad he wasn't there, even though that was precisely where he was supposed to be.

Now where the hell was the Captain!

"Bos'n?" he snapped into the phone.

"Yes, sir?"

"Mr. Peale," broke in the excited voice of the engineer in the Engine Room, "the fucking shutoff's bent. I can't get it completely closed."

"Do the best you can!" Peale snapped. "Bos'n!"

"Yes, sir?"

"Get your fire party below. You're going to have to go in through the starboard passageway and the machine shop."

"Yes, sir. Mr. Hawkins is on his way there already with two men."

"Good," he replied, noticing that thin, greasy streamers of smoke, bearing an unpleasant resemblance to Reilly's hair, now seemed to be jetting out from the inner bay wall itself.

Good Christ! he thought. It's burning through the plates! How much longer before it gets through the outboard plates, the ones between the ship and the water?

"Frank, this is Paul."

"Yes, Paul?"

"I can't get into the machine shop. Somebody left the watertight door between it and the Generator

301

Room open. It's like a hurricane here, the wind's roaring into the shop and I can see the flames from the Generator Room shooting back through the door into the shop, sucking up the air. Sometimes they're filling the whole shop!"

"Where are you?"

"In the starboard passageway. At the forward door of the shop."

"Close it! Cut off the air supply!"

Before the young mate could carry out Peale's order, Reilly appeared from only God knows where and charged up to him.

"Don't close that fucking door, Hawkins! That won't cut off all the air. I want that fire extinguished and that's our only access."

Reilly grabbed the phone. "Frank! Where the fuck's that fire party? I want it down here now!"

"It's on its way, Captain," replied Peale.

"*Johnson*, this is *El Dorado*," the radio announced. "Did you know the paint right above your waterline is smoldering? Jesus! It's not just smoldering, they're red-hot. The plates are red-hot, and one looks like it's crumpling!"

"*El Dorado*," Peale shouted into the mike, beginning to wonder, for the first time, whether the ship would survive the day, "come along our starboard side and direct your fire hoses on the smoldering plates."

"Roger, *Johnson*."

The phone buzzed. "Mr. Peale. This is Jake Smith. Me and my men are securing the weapons, rigging them to jettison if necessary."

"How many will it take to actually dump them overboard?"

"One can do it."

"All right. After you've done whatever you're doing, two of you join the fire party."

"Roger."

The fire's throaty, blast-furnace roar was becoming increasingly noticeable even on the bridge as its dense blackness, in increasing quantities, belched out into the well and, after oozing over the gate, trailed off slowly astern.

She's heaving her guts out, thought Peale as he watched the smoke. She's dying. He then buzzed the Engine Room on the phone and got the Chief Engineer. "Chief, light off all pumps and get all your eductors on line. In addition to the firefighting water, it looks like a hole's burning through the side at the waterline."

"Aye."

The phone buzzed. "Where the hell you been, Frank? I've been trying to get through to you!" demanded Reilly.

"Telling the Chief to light off all pumps and eductors, Captain. The fire's starting to burn through the hull, just above the waterline."

"Fuck! All right! We're going to have to go in through here, just as I thought."

Dropping the phone before Peale could express his doubts, Reilly turned to watch the arrival of the Bos'n and the rest of the fire party.

"Over here, Bos'n," he shouted, waving as he did and struggling to be heard over the hellish roaring in which they were all immersed. "We're going to go in through the machine shop."

The Bos'n blanched, then nodded. Almost simultaneously, one of the small air flasks in the shop exploded from the heat.

"I want two hoses rigged," Reilly continued. "The first is going to be charged with firefighting foam and the second's going to use fog to protect the first. I'm going to lead the first into the shop so we can pump the foam into the Generator Room. I want you to take the second hose. You understand?"

"Yes, Captain."

"What about me, Captain?" Hawkins shouted. "What do you want me to do?"

"I want *you* to keep the fuck out of the way!"

Stunned, Hawkins stepped back, away from the door, and watched while the hoses were rigged and laid out along the nearly dark passageway and the two hose parties tried again to get their masks and oxygen tanks adjusted correctly.

"Ready, Bos'n?" Reilly shouted, finally losing his patience.

"As we'll ever be," mumbled the Bos'n, giving Reilly the high sign.

"Let's go, then!" Reilly shouted as, with water from the second hose drenching them, he led the first hose team into the shop.

When Reilly first advanced into the shop, the flames seemed to shrink from him, retreating, taking cover behind the drill presses and milling machines.

Suddenly there was a "boom!" in the generator room and the fire counterattacked. With astounding speed, the black-yellow flames lashed out. They raced along the sides of the shop, roaring, curling, hissing, smoking, snapping, lunging, and grabbing in all directions, threatening to engulf both hose parties in a pincer movement.

"Stay where you are!" the Bos'n shouted into his mask as he saw some of the men on the number-two hose starting to fall back. "Keep that number-one hose party covered!"

"This is bullshit!" shouted Bobby Bell, who was one of the men on the number-two hose. "They don't pay us enough to die like this! Follow me, men!"

With that, Bell dropped his hold on the hose, turned, and tried to run—only to slam into the men behind him. It took less than an instant for the Bos'n to completely lose control of the second hose party as they all dropped the hose and tried to run before the advancing flames.

The first hose party, being all that much deeper in the crackling shadow of death, needed no further encouragement to retreat. Dropping their own hose, they turned and stumbled blindly into the second hose party, causing a near-fatal pileup at the door.

So intent on escaping those terrible flames were all members of both parties that Paul Hawkins, that most unwilling spectator, was the only one to realize that Reilly was not participating in the retreat.

Still unrecovered from Reilly's mortal abuse, Hawkins stood, both paralyzed and fascinated, and stared at the Captain's dark, stick-figure form as it was distorted and made unnaturally fluid by the shimmering, blasting heat and fury.

He's dancing, thought Hawkins, a smile of some sort, or maybe a grimace, forming on his soot-covered face. The son of a bitch is doing a jig! He's dancing all the way to Hell.

Burn, motherfucker, burn!

After watching in rapt fascination for several moments, he felt a sudden wave of nausea sweep over him.

God damn it to Hell! he thought. The fucker's won! I'm just like him now. He's turned me into another Reilly just like himself!

He slammed his hand into the smoking-hot bulkhead, then looked down at the tangled mass of humanity in front of him.

"Up, you men!" he bellowed. "Get up and grab those hoses!"

While several members of the still-tangled, panting mass turned dulled eyes in his direction, not a one moved.

"On your feet!" he shouted. "Reform the two hose parties! We'll start by cooling down this door and bulkhead."

"Fuck you, you little shit!" Bobby Bell snarled from the pile of humanity. "What the fuck do you know!"

The Bos'n looked at Bell, then at Hawkins, but neither said nor did anything.

In a fury, Hawkins grabbed the second hose. Leading it over his right shoulder and leaning forward, he dragged it into the shop, moving the nozzle in large circles, determined to drive the flames before him.

As he struggled forward, the flames once again retreated, inviting him to continue to chase them among the smoldering lathes and benches. Hawkins knew they'd be back, just as they'd returned to get Reilly, but he also knew he had to take the chance; that he had to go in and try to get the Captain out before the fire had time to regroup and counterattack yet again.

It wasn't for Reilly that he was doing it; that fucker was right where he belonged! Paul Hawkins was forcing entry into the crematorium for his own sake.

When the Bos'n reported both Reilly and Hawkins were dead, and that the fire was as out-of-control as ever, Frank Peale cursed more violently than he ever had before in over thirty years at sea.

Reilly, he snarled to himself, had been a good seaman, but he was a shit-for-brains Master. He'd never understood his position, his role. He should be standing now where Peale was, doing what Peale now had to do.

It was Reilly's own Goddamn fault that he'd died.

Peale walked out to the starboard wing and looked down at *El Dorado*. She was still alongside, doing her best despite the searing heat, loyally playing her puny, two-inch fire hoses on *Johnson*'s steaming plates.

Only then did his attention leave the fire long enough to notice the change in the ocean's face. The surface was still smooth, but no longer flat and blue. Brought to life now by the long, unmistakable roll of distant swells, the blue was turning gray. He glanced aloft, and noted the solidifying mare's tails, the thin, milky halo around the sun, the irregular puffs of wind. Without even looking, he knew the glass was falling, that another trough was forming, that a storm would soon follow.

If worse came to worst, the little treasure hunter could save *Johnson*'s crew, but he'd need more help if the ship herself was to survive.

Returning to the pilothouse, Peale grabbed a pencil and paper and walked over to the navigational plot. After glancing at it several times, he started writing.

"Gomez!" he called, finishing his hateful task.

"Yes, Mr. Peale?" Gomez replied, hustling toward him.

"I want you to transmit this on all distress frequencies, international and radio telephone, and keep transmitting it until somebody replies."

"Yes, sir."

Taking the paper, Gomez read:

SOS SOS SOS/RV IRVING JOHNSON/KWB 1537/POSIT THIRTY THREE DEGREES FIVE MINUTES NORTH SEVENTY SIX DEGREES TWENTY EIGHT MINUTES WEST/ON FIRE AND TAKING WATER/ FIRES OUT OF CONTROL/ GLASS FALLING/MASTER-SECOND DEAD/PEALE ACTING MASTER/SOS SOS SOS.

Twenty-nine

Goddammit to Hell! Madeira thought when he heard Higgins's words and fully grasped that *Johnson* was in danger. It's happening all over again!

A familiar sensation of helpless, powerless dread surged through him. Was he, once again, to be the absent commander, forced to watch, from a distance, that which it was his responsibility to avert?

The first time he'd been ashore. While he was sleeping soundly in Maine, Cabot Station, the subsea station he'd commanded, had shuddered violently, then entered its death throes under three hundred feet of icy North Atlantic water.

Yes, there'd been a rescue force in which he'd been permitted to participate, and yes, much of the crew had been saved, but it was not those facts that dominated his memories. In Madeira's mind the disaster was defined by the shock and fluid despair he'd first felt, a shock and despair quickly followed by horror; by a sickening certainty of his own criminal negligence and failure, of dereliction and guilt; by a mortifying sense of shame and self-contempt. Because he'd failed to do his job properly, others, shipmates and friends, were suffering and dying and it was too damn late to ever correct his mistakes.

Somehow, it always turned out to be too late.

Almost from the very first day, he admonished himself, he'd noticed a dangerous slackness aboard *Johnson*, a laid-back, fuck-em-if-they-can't-take-a-joke attitude among much of the crew.

Yet he'd failed to take action to correct it. He'd permitted Reilly to run an arbitrary, slack ship, and to conduct sloppy, incomplete exercises, and his failure to do something about it had now burst into flames.

"Tina," he finally said, "we're going to secure the excavation and prepare to surface, just in case there's some way we can help. So recall the divers and the ROVs. I want to be able to lift off in half an hour. You won't have time to backfill."

"That's okay, Al. I understand."

"Have Dale and Rafael stow and secure any loose artifacts."

"Roger," Tina replied.

"Higgins, wake Carol and have her meet me in the bubble."

"Roger."

Madeira was seated in the bubble, looking out as the divers secured the job as best they could in fifteen minutes, when Bannerman slid in beside him.

"Higgins tell you?" Madeira asked.

"Yes, there's a fire on *Johnson*."

"I'm not sure what we can do to help, but I want to be ready to lift off in twenty minutes."

"Roger," Bannerman replied, reasonably certain there was little they could do to help. "I told Higgins to make sure everything's secured."

"Good. The divers will be finished in a few minutes."

"MOHAB, this is *Johnson*," Gomez reported in the first of several updates. "Be advised that we are unable to extinguish the fire from the main deck. The fire party is now attempting to get at it through the machine shop."

"Roger, *Johnson*."

"Al," Tina announced a few minutes later, "we've recovered all the filled baskets. The divers are coming aboard now, and I'll have the ROVs back in bed in about five minutes."

Before Madeira could acknowledge her report, Gomez's voice boomed into the bubble again. "MOHAB, this is *Johnson*, The fire has burned through the inner bay wall. I say again, the fire has burned through the inner bay wall and is still out of control. We will be unable to recover you."

"Roger, *Johnson*," replied Madeira, "I understand fire has burned through bay wall and you are unable to recover us."

Shit! he thought. They probably couldn't have recovered us anyway; they're all too busy fighting the fire.

"We're not going anywhere for the time being," he mumbled, not expecting to be heard.

"Roger," Bannerman said.

"Now attention all hands," Madeira said into the PA. "The fire aboard *Johnson* has burned through the inner bay wall so it is now impossible for them to recover us. Accordingly, we will not lift off at this time. However, I want all hands to continue recovering and securing all gear and securing all hatches. I want to be able to get under way at any time. Any questions?"

There were none.

Sitting in the bubble, waiting, imagining the hell that must exist above them, remembering the hell that did once exist years ago at Cabot Station, Madeira was desperate to do something, anything.

He had to force himself not to pester *Johnson* with questions. What was being done to fight the fire? What was *El Dorado* doing? Any sign of *Fortune Hunter*?

Despite the madly itching temptation, he resisted the almost irresistible impulse to scratch, to tell Gomez to put Reilly on.

Reilly undoubtedly had his hands full.

Then, "MOHAB, this is *Johnson*. Be advised that Captain Reilly and Mr. Hawkins have both been killed in the fire. Mr. Peale is now in command and the fire is still out of control. We are now transmitting an SOS."

Madeira slumped forward slightly, all spirit, for the moment, gone.

Poor Hawkins! He never got, not once, the chance to tell himself he'd beaten the sea; the chance to taste the sort of the triumphs that only a sailor could appreciate—and that constituted just about the only reward the average sailor could ever expect to receive.

And Reilly? Whatever the man's infuriating shortcommings, the thought of his death made Madeira feel sick.

"MOHAB, this is *Johnson*."

"Roger, *Johnson*," Madeira replied glumly.

"The engineers have finally succeeded in cutting off the fuel supply to the fire. Mr. Peale says he thinks it's going to burn itself out within a few minutes. The fire parties are concentrating on cooling down all surrounding decks and bulkheads."

Madeira sat up straight again, muscles tensing, and grabbed the microphone. "*Johnson*, this is MOHAB. As soon as he can get a chance, ask Mr. Peale to get on the circuit."

"Roger, MOHAB."

"Have the owners, and the syndicate, been notified?"

"We are doing so now, MOHAB."

"Roger."

"Tina," Madeira said into the intercom after several minutes of silence.

"Yes, Al," she replied quietly, her breath reaching his ears.

Startled, he spun around to discover her worried face, along with those of Higgins and Dale, all looking at him through the hatch.

"How much longer will it take you to complete this project to your satisfaction?" he asked.

"I could probably spend years sorting through the sand and gravel, but in another seventy-two hours, the way we've been going, we'll be done for all practical purposes. We've already got enough for a lifetime of analysis and study ashore."

"Okay. Is Rafael there?"

"Yes, Al," replied the Cuban, peering hesitantly into the bubble.

"Do you, or do you think the syndicate will, have any problem with my sending *Johnson* to Charleston, assuming I have any choice in the matter, and us staying here another three days to finish up, then going in ourselves under our own power?"

"Is that possible?" the Cuban asked, already knowing perfectly well that it was.

"We'll be pushing it, but yes, it should be possible. If we see that our power reserves are dropping too fast, we'll head in earlier. Either way, Carol will make sure we all get in safe and sound. Right?"

"Right!" Bannerman replied with more enthusiasm than Madeira could ever remember seeing her show. "I can do anything!"

"Clearly, then," Cienfuegos said, "we would wish for the excavation to be finished, but we have no desire to further endanger any lives. We leave the decision to you."

"Very well," replied Madeira. "We all seem to agree."

"MOHAB, this is *Johnson*," sighed the digital encoder a few minutes later. "Peale speaking."

"Frank, what's the situation up there now?"

"It's a fucking mess, Al. The fire's about burned itself out, but it burned a big hole into the bay and a number of external plates are buckled and cracked and I think a storm is making up. We're taking water, which we've been able to handle so far, but unless you have other instructions for me, I want to head into Charleston just as soon as I can shore up the buckled plates.

"I'd leave *El Dorado* for you, but she's getting low on fuel again. I think the best plan is for me to send her in right away to refuel. She can then return and cover you."

"Then who will be standing by you?"

"Three shrimpers, a tanker, and the Coasties are all on their way, so we'll have lots of company."

"Are they there yet?"

"Who?"

"The shrimpers, tanker, and Coasties. Are any of them there yet?"

"Negative."

"What about the weapons?"

"Jake did a good job of securing them. They're okay."

"Tell him to get the missiles over the side this instant, before he has an audience!"

"Jesus! I hadn't thought of that!"

"Do it! Right now!"

"Roger."

"And send *El Dorado* in to refuel."

"Roger."

There was a long pause, then. "MOHAB, this is *Johnson*. Smith is disposing of the missiles right now. In fact, he was already preparing to do it when I called him."

"Very well," Madeira replied. "You head on in ASAP. Unless something else goes wrong, I intend to spend another seventy-two or so hours here, finishing up. Then we'll come on in and join you."

"Roger."

"And Frank. I want you to offload the artifacts in Charleston. Have Jake arrange to put them in some bank vault and ask Señor Velazquez to notify Judge Weaver in Miami. Don't keep that stuff aboard one second longer than absolutely necessary!"

"Roger."

"Make sure Customs is there when you do it!"

"You don't think they trust us?"

"No. And good luck."

"Thanks, Al, but don't worry about us. We'll be okay. . . . Stand by!"

Madeira waited again.

"Gomez just handed me a message from Señor

Velazquez, a reply to our message. They're sending another security party to you by worksub. They hope to be under way from Jacksonville in about twenty-four hours."

Madeira nodded. The possibility had been discussed during the expedition's planning sessions.

"Roger, *Johnson*," he acknowledged into the digital encoder.

Thirty

Even before *Johnson* and the shrimp boat —which was the first of her escorts to arrive—had cleared the scene of the wreck, Madeira had instructed Bannerman to launch the emergency radio antenna buoy. Tina immediately started to transmit her data directly to Miami. As she did, everybody crossed his fingers that the buoy would not be torn off its half-mile-long cable by the storm that was rapidly developing on the surface. The Crab was put back to work, as were all the humans, who were divided again into two shifts.

"How are we doing, *mi nina*?" asked Cienfuegos as he walked into MOHAB's small dining area and found her taking a coffee break about twelve hours after Johnson's departure.

"Rafi," replied Tina, "this is turning out to be the greatest underwater excavation ever done. We're going to know more about this ship than her builder and her captain did."

"Excellent!" Cienfuegos beamed, his gold tooth glinting even in the energy-preserving dim light. "I'm very pleased the project is proving to be so successful and that you are enjoying it. And I'm sure Diego and the others will be also," he added as he poured himself some coffee, added a large amount of milk, and sat down at the rectangular stainless-steel table.

"This is all going to look very good in Diego's museum . . . the museum all of you are working so hard on," Tina said.

"If so, it will be because of *your* very hard work."

Rafi smiled as he spoke, despite the rippling pressure he felt along the rubbery channel that twisted around and around in the space below his stomach.

The disorder from which he was suffering was fear, and he knew it. It was that same fear of dying under thousands of feet of water that had plagued him all along. It was also a new fear, the fear that he would fail to act, that he would be unable to do what he now knew had to be done.

"And MOHAB, Rafi. And Al."

"Yes, of course," Cienfuegos replied. "It would not have been possible without them. It will be a great victory for all of you."

"Us, Rafi. For all of us."

"Of course."

"Please excuse me. If we're going to have our great victory, I'd better get to work again."

He stood when she did and followed her, with his eyes, as she walked aft toward the work compartment. Then he sat back down again and stared into his coffee as the blackest of despairs settled back over him.

Thanks to Agustin Ramirez, Cienfuegos had

never loved any of the women with whom he had been, discreetly, over those long years of service to the revolution. He had been programmed to avoid such pitfalls, such dangers.

But during the past few months everything had changed. The revolution had become obsolete, and even Ramirez had jumped ship.

And Tina had come into his life.

How he wanted to love her, to be with her on almost any terms, but he knew that was impossible. He was convinced that the problem was not really one of age. The problem was that he and Tina existed in different universes. She was a creation of God. He was the creation of Agustin Ramirez.

It was a case of mixing matter and anti-matter. Close co-existance was utterly impossible.

Yet her love, and his liberation, might yet be achieved.

Somehow.

He must remain alert, he told himself, and prepared. He must not permit any weakness to interfere!

Thirty-one

"Al," Carol Bannerman said as she walked into the work compartment, "that short in the antenna buoy cable keeps getting worse. I'm not sure how much longer we're going to be transmitting. In fact, I'm not even sure anything's getting out now. We've got close to ninety-percent feedback most of the time."

Madeira, who had been bent over, sorting endless piles of soggy artifacts, straightened up with a grunt. As he did, he thought of the full gale blowing on the surface and of the buoy tugging and jerking violently on the end of its half-mile-long cable. If the cable was shorted out, then the skylink with Miami—virtually all long-range communications, for that matter—was broken until MOHAB surfaced.

"It's too bad Freddie isn't here," Bannerman remarked. "He'd find a way to fix it!"

It was too bad, thought Madeira, but then the antenna was only designed for emergency and temporary use. Not for continuing operations.

If *Johnson* were only still here, he thought, to relay the data. At least she was now safe in Charleston, most of her crew sent home while the ship was repaired.

Madeira looked around him, first at the priceless stew of cultural artifacts spread on the worktable, then at the immodest mounds of silver and the locked sarcophagi containing hundreds of pounds of gold and jewels. He thought of Judge Weaver and his very convincing threats. The minute the data stopped flowing, the IAA people would undoubtedly start screaming their heads off.

Unless, of course, they never even noticed.

"How much longer until that worksub arrives with the new security people?" he asked Bannerman.

"Sometime tonight or early tomorrow."

"Very well," he replied.

"What about the buoy?"

"Keep transmitting until you're sure it's completely dead. Then recover it."

"Roger."

After placing a handful of musket balls in a baggie—at least that was what they looked like to him—he dried his hands and arms and walked around to behind the console. He stood for several minutes, watching in silence as Tina guided The Crab to vacuum up a horde of who-knows-what from a particularly promising pocket of silt exposed by the removal of several ballast stones.

"I don't think I'm going to be able to keep up with you," he finally remarked quietly. As he spoke, he wondered if the musket balls might really be grapeshot.

Couldn't be, he decided. Wasn't grape usually made of iron?

"I don't see how you could," replied Tina. She turned in her chair and smiled over her shoulder while she used one hand to guide the ROV clear of The Crab's snapping claws, which she was controlling with her other hand. "I have all these marvelous machines of yours, while all you have is your fingers."

"Goddamn it to Hell!"

"What's wrong, Carol?" Madeira asked into the still-vibrating intercom.

"The damn buoy just carried away!"

"You mean the cable parted?"

"Affirmative."

Hell! he thought. "Have we heard from the work-sub yet?"

"Negative."

"Very well. Recover whatever's left of the cable right now. I don't want the current laying it out downstream where it'll get tangled in the framework."

"Roger."

"Tina?" Bannerman demanded over the intercom a few seconds later. "How many ROVs you working with?"

"One," Tina replied.

"Well, there's something else out there then."

Frowning, Madeira bent over the console and looked at Tina's short-range Sonar plot. All he saw was Tina's one ROV. He then turned on one of the monitors not currently in use. "Carol, please patch your Sonar display into our video unit six."

"Roger," Bannerman said as she patched the output of the long-range Sonar into the remote unit.

"There!" Madeira said, primarily to himself, as he

pointed at the blip. It was about ten miles to the east and almost a thousand feet above them.

"It's not on mine yet," Tina said.

"It should be soon," replied Madeira.

"Carol," he continued, "raise the angle of your transducer and see if we can scan the surface."

"Roger."

The image on monitor six did not, at first, seem to change. Then, almost instantaneously, it burst into a solid, brilliant mass of light.

Well! What the hell did you expect! thought Madeira. There're fifteen-foot seas breaking and churning up there. Only a very advanced computer system could pick out the reflection made by a ship's hull, especially if it was a relatively small ship, from among that mess.

"This ain't going to tell us a damn thing!" Bannerman said.

No it ain't, thought Madeira. "Carol, please lower the transducer again and see if we still have that other contact."

"Roger."

The display cleared within seconds, leaving only The Crab, Tina's ROV, and the unidentified contact, which was headed more or less directly for them.

"Whoever's driving that thing must he high," Bannerman said. "It's wobbling all over!"

"I've got it now," Tina reported.

"Al," said Bannerman over the intercom, "I've just picked up the worksub's signal. It looks like that's them. Should I activate our beacon?"

"I thought they weren't due for another eight or ten hours!"

"You got me."

"Why did they wait until now to identify themselves?" Cienfuegos asked.

"Maybe they were having some sort of mechanical trouble. They did look like they were wobbling a few minutes ago. Go ahead and turn on the beacon. Then call them up on the digital encoder and exchange passwords."

An hour later, the approaching worksub turned into the current and started to sidle up to the much-larger MOHAB. As he watched the maneuver on the Sonar screen, Madeira found himself wondering what the new security group would be like. He wondered if it would be as colorful, and as efficient, as Rambo's crew. He discovered he actually missed Jake and his big, blond, frowning mustache.

"All watertight doors are secure," reported Bannerman, who was sitting beside him in the bubble.

"Stand by, MOHAB," squawked the digital encoder. "We are now making our final approach."

"Roger," Bannerman responded.

Madeira leaned forward and craned his neck around, trying to look aft, but could see nothing. He then looked at the video monitors, and could finally see the worksub as it crept up from astern, headed for the big lock located aft of the conning tower.

The sub was about sixty feet long and painted white. It could be any one of a hundred similar vessels in use around the world.

Then he heard the gentle scraping sound made by the rubber skirt of the worksub's airlock as it rubbed along MOHAB's back.

The sub seemed to stop a moment, then rise slightly.

It backed and settled, and there was a clank and thunk as the two locks came into contact.

"Mating locks . . . now!" reported the digital encoder.

There was another thunk, then silence.

"Okay," Bannerman said as she looked up from the green status diagram on the control panel. "That lock's solid!"

"I'm going aft to meet them Carol," Madeira said as he stood up. "You stay here just in case something goes wrong."

"Roger, Al."

When Madeira reached the aft storeroom, the storage area between the work compartment and the motor room, the airlock's inner hatch was just opening. Within a second or two a very slender, squared-away-looking young man with a very short haircut was dropping down to the compartment's deck.

"Captain Madeira! It's a great pleasure to meet you, sir," said the very military-looking character as he emerged from the airlock.

"My name is Ortega, Bernardo Ortega," he continued, offering his hand.

After a brief handshake, Ortega turned to Rafael Cienfuegos, who had appeared—or so it seemed later to Madeira—from nowhere.

"And to you, *señor*," Ortega said to Cienfuegos, "Don Diego and Dona Elena send their very warmest regards."

Cienfuegos accepted the proffered hand and shook it. But he never took his eyes off those of the hand's owner.

"And this, gentlemen, is the balance of the team," Ortega said gesturing toward Sandra Argento as she dropped down from the lock. "Amanda Vega."

While Sandra shook hands with Cienfuegos,

Madeira studied the pair. Dressed in coveralls much like those MOHAB's crew was wearing, the new arrivals had only one distinguishing characteristic, the small-caliber side arms hanging at their hips.

At least they hadn't arrived with pigstickers strapped to their legs and bandoleers of hand grenades across their chests! thought Madeira.

"Mr. Ortega," he asked, "what's your background?"

"I was a SEAL, sir. Eight years," Ortega replied, glancing around him at the sarcophagi and the stacks of silver waiting to be lowered into the lower hold. "Then three more in corporate security. Ms. Vega's experience is comparable."

Madeira nodded, thinking the security group leader looked younger than he was. "What about the worksub crew?"

"They're all very well qualified, sir. After Ms. Vega and I have had a chance to become familiar with this vessel, I will have the worksub stand off and patrol.

"Very well. Tina de Navarre, our archaeologist, says she has about six hours more work to do. Then we'll recover our equipment, which should take another six to eight hours, and we'll be ready to head in."

"Yes, sir."

"In the meantime, Geoff Higgins here will give you a tour of MOHAB."

"Sounds good to me, sir," Ortega said with a smile.

"*Hola!*" Tina said, turning from the console and standing to greet the party as it entered the main workroom. "Welcome aboard."

"*Hola*, Dr. de Navarre," Ortega replied. "We're very pleased—"

"Where's Ramirez!" Cienfuegos shouted before

Ortega could complete the greeting. "Where's Agustin Ramirez?"

"Who?" Tina demanded as Cienfuegos drew a small-caliber pistol from the big pocket of his own coveralls. It was the same weapon he'd purchased so many years before for protection when he took his cash-register receipts to the bank every day.

Crack! The little pistol spoke before Ortega and Sandra could draw their weapons.

Crack! Crack!

Thirty-two

Ortega staggered as he clutched his bleeding chest. He then collapsed to the deck.

"What the hell are you doing, Rafi?" Madeira shouted.

"These two don't work for the syndicate, they work for Agustin Ramirez," Cienfuegos panted. He kept his eyes and his pistol pointed at Sandra, who had still not managed to unholster her own.

"Who's Ramirez?"

"He's one of Fidel's men. But now he has gone out on his own. He plans to steal Tina's treasure."

"What! How the hell do you know all this?"

"I'm right here, Antonio," Ramirez said quietly as he stepped into the work compartment, a riot gun in his hands.

Before Cienfuegos could shift his target, the riot gun roared and a full load of lead shot slammed into his chest.

"Rafi!" Tina shouted as Cienfuegos slumped down to the deck, his back against the electronics console.

Silence reigned for a second or two, and then Sandra got her pistol out of its holster.

Using both hands and shaking violently, Cienfuegos opened fire on her, and she returned the compliment. Meanwhile, everybody else dove for whatever cover they were able to recognize and reach.

The furious fusillade clanged and banged, roaring and echoing horribly in the closed, metallic space as the lead pellets and small-caliber projectiles splated against MOHAB's sides. It then stopped as quickly as it had started when, with a deep roar, Ramirez put an end to his creation for once and for all.

Rafael Cienfuegos, his chest and face covered with thick, red blood, lay crumpled in a heap in the center of the compartment.

Although fewer holes had been punched in his body, Ortega lay equally dead, and Sandra was wounded in her non-shooting arm.

"Ms. Vega . . . " Madeira started, appalled at the horror that had resulted from Cienfuegos's madness.

"What the hell's going on in here?" Bannerman shouted, her head appearing at the hatch to the galley and berthing space before Madeira could complete his sentence. "Oh my God! Jesus Christ!"

"Shoot her!" Sandra shouted, turning and shooting at Bannerman as she told Ramirez to do the same.

Bannerman lept back, closing the hatch behind her as the wave of lead slammed into it.

As the Chief Operator's head disappeared, and

the hatch slammed shut behind her, Madeira dove for Ortega's pistol.

"Don't shoot him!" Tina shouted, leaping at Sandra as the latter's weapon swung toward Madeira.

Almost the instant Madeira wrapped his hand around the pistol's handle, Sandra's exploded to life, tearing a hole in Tina's left shoulder and slamming her around and down.

Silence again fell, a silence broken only by the roaring that continued to echo in Madeira's ears. Glancing to his right, he noticed the worksub's two-man crew looking through the door between the storeroom and the workroom. They both appeared to be holding pistols and looking for an opportunity to get a shot in. He also noted that Sandra and Ramirez had both taken cover.

Meanwhile, below the work compartment deck, Crown and Savage were still serving their time in the hyperbaric suite. Trapped as they were by the laws of physics, and dependent on Bannerman for their information, all they could do was fume and wonder what was really going on.

Madeira looked down at the pistol in his hand. He had no idea how many more rounds it contained. Nor, for that matter, could he even guess how many more Sandra might have.

And then there was that Ramirez guy with the riot gun!

Stunned by the crushing, echoing concussion and unsure of their next move, everybody remained where they were—crouched behind consoles, tables, or sarcophagi.

Madeira glanced down at Tina, lying on the deck. Her eyes were tightly closed, her lips drawn back in pain, her right hand clutching her bloody shoulder.

"Tina?" he shouted.

"I'm still here, Al," she replied faintly, through gritted teeth.

"Shit!" he mumbled. Then he aimed the pistol in the general direction of Sandra and Ramirez and pulled the trigger, not having the slightest idea if anything would happen.

Blam!

That should keep their heads down, he rationalized. While I figure out what to do.

There was no response.

Then the PA burst into life. "Now listen up, you shitheads," Carol Bannerman thundered. "In exactly three minutes, that's one hundred and eighty seconds, I'm going to trip the airlock manual override. That means I'm going to close our lock and dump your Goddamn submarine with its lock wide open. Think about it! But think quick!"

It took a moment for the meaning of Bannerman's words to sink into Madeira's mangled brain.

The woman's a Goddamn genius, he thought. He wasn't sure if she really could do everything she threatened, not without the sub's cooperation, but he doubted Ramirez and the Vega woman could be sure either.

"You hear that, Ramirez?" he shouted. As he spoke he could hear a rustling, and a clanking, in the storeroom. It was the sub's crew, he assumed. They didn't need any more hints.

"Yes, Captain, I did," Ramirez said from behind a sarcophagus. "We accept your offer."

There was a sliding sound. Then Madeira caught a glimpse of Ramirez as he dove through the hatch into the storeroom. Madeira couldn't be sure, but it looked as if the son of a bitch was wounded in one leg.

Madeira's attention quickly shifted back to Sandra, who was backing slowly toward the storeroom hatch with her pistol pointed at Tina.

As Sandra backed away, Madeira kept his weapon aimed at her chest.

The standoff continued in silence.

Suddenly, with a brief but radiantly vicious smile, Sandra fired. She then slammed the hatch shut before Madeira could fire back.

Tina screamed once, then passed out as a reddish-purple stain began to spread on one leg of her coveralls.

"Take this," Madeira snarled as he handed Higgins the pistol. "You're to guard that hatch. If any of them comes out again, kill them."

"Kill them?"

"Yes! You do know how to shoot a pistol, don't you?"

"Only targets."

"Just make believe they're cardboard."

After the thumping and scraping of the worksub's unmating sequence had ended, Higgins turned away from the hatch and found Madeira kneeling next to Tina, working with Dale to control the bleeding.

"How is she?" asked Bannerman, who had just appeared from forward.

"I don't know!" Madeira said, his face a mixture of agony and horror. "I'm afraid she's gone into shock. One leg's definitely broken, and the shot to her shoulder came out her back. I think it may have hit some bones on the way."

"What about the sub?"

"The sub?" It took a moment or two to register. Yes, thought Madeira finally. He breathed deeply of the sickly scent of blood and burnt black power.

The sub! The sub could, probably would, still attack MOHAB.

He wasn't sure exactly how they'd do it, but they'd find a way. They had to! Just as soon as they had a chance to think about it, they'd realize they had to kill all the witnesses.

As long as they were alive, they'd be a threat.

His roving eyes settled on Tina's console.

The ROVs!

Then he looked back at Tina herself. He reached forward and touched her hand. He placed his hand on her forehead. How cold, how lifeless her flesh felt! How pale she was! Yet she was still alive. He could feel her breathing.

An icy coldness, an inhuman numbness filled his entire body and soul. There was no past and no future. No good and no bad. No Al Madeira and no Tina. There was only the action that must be taken.

The threat it still represented was more than enough reason for Madeira to attack the worksub, but that wasn't the reason that compelled him to do so. His reason was simple. Burning hatred. He'd send them to Hell—the prick with the riot gun who was behind it all and the vicious bitch who'd shot Tina—and he'd send them there before they even died!

But could he get an ROV under way quickly enough? Before the worksub had time to launch some sort of attack on MOHAB?

"Carol!" he snapped. "You and Geoff see what you can do to stop Tina's bleeding and get something on her to keep her warm."

"Roger," responded Carol, kneeling at his side as she did. "Geoff, you get the medical kit from the hold. And don't forget the splints and some blankets.

"You, Dale," she continued, turning to Tina's assistant, "you get the stretcher."

While Bannerman took charge of treating Tina, Madeira stood and stepped toward the console Tina had been using to control The Crab and the ROVs. On his second step he stumbled, tripping over Cienfuegos's body.

He looked down at the mound of blood and rags a moment, then stepped over it. Rafi was a mystery that would have to be solved later.

He reached the console on the next step.

Christ! The damn thing was full of holes! While all the flying lead had barely scratched MOHAB's hull, it had shredded the fiberglass console.

It would work! he reassured himself with cold certainty. Even before sitting down, he flicked on all MOHAB's external lights and TV monitors.

There they were, Goddamnit, still backing away from the habitat. In the process, they were being carried to the northeast by the Stream.

Concentrating intently, wasting none of his attention on visions of what might be happening on the bloodied deck behind him, Madeira powered up one of the ROVs. He then turned on its lights and TV monitor and tripped the release switch. He watched on the monitors as the ROV rose slightly from its cradle, then spurted clear of MOHAB.

He'd been right. The console's exterior looked like hell, but the insides were okay.

He glanced up at the Sonar plot and saw the sub clearly. Still to the northeast, it was driving southeast, into the Stream, directly toward MOHAB.

What did they have in mind? he wondered with cold calculation.

Guided by the Sonar and sweating profusely—despite the iciness of his emotions—he aimed the ROV toward its fast-approaching target.

Damn! The worksub was turning sharply to port, heading for Africa. They must have spotted the ROV on their own Sonar!

But they'd made the discovery too late! he thought with something approaching glee. The ROV could get them now before they got too far.

As the blip that was the ROV approached the blip that was the worksub, Madeira concentrated his attention on the ROV's TV monitor.

There the sub was, ahead of and slightly above the vehicle.

The sub turned again, to the left.

The maneuver was fruitless! Madeira pulled back and to the left on the small joystick, and the ROV slammed into the sub's spinning propeller, destroying the TV in the process.

Although unseen by Madeira, the target shuddered as its stern rose and its propeller shattered against the propeller guard, which had been bent inward by the ROV.

Within seconds, the sub sank slowly to the dark, hard bottom.

Panting, his eyes still blazing in fury, Madeira stared at the Sonar plot in silence. The worksub was without doubt crippled, but his work was far from being finished. Ramirez and the woman could still escape.

Concentrating intently, he activated a second ROV and sent it swimming in the direction of the worksub. Within a minute or two he could see his target on the ROV's TV.

He could imagine what was going on in the worksub. The crew and passengers would be bruised and disoriented—some might even be panicking—but at least one would be trying to restore order and save them all.

If he were there, what would he do?

Blow the ballast tanks, of course!

The worksubs were designed so that if motor power was lost, they could be safely surfaced by blowing the tanks.

But you can't blow a tank with a hole in it. Not when the surrounding waters were under a thousand PSI of pressure!

As the ROV approached the crippled worksub, Madeira armed the ROV's stud-gun attachment with a hollow stud—a pipe-like, pointed length of hardened steel normally used to permit air to be pumped into a sunken ship.

He had to hurry! They were bound to recover their wits any second now.

The ROV was soon alongside the sub.

Madeira studied the TV image, and realized the sub was listing well to starboard. He guided the ROV around to the port side and slammed the first stud into it just about amidships, where he knew one main ballast tank had to be. Then, with almost surgical precision, he fired in five more in two horizontal rows, one row well above the other.

Certain now that the sub was on the bottom to stay, Madeira backed the ROV off. He noticed that his hand was shaking, but paid no attention to it. His work would not be completed until he'd done something about the sub's day-glo escape pod.

With a snarl he drove the ROV down toward the

pod. It hit, as aimed, right on the pod's edge. The shock slammed the pod to one side, wrenching the airlock that connected it to the sub and jamming the release mechanism.

The devil's work is never done, thought Madeira as he activated the third, and last, ROV. He repeated the previous attack, leaving the pod dangling crookedly out of its recess, like a partially plucked eyeball.

Satisfied at last that his mission was completed, Madeira settled back and stared at the Sonar display.

A few minutes later the sub started to rise off the bottom. One foot! Two feet!

Madeira began to worry.

Then, long jets of bubbles suddenly appeared at the ends of the three upper hollow studs as the surrounding high-pressure water forced its way through the studs in the lower row.

Madeira grinned.

The worksub sank back to the bottom again, rolling to port as she did.

And there she remained with her precious—and very limited—supply of air leaking out into the deep waters.

He'd use an ROV to cripple the bastards! They would suffocate now, die in agony, knowing full well no escape and no rescue were humanly possible at twenty-four hundred feet.

Ramirez and the woman, he thought with grim satisfaction, had started the infinitely long, final leg of their voyage.

Carried toward the northeast by the Stream, the sub would drift and bounce along the bottom toward the great, abyssal depths east of Hatteras. There, somewhere, it and its passengers would finally come to a stop. And in time, they would become just one more assemblage of fossils buried in the thick, silty ooze.

God damn them!

Thirty-three

"Al!"

"Al!"

"Al, Goddamnit!"

Madeira was staring intently at the Sonar plot, watching the little speck that was Sandra, Ramirez, and their all-too-willing crew as it skipped and bumped its way to eternity. So focused were his thoughts that he had been unaware Bannerman was standing next to him.

"Yes, Carol?" he asked, as if in a daze.

"We've got Tina in her rack and I think we've stopped the bleeding—at least for now. We're trying to keep her warm and I gave her some antibiotics. I also gave her a shot for the pain—I'm not sure if I should have done that, what with the shock. . . ."

"I'm not sure either, at the moment," Madeira replied, his eyes wandering back to the Sonar plot.

"Al, you're done with them! They deserve everything they're getting, but now we've got other work to do!"

Madeira stared at her a moment. The numbness slowly oozed out of him as he thought of Tina.

"We've got to get her ashore. None of us are qualified to save her."

Then he realized just how far he'd fallen into himself. He'd lost sight of his responsibilities.

"We've got to get Tina ashore, Carol, and we've got to save ourselves and MOHAB."

"I'm with you all the way, Boss. Let's hit it."

"I want somebody to stay with Tina at all times—have Geoff and Dale swap off. You and I will handle the driving."

"Roger."

"Then prepare to surface."

Slightly less than an hour after Madeira gave the order to lift off, MOHAB's upperworks broke through the churning, storm-maddened boundry between water and air.

"Oh, Christ!" he growled, a note of despair in his voice as he watched the immense seas breaking against, and over, the conning tower. "We'll never be able to medevac her in this."

As he spoke, the habitat snap-rolled to port, almost throwing him out of his chair.

"Very well," he continued after a brief pause. "Come to Two Six Three and floor it, Carol. I'll get the Mayday out. I'm going to tell them to stand by for a medevac, as soon as the weather permits, and that we need medical advice right now!"

"Roger."

"And we'll dive again as soon as we get that advice."

"I'll second that!"

"We'll run at two hundred feet and surface every change of the watch to check the weather and reestablish radio contact."

"Roger."

Thirty hours to Charleston, thought Madeira as he prepared to transmit. Maybe more. Would she survive that long without proper attention?

While MOHAB plodded through the dark waters and across the Gulf Stream, surfacing only long enough to maintain periodic radio contact with the Coast Guard, there was no break in the weather. The storm, which had developed into a long-remembered, monster nor'easter, lashed the sea incessantly and laid bare large portions of the bordering shore with the brutal efficiency of a cat-o'-nine-tails.

Every now and then the sky would seem to lighten for a few minutes, but without fail, another squall would soon roar in. The darkness, the howling wind, and the pounding rain would all return as violently as before.

If not more so.

When not on watch, Madeira split his time between cleaning up the carnage in the workroom and sitting beside Tina, who, heavily sedated and strapped into her bunk, seemed unaware of his presence or anybody else's.

Beneath him, in the hyperbaric chamber, Crown and Savage remained prisoners of the laws of physics.

Should I turn north? he asked himself time and time again during those long, dark hours. Head for Georgetown maybe, Winyah Bay, where the approaches might offer a slight lee?

As he studied the chart looking for, hoping for, some haven, some shortcut he'd overlooked, a powerful sense of bleakness, of impending loss, settled over him.

What about Savannah? he thought. Maybe I should angle south.

Madeira stood in the berthing compartment and looked at Tina, strapped into her bunk and locked away in her own very personal Hell. He tried to smile, tried to think positively, but found it almost impossible. Touching her forehead, he confirmed that her deathly chill was now a raging fever.

She's shrinking, he suddenly thought in terror. She's shriveling away before my eyes!

He looked around the compartment. Except for the quiet rasping of Tina's erratic breathing and the fluttering of the air as it emerged from the ventilation duct, the end of the world was occurring in almost total silence!

In the end, Madeira stuck with Charleston, and ran out of water long before any medevac was possible.

Roughly twenty-five miles from the sea buoy, the shoaling coastal waters forced MOHAB, now running on her emergency power reserves, to the surface. She would have to roll and wallow the rest of the way in—through the angry seas and heavy rain—like a waterlogged coffin.

The sky started to brighten as they approached the sea buoy. In fact, for a few minutes the sun was faintly visible, a pewter circle showing through the clouds. Then the clouds slammed shut again.

"This is it, Carol," said Madeira a few minutes

later. As he spoke, both studied the video monitor, which showed the two stone jetties, about a half mile apart, along with the harbor tug waiting prudently inside them. "The water's pretty close to slack, but there's a strong set to the south from the storm, so you're going to have to steer right for the North Jetty. With any luck at all, we'll slip gracefully between them."

Bannerman, who still didn't believe MOHAB was capable of doing anything gracefully, just grunted.

Madeira glanced out the bubble just in time to see a wave break over it. He looked up at the video display—whose camera was mounted on the top of the conning tower—and watched the huge plumes erupting from the North Jetty as the storm waves attempted to destroy it.

"As soon as we're inside the jetties, Higgins and I'll get out on deck to handle the tug's lines."

"Don't forget to hook up your lifelines," she replied.

"Roger," he said absently.

Fifteen minutes later, Bannerman turned slightly and prepared to thread her way between the jetties. Madeira glanced up at the video monitor, and was no happier with what he saw than he had been before. The dirty-gray seas were pounding against, and in some places over, the North Jetty. Even worse, they were curling around the entrance and steepening as they met the powerful outbound current.

He glanced at a second monitor, which showed MOHAB's deck, aft of the conning tower, and the shoulder-deep waves that were boiling over it.

"There's no way we can get out on deck, Carol. Even if we go up through the conning tower. We're going to have to continue on our own up the channel for another few minutes."

He then picked up the radio mike and called the tug. "*Ashley Number One*, this is MOHAB."

"Come back, MOHAB."

"We still can't get on deck to receive your lines, so we will—"

"Goddamnit! I'm losing her. There's some Goddamn eddy here, right at the entrance," Carol announced.

Madeira paused, then realized that he could feel it. MOHAB's bow was being forced to port. He looked up at the video, on which the course change was now becoming evident, and then down at the green outline of the habitat on the control console.

The forward port thrusters, and the starboard aft ones, were all flashing madly.

He raised his eyes again to the video monitor, and saw a puff of black smoke explode out of *Ashley Number One*'s stack. Within seconds the tug was surging at them, her bluff bow battering the gray seas as she strained to slip in between the habitat and the South Jetty.

"I'm backing full now, Al, but nothing seems to be working!" Carol said.

The frustration and anger in her voice were evident, but there was no hint of panic.

"You're doing fine, Carol. You're doing everything that can be done."

The South Jetty was now clearly visible, even through the bubble, as it rushed at them. And off to the right he could see the red-and-gold tug, her bow foaming and frothing like a mad dog as she charged toward them.

It's going to be damn close, he thought as he clenched the arms of his chair and ground his teeth together. The tug was making a furious try, but the jetty was approaching much too fast.

He leaned forward and picked up the PA mike. "All hands strap in and hang on. There's a chance we will—"

Before he could finish his warning, there was a loud "thunk" and a violent shudder as MOHAB's forward runners bounced off the base of the jetty.

Madeira and Bannerman looked at each other, but said nothing.

There was a second, even louder "thunk," and they were almost pitched forward, through the bubble.

A hundred yards away, *Ashley Number One* was backing full now and trying to turn to port to avoid both MOHAB and the jetty.

With her bow firmly aground, the habitat's stern swung around and slammed against the sharp, hard rocks, rolling violently as she did.

As the wave passed, the habitat rolled the other way and slammed down again on her runners, only to be picked up again by the next wave and thrown against the jetty's sharp teeth.

The merciless beating continued—although by the second blow Madeira knew that MOHAB was lost.

"All hands prepare to abandon ship," he said as calmly as he could over the PA. "Geoff and Dale, get Tina strapped into a litter. Bannerman to release Crown and Savage from the hyperbaric suite, then help with Tina. All hands to assemble at the base of the conning tower. The plan is to go out through the tower."

After he'd finished, Madeira wondered briefly about the two divers. They still had six or eight hours to go on their schedule, but at this point a very possible, but by no means certain, case of the bends was the least of their worries.

As soon as the two "Rogers" came back over the intercom, Madeira turned to Bannerman. "You get all that, Carol?"

"Roger."

"I'm going up the conning tower now to make sure we can get out there. If anything happens to me, you're in command. Do what you think is best."

"Roger."

"And Carol . . . remember that your job is to save as much of the crew as possible. Tina is just one member of the crew."

"Is that how you feel about it, Al?"

"Yes!" He didn't add that, once everybody else was out, he planned to stay if he couldn't save Tina.

MOHAB rose, then rolled and slammed down again. The lights blinked, then went dead, and the faint whine of motors and gyros and blowers stopped abruptly, leaving only the hammering, banging, and grinding of the hull on the rocks.

The emergency lighting came on before Bannerman could reply to Madeira, assuming she planned to.

"Okay, Carol, I'm off," he said as he stood up and grabbed a handrail to steady himself. "I'm going to try to contact that tug with one of the handheld radios in the conning tower. You get everybody organized. If it doesn't look like we can make it out the tower for some reason, I guess we'll aim for the main airlock."

They both knew that with the waves rolling in as they were, the lock was an even less likely route than the tower.

While Bannerman worked her way aft to release the two divers, Madeira struggled through the lower hatch leading into the conning tower, and then up the ladder. He reached the small, chariot-like bridge at the top of the tower just as MOHAB was slammed by yet another pounding wave. The resulting roll came close to pitching him over-board.

"*Ashley Number One,* this is MOHAB," he shouted into the phone-sized handheld radio he'd picked up in the tower. As he spoke he looked around at the thoroughly disheartening scene, and decided Tina's only hope was the South Jetty itself, the very rock pile that was pounding MOHAB to pieces.

"This is *Number One,* MOHAB."

"We are about to abandon ship."

"Roga. We've called for a helicopter. Should be here in about fifteen minutes, maybe less."

MOHAB rose, rolled, and slammed into the rocks again. Then Madeira realized that somebody, Bannerman, was shouting up the tower at him. He knelt and stuck his head into the hatch. "What was that?"

"We're starting to flood down here, Al."

"Roger," he replied, not knowing what else to say at the moment. He then stood up and looked out over the side. MOHAB did seem lower in the water. Less lively. There was a very good chance she'd sink long before the helo arrived.

He looked at the jetty. It was possible, faintly possible, that somebody might survive on it long enough to be plucked off by rubber boat. Or helo.

That was assuming that somebody could get up on the rock pile without being beaten to death against it.

He looked around the sky and saw nothing but thick, wet clouds and driving rain. Then he looked over at *Ashley Number One* and thought how solid and comforting she looked.

"*Ashley Number One,*" he shouted into the radio, "this is MOHAB."

"*Number One* here."

"We're taking water fast and may not stay afloat until the helo arrives. Can you stand off to windward and put a line over to us with a rescue yoke in the middle? You should be able to haul most of us back to you."

"Ah can do it, MOHAB, but Ah understood you have a wounded crew member. Will she survive the trip?"

The tug captain was right. If he could hold position, there was a good chance his deckhands could pull them all aboard, one at a time. They'd be wet, cold, and battered, but they'd probably be alive.

All except Tina.

For her, the trip to safety would be deadly!

But he'd known that when he made the suggestion. Goddamnit! He didn't have time to dither like this! He had to get the rest of the crew off before the habitat sank. He'd stay with Tina and hope the helo showed up in time. Or maybe he'd get her up on the jetty somehow.

"Crown and Savage," he shouted down the hatch, "come on up here."

Then he pressed the "transmit" button on the radio. "*Ashley One*, this is MOHAB. You're going to have to drag as many of us over as you can. Come on in and get those lines over as soon as you see my two men on deck."

"Roga, MOHAB. We're on our way."

The two divers appeared almost immediately.

"The tug's going to put over a line," he told them, "and use it to pull us back, one at a time. I want you to to inflate your life jackets, get that line when it arrives, and bring it up here. You can then tend it from here."

Crown and Savage looked at each other a moment. "What about Tina?" Savage asked as MOHAB rolled.

The habitat's motion was considerably more sluggish than it had been a few minutes before.

"Let me worry about her," Madeira replied. "Now here comes the tug, so you two get down and grab that line!"

"Our pleasure!" the two said in unison as they pulled the lanyards to inflate their life jackets and then started down the side of the tower.

Madeira leaned on rail a moment and watched as *Ashley Number One* approached to within about fifty yards, and then turned to port so her bow was into the seas and MOHAB was slightly aft of her starboard beam.

Almost immediately there was a crack as one of the tug's deckhands fired a line-throwing gun, a rifle-like weapon that shoots a metal shaft with a soft plastic cylinder at one end and a light line trailing out behind.

The shaft flew across the wind, sailed over MOHAB just aft of the conning tower, and fell onto the jetty. The orange messenger line it was hauling floated down onto the habitat's deck at the base of the tower, well within Crown's reach.

While the two divers hauled rapidly on the messenger, and the tug backed and filled and managed to hold position remarkably well, Madeira shouted down the tower.

"It's time to get Tina up here. Geoff, you come up first and help me while Carol and Dale push."

"Roger," Bannerman shouted as Higgins started up the ladder, bringing with him the ends of two short lines that were connected to the head of Tina's litter.

When Madeira knelt down to grab one of the lines from Higgins, he couldn't miss the sight of the ankle-deep water sloshing around the work compartment deck.

He stood and looked quickly over the side of the tower at Crown and Savage, who now had one end of the one-half-inch nylon rescue line. While Savage hauled more in, Crown was madly coiling what they had. Both were frequently waist-deep, even chest deep, in the surging seas.

"You ready up there?" Bannerman demanded. "It's getting a little deep down here."

"We're ready," replied Madeira after he and Higgins had braced themselves.

"Here comes Tina," Bannerman said.

The next thing Madeira saw was one end of the litter, and the glint of Tina's red-brown-gold hair. While Madeira and Higgins pulled, Bannerman and Dale pushed, and it was the work of a minute or so to get Tina out onto the tiny bridge.

She looked so small, Madeira thought as he looked down at her. It was hard to see her, in fact, lashed as she was every which way to the litter.

"We've got the yoke," Crown bellowed.

"Then get back up here," Madeira shouted. "You can tend as well from here as on deck."

"Roger," they both replied as they started to climb, one after the other.

Madeira turned to Higgins, just as another wave slammed into and over MOHAB. "You're going to be the guinea pig, Geoff. Inflate your vest, let Savage slip that yoke around you, then go for it."

Higgins just nodded. After he was all rigged up, he climbed partway down the ladder.

Everybody watched as the next wave approached. Just before it hit, Madeira signaled the tug to begin heaving around on the line. Then, just after the wave had passed, Higgins launched himself into the racing seas.

Madeira watched MOHAB's assistant operator until he was clear of the habitat, and then looked over at the tug and watched as half-a-dozen people hauled Higgins over, and through, the breaking waves.

After what seemed an hour, but was actually only a few minutes, Higgins had been hauled aboard the tug and the yoke was headed back toward them.

"Dale, you're next," Madeira said as the next wave hit. MOHAB ground against the rocks without making any effort to rise beforehand.

The archaeologist's trip was as uneventful as had been Higgins's.

"Carol—" Madeira said.

"No, Al. I'm the captain, remember? You may be the admiral but I'm MOHAB's captain. Send Crown and Savage. They should be getting their asses back into a chamber anyway. I'll tend."

Madeira smiled grimly. "All right, you two. You have thirty seconds to toss for the honor of going first."

The two divers looked at each other a moment, then nodded. Neither moved.

"Time's up," Madeira said. "We're going alphabetically. Hit the road, Crown."

Crown looked as if he were going to argue, but didn't. And neither did Savage when his turn came.

"Good luck, Carol," said the second diver as he swung his leg over the rail. "Good luck, Al."

Then he looked down at the litter.

"Good by, Tina," he said very, very quietly.

Thirty-four

By the time Savage was hauled aboard *Ashley Number One*, MOHAB had stopped responding to the waves and her hull was no longer visible, probably hung up temporarily on the jetty's rock face.

"The way I see it, Al," Bannerman shouted, "we have two choices. We can either lash another dozen life vests to the litter, then tie it to the line and swim along with it, keeping Tina's head out of the water . . . or we can try to get her up on the jetty."

Madeira just shook his head slowly as MOHAB lurched and the conning tower tilted sharply away from the jetty.

"Or," Bannerman continued as she squinted into the surrounding murk, "we can give her to that helo."

Madeira glanced toward Charleston and, within a second or two, spotted the approaching orange-and-white Coast Guard Rescue Hawk that Bannerman had already seen. He then reached for the handheld radio.

"Coast Guard helo, this is MOHAB. Over."

There was no response.

He tried again, and again there was no reply. Nor was there any static either. And no number showing on the channel indicater.

"Hell! This radio must be waterlogged."

By this time, the helo was almost overhead, the roar of its rotors clearly audible above the storm.

As Madeira and Bannerman both pointed with exaggerated motions at Tina, the helo hovered. At the same time it lowered a weighted hook, which Madeira allowed to land solidly on the deck in order to ground any static electricity that had built up on the helo.

Satisfied he wasn't going to get the shock of his life, Madeira grabbed the hook and snapped it onto the litter's lifting bridle. He then signaled the helo to heave around.

As he waved his arm in a big circle, MOHAB shuddered, then rolled sharply to starboard, away from the jetty. It was as if she was falling into the trough of the wave as she slipped down the rock pile's face.

Tina, in her litter, flew up and away as the conning tower sank, while Madeira and Bannerman found themselves grabbing the line to the tug as they were pitched into the angry gray waters.

Hanging on for dear life to both the yoke and the line, the two tried to kick to help the tug's crew haul them in. The water was cold, but not as unbearable as the strain on their arms and the steady mouthfuls of salt.

They eventually found themselves alongside the

tug's low, fender-covered side, where arms reached down to drag them up.

Coughing and shaking, Madeira lay on the cold steel deck a moment. When he finally stood and looked around, the first thing he saw was a big, blond moustache.

"It's very good to see you alive, Captain Madeira," said Jake Smith, a slight smile showing on that portion of his face that was visible. "I can't tell you how much I hope that Dr. de Navarre recovers."

"What the devil are you doing here, Jake?" Madeira gasped, his lungs half-filled with seawater.

"The syndicate has chartered this tug. After seeing you all safely ashore, my staff and I are to keep an eye on MOHAB to maintain our claim until you can get the salvage operation organized."

"Oh!" Madeira replied. Once again, Rambo had provided a big surprise.

Upon returning from the hospital a week or so after they were dragged aboard *Ashley Number One*, Madeira spotted Carol Bannerman standing on *Johnson*'s bay wall. She was leaning on a rail, watching two welders as they cut out the burned-through plates.

"How's she today?" Bannerman asked as he joined her.

"Much better," he replied. "The doctors have decided she'll be almost as good as new after they install some replacement parts." He chose not to dwell on the additional operations and the year or more of therapy she'd also have to suffer. "Although they do admit her freestyle's going to look a little strange."

William S. Schaill

"That's good. I'm glad to hear that," Bannerman drawled. "Will the parts be waterproof?"

"Certified to a hundred and fifty feet."

As he spoke, Madeira thought of Tina lying in Intensive Care, frighteningly fragile and pale, conscious but still not totally aware, and of Diego Velazquez haunting the hospital corridors, frantic with worry and frothing with self-condemnation.

Aside from his continuing worries about Tina, though, Madeira had to admit that everything had gone very well the past few days.

Even before the tug had returned to its berth, Madeira had been on the phone arranging for the owners to charter the nearest available heavy-lift crane, which happened to be in Jacksonville, Florida.

By the next afternoon, the storm had passed and conditions had improved enough to allow Madeira, Bannerman, Crown, and Savage to survey MOHAB's wreck in SCUBA gear.

They found the habitat resting on the sand and mud between the jetty and the dredged channel. Of greater importance, they found that while the habitat had been holed in its lower portions, the upper half seemed intact.

The following morning they returned aboard *Ashley Number One*. After several lines were rigged between MOHAB and the tug, Crown was given the honor of closing the conning tower hatch, and Savage that of driving the hollow stud into the work compartment.

Crossing his fingers, Madeira then ordered that air be pumped into the wreck through the hollow stud.

To Madeira's great delight, MOHAB was more or less afloat—awash anyway—forty minutes later.

The habitat was safely parked in one of the floating drydocks at Lowcountry Shipyards by sunset. And guarded by Rambo and his crew along with half-a-dozen police officers.

Within another twenty four hours, Jake had unloaded all the silver and sarcophagi and arranged for their shipment to Miami, and after payment of appropriate cancellation fees, the heavy-lift crane's charter had been canceled.

"What about MOHAB and *Johnson*, Al?" Bannerman asked.

"The owners haven't decided yet. I think it'll take them a while."

"What about me? Us?"

"They'd like to keep you and me on the payroll for a while. To help them figure out what happened and what to do next."

As he spoke, Madeira was faintly aware of a telephone ringing someplace nearby.

"What about the wreck? And The Crab?"

"I assume that someday somebody will go back to them. It won't be me, though. I don't think Tina wants to go back either. She's got enough already to spend the next two hundred years on." Madeira smiled. "You want to go back?"

"Don't know. This project ain't been no fun, as they still say some places in Texas, but I will admit that I've learned a lot. I also like the idea of finishing what I've started."

"Madeira!" shouted a shipyard worker, his hard hat sticking out a door into *Johnson*'s superstructure. "There somebody here named Madeira?"

"That's me."

"You got a call."

"Very well," he replied, walking towards the door.

"Al," said Diego Velazquez's voice over the phone

after Madeira had identified himself, "she is dead. Tina has died."

A cold numbness settled over him, his eyes lost their focus, and his right hand contracted on the phone in a spasm of almost inhuman strength.

"What happened?" he asked.

"It was a blood clot. A heart attack. They think it started in her leg and moved to her heart. They had given her drugs to prevent this sort of thing, but . . . "

"Was it quick?"

"They say it was."

There was a long pause. "I'm very sorry, Diego," Madeira said finally, conscious that Velazquez had lost almost as much as he had. Then, before the Cuban could reply, he hung up gently.

So that's how it's to end, he thought. His eyes started to regain their focus, penetrating the numbness and settling first on the harbor's slick, dark waters, and then on Carol Bannerman.

"That was Diego, Carol. Tina just died. A blood clot from her leg got into her heart."

Before she could reply, Madeira turned and headed slowly down the brow toward the pier.

Maybe it never happened, he thought.

Tina. MOHAB. The past few weeks. Maybe it was all a fantasy.

It certainly felt that way now.

SEAGLOW

WILLIAM S. SCHAILL

A sunken Soviet nuclear sub lies off the coast of Puerto Rico, quietly leaking radiation into the sea. Hired by the Russian government, famed U.S. savage expert Al Madeira sets out to retrieve the deadly cargo, only to be caught in a vise between the U.S. and Russian governments, the Russian mob . . . and Saddam Hussein, with global security hanging in the balance.

___4429-3 $5.50 US/$6.50 CAN

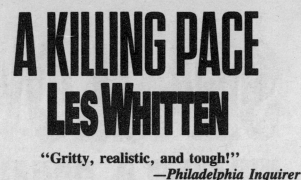

A KILLING PACE
LES WHITTEN

"Gritty, realistic, and tough!"
—Philadelphia Inquirer

For George Fraser, dealing and double-dealing is a way of life. But with the body count around him rising higher, he decides he wants out of the espionage business. As a favor for an old friend, Fraser agrees to take on one last job: just running some automatic weapons—no big deal. Then the assignment falls apart, and Fraser is caught in the sights of terrorists determined to see him dead. Suddenly, Fraser is on a harrowing chase that takes him from the mean streets of Philadelphia to the treacherous canals of Venice. He is just one man against a vicious cartel—a man who can stop countless deaths and mass destruction if he can keep up a killing pace.

_4017-4 $4.99 US/$6.99 CAN

LADY OF ICE AND FIRE
COLIN ALEXANDER

Colin Alexander writes "a lean and solid thriller!"
—*Publishers Weekly*

With international detente fast becoming the status quo, a whole new field of spying opens up: industrial espionage. And even though tensions are easing between the East and the West, the same Cold war rules and stakes still apply: world domination at any cost, both in dollars and deaths. Well aware of the new predators, George Jeffers fears that his biotech studies may be sought after by foreign agents. Then his partner disappears with the results of their experiments, and the eminent scientist finds himself the target in a game of deadly intrigue. Jeffers then races against time to prevent the unleashing of a secret that could shake the world to its very foundations.

__4072-7 $5.50 US/$6.50 CAN

WAR BREAKER
JIM DeFELICE

"A book that grabs you hard and won't let go!"
—Den Ing, Bestselling Author of
The Ransom of Black Stealth One

Two nations always on the verge of deadly conflict, Pakistan and India are heading toward a bloody war. And when the fighting begins, Russia and China are certain to enter the battle on opposite sides.

The Pakistanis have a secret weapon courtesy of the CIA: upgraded and modified B-50s. Armed with nuclear warheads, the planes can be launched as war breakers to stem the tide of an otherwise unstoppable invasion.

The CIA has to get the B-50s back. But the only man who can pull off the mission is Michael O'Connell—an embittered operative who was kicked out of the agency for knowing too much about the unsanctioned delivery of the bombers. And if O'Connell fails, nobody can save the world from utter annihilation.

_4043-3 $6.99 US/$7.99 CAN

THE SEA

R. KARL LARGENT

At the bottom of the Sargasso Sea lies a sunken German U-Boat filled with Nazi gold. For more than half a century the treasure, worth untold millions of dollars, has been waiting—always out of reach. Now Elliott Wages has been hired to join a salvage mission to retrieve the gold, but it isn't long before he realizes that there's quite a bit he hasn't been told—and not everyone wants the mission to succeed. The impenetrable darkness of the Sargasso hides secret agendas and unbelievable dangers—some natural, other man-made. But before this mission is over, Elliott Wages will learn firsthand all the deadly secrets cloaked in the inky blackness.

____4495-1 $5.99 US/$6.99 CAN

R. KARL LARGENT

RED WIND

When a military jet goes down off the California coast, killing the Secretary of the Air Force, it is a tragedy. When another jet crashes with the Undersecretary of State on board, it becomes cause for investigation. When a member of the State Department is found shot in the back of the head, his top-secret files missing, it becomes a national crisis. The frantic President turns to Commander T. C. Bogner, the only man he can trust to uncover the mole and pull the country back from the brink before the delicate balance of power is blown away in a red wind.

___4361-0 $5.99 US/$6.99 CAN

SILENT DOOMSDAY

ROBERT PAYTON MOORE

The U.S. military has developed a new technology so effective it will render modern weapons of destruction totally useless. But the dream turns deadly when a mole in the lab leaks the technology to a Libyan despot with dreams of a unified Middle East under his iron rule, with no country able to stand between him and his terrifying goal. Suddenly the U.S. is confronted with their own super-weapon, and a total, all-out war to save the world from a silent doomsday.

___4395-5 $5.99 US/$6.99 CAN

Dorchester Publishing Co., Inc.
P.O. Box 6640
Wayne, PA 19087-8640

Please add $1.75 for shipping and handling for the first book and $.50 for each book thereafter. NY, NYC, and PA residents, please add appropriate sales tax. No cash, stamps, or C.O.D.s. All orders shipped within 6 weeks via postal service book rate. Canadian orders require $2.00 extra postage and must be paid in U.S. dollars through a U.S. banking facility.

Name_____

Address_____

City_____State_____Zip_____

I have enclosed $_____ in payment for the checked book(s).

Payment <u>must</u> accompany all orders. ❑ Please send a free catalog.
CHECK OUT OUR WEBSITE! www.dorchesterpub.com